Books by

Bakkian Chronicle[illegible] cy

Bakkian Chronicles, Book II – Insurrection

Bakkian Chronicles, Book III – Amulet of Aria

"This is an extremely well written story with great dialogue that had me engaged with the character and even laughing a few times." – Scott P., IndieBookBlogger

"Entertainment at its finest!" – Robert Day, author of the Demon Gates Saga.

"A light-hearted fantasy read with good action and dialogue!" – B Throwsnaill, author of Hemlock and the Wizard Tower

"Truly amazing!" – Ryne Billings, author of Sword of Kirakath series.

"A debut worth reading!" – Eric Jones, author of The Door to Canellin.

"I really enjoyed reading both books 1 and 2. The story was easy to get into. The characters were likable and the action kept me engaged." – Anonymous, Barnes & Noble review

"Many years from now, it will come to pass,
A child will come, born unto class.
The mark of the Gryph, found upon his arm,
Indicates to all: protect from harm..."

Unknown

Bakkian Chronicles,

Book I

The Prophecy

By

Jeffrey M. Poole

www.Lentari.com

3rd Printing – May, 2012
4th Printing – September, 2012

International Standard Book Number: 978-01477400630
Published in the United States of America

Cover illustration by Rachel Marks (falynevarger.deviantart.com) and title graphics by her husband, Richard. Great job once again, guys!!

BLNT Rocks!!

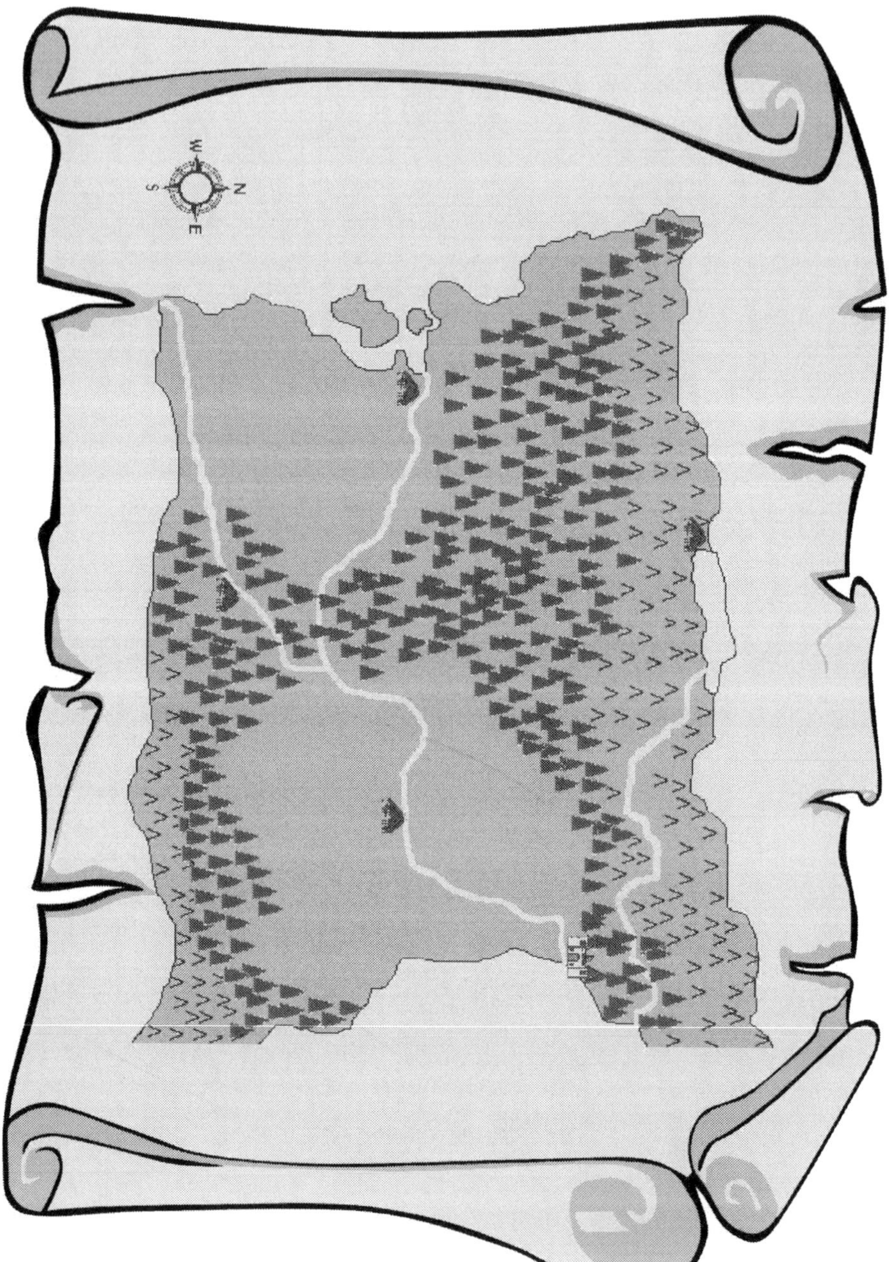
W
S
N
E

Contents

For Giliane –

My one true love, my soul mate, my everything.
Thank you for believing in me!

Chapter 1 – Beneficiary

Mondays typically didn't bother him too much, but this particular one wasn't off to a good start. He had just let out a monster yawn, the kind where once finished, your jaw muscles are left hurting and the insides have long dried out. He hadn't even made it in to work yet, and here he was, already wishing he was back home. The simple fact of the matter, he thought glumly, was that he was bored with his job. Sure, it paid the bills, and with the economy the way it was, he was thankful to have a job. Nevertheless, the fact remained that he needed something more challenging to do than solving the same type of problems day in and day out.

Thanks to his job in tech support, his social life had become practically non-existent. Being able to treat his wife to a night out was a rarity anymore. He sighed. He couldn't even remember the last time that they had not been interrupted over a weekend. All he had to do was think about going out for the night and within the hour plans would have to be cancelled. It was as certain as washing your car and then watching the thunder clouds roll in.

Take last Friday, for example. He had just finished placing reservations at the new steak house in town when a major client's system went down. It had taken him three hours of remote dial in service to resuscitate the stubborn machinery. Was he thanked for putting in the long hours, especially on a Friday? Of course not. Would he see any part of the exorbitant fee that his boss would charge the client for the after-hours support? Nope. Part of the job description, his sadistic supervisor had informed him.

His reverie was shattered by the Bane of his Existence, his business cell. The blasted thing had begun ringing well before his 8am start time and he hadn't even made it to the office yet. A quick glance at the caller ID had him cringing. Unfortunately, it was a client's number that he knew all too well. Well, they were just going to have to wait. Pushing the ignore button on the cell, his attention returned to the road. Moments later, his cell chimed: new voicemail. His irritated eyes flicked momentarily over to the time indicator on the SUV's dashboard. Ten minutes to eight. If there was one thing he was adamant about, it was not letting any of the numerous clients who had been given his cell phone number know he was available before his allotted start time. He might not have a say as to who is given his cell number, but he could certainly control when he answered it.

Steven Miller was the senior computer tech for a medium-sized company that sold and maintained telephony software and hardware. Out of five full-time techs that his company employed, not one person knew the system better than he. It was a bitter point of contention that consistently fell upon deaf ears.

His cell phone chimed again a few moments later. It didn't like being ignored. Steve sighed irritably. It would be dealt with as soon as he made it in to the office. What had happened to the weekend, anyway? How was it possible that two days could pass by in the blink of an eye? Wasn't it just Friday?

Well, I can't say that we didn't do anything fun this weekend, he thought. Since he and his wife truly (gasp!) enjoy playing video games together, they had decided to buy Nintendo's latest video console, the Wii. Nothing will make you lose your dignity faster than yelling at the television while waving around a set of game controllers that strongly resemble a set of martial arts nunchuks, and, to top it all off, getting beaten horribly by your wife. It was debilitating.

At least the summer was finally over, Steve mused. The start of fall had always been his favorite time of the year. Maybe he might be able to swing some time off in September, for their anniversary. His bosses owed him at least that. Being huge Disney fans, he and his wife liked nothing more than walking around Disneyland, hand in hand, admiring the –

A horn honked loudly nearby, snapping him out of his second daydream of the day. Groggily rubbing both eyes, Steve glanced in his mirror to see who had honked their horn, and why. Not one car had moved an inch since he became stuck in this lousy traffic jam. Sighing again, he started tapping his fingers on the steering wheel. Jeez, how much longer were they gonna be stuck here? This had better be one hell of an accident.

Ordinarily, the traffic in Twin Falls, Idaho was minimal at best. Sure, it was a larger town, at least when it came to the Spud State, but traffic here was typically not something you complained about. Today, however, there were at least twenty cars ahead of him, not to mention at least that many piled up behind. Even the oncoming lanes of traffic were also snarled, which usually meant that there was some serious rubber-necking happening up ahead. This must be one nasty accident. He hoped no one was seriously hurt. Cars mangled, sure, that's fine, but no one hurt.

Steve glanced over at the passenger seat and noticed a corner of an envelope sticking out between the seat and the car door. He reached over and pulled it out.

"Oh, yeah, forgot about this," he mumbled. The certified letter. It had arrived the previous day, courtesy of some young kid in a beat-up VW bug. "You Steve Miller?" the courier had asked, with a not-so-bright look on his face. The unprofessional manner in which this "certified" piece of mail had been delivered had denigrated its importance to that of an unwanted piece of trash. As a result, it had been tossed into his SUV to be dealt with later. Well, no time like the present. Might as well see what it says.

Steve tore open the cardboard mailer. A white envelope fell onto his lap, along with a folded piece of newspaper. Okay, so what's this? He glanced up to check on the status of the (non-moving) traffic and unfolded the newspaper. It was a clipping from the Coeur d'Alene Press, the local newspaper that covered the northern Idaho panhandle region. He was holding the obituaries page, and there were two. However, only one held his attention:

> Simon & Grace Miller, 81 and 80, long-time residents of Coeur d'Alene, passed away suddenly from an automobile accident. They leave behind one son, Stan (& Bonnie) Miller of Phoenix, AZ, and one grandson, Steven (& Sarah) Miller, of Twin Falls, ID. Funeral arrangements will be handled by C. Baron Funeral Home.

Steve blinked a few times. He recognized the names of his paternal grandparents, of course. They're dead? When did that happen? Steve turned the paper over, looking for the date. Hmmm, nearly three weeks ago. Who would send him a copy of their obituary? He reached for the white envelope, opened it, and pulled out a single folded piece of paper.

Dear Mr. Miller,

My name is Arthur C. Carroll. I am the attorney for your grandparents, Mr. and Mrs. Simon Miller. I regret to inform you that your grandparents have passed away. I will be handling their estate.

The reason for my letter is to inform you that you are named as the beneficiary in their will. Please call my office so we can arrange a visit to review their will together. Again, my most heartfelt sympathies for your loss.

Sincerely,

Arthur C. Carroll

The attorney had even personally signed the letter. Well, it looked like an authentic signature. Steve squinted at the paper. Could be fake. Those computer printers were getting really good at making a phony signature look real.

Steve reread the letter. His grandparents were dead? Should he be upset? He didn't feel it. Hell, he hadn't even known his father's parents. Sure, he knew them by name only, and knew what they looked like from his mother's photo albums, but he himself had never talked to them.

Steve drummed his fingers on the steering wheel again. I'm named in their will? Did dad also get a letter like this? He pulled his cell out of his pocket and called his parents. His mother picked up on the second ring.

"Hello?"

"Hi mom. How's it goin'?"

"Steven! What a pleasant surprise! Aren't you supposed to be at work?"

"Well, yeah," he admitted, "but I'm presently stuck in traffic. Must be an accident or something up ahead."

"Traffic? In Twin Falls? Please. Unless it's four lanes deep, and several miles long, don't complain to me about traffic."

His parents had retired to Phoenix to soak up the desert sun. A simple trip to the grocery store usually resulted in a thirty minute drive. Being the fifth largest city in the United States, Phoenix's traffic naturally, well, stunk.

Steve laughed. "Yeah, yeah, you have a point. Hey, listen, I have a question for you. Have you or dad received a certified letter in the last couple of days? From an attorney named Arthur Carroll?"

His mother thought a moment. "No, nothing like that here. An attorney sent you a certified letter? Are you all right? Is someone trying to sue you?"

"No, no, nothing like that. He sent a letter stating dad's parents had died in a car accident, and that I'm named as beneficiary in their will. I just figured dad was named as well. I mean, I know they had their differences, but I just figured the attorney would have contacted the two of you first."

Bonnie Miller sighed and sat down. Her husband had most definitely not gotten along with his parents. How could a happily married couple neglect their only son?

"No, we haven't received anything. When did this happen?"

"Just about three weeks ago."

"I'm really sorry to hear that. I didn't know them that well. I only met them once. I don't know how your father is going to take this. He's playing golf at the moment. I'll have to tell him when he gets back. He didn't take his cell."

"But why would they name me beneficiary and not dad? Were things that bad?"

"Yes, honey, they were. They hadn't spoken to each other in years."

"I sure as hell don't remember talking to them, either. Why name me?"

"I don't know why they did. They must have had some reason to. What are you going to do?"

"Well, I guess I can call this lawyer to see what he needs me to do. Do I have to go to his office? Can't he just tell me over the phone what they left me?"

"You'll have to talk to him personally. When going through a will, I've never heard of a reputable lawyer disclosing the contents over the phone. Just let me know what happens, alright?"

"Is dad going to be okay?"

"Leave your father to me."

"Okay mom, thanks. Bye."

"Goodbye, Steven."

Steve sighed inwardly. Figuring his boss wouldn't give him any problems about dealing with a death in the family, he picked up his phone again and called the attorney's office and made an appointment for the following day. That done, he decided to call his wife whom he had just dropped off fifteen minutes ago at the hospital. Sarah Miller was the supervisor for a company that provided medical billing on behalf of the local hospital. Her job was to oversee a team of people who relentlessly nagged the insurance companies on the hospital's behalf until they paid the claims that she and her team had submitted.

"Hi honey! What's up?"

"Hey. I'm stuck in traffic at the moment. Haven't even made it to the office yet. Hey, listen, remember that certified letter that I got yesterday? Forgot about it until just now. I decided to open it. It looks like my grandparents passed away. They…" and was quickly cut off.

"Omigod! What happened? When did this happen? Ummm…" Sarah paused a moment. She only knew of one set of Steve's grandparents, and his grandfather had passed away a number of years ago, leaving only his grandmother. He had clearly said "grandparents". Plural. "Who?"

Steve smiled into the phone.

"They were dad's parents. You've never met them. Hell, I can't remember ever meeting them before. Mom claims that I did, but being only two years old doesn't count. Anyway, they were always out of town. They never came to family get-togethers. They were the family outcasts."

"Oh honey, I'm so sorry. Is there anything I can do?" Now Sarah sounded upset.

"I know this is cold-hearted, but I didn't know them. They never made an effort to get to know us, so I really didn't worry about it. Apparently I'm named in their will. So thanks to that, I have to go see their lawyer tomorrow morning, see what's up. I have plenty of PTO, so I'll take the day off and pretty much spend it on the road. Just what I always wanted to do on a day off. He's probably gonna try and make me pay some type of legal fee, isn't he?"

"You're not responsible for any debts or fees," Sarah pointed out. "If anything, you'll have to liquidate the assets to pay for anything that's owed. Be cordial to him tomorrow. I don't want you scowling at him, or anything like that. Promise." It wasn't a request.

"Okay, okay, I promise. I'll wait to see what he has to say before I start scowling."

Sarah laughed and hung up.

As it turned out, the lawyer was surprisingly polite. Of course, he was in Boise, a two hour drive from his home in Twin Falls. Fortunately, the drive gave him plenty of time to come up with excuses to get out of doing too much work or paying any money.

Arthur C. Carroll had seen better days. He appeared to be in his sixties, was overweight, balding, and had stained teeth. Well, that's what you get when you drink too much coffee, Steve thought.

"Mr. Miller, thank you for coming," the attorney shook hands with him. "Please sit down. I know you had a long drive, so I'll make this as short as possible."

Steve smirked. *I'll believe that when I see it.*

"I can tell from your expression that you're expecting the worst. So I'm pleased to disappoint you. You're the sole beneficiary of the Miller Estate in Coeur d'Alene. That includes their home and land, about a hundred and fifty acres."

Steve's eyebrows shot up, his jaw clanging noisily on the floor.

"A hundred and fifty acres? In Coeur d'Alene? Wow."

"That is correct, Mr. Miller. Their residence and the land it's sitting on now belong to you. What you do with it is entirely up to you. Sell it, live on it, demolish it, it doesn't matter to me. Please sign here. The transfer of title will take about thirty days. Then the estate is officially yours."

"Free and clear?"

"Free and clear," the lawyer confirmed.

Steve shook his head in amazement and signed the papers. Once the documents were signed and given back to the attorney, he was handed a set of keys. And a map.

Steve was puzzled.

"What's the map for? I know where Coeur d'Alene is."

"Their property is northeast of the city, bordering BLM land. I've only been to the estate once. Trust me, you'll find the map useful. Good luck, Mr. Miller."

And with that, he again shook hands with the attorney and left the office.

Steve's mind was spinning. He owned a mansion now? And a hundred fifty acres of land? He had to call Sarah, as this was Breaking News. They were going to have to celebrate! But how? How could he keep this a surprise from Sarah? How could he, the world's worst secret keeper, keep his big mouth shut? Oh, why bother. She'll see through me in a heartbeat, he thought. Fine, dinner it is.

Of course, Sarah knew something was up the moment his little 'let's go out for dinner' suggestion escaped his lips. Was he upset and wanted to get his mind off of his grandparents? Was the trip to the lawyer's office a waste of time? No, she shook her head. That couldn't be it. If that were the case, they wouldn't be eating out. Okay, so why are they going out then? Wait a minute. Out to dinner? On a weekday? Did he inherit some money? Why won't he tell me? She sighed. Steve and his surprises. This had better be a pleasant surprise.

After they had placed their orders, Steve then proceeded to fill her in on what had transpired at the lawyer's office.

"A mansion? You never said they were rich. And a hundred fifty acres? That's gotta be worth something up there. Coeur d'Alene is a resort town, you know." Sarah clapped her hands. "I wonder if it's a pretty mansion with a garden? Wouldn't that be great?" Sarah looked at Steve and sobered instantly. "Oh honey, I'm sorry. I didn't mean to sound so excited about your grandparents' death."

"Hey, don't worry about it. Like I told you, I didn't know them. I say we contact a realtor up there and put the property up for sale. Let's see what kind of offers we can get on it. I want to be done with it. The way I see it, we should be able to make some good money off this whole deal. Real estate is worth a lot up there."

Sarah clapped her hands again, back to being instantly excited.

"We don't have anything planned this weekend. You should be able to take Friday off. Just tell 'em that since there's been a death in the family, you have to go to the funeral. I'll take it off, too. We can go up there to see what the place looks like."

Steve shook his head.

"You want to drive up there? Going through someone's house is not my idea of fun. The place probably has orange shag carpeting. Lime green appliances. Formica countertops." He chuckled at the mental picture this formed and returned his attention back to Sarah. "Did you know that when dad moved out of his parents' house, I've never once heard of him returning to visit? Hmmm…" Steve's voice trailed off.

Sarah waited. Was there more to this story?

"They never attended family reunions," Steve continued on, moments later. "No Christmases that I can remember. No phone calls to say hello, how are you? And for my birthday, they always sent three lousy bucks in my birthday card when I was a boy. And now I learn they have, er, had a mansion." Steve paused, and looked at his wife. "I never knew these people. I always thought they were cheap and wanted nothing to do with me. Then I find out they've given me essentially everything they own. I don't understand why.

What's the logic behind that? Sure, I'm flattered that they chose to give everything to me, but why should I bother with them?"

Sarah had remained quiet the whole time Steve had been rambling, nibbling on a bread-stick. Now that he appeared to be done, she took a breath. "I think that since they've named you in their will, they thought highly of you. You should at least go to their house up there and see for yourself what you were given. I think you owe them that."

Steve wasn't ready to commit to a day long drive. Not yet, anyway.

"I looked it up. The directions I found online says that Coeur d'Alene is a twelve hour drive from here. Twelve hours!! Wouldn't it be a better idea just to call a local realtor and put the house and property up for sale? We could get some bids for cleaning the place up, tossing trash, etc. I'd be willing to pay for that provided I didn't have to be involved. I wonder if Lynn has any contacts up there."

Lynn was one of Sarah's close friends that they periodically hung out with. She just happened to own her own real estate brokerage.

Sarah fixed him with a glare. "You can call her if you like. However, we're going. This is important and you'll feel terrible if you don't go."

Steve mentally scratched the remaining items off of his list of issues and resigned himself to the trip. A day-long drive up the northern Idaho panhandle.

Steve sighed. How much longer was this drive going to last? When he had looked at the map to plot their course, he still couldn't see how it could last twelve hours. The starting point and ending point were in the same state for crying out loud! They had passed Boise several hours earlier. Now they were on a straight stretch of SR-55, in the middle of nowhere, with nothing to see. The steady humming of the SUV's tires on the asphalt was beginning to make him drowsy.

Sarah had gone to the library to check out several audio books. Steve had to admit, it was a good way to pass the time. Provided that they were murder mysteries, and not romance novels. Although he'd deny it under the most heinous of tortures, some of them weren't too bad.

This novel, however, was boring beyond belief. The story was very slow to start. He had believed (prayed!) that the pace would pick up, but after three cds, it was apparent that it wasn't going to happen anytime soon. And what was with the narrator? Flat, emotionless, unenthusiastic voice that could put even the most caffeinated person to sleep in just a few minutes. Which moron listened to her and thought, "Gentlemen, here's an idea, let's have her make an audio book"? How many accidents was this lady responsible for, anyway? **Groan**. Seven more CDs to go.

Steve glanced over at Sarah. She was staring idly out at the passing scenery. She clearly wasn't paying attention to the book anymore, either. Time for Plan B. He reached behind his seat to pull out a bag of beef jerky, procured at the last gas stop they made. Knowing his wife could never resist her favorite road trip snack, he tore off the top and opened the bag. A split second later, Sarah's head snapped around.

"You sneak! When did you get that?" Sarah was trying to act insulted that he hadn't offered it to her the instant he had bought it, but she knew Steve liked to surprise her. If her playful tirade of insults would have lasted any longer, then she would have ended up spraying jerky everywhere. Happily chewing away, the boring audio book was promptly ignored, which might be due to the fact that Steve had surreptitiously turned the volume down.

"What do you think we'll find up there? Run-down house, trash everywhere, junk cars in the yard..." Steve was drawing himself a pretty good mental picture of this when Sarah finally swallowed.

"Hon, I don't think they were rednecks." She stifled a giggle. "Maybe an outdated house in need of a new paint job, and a couple of pink flamingos in the front yard." She grabbed another piece of jerky. "I'm curious about the land, though. According to your map, their tract of land extends well into the forest. The land is probably worth more than the house itself." She bit off another piece of jerky.

"I wonder what type of people they were," Steve mused, clearly not on the same page as she. "I don't understand why they wouldn't want to have contact with their family."

"Maybe they wanted to, but didn't know how to." Sarah was still chewing on her jerky. "Maybe your dad and his parents had an argument, and your dad decided to sever the relationship. That's what I think happened."

"Dad never talked about his parents," Steve said. "Every time I tried to bring the subject up, and wonder why we never went to visit, or why they never visited us, he always said he had no desire to see them. Never said what he had against them. I wish I knew. Sad way to live, if you ask me."

Sarah nodded. She bit off another piece of jerky. "Let's listen to some music, 'k?"

Two bags of jerky, four music CDs, and a hasty overnight stay at a run-down motel later, they pulled in to a Coeur d'Alene gas station just off of I-90 to verify the directions they were given. Steve got out of their SUV and headed inside. Sarah decided the station looked nice enough to get out and use the restroom. She passed her husband and headed to the back of the store. The attendant was studying the map.

"Holt Lane. Hmmm. Your map says it's off of French Gulch St. Haven't heard of that one, but if your map is correct, then go out to that stop sign and hang a right. Keep going until you hit Harrison. Turn right. Harrison will turn into French Gulch. It should be on your left."

Steve thanked the attendant and got back in their car. Sarah returned several minutes later with a fresh, cold bottle of water and they were on their way.

They found Holt Lane without any problems. The street ended in a cul-de-sac, backing up against the forest in all directions but the east. There were three houses that met their gaze. All of them, Steve thought joyfully, were large manors with well kept grounds. A fourth driveway could be seen, only it had locked gates securing the entrance, with the private road disappearing off into the woods Steve looked at the first house on the left.

"439 Holt Lane. Look at the size of that sucker! It's gorgeous!! That's gotta be worth at least a half mil, easy!"

Sarah looked at the large, Tudor-style manor. "That's a beautiful house. They all are. Great neighborhood. Lots of land around. Forest for a backyard."

Steve had unfastened his seat belt and was reaching for the ignition when Sarah grabbed his hand.

"Umm, wrong house. We're looking for 419 Holt Lane."

Steve looked over at the next house on the right. "Hey, fine by me! That one is even bigger."

Sarah, however, was looking at the gated driveway. She pointed to it. "I think that's ours."

"Huh? How can you tell? I don't see an address."

Sarah unbuckled her seat belt and got out of the SUV. Walking over to the gates, she moved some of the brush aside, revealing a tarnished brass plaque set into the brick wall.

"See? 419. This is it."

The gates were old, thick, and very formidable. They were set into solid brick foundations and, Steve was willing to bet, would be able to withstand any attempts of forced entry. A large, weathered lock kept the gates chained securely together.

Steve got out of the car and started trying the various keys he was given. After a couple of attempts, he found the correct one and pushed the gates open. Belying their rusty appearance, the gates effortlessly opened, smacking into the brick wall with a resounding clang. Ahead of them, the driveway stretched on for about a hundred yards before disappearing into the forest, curving off to the right. It looked as though someone had cut a swath right through the middle of the trees, clearing just enough room for a car to squeeze by. Steve glanced at the other driveways. The houses at the end of each were situated about fifty feet away. He looked back at the gate and chuckled.

"What's so funny?" asked Sarah, once he was back in the car.

"I keep expecting to see a green van with a great big dog in the back seat."

Sarah stared blankly at him.

"You know, like Scooby Doo. Are we going to find some type of mystery that needs to be solved? This is how they always seem to…" He trailed off after noticing his wife's look, which clearly said, 'You're a dork.' in any language. "Right. On we go."

Steve nudged the car through the gates and drove slowly down the lane. After they rounded the bend, it took a full ten minutes of driving (at ten mph - for some reason Steve couldn't bring himself to drive any faster) before they passed what could only be referred to as an authentic fruit orchard. They slowly drove by apple trees, pear trees, apricot trees, and several Sarah couldn't identify. At last, the trees cleared and their newly acquired house came into view. And what a house it was!

The manor was roughly 12,500 square feet, three stories high, and built in the early 1900's (by none other than Steve's great-grandfather, Luther, which he would not discover until much later). The house sat on a huge tract of land, with the forest encroaching from the north and west. Steve was not an architect, so couldn't pinpoint what style the house was built to conform to, but it did look part Victorian, part

Mediterranean, and it even had a medieval feel about the place. That turret on the western side of the house, for example. He blinked. No, that wasn't a turret. More like a round anteroom off of another room. The second and third stories also incorporated the same design as the first floor, so it certainly could be mistaken for a turret.

Flagstone decorated the base of the house, extending halfway up the second floor. Situated on the northern side of the house was a detached garage with enough room for four full-sized RVs with room to spare. The southern side of the house contained the beginnings of an immense Victorian garden that wrapped around the western side of the mansion, stretching all the way up to the edge of the forest. A small, gurgling creek wound through the gardens before returning to the forest at the northwestern perimeter of the property.

"You know, I would prefer it if you could pull all the way up to the house. I really don't want to walk the rest of the way in." Sarah was smiling, shaking her head. She was anxious to check out their new-found fortune. Steve had stepped on the brakes the moment their new house had come into view as they were still a good hundred yards away.

"Sorry. Just taking it all in." He drove to the front of the house and parked their car. Look at that garage! Room for all of your toys. That'd be an apt description for a real estate listing, he mused. Sarah was out of the car first.

"This thing is a mansion! Omigod! It's enormous!!" Sarah was slowly turning in place, trying to take in as much as possible. It was then that she looked to the south of the gigantic manor and saw the gardens. Her gardens. "Look at that! Do you see the gardens? Let's go check it out! Please??"

"Knowing you and gardens that could take a while." Steve immediately sidestepped to his left about three feet in order to avoid the imminent hit. "Tell you what, as soon as we're done checking out the inside, we'll look around the outside. Okay?"

"As long as you promise to not rush me."

Steve smiled. "Deal."

They both approached the front entry. Steve dug out the keys again and started going through them.

"Got it. Shall we?"

Sarah smiled as her husband held the door open. However, Steve had a change of mind when, instead, he decided to be the first one in. Sarah nodded, saying nothing. She was rather glad he had gone first.

What if something jumped out at her? Besides, it was best to let him walk through any cobwebs first.

Steve and Sarah Miller stood in a foyer the size of their first apartment. The first thing he noted was how everything inside looked as though it belonged in a museum. There were several cast iron coat racks to the left of the main doors; a huge mirror with a carved, mahogany frame was directly on the right. Two sets of staircases, one on the left and the other on the right spiraled up and joined together on the second floor, and then continued as one up to the third floor. A fireplace was just visible through a set of double doors on the left side of the room. It was so big that the two of them could have stood in it without hitting their heads. The right side of the room also contained a set of double doors, but those were closed.

Both of them hadn't moved more than a few feet from the front door.

"How in the hell did they keep a house this big clean?" Steve wondered, looking around.

Sarah didn't have to think of the answer. "Easy. If you can afford a house this size, you hire maids."

"You have a point." Steve walked over to a narrow table that was just below the mirror. He ran his finger along it. "Do they still have maids coming to take care of this place? No dust."

"Do you usually go into someone's house and check for dust?"

"Hey, I'm just saying that this room isn't dusty."

"Well, you don't know how long it's been since your grandparents were here, do you?"

Steve admitted that he did not.

Together, they walked through the ground floor, going from room-to-room. Steve started a mental list to keep tabs of everything they had come across so far: foyer, kitchen, dining room, formal dining room, sitting room (Sarah's term for the round anteroom), two rooms that could pass for studies or offices, three bathrooms and a laundry room. There was no way they were going to be able to remember everything they had found. Ascending to the second floor, they started looking around. They found a well-stocked library, three guest rooms, two more bathrooms, another sitting room and a hobby room (Sarah discovered several sewing machines, an actual spinning wheel that looked as though it would still work, large stores of fabric and yarn, and great quantities of blank parchment).

The third story had enormous vaulted ceilings spanning the entire floor. This level yielded what could be described as an observatory (a large, powerful telescope had been set up in the "round room"), a huge sitting area with numerous bookcases lining the walls, an enormous bathroom, and a massive set of carved doors leading into the late Simon and Grace's personal bedroom. The vast doors were wide open.

Steve moved closer to inspect the unusual doors. The door frames stood at least fifteen feet tall and had hand carved dragons, fairies, swords, and other symbols covering every square inch of the surface. The doors also had carvings covering the entire surface area. Whereas the frames had multiple figures carved onto the surface, the doors themselves depicted one carved relief that spanned both doors. It was a scene of a valley, with mountains to the north, a sea to the east, with a multi-turreted castle to the northeast bordering the coastline.

"Someone sure had plenty of time on their hands when they carved this." Steve ran his hands along one of the swords carved into either side of the frame. "This has got to be the coolest looking door frame I've ever seen. Have you ever seen anything like this?"

"No, I haven't. Something this intricate, this detailed has got to be documented somewhere." She leaned forward and peered closer. "We could do some research online when we get a chance. Remind me to take a couple of digital pics for later."

Steve and Sarah walked through the doors into the master bedroom. This room, along with every other room they had explored thus far, conformed perfectly to the antique motif of the rest of the house. Paintings, tapestries, bookcase-lined walls, large comfortable-looking armchairs, and even a fireplace a shade smaller than the one on the first floor met their eyes. Everything seemed to be in its place.

Sarah walked over to the nightstand on the right side of the bed and picked up a small, leather-bound book.

"What do you have there?" Steve inquired.

"Looks like some type of diary. A journal, maybe." She flipped it open and read the inscription on the inside cover. Or at least tried to.

"I can't make this out. Take a look." She offered him the book.

Retouk e R'Tal dedonde lu manis er' fasim olande djeren – Kri'Entu er' Ny'Callé

Steve was perplexed. "What language is that? It's not Spanish."

"It's not French either. I can't make out any words at all." Sarah looked as stumped as he was.

He started to flip through the book, fearing it was all written in this unknown language, when he chose a random spot near the middle of the book and stopped. It was clearly written in English. He read aloud to Sarah.

"'We finally located the manuscript in Capily. I'm anxious to start reading about Volan's legendary travels, but Grace is anxious to return. The Nayan is very eager to see the manuscript, and I believe Grace would like to share the discovery with her.'" Steve closed the small book. "Capily? Where's that? I haven't heard of it."

"Me either. Probably somewhere in Europe." Sarah looked thoughtfully at the journal, then at Steve. "You ought to read that. It might help you to get to know your grandparents better. Maybe find out why they wished to seclude themselves up here all the time."

Steve frowned. "Isn't that a violation of privacy? I don't want to pry into their lives. I wouldn't want someone I don't know reading my journal."

"Hon, they were your family. You're the self-appointed family historian. I'm sure it's okay. Besides," she pointed out, "I don't think they would care. They're dead!"

Steve finally conceded the point and slipped the journal into his jacket pocket. They continued to look around the master bedroom before returning to the ground floor. He didn't know about Sarah, but he was starting to have second thoughts about putting this place up for sale. This wasn't the dump he figured it would be. Everything they had discovered thus far had been tasteful and elegant, indicating subtle wealth everywhere he looked. This was the home of a very civilized couple that enjoyed a comfortable lifestyle, surrounding themselves with unique possessions that interested them. Besides, the house was freakin' huge!

With each passing moment as they explored the manor he was starting to visualize both he and Sarah living there. In fact, he was already mentally claiming the study/office on the northern side of the first floor for his own when Sarah spoke.

"What are you smiling at?" Sarah's question yanked him back to the present. She had been watching him, trying to figure out what was going through that head of his. Just then, Steve's cell phone started ringing. He unclipped his cell from his belt and checked the display.

"It's your sister. Wonder why she didn't call you?"

"She probably did. My cell is charging."

"Probably ought to go outside. Better signal."

Sarah nodded. She took the cell and headed outdoors.

"Seester!!"

Steve shook his head and chuckled. Hearing Sarah call her sister that always made him smile. Sarah and Annie were as close as sisters could be, which meant this call could last quite a while. He sat down on one of the couches in the sitting room and pulled the journal out of his pocket.

Outside, Sarah had wandered (deliberately) over to the gardens while chatting with her sister.

"Omigod Annie! You should see this place! The house is beautiful! Not at all what I expected! The grounds are gorgeous! And I wish you could see this garden! I think I'm in heaven!" Sarah sank blissfully down onto a stone bench in the middle of a group of hydrangea bushes.

"Do I really have to hear this?" Annie sounded jealous. "You get this fabulous mansion for free, along with your dream garden, and now you gotta brag about it?"

"You better believe it! I so wish you could see this with me!"

"Where's Steve?"

"Oh, I left him in the house. I think he's probably looking around. Annie, I don't want to sell this place."

"Then just tell him. Steve's a reasonable guy. I'm sure he'd understand."

"You didn't hear him. He truly sounded like he didn't want this place. Almost like he was offended that he was given it"

Annie rolled her eyes. "Yeah, tough break."

Back inside the house, Steve was flipping through the journal when a sentence caught his eye.

We'll place the necklace in the safe...

That got his attention. A safe? In this house? He stood up and walked to the living room with the ridiculously large fireplace. He scanned the room. Where would somebody hide a safe? Where else! Behind a painting! He practically ran to the closest painting and tried pulling it away from the wall. He promptly succeeded in knocking it off its holder. The gigantic painting fell noisily to the ground with a loud crash. A plant stand, complete with an exotic-looking plant, were also knocked over in the process.

Sarah came sprinting back into the house. There was her husband, down on his knees, hastily scraping spilt dirt back into the base of a large potted fern.

"Fifteen minutes! I leave you alone for fifteen minutes and you already break something! What did you do?"

A five-year-old child caught with their hand in the cookie jar couldn't have looked guiltier.

"Umm, well, the thing is…"

Sarah looked at the blank spot on the wall. Her gaze traveled down until her eyes rested on the painting and the fallen plant.

"What were you doing? Don't tell me you were looking for a hidden safe."

"Actually, I was. Get a load of this." Steve showed the journal entry to his wife.

Sarah was silent as she studied the journal. Steve noticed with satisfaction that his wife's head was slowly swiveling about as she took in the layout of the room.

"See? That's what I was doing! I was checking to see where they might have hidden a safe."

"Okay, for the sake of argument, let's assume there is a safe somewhere in this house. Do you actually think it would be hidden behind a painting?" Sarah paused. "They have safes that are hidden in the floor, you know. For that matter, they've hidden safes behind panels, bookcases, etc. We could search for days in here without finding any traces."

Steve looked thoughtful. "Remember those two rooms on this floor that could pass for offices? Let's check there. Umm, I'll take the one on the left; you take the one on the right."

"Sounds good. I don't want to waste too much time on this, though." Sarah thought a moment. "Let's give it about ten minutes, then go on to something else. We can always search later."

They split up, Steve going to "his" office and Sarah to hers. Where to start? There was a mahogany desk on the far wall, bookcases everywhere, several plants, and he counted five paintings on the wall. Oh, and in the corner to the right of the desk was a statue of some mythological creature. Steve had to delve into his fantasy encyclopedia to come up with the name: griffin. A creature with the head, wings, and forelegs of an eagle, and the rest of the body resembling a lion. Cool!

He went to the desk first and rifled through the drawers looking for any clues that might indicate the location of the safe. Nothing. He checked the paintings, carefully this time, and discovered bare walls behind them. He eyed the bookcases. There were five of them that were all filled with huge, musty tomes that looked as though they'd fall apart if he so much as touched them.

He moved to the first bookcase when he stopped and listened. There was a faint humming noise that hadn't been there before. He pivoted in place, trying to pinpoint where it was coming from. The odd thing was that it sounded like it came from everywhere in the room. Not a loud, unpleasant noise, but a constant soft, musical humming.

Was this noise in all the rooms? Steve started moving toward the door when he froze. The humming had stopped.

"What the hell?"

Steve spun around and eyed the room again. He still couldn't determine where in the room the sound was coming from. Eager to see if it would start up again, he stood in front of the same bookcase and waited. Sure enough, the humming returned.

"Where in the hell is that coming from?" Steve spun in place again. Nothing out of the ordinary. He took a step toward the bookcase and cocked his head toward the books, fully expecting the humming to increase in volume. It didn't. He experimentally took a couple of steps back and the humming ceased. Bemused, he stepped forward again, and the humming started. Back, and it stopped. Started, stopped. Stopped, then started. Stopped again.

Sarah came around the corner and started to enter the room when she saw her husband. She stifled a laugh. What was he doing, the Hokey Pokey??

Unable to refrain any longer, Sarah burst out laughing. "What are you doing?"

"Hey, don't laugh! Check this out!" Steve stepped towards the bookcase. The humming started.

Sarah stopped laughing and cocked her head. Was someone humming?

"What's that? Where's it coming from?"

"I have no idea. It seems to be centered on this spot. If I move from it, like this…" Steve stepped away from the bookcase. The humming stopped. "See? It stopped. And if I go back, it starts again. What do you think?"

"Something is reacting to your presence. But what?" Sarah looked around the room. Nothing was out of place and there didn't seem to be anything in the room that had an electronic brain.

"Here, you stand here and let me see if I can tell if anything changes." Steve stepped back to get out of the way as Sarah took his place. Both of them froze as they realized that the humming did not resume.

"What the hell?" both said, in perfect harmony.

Sarah stepped to the left and motioned Steve to join her. He returned to her side and was shocked to discover that the humming had resumed.

"It's you! Not me, but you! This is really spooky!" Sarah's eyes had widened until they were the size of saucers.

"Okay, I'm gonna move around the room. Something is making that noise. Stand over by the doorway and see if anything changes." Steve walked the length of the bookcases on the far wall.

"The STATUE!! Stopstopstop!!! Look at the statue!!" Sarah was practically jumping up and down as she gestured wildly at the stone statue of the griffin, whose eyes were glowing green.

Steve froze in place as he looked at the statue. The griffin's eyes were definitely glowing. The eyes grew brighter as he ventured closer. Stepping directly in front of the statue, the griffin raised its right foreleg, revealing a button that was recessed into the pedestal it was standing on.

Steve was silent as he stared at the button. "Oh well, what the hell." He pushed it.

The front panel of the pedestal swung open. Inside the hidden chamber was a brass container the size of a shoebox, several stacks of papers, a small pewter box, and several sacks of an unknown substance.

Steve reached in and pulled out a sack. The weight of the bag surprised him. He opened it and let out a shout.

"Holy cow! It's gold! This thing is full of gold coins! Not American. Or European. Ummm…" he picked up a coin and squinted at it. "I have no idea where it's from. Some marks on the front and a picture of a griffin on the back. That's odd. It kinda looks like that griffin," he said, pointing to the griffin standing on the pedestal.

"Do you think that's real gold? What are in the other ones?" Sarah asked, pointing to the other two sacks.

Steve reached in and pulled out the other two. He opened one and pulled out something that shimmered in the light.

Sarah took the object from Steve. "What's this?"

"No clue. There's about half as many of these as there are of those."

Sarah studied the object. It appeared to be made of some type of crystal, and was practically transparent with a slightly smoky color to it. The crystal was shaped roughly like a coin, but had (she counted) nine sides to it. She couldn't make out any markings on its surface.

"Another type of currency?" Sarah wondered aloud. Then with a sudden jolt of realization, she looked at Steve. "Hon, this is the safe. It has to be! Think about it! A sack of gold coins and a sack of these things. What's in the last one?"

Steve opened the bag to reveal... marbles. Smoke-colored marbles. Steve pulled one out and almost dropped it.

"It's vibrating! This thing is vibrating! And it's warm, almost like it's generating its own heat!" He handed it to Sarah.

As she studied the marble, Steve pulled out the small pewter box and opened it. The object inside reminded him of those old skeleton keys you'd find in those big, ancient houses. However, this key didn't appear to be made of metal. It looked like it was made from another type of crystal. A deep, vivid dark green colored crystal. He had to admit, it was the prettiest key he'd ever seen.

"Hey, forget about that marble and take a look at this!" Steve passed the key to his wife.

Sarah took the key out of the box and ran her fingers along the surface.

"I'd love to see what this opens." Then Sarah fell silent as she thought for a moment. "Actually, there's only one possible door that this could unlock."

"Hon, maybe you've noticed, but we checked out the house. There's no green, crystal doors in there."

"Steve, think about it!" Sarah sometimes had to explain the obvious to her husband. "Of all the rooms and doors we saw in that house, do any of them stand out to you?"

Steve detected the I-can't-believe-you-haven't-figured-this-out-yet tone from his wife and decided not to make too much of an issue out of it. Yet.

"If you're going to tell me we saw a green door and I don't remember it, then I'll personally run out to Walgreen's and pick up some ginkgo."

Sarah sighed.

"The master bedroom. With the huge, carved doors? Remember them? I'll bet this key is for the lock on those doors."

"Well, maybe you're right" Steve admitted, "but if that key is for those doors, then we don't need it. The doors are unlocked and open, remember?"

"I remember." Sarah's curiosity had been piqued. "But I still want to see if this key does fit those doors and why it needs such an unusual key to lock them."

"Okay, I'm game."

Steve put the sacks back into the safe, closed the panel, and followed Sarah out to the foyer.

They started climbing stairs.

"Hon, I've been thinking…"

"What would you think…"

Both of them laughed as neither one heard what the other said.

Steve smiled. "You first."

"Okay. I'll be honest with you. I really like this house. I don't want to give it up. I think we should keep it." Sarah gave her husband her best attempt at her Bambi eyes. Steve, staring straight ahead, didn't notice.

"Well, that makes what I was going to say a lot easier. I don't think we should sell it, either. There's something about this place. I'm seriously starting to consider relocating here. I know it's a resort town, but hey, we don't have any family in Twin Falls. And I can finally start up my own business." He paused. "I'm getting way ahead of myself. Why don't you want to get rid of it?"

Sarah simply stared at her husband. "Did you not *see* the garden?"

They reached the top floor and proceeded to the master bedroom. The doors were massive and looked as though they weighed a ton each.

"Okay He-Man, close 'em up."

Steve eyed the doors. "Yeah, sure. Give me a minute."

The doors were much easier to move than he had anticipated. They smoothly slid into place and with a resounding clang, both doors were closed.

Sarah approached the doors and ran her hands over the picture that was carved onto both of them. She took out the key and automatically started moving toward the doorknob, only no doorknobs were to be found.

Steve blinked. "No doorknobs? Now what?"

Sarah, too, was studying the doors. This key couldn't be for a set of doors without doorknobs. Maybe she was mistaken. She was about ready to tell Steve she was obviously wrong when she noticed the carving of the castle. It was carved with exquisite detail, including the drawbridge and windows. One window didn't have a regular, rectangular window, but had what appeared to be a hole. A key hole.

"Hon, I think we have a winner! Look at this window on the castle!"

Without waiting for his reaction, she inserted the key into the opening and turned.

Chapter 2 - Portal

At first, nothing happened. Steve was glancing around the room, waiting for a hidden door to appear, when both of them felt the floor shudder slightly. Sarah let go of the key and shared a glance with her husband. The two of them looked around the room once more. So what was supposed to happen? Maybe a secret panel would appear on one of one of the walls?

"Well, I don't see…" Sarah suddenly pulled her husband close and pointed to the massive doors. "Honey! Where's the seam?! There's supposed to be two doors!!"

The huge doors had merged seamlessly together and the frames had started to glow. The carved relief rippled outward from the castle, as if a stone had been dropped in the middle of a pond.

"Listen! Do you hear that?" Steve motioned for Sarah to be quiet. "The humming is back. It's stronger, and this time there's no mystery about where it's coming from."

The surface of the doors became increasingly turbulent, and then faded out to reveal a realistic, life-sized scene of an outdoor path winding through a coniferous forest. Pine trees nearly a hundred feet high were visible as far as the eye could see.

Coeur d'Alene's newest residents reacted with astonishment as wafts of fragrant air flowed through the doorframe on the back of a gentle breeze. The sounds of a distant waterfall could also be heard. Small mammals were seen darting through the treetops at amazing speeds.

Since most people do not normally discover a doorway leading into a forest on the third floor of their house, both husband and wife were naturally left quite speechless. Sarah recovered her composure first.

"Now there's something you don't see everyday."

Steve's response was a few degrees less than formal. "That is no bullshit, hands down, the freakiest thing I've ever seen." He took several steps toward the "doors" and stopped. "That looks real! It looks like we could stroll right across and be walking on that path!" He grabbed Sarah's hand and started pulling her towards him.

"Now wait." Sarah was struggling very hard not to lose her grip on her sanity. "I'll grant you that it looks very realistic, but there's no way that we can go strolling through that and find ourselves in that forest. It *has* to be some type of optical illusion."

Steve shook his head. "Do you smell that? I can smell pine trees. Flowers. I think I even smell water as well. It sounds like there might be a waterfall or something in the area."

"Okay, I haven't figured out how it can smell like there's a real forest, but I'm working on it! I mean, if that ride at Disneyland can use aromatics, so could this thing."

"I doubt this is an illusion. Wait a minute. I have an idea." Steve walked over to the desk and grabbed a piece of paper. He folded it into a pathetic-looking airplane and tossed it through the doorway. The airplane sailed through the air and landed nose first on the path.

"Hah! Did you see that? This is a portal! A portal that will lead us to, ummm, to…" Steve shrugged and hooked a thumb in the direction of the activated portal, "wherever that is."

Steve took Sarah's hand again and pulled her up to the threshold of the door.

"Now. You're telling me that if we walk through that," he looked pointedly at the portal, "then we won't end up on that path, but instead we'd end up walking into the master bedroom? No, better yet, since the doors are closed, we'd run into them?"

Sarah was reluctant to abandon her common sense. "There has *got* to be an explanation for this. This type of thing just doesn't exist. It has to be an illusion of some type."

Steve held out his hand. "How certain are you of that?"

Her hand smacked into his. Together, they walked through the door. Through, he noted, but not into.

To Steve, it passed as smoothly as stepping into the outdoors. They stood blinking in the bright sunlight, staring at the scenery before them.

"We're through! Omigod, we're in the forest!" Sarah bent down to smell the pretty blue flowers she had noticed from the house. "It's so beautiful here!"

Steve couldn't stop grinning. He was going from rock to tree to flower as if verify this wasn't a figment of his imagination.

"There's nothing that's illusory about this place, believe you me!" He took a deep breath. "Smell that air! I wonder where we are. Nowhere near a city, that's for sure."

It was at this time that Sarah regained most of her senses.

"Okay, why in the world…" She paused. "No, better yet, how did a magical door get into your grandparents house? Hmmm, let me backtrack a little more. Who made it? Certainly not by us. The Japanese are good, but not that good." Sarah began to pace.

The light of comprehension finally shone a few rays in Steve's direction.

"Are you saying that, uh, someone *else* created those doors? Alright, alright, let's think about this." His turn to pace. "You're right. There's nobody out there that has successfully teleported something, let alone someone, from point A to point B. This sort of thing is straight out of Star Trek."

"There's something else that's bothering me." Sarah thought for a moment. "Okay, the creators of those doors are obviously more technologically advanced than we are. By leaps and bounds, I'd say. Who knows where we are now? I mean, there are tons of trees, plants, and flowers around here and I don't recognize any of them!"

Steve sighed. "Hon, there are thousands of trees and flowers. Can't be expected to know all of them."

"True. However, I can usually recognize something. My grandmother ran a floral shop for years, remember? I've spent a lot of time with her. Steve, nothing here is familiar. I mean, look at this flower, for example." Sarah pointed to what looked like a brightly colored rose.

"That's a pretty rose."

"It sure is, isn't it?" Steve nodded, so she continued, kneeling close by the multi-hued flower. "However, this one has at least four different colors in it, maybe more. Look, on this one petal alone you have dark blue, which turns purple, then pink, and then yellow."

"Looks kinda like a sunset," Steve commented.

She nodded. "It does. However, roses don't have that many colors on the same flower. Don't even think about rolling your eyes at me."

Steve's gaze snapped back to neutral.

"Besides, look! It has blue thorns!"

"Flowers and thorns. Not an uncommon match, ya know."

It was Sarah's turn to roll her eyes. "Just trust me. This flower isn't natural."

They continued exploring the surrounding plant life when a large shadow passed over them, a loud screech shattering the air. Both of them froze instantly.

"What was that? A bird?" Sarah looked up at the trees.

"A bird that big? Did you see the size of that shadow? It was as big as the car!" Steve nervously scanned the immediate vicinity. It was then that he finally looked behind them.

"Houston, we have a problem."

Sarah detected the note of alarm in his voice. It got her attention. Instantly. "Honey? What's the matter?"

"The, uhh, there's..." Steve ran his hands through his hair and cleared his throat. "The portal's gone."

"WHAT?!" Sarah spun around and looked behind them. "This is not good. This is SO not good. What do we do?"

Steve noted the panic in his wife's voice. It spooked him more than he would ever care to admit. Here they were, in an unknown land, with no signs (or sounds) of civilization anywhere in the vicinity. If he were by himself, it would be one thing. But to have Sarah suffer the same fate as he, it was almost unbearable. He had to think of something to do, quickly, before he started showing signs of panicking himself.

"Ummm, maybe the doorway is there, but we just can't see it." He grabbed her hand. "Come on."

They hurried to the exact spot where they stepped onto the path.

"Alright, one more step and we should be back in the house." Together, they stepped forward. Unsurprisingly, nothing happened. "Maybe it's a little farther than I thought. Let's keep going."

They continued down the path another twenty paces before Steve stopped and reversed his course, figuring an approach from the south would have better results. No luck. They tried from the east and then the west, still with no luck. They were stranded.

Sarah was furious. "We're stranded? We're STRANDED?? This is all your fault!!"

Steve whirled on her. "My fault? I'm not the one who stuck that damn key in and turned it, causing that portal to appear."

"No, you're right. YOU are the one that pulled us through without thinking about the consequences. And now look at us. We're screwed!"

"Hey, wait a minute. I've got my cell. I'll just call someone, like 911, and they can trace the signal." Steve unclipped his cell. "Problem solved."

He started punching in numbers when he frowned, spun to the left, then to the right, then started moving aimlessly around. "No freakin' signal. Must be all the trees. Dammit!"

"Well then, come on. Let's find a clearing or something." Sarah started to head north when Steve gently pulled her to a stop. "What's the matter?"

"That waterfall sounds like it's coming from the other direction. Let's go that way."

"Okay, the waterfall is that way. So?"

"Usually water increases the signal from cell phones. Right?"

Sarah shrugged. "Makes sense."

For half an hour they traveled south. The trees were just as thick as ever, with no signs of thinning. There were also, Steve noted, no signs of civilization yet (or traces of it). For all he knew, they could be following a deer trail. However, one positive note was that the sound of the waterfall was getting progressively louder.

Sarah's legs were getting tired. She wasn't used to this much continuous walking. She was about to suggest they stop to rest when the path took a sharp turn to the left and they found the waterfall. It was, she noted, very pretty. As Steve attempted to get a signal on his cell, she craned her head to look at the top. She estimated it to be at least a hundred feet tall. The falling water had formed a small lake, with the excess water flowing off to the east as a small river.

However, what held her attention at the moment was the pair of griffins that were satisfying their thirst from the pool. Panic spread through her like wildfire. Where was Steve? She scanned the immediate area, but couldn't see him.

Cra-ack!! The snapping of the twig echoed like a gunshot all throughout the clearing. Sarah groaned. Steve had just announced his presence, existence, and location to every living creature within a two hundred foot radius.

Both griffins jerked their heads up. Steve came out of the trees and stumbled toward the lake, eyes still down as he attempted to get a signal on his cell.

"Steve!!" Sarah hissed.

Steve finally looked up. "What?"

"Don't move!" Sarah whispered, panic evident in her voice. "Remember that statue in the office? The one with the safe?"

"Yeah, what about it?"

"Look to your right! Just don't move," Sarah pleaded, "and don't panic!"

Don't move? Don't panic? What, had a bee landed on him? What did that office safe have to do with anything? Steve glanced to his right. Not more than fifteen feet from him were two sets of avian eyes staring straight at him.

"Awww crap..."

It was hard to say who was more surprised, the griffins or Steve. Normally, prey didn't come stumbling right up to them. What was wrong with this human? There was no fear! Humans without fear usually meant wizards or sorcerers. It was bad luck to eat a wizard.

Both griffins appeared undecided, and then with a loud squawk, they took to the air and flew away.

"Could it hurt to once, just once, look where the hell you're going?" Sarah surprised herself into feeling both happy and furious at the same time.

"Those were griffins! Holy crap! Actual live griffins!!" Steve sailed right past fear to land squarely on amazement. "Those are mythological creatures! Half eagle, and half lion!" His smile then melted into a frown.

"Yeah, that's right, Einstein." Sarah was still mad. "Griffins, along with multicolored roses. They don't exist. At least, not in the States. And, if I'm not mistaken, anywhere else. We're nowhere close to home. I hate to sound like a sci-fi geek, but I think we're in another reality, or on an entirely different world!"

"Another reality? You mean like a parallel dimension??" His brow furrowed as he frowned harder.

"Yeah, that's exactly what I mean." Sarah noted her husband's skeptical tone and body language. "Come on! You're more into sci-fi than I am. I would think you'd believe this sort of thing more than I would."

"Hey, reading about it and experiencing it are two very different things. However..." Steve looked in the direction the griffins flew off. "I better start believing it before I go crazy."

Steve walked over to the closest rock and sat down. Sarah joined him an instant later.

"Let's recap, shall we? We discovered a portal in my grandparent's mansion. A portal that brought us here, to a place where apparently fantasy creatures can and do exist. Where, according to you, (and I do trust you!) the flora is unique and unknown as well." He looked at Sarah. "I think it's obvious that my grandparents used the portal. Why else would it be there?"

"Well, if they came here before, then where did they go? They must have known people here, or frequented a known spot." Sarah looked around. "Let's keep moving. The last thing I want right now is for something else to come here for a drink."

They both stood up. "Any ideas on which direction to go?" Steve's eyes followed the flowing river as it trailed off to the east.

"Let's follow the river. We'll have a better chance of finding some people if we stick to the water." Who knew watching the Discovery Channel would have eventually paid off?

Sarah nodded. Made sense. She looked further downstream. Still no signs of civilization whatsoever. Steve took her hand and together they headed east.

Several hours had passed. Both were still walking along the same river still eagerly scanning the horizon looking for the same thing: some sign of human presence. So far, no luck. At times, the tiny path was practically impossible to follow, cutting through dense, squat brush that even a rabbit would have been lucky to get through. Other times the path inexplicably swerved in a different direction, almost doubling back on itself. Since the path they were following appeared to be used regularly, if it swerved to avoid harmless-looking trees, then so be it.

The path rounded a bend on the left and they came across a field of shoulder-high pale, blue flowers. These, too, had thorns. Inch long thorns, to be exact. However, the trail proceeded straight through the flowers. Sarah pointed to the river.

"Water looks shallow. I think we can make it around these things. I personally don't want to go wading through those flowers."

"No arguments here."

Together they walked along the riverbank until they were finally forced to enter the water. Steve, who considered himself very chivalrous, gave Sarah a piggyback ride so she wouldn't have to get wet. It was slow going, and the two of them nearly pitched into the river when Sarah started tickling him, but they eventually made it past the thorny flowers.

The more they traveled on the path, the more Steve was convinced that they were following an animal trail. And he was willing to bet all the gold in Fort Knox that it wasn't a deer trail.

"Uh, oh." Steve abruptly stopped, causing Sarah to plow straight into him.

"What's the matter?" Sarah leaned around her husband to see the source of the holdup.

One of the hundred-foot high trees had fallen and now the mammoth tree was blocking the path. Steve surveyed the tree to determine the feasibility of hiking over it.

"It's not bad. We can climb over it." The tree had a diameter of about ten feet and appeared to be a pine tree. Fortunately, there were many smaller limbs that were sticking out at all angles, making footholds plentiful. Steve had started breaking off the smallest of the limbs when he abruptly stopped. He bent to pick up one of the broken limbs, scrutinizing it closely. He looked at Sarah, grunted, and dropped the limb.

Her interest had been piqued. "What is it?"

"This pine tree," Steve gestured at the fallen tree, "has pine needles."

Sarah looked at the tree and then back at her husband. She raised an eyebrow. "With you so far."

He retrieved the limb and handed it to her. "The needles have multiple points. Some have two points, others have three."

Sarah studied the needles. Yes, there were multiple ends, some resembling a snake's forked tongue. With the exception of the needles, it looked like a typical pine tree.

Steve climbed to the top of the massive trunk and helped Sarah up. Once she was safely standing next to him, he slowly lowered her to the other side. From this vantage point he could see the path along the river stretch out for several more miles before it disappeared around a hill. Still no signs of civilization. He dropped to the other side next to Sarah and they resumed walking.

Steve watched his wife closely. How scared was she? This place would give anyone the creeps. The eerie silence was enough to give anyone the willies. What if they run into one of those griffins again? What if they don't fly off? What if it's something worse? What if… Why was Sarah smiling at him?

Sarah was grinning from ear to ear. One thing about Steve, it wasn't possible for him to be sneaky without a neon sign above his head blinking 'I'm up to something'! He was as easy to read as a book with large print.

"What?" she asked, with all innocence.

"Nothing. Just seeing how you're holding up. You look so calm. Aren't you worried about what might happen to us?" She shook her head no. "How are you doing?"

"All things considering, not bad. There's nothing we can do about where we presently are. Why dwell on it? We're here, and we will have to do what's necessary to get out of this mess." Her eyes flickered momentarily to his. "The mess that you got us into."

Steve stopped dead in his tracks. He whirled on her. "My mess? I thought we went through this. I…" he broke off as his darling love-of-his-life wife start laughing at him. "You're mocking me, aren't you?"

Sarah couldn't stop laughing. He looked so flustered! Every time she managed to compose herself, she took one look at her husband and broke out in giggles again. Even Steve started laughing, too, and when he started laughing, there was no telling when they would both be able to stop.

"What are you trying to do??" Sarah gasped. "I can't breathe! Sides h-hurt! Stop - laughing!"

"Absolutely no sympathy. Whatsoever." He turned to her and pulled her in to an embrace. "We'll get out of this. I promise you."

"I know we will. It's just frightening, that's all. If the trees and flowers are different, and creatures like those griffins live here, what else are we going to find? What if the people here are savages? Provided some people actually live here, that is."

Steve thought a moment. "If there are people here, I can guarantee that they aren't savages. Or cannibalistic, if that's what you're wondering."

"How? How can you be certain?"

"My grandparents. If this was such a horrific place, I doubt they would return here. The fact that they were always gone suggests that they were always here. I would go on to say that they might have a home here, or have at the very least some friends here that they visited often. Someone that knew them. Someone that would know they weren't from around here. And if they did have friends like that, they obviously had a way to return home."

For the first time since she arrived in this strange world, Sarah felt a little relieved. It made sense. Play the tourist, but have that round trip ticket to return home. The portal was installed in that house so they could visit here whenever they wanted, so there must be a way to return back. So how do you get the return ticket?

"So we just need to find someone that knew them? That's the plan now?"

"Yeah, don't you agree? If we can find any friends of theirs, then they would have to know that my grandparents weren't natives here. They would know that they returned to their home occasionally. If we're lucky, they will know how they did it. Or at least point us in the direction of somebody that might know."

"What if they didn't have any friends?" Sarah was doing an excellent job of playing the devil's advocate. "What if they preferred their solitude?"

Steve suddenly smacked his forehead with the palm of his hand. "The journal! Remember the journal? That entry I read to you. Hey, in fact..." Steve began systematically patting his pockets. With an exclamation of triumph, he pulled the small, leather book from his inside jacket pocket. He opened it and started flipping through pages.

"Oh sure, found it before, can't find it now. Damn. Where is that freakin' passage?"

"You mean Capily?" Sarah's short-term memory was a shade better than his, a fact that she didn't hesitate to remind him of from time to time. "I thought that entry referred to a place, not a person."

"Capily," Steve repeated. "I remember that now. Wasn't what I was referring to, though. I thought there was something else. Where is that friggin'... Ah! Here it is. Listen, listen to this: 'The Nayan is eager to read about Voltan's legendary journeys...'"

He snapped the journal closed and looked at Sarah.

"That's two names to work with. Nayan and Voltan. Although, now that I think about it, I think Voltan refers to some historic figure. 'Legendary'. Doubt that dude is still alive. No," Steve shook his head, "I think we need to concentrate on Nayan, whoever that might be."

"Nayan? That passage said 'the'. I thought that referred to a title, not the name of a person."

"Name of a person, or a title." Steve shrugged. "It's still something to go off of."

"I just hope 'the Nayan' doesn't refer to the lady of the house, or some other generic title. Or could be..." she trailed off. Steve was staring at her. "What?"

"What is it with you??" He started laughing. "Let's try and be a little optimistic, huh?"

Sarah took a deep breath. "Okay, until evidence suggests otherwise, let's assume 'the Nayan' refers to just one person."

They proceeded east for another couple of hours. Steve noted with dismay that it was starting to get dark. He hadn't realized it until now, but he was also quite famished. He was fairly certain that Sarah was hungry as well. He nervously scanned the area, looking for a suitable place to camp for the night, when his luck held out. About two miles down the river a tiny cottage had appeared, complete with a thatched roof. A single stone chimney was sending out tendrils of smoke against the darkening sky.

"Oh, thank God! Look, honey!" Sarah was pointing to the cottage. "Do you think they'll help us?"

"Only one way to find out." He took her hand. "Come on."

As they approached the small house, the flowers in the flowerbeds that were scattered all about the house pivoted in unison until they faced them.

Steve blinked a couple of times. Were those flowers watching us?

Several of the violet-colored flowers were actually starting to glow, and the orange-colored ones started vibrating. In fact, they started producing a ringing noise that was growing steadily louder.

Sarah was dumbfounded.

"They're protecting the house! Amazing!!"

Muffled shouts could be heard coming from the dwelling. The door banged open and a young, bearded man barged out holding a long stick with an equally long metal blade attached at the end. He was dressed in worn, non-descript clothing. The man took one look at them and assumed a menacing stance.

"Ummm, take it easy friend." Steve raised his hands, palms up. "We mean you no harm. We were hoping to…" he broke off and looked at Sarah. "New problem. I doubt this guy can even understand me." Steve sighed. He turned back towards the bearded man. He took a breath but was instantly cut off by the young stranger.

"And why would I not understand ye? Ye are human, are ye not?" The weapon remained trained on them. "Who are ye? What do ye want?"

The peasant looked beyond Steve and saw Sarah standing quietly. His eyes widened.

"Ye took yer woman out at night? I see no sword, no weapon. If ye are attacked, what then??"

"You can understand me? How is that possible?" Steve shook his head. "Scratch that. Listen, we mean you no harm. But we need your help. We're lost, we don't know where to go. It's late. Can you help us?

The peasant looked them over again. Apparently they were deemed harmless, because he straightened up and lowered the weapon.

"Ye seem to be decent folk. Aye, I will help if I can. I am Kornal." He extended his arm. "What kind of assistance would the two of ye be needing?"

"My name is Steve. Steve Miller." Steve went to shake the proffered hand, but before he could grasp his hand, Kornal had grabbed his forearm and gave it a friendly shake.

"Glad to meet ye, Stevemiller. Strange name." Kornal looked over to Sarah, then back at Steve. He nodded in Sarah's direction.

"Oh, sorry. This is my wife, Sarah."

Sarah stepped forward and clasped his arm in the fashion she had seen Kornal use. "Pleased to meet you, Kornal."

Steve stepped forward. "Kornal, we really need your help. We're not from around here. We need a place to stay for the night. I really hate to impose, but can you help us out? And tell you what, call me Steve. It's easier."

"Steve. Aye. Sounds better." Kornal gestured to the cottage. "Let us go inside. It is safer and ye can meet my woman."

He opened the door and beckoned them to follow. Steve glanced at Sarah. They stared at each other for a moment. Taking a deep breath, Steve stepped inside, with Sarah following close on his heels.

Kornal had disappeared somewhere in the back of the cottage, presumably to bring his wife out to meet the visitors. As Sarah entered, she caught the last parts of a whispered argument.

"Are ye crazy??" A woman's voice was hissing out the words. "Ye meet total strangers and invite them into our home? What the blazes are ye thinking??"

The man was trying to smooth things over.

"Nilly, just come and meet them. Ye will see that there is something different about them."

The lady of the house, followed closely by Kornal, came out of the back and stared at her guests. She spoke but one word:

"Greetings."

Steve glanced quickly at Kornal. Being a married man, he recognized the danger signs brewing in an irritated female. Kornal smoothed down his beard and took a deep breath.

"This is my wife, Nilhanu."

Nilhanu deliberately met each of their eyes.

Kornal gestured to their guests. "These are the people that need our help."

Sarah spoke first.

"I'm really sorry to impose on you like this, ma'am. We don't mean to be an inconvenience to you. Truthfully, we're lost. Very lost. Your husband has very generously offered his help."

"As you can see," Steve added, "we're not from around here."

Nilhanu eyed her husband dangerously before returning her gaze to Steve. "Aye, I can tell ye are not from these parts. Who are ye and what are ye doing here?"

"My name is Steve, and this is my wife, Sarah."

Sarah, remembering how Kornal clasped Steve's forearm, duplicated the gesture of greeting with the lady of the house.

Nilhanu stared in disbelief at the stranger. She had just been greeted as though she were a man! Either this was an elaborate prank concocted by her oaf of a husband or else these two were truly not from this kingdom, or any of the neighboring kingdoms for that matter. She looked to Kornal to see what his reaction would be, but discovered instead he was engaged in conversation with the strange man.

"I'm so sorry! Have I offended you?" Sarah was upset. She had watched Nilhanu's eyes open with surprise, so she knew something had transpired. The question was, was it good or bad? She looked to see what Steve's reaction was. Her husband, however, was trying to unsuccessfully describe to Kornal what a telephone was and where the closest one could be located. "If I have, I am truly sorry. I'm unfamiliar with the ways of this land. In fact, I don't even know where we are."

"I was not certain of ye before," Nilhanu admitted, "and since ye have greeted me as a man would greet a man," (Sarah blushed and looked down), "I am more convinced that ye and…" she gestured to Steve.

"Steve," Sarah supplied helpfully.

"Aye, right. Steve. Apologies." Nilhanu took a deep breath. "Ye and Steve must be true strangers here. And as such, Kornal and I will do our best to help ye out."

Sarah was so grateful that she sank down wearily into the closest chair. Tears started forming in her eyes. She took Nilhanu's hand this time and clasped it tightly. "Thank you."

"Are ye hungry? We were about to have our supper. There is plenty here for four."

"Yes, we are. We are very grateful." Sarah looked to Steve, still in conversation with Kornal. "We haven't eaten anything for the better part of the day. The last thing I had was a couple bags of beef jerky."

"Beaf jerkie? What is that?"

"Ummm, dried strips of meat. For traveling."

"Ah! I understand." Nilhanu gestured towards the hearth where a small iron kettle was hung over the flames. "I have put some dried meat in the stew. Bolger meat is quite tasty, dried or fresh."

"Bolger?"

"Aye, bolger. Is that not the type of meat ye ate earlier?"

"Ummm, no. It was, well, it was cow meat."

"Kow?" Nilhanu said the unfamiliar word slowly. "What manner of creature is that?"

"One that is bred for its meat in my homeland." Sarah paused, never believing in her wildest dreams that she'd one day have to describe what a cow was. "It's quite good."

Nilhanu smiled hospitably. She still didn't know what a *kow* was, but it was not important to her. She rose and left the room, returning moments later with four bowls and four flat, wooden spoons.

Sarah again looked over to Steve. He was still talking with Kornal.

"Steve?"

Steve's eyes snapped over to lock on hers. "Yes?"

Sarah gestured to the bowls. "Have some stew."

"Great! I'm starved." Steve walked over to his wife and took his bowl of steaming stew. The spoon was half-way up to his mouth by the time he sat down in front of the fireplace. The fire flared just then, giving off enough light for him to catch sight of the contents of the bowl. Chunks of green meat caught his eye, with unfamiliar vegetables and bits of leaves and other unknown greens floating around in a light green broth. His eyes widened, and then narrowed in speculation.

Sarah, who had suspected this behavior would come from her culinary-retarded husband, elbowed Steve discreetly in his ribs. Hard, but not hard enough to spill the stew. Fortunately, their hosts were busily consuming their own bowls.

Sarah whispered a fast set of instructions to her hesitant husband. "Hon, just eat it. Don't ask."

Steve looked at his wife, back at the bowl of stew/glop, back to his wife and took a bite. Fortunately, his hunger prevailed. Besides, it wasn't that bad. With a side-long grin at his wife, he ate another spoonful. And another. "It's very good."

Chapter 3 - Encounter

Steve awoke the following morning blissfully unaware of where he was. He turned on his side and snuggled closer to his wife, only Sarah wasn't there. Nothing to worry about. His wife usually started moving around long before he did.

He smiled. Today was Sunday, wasn't it? That meant that Sarah was most likely in the kitchen cooking something wonderful for breakfast. Sighing contentedly, he started daydreaming, wondering if it would be fresh cinnamon rolls, or maybe some french toast and bacon.

I really should get up, he thought. See if I can be of some help.

He cracked open his eyes and inhaled, hoping to smell something good. Instead, he instantly locked eyes with his wife from across the room. She wasn't smiling.

"So you're finally up, huh? Good. There's a lot to do and I don't want to appear like ungrateful guests. Go see if you can help Kornal with anything."

"Kornal? Oh, man. It wasn't a dream." Steve sighed. "Okay, okay, I'm up. Where is he? Probably outside chopping wood or something, huh?"

"He's outside, but I'm not sure doing what. I'm going to go try and help out with breakfast. You just try not to hurt yourself, okay?"

"Hurt myself, huh? Think highly of me, don't you?" Steve grinned at his wife.

"Do you really want me to answer that?" Sarah smiled back as she walked to the opposite side of the small cottage.

Steve stretched and sat up. His gaze traveled about his immediate surroundings. The hearth on the far wall already had a steady fire going. An iron kettle was hanging over it with some steam escaping now and then from the lid. It smelled wonderful. He didn't want to think about what it might have in it. Nilhanu was busy mincing some type of root and adding diced something-or-other to the mixture whenever she paused. She gestured for Sarah to stir the kettle on the fire.

Steve got up and walked to the door. Kornal was nowhere to be seen. Okay, now what was he supposed to do?

The flowers that had previously acted as sentinels swiveled again to face him, but did not start chiming, or glowing, or whatever it was that they were doing last night. Steve got the feeling that they were keeping an eye on him.

"Kornal? Are you out here?"

There were rustling sounds coming from around the back of the cottage. Jamming his hands in his pockets, he headed off to investigate.

When he made it to the back of the house, he still didn't see or hear anything. Just then, he heard a shout of surprise, followed closely by several splashes and a slew of curses coming from the general direction of the river.

Steve sprinted towards the riverbank, ready to help out in whatever way he could. What he saw when he got there, however, drew him up short. What the hell? Steve blinked a couple of times.

Kornal was wrestling with what appeared to be a salmon-sized, eight-legged fish that was making it quite clear it preferred not to be a meal. The "fish" kept wriggling and kicking its way out of Kornal's grip and managed to flop back into the water. With a fresh string of curses, the young man dove after the creature.

"Get back here, ye stinkin' pile o' naka dung! I am not finished with ye!"

More splashes and angry shouts. After a few more moments, Kornal emerged triumphantly with his catch. He strode out of the water with the limp fish and spied Steve.

"Ah, Steve, good mornin' to ye." He held up the creature. "I caught breakfast!"

Steve gestured to his catch. "What is that? We sure don't have any fish that look like that where I'm from."

"This is a rypo. There are plenty of them all throughout the river. They are a bugger to catch. Practically impossible to see in the river. Ye have never seen a rypo before?"

"No, I'm sorry, I haven't. I'm curious as to what other types of creatures live around here. Anything dangerous?"

"Dangerous? Well, there are the dragons, naturally. Ye do not want to tangle with one o' them. They can be... Steve, are ye well? What is the matter? Do ye not know what a dragon is?"

Steve's eyes had gone wide open and had an utterly shocked expression on his face.

"Dragons!! Hell yeah, I know what a dragon is. Holy crap, are there really dragons here? Are they big? Do they breathe fire?"

"Ye sound like ye want to encounter one. If ye did, ye would not live to see another day. Very dangerous, are dragons. Thankfully, there are none in these parts." Kornal pointed to the mountains far to the north. "Ye would have to journey many days into the Bohanis if ye truly wanted to see one."

Steve thought a moment. "Okay, no dragons around here. What other types of animals live in this land? We saw a pair of griffins yesterday. I was almost dinner for them."

"Aye, there are plenty of griffins in these parts. They can be very dangerous if provoked. Ye are not allowed to hunt or kill a griffin. Considered to be sacred. Not sure why." Kornal scratched his beard. "There are no shortage of griffins here, that is for sure. The best advice I could give ye would be to steer clear of 'em."

"How many people live here? Are there others like yourself and your wife?"

"There are several large villages. The closest can be found to the west. Avin. "

"Kornal, think carefully, have you encountered any other travelers that appear to be total strangers, like us? More specifically, an old man named Simon, or a woman named Grace?"

Kornal thought a moment. "We do not get many travelers throughout these parts of the mountains. Of the few that we have met and spoken with, there has not been anyone calling themselves by those names."

"What about people that looked completely out of place, such as ourselves? Do you get many visitors like that?"

"Nay, no one like that."

Steve suddenly brightened. "What about points of interest? If someone were to come to this place from a far away land, what do you think they would like to see? "

"A'poynt o' intrehst'?"

"Okay, okay, let me think. What about a ruler? Someone in charge? If a distant traveler came to this land looking for the representative of…" Steve paused a moment. "Exactly what land is this? What do you call it?"

"Ye are standin' smack in the middle o' the kingdom o' Lentari."

"Kingdom? Then there must be a king and queen?"

"Aye, Kri'Entu and Ny'Callé."

"Where do they reside? I mean, how would I find them? They might be able to help us."

"Their majesties are very kind and generous. They would find a way to help ye. The king and queen hold court in R'Tal. That's several days journey from here, due east as the griffin flies."

"How difficult do you think it is? I mean, do you think Sarah and I could make it?"

"Aye, there are several roads that will lead to R'Tal. We will give ye enough supplies so that you can make it there."

"Thanks. Again. We really do appreciate all you've done for us." Steve paused for a moment. "Is there anything that can pose any problems to us on our way there?"

"There is always a chance that somebody or something would do ye harm if given a chance. Their majesties, however, have enchanted the roads to keep folk from harm." Kornal's look became stern. "Do not risk yer lives. Do not stray from the passageway, at least until ye have the castle safely in sight."

"If the roads are safe, then we have nothing to fear, right?"

Kornal shook his head. "Friend, ye do not have knowledge of our kingdom nor our ways. That in itself will put ye in grave danger. Just get to the king an' queen as soon as ye can. Do not stray," Kornal repeated.

"Stay on the road. Got it."

Kornal went around to the back of the hut to clean the rypo. Suspecting their host was going to prepare the fish for breakfast, Steve wisely walked the other direction, deciding to seek out Sarah. He was pretty sure he'd be unable to eat the fish if he saw the poor thing cleaned.

He ducked back inside the hut and discovered his wife and Nilhanu seated at the table, chatting away as though they were the best of friends. It never fails. Leave two women in the same room and even if they didn't know one another, they'd find something to talk about.

Sarah looked up at him and smiled. "Hi! Were you able to help out?"

Steve looked down and shuffled his feet. "Well, not exactly. I had a feeling that if I tried to jump in and lend a hand that I'd be in the way. He's very versatile. I do have some info for you that might help us out."

"You do? That's great! Nilhanu and I have been chatting as well. After breakfast, we'll compare notes."

They feasted on roast rypo and boiled grains. It was not his favorite egg breakfast sandwich, but it wasn't too bad. The rypo didn't taste like fish at all, more like pork. The meat had too much fat in it, but that didn't seem to stop Sarah from enjoying it. Steve, meanwhile, was nonchalantly trying to trim the fat off of his piece of fish without making it look too obvious what he was doing. He was determined to eat this meal without making too much of a fuss.

Once they finished their breakfast, Sarah helped Nilhanu clean up while Kornal presented Steve with an old, used knapsack. Together, they packed the sack with dried meats and other foodstuffs that would see them through the several day journey to R'Tal.

"Kornal, I can't thank you enough for your hospitality. I'm quite convinced we wouldn't have been able to survive last night if it wasn't for you and Nilhanu." Steve offered his hand to Kornal. "I won't forget this."

Kornal grasped his forearm warmly.

"Steve, it has been my pleasure. I hope ye and Sarah find what ye are looking for and have a safe journey to R'Tal."

Nilhanu and Sarah joined them outside. Steve hoisted the pack onto his back.

Their hostess smiled at the both of them. "Please, if at all possible, send word back to us that the two of ye arrived safely. I will not rest easy until I know ye are safe in the castle."

Sarah stepped up and hugged Kornal, then Nilhanu. "We will, I promise."

Steve cleared his throat. "Ummm, exactly how do we do that? Send word to you, that is. Tell me how and I will."

"My apologies, I keep forgetting that ye are not familiar with our ways. Ye can send word by trained kytes. All villages have them. Very useful. Or," Kornal paused, "if ye gain the favor of their royal highnesses, ye could send word by jhorun."

"Kites. Jorren. Got it."

Kornal picked up a stick, smoothed the dirt in front of them.

"Now, we are here." Kornal drew a small house in the dirt. "A day's walk should bring ye to here, where the Wanlu breaks off from the Zylan River." Kornal drew a line about five feet long and drew a connecting line from the south that joined the main line at roughly the halfway point. "Ye can choose to follow either the river, or travel along the forest edge. Both will take ye to the great sea." Tapping the line that stretched straight toward to the water, Kornal continued. "I would follow this. Ye will find the village of Donlari along the way if ye go that way."

"What about the other way? Any advantage to taking that route?" Sarah asked.

"The forest path is less travelled than the river." Kornal drew more marks into the dirt. "If ye choose, ye can follow that around the valley perimeter. That would take you directly to R'Tal. It is shorter, but there are no villages if ye need help. The other way, leading to the sea, ends here. From there, ye would have to turn north, following the coastline. In two days ye would find yerself before the castle. All told, this path," Kornal pointed to the east-west path, "will take ye about three days, two if ye hurry."

"Which way would you take?" Sarah asked Kornal.

Kornal pointed toward the line depicting the river.

"Ye would be wise to take the river path. If ye encounter trouble, or need more supplies, ye can find what ye need in Donlari."

"Whereabouts would we find Donlari on this map?"

Kornal made a small indentation in the dirt about halfway along the river to the sea. "About here."

Steve suddenly straightened up and glanced at Sarah, then back to Kornal. "When you mentioned if we needed anything we could stop by Donlari, what do you use for currency?" At Kornal's blank look, Steve went on. "What do you use for money? If you wanted something, say, some food, how would you pay for it?"

Nilhanu stepped forward. "I believe Steve is referring to our coinage. There are grifs, which are gold; tags, which are silver; and werts, which are iron." She went back into the house and returned with a small, leather pouch. "Here, we do not have much, but we do have two tags and several werts."

She reached into the bag and pulled out two silver coins and several iron ones. She offered them to Steve, who started to reach for them when Sarah cut her off.

"Wait a minute, there's no way we're going to take your money. There has to be something we have that… Hold on a sec." Sarah started patting the pockets in her jeans. She reached into her right front pocket and pulled out the gold coin, the nine-sided crystal disk, and the marble, all taken from the forgotten safe.

"I forgot about these." Sarah held out the gold coin. "Is this a grif?"

Both Kornal and Nilanu's eyes widened in disbelief.

Sarah was confused. "What's the matter? This has got to be a grif. Look, it has a picture of a griffin on the back of it."

Kornal was gesturing at the marble.

"Ye have a jorii! Blessed be the Wizards!!"

"A what? A jore-eye? What did you call this thing?" Steve picked out the marble from Sarah's hand and looked at it. The marble was still warm to the touch.

"Only wizards and kings possess jorii! Ye did not tell us that ye were of noble blood!"

Steve scoffed. "Noble blood? Nope, sorry, we don't have any royal blood in us. At least, not that I'm aware of. Why? Do you have to be a member of royalty to have one of these?"

Sarah took the marble from Steve. "Exactly what is this? What does it do?"

"It is a jorii," Kornal explained, refusing to hold it when Steve offered. "I have only seen one, when I was but a lad. It enhances the jhorun inside of ye and amplifies it. Most jhorun is minor. A jorii is capable of raising the level of yer own jhorun to that of the wizards. Kings and wizards have powerful jhorun, but do not want others to have a level equal or greater to their own, so they hoard their jorii. How did ye get that??"

Sarah held up her hand. "Wait a moment. What exactly is 'joarrun'?"

Nilhanu tapped her chest. "Jhorun is inside of ye. Every human is born with it. Some manifests itself physically, whereas other jhorun manifest itself without ye even being aware of it. My jhorun enhances pontal. Ye might have noticed them by the door." She gestured to the "sentinel" flowers Steve and Sarah had seen when they first arrived.

Steve approached the flowers. "You enhanced these? What does that mean? You fertilized them?" Comprehension clearly still eluded him.

"What I do is raise these from seed, enhance them, and have them perform tasks for me that they otherwise could not do." Nilhanu started stroking the orange flowers.

Sarah blinked. The flowers were all swaying softly back and forth under Nilhanu's hand. Understanding was dawning on her.

"You mean these flowers don't ordinarily move?"

Nilhanu smiled. "These pontal have been enhanced to warn us of intruders. Did ye not hear them ringing last night when the two of ye arrived?"

"I do remember that. So these, uh -" Sarah pointed at the orange flowers again, "flowers don't typically warn the occupants of the house that there are strangers lurking about? What do these, uh, pontal normally do?"

Nilhanu gazed blankly at Sarah. "Do? They share their fragrance with whoever admires them."

Steve suppressed a chuckle. Sarah fired a dangerous look at him.

"Sarah, do ye not have pontal where the two of ye are from?"

"Yes, we do. It's just that there isn't anyone that can take the function of a plant such as this and modify it to perform some other function. And your joarrun was able to do this?"

"Aye. My jhorun is minor, but I have found ways to make it useful around our home."

Sarah turned to Steve. "Honey, I think they are talking about magic. They have to be."

"Magic? Why do you say that?"

"She's saying she took these basic flowers and modified them into something else."

"They still look like flowers."

Sarah sighed and faced Kornal and Nilhanu. "Let me see if I understand you properly. When you refer to joarrun…"

"Jho-run," Nilhanu said slowly, putting stress on the first syllable.

"Jho-run. Jhorun. Got it. Thanks." Sarah took a deep breath. "Okay, when you talk about jhorun, you're referring to an ability that each person has to do something that typically they wouldn't have been able to do without their jhorun, correct?"

Nilhanu smiled. "Aye, that is correct. Without my jhorun, these pontal would be just average pontal and serve no useful purpose."

Sarah gave Steve her victory smile. Steve, however, was wearing a frown and thinking deeply. Sarah decided to move in for the kill, so she faced Kornal.

"If you don't mind me asking, Kornal, what is the nature of your jhorun?"

"It is no important ability. My jhorun lets me predict where rypos will be the following morning." He smiled at his wife and took her hand. "Makes catching breakfast easier!"

Nilhanu smiled back. "It is very fortunate that rypo taste delicious and we live near a river."

Steve was still mulling over the existence of magic in this reality and therefore didn't say anything. Yet. Sarah stepped forward and met Kornal's gaze.

"Kornal, that is a very important ability. You can locate food to help support your family. I can't think of a more noble jhorun."

Kornal was all but glowing at this remark.

Nilhanu looked at Steve, then to Sarah. "If ye don' mind me asking, what is the nature of yer jhorun, Sarah?"

Sarah let out a breath. She knew they were going to ask that. What should she tell them? She looked to her husband for help. She didn't want it known that they were from another world/reality. No sense in scaring the hell out of their newfound friends.

Steve caught the 'request for help look' from his wife. They gazed at each other for a few seconds, an unspoken argument raging full on. Steve finally stepped forward. "We come from a group of people that don't have jhorun. Nothing to be alarmed about. Quite truthfully, I wish we had some."

Kornal shook his head. "I did not know that there were humans who did not possess jhorun. Amazing! Perhaps the castle wizard could grant ye jhorun."

Steve raised an eyebrow and looked at Kornal with disbelief. "Really? Can a wizard actually do that?"

"Aye, friend, wizards are very powerful. If they wished it, or if their majesties ordered them to, they can give ye jhorun."

"Have the wizards given jhorun to people that haven't had it before?"

Kornal scratched his head. "Come to think of it, I do not recall ever hearing of a wizard that granted that gift because I have never heard of anyone that did not have jhorun."

Now Sarah was frowning. What was he doing? Was he trying to provoke an argument? Let's not upset the locals, dear.

"I have yet to meet another human that did not have jhorun of some type." Nilhanu said. "Ye may yet have jhorun in ye that ye aren't aware of or have not yet discovered how to invoke it yet."

Steve kept his best poker face on. "You may be right. We haven't ever tried to use our jhorun, so it may be lying dormant." Steve mentally rolled his eyes. Yeah, right. I have some type of magic ability that I've never discovered until now? What was in these people's drinking water? Best to humor them. "Hey, if we had jhorun and wanted to learn what it was, what would we do to bring it out?"

Nilhanu opened her mouth to speak, closed it, and then looked at Kornal. Kornal noted his wife's behavior and interpreted it (correctly!) as it being his turn to answer a question.

"Each person has a different type of jhorun. Where there may be jhorun that will accomplish the same task, the method of accomplishing that task might be different. It is difficult to say." Kornal thought a moment. "Ye might try to *will* something to happen."

Steve took a breath but was cut off by Sarah. "I promise you, Kornal, we will try. Won't we, dear." Sarah's tone indicated this wasn't a question.

Steve adopted a cheery expression. "Yeah, we'll try our best!"

Sarah looked back at the young peasant couple and smiled at both of them. "Again, we appreciate your hospitality. You have given us a lot to think about!"

Steve spoke up. "Thanks again guys, for everything. We'll send word when we reach R'Tal, that I can promise you."

They bid farewell to their new friends and started down the path. Once they were out of earshot Sarah smacked Steve on the arm. Hard.

"What was that all about? Why did you have to press them? They have been nothing but nice and hospitable to us the entire time. Was making your point that important?"

Steve looked down and shrugged his shoulders. "I didn't mean to be an ass about it.

"So what exactly did you mean to do?" Sarah was pissed. "Just because you don't believe in magic doesn't mean that it doesn't exist! Look around you!" Sarah swung her arm in a wide arc. "This isn't our home. It's not even close! We got here by some magic portal in your grandparent's house. Griffins exist here and apparently so does magic. You'd better get used to it."

Steve sighed. "It's just hard for me to accept this. Like I said before, it's one thing to read about this sort of thing. It's quite another to experience it firsthand."

They continued on, heading east along the river. They had stopped for a drink and a brief rest when they heard a distinctive screech in the distance. Both husband and wife jumped to their feet. Steve started scanning the distant horizon. "Crap. Griffins. Let's find some cover!" He pulled Sarah over to some fallen trees and several squat bushes. "Get under, quick!"

They crouched in silence until they were sure that whatever it was had flown upriver and were out of range.

"There's got to be a way to safely avoid those things." Sarah was still looking up. "Who knows what else calls this place home?"

Steve smiled. "Funny you should say that. I asked Kornal the very same question."

"And?"

"Well, he said the most dangerous creatures here were the dragons, and -"

"Dragons!! Omigod!!!" Sarah rubbed her temples. "Oh, this is perfect. Just perfect. What happens if we run into one of those? We'll be done for!"

Steve tried to calm his wife. "Yeah, we probably would be if we were to seek them out. Relax. Kornal said that we'd have to walk many days north past those mountains there in order to enter their territory. We're safe."

"Oh, thank God." Sarah let out the breath she had been holding.

"One other thing."

Sarah froze. Again.

"No, nothing serious. Well, it kinda is. Anyway, we need to stay on the road. It's supposed to be enchanted against harm. So as long as we stay on the road, we should be good."

Sarah glanced down and then followed the road east with her eyes. "If we step off, we could be hurt? Got it. No straying."

Steve picked up the knapsack, slung it over his shoulder, and helped his wife up.

"Do you really think that we might have some magic ability?" Steve asked.

Sarah bit her lip, thinking. "I'm not sure. I think it would be really cool if we did. I doubt it would be anything major, though. Still, I'm curious."

Hours later, Steve was tired. He was tired of walking, tired of listening for medieval monsters, tired of a general lack of civilization. "How much longer before we hit the fork in the river? We should be getting close." Steve was looking north.

Sarah chuckled. "If you're looking for that other river, then you should be looking east, not north."

"Hey, according to that map Kornal drew, that other river, the main one, should approach from the north. We've been traveling northeast for the last two hours."

Sarah blinked. "You paid attention to the directions Kornal gave you? I'm impressed!"

Steve shot her a dark look. "That's a common misconception women have nowadays. Guys do pay attention to directions, and have been known to ask for them. Lordy, woman."

Sarah laughed.

They continued on in silence for another half an hour when they reached the source of the river they had been following. The impressive Zylan River stretched out from west to east as far as the eye could see.

"That sucker has got to be the size of the Mississippi! Wow!!" Steve whistled in amazement. "I sure do hope we don't have to cross that."

The Zylan River stretched a mile and a half across at its widest point. The murky water was gently flowing east, prompting Steve to yet again wonder if he might be able to make a raft. Just as quickly as before, he dismissed the idea. A flock of light blue birds were floating on the river and another flock was circling overhead. The road, fortunately, continued east, running alongside the river as well as heading off west.

"So far, so good," Steve mused. "We have to head east for close to a day. That should bring us to that village. Piece of cake!"

"Can we stop for a bit? My legs are tired." Sarah sat down on the nearest rock. "Why don't we have something to eat?"

"Good idea." Steve set down the knapsack and started rummaging through it. He handed some dried meat to Sarah and took a piece for himself.

"I'll say this," Steve said, "I'm really starting to like jerky. Funny thing is, I'm pretty sure this ain't beef jerky, but at least it ain't green." He gave Sarah a lopsided grin.

"Think anyone will ever believe this when we tell this story?"

Steve leaned back against the rock and looked to the east. "As long as we get to tell the story, I really don't care."

After a brief rest, they resumed their trek east. Steve turned to Sarah. "Did you hear that we're in the kingdom of Lentari?"

Sarah nodded. "Yeah, that's what Nilhanu said. She also said that Lentari is ruled by a king and queen."

"Right. Kornal said that, too. He said they are Cree Entoo and Nigh Kuhlay, or something like that. And Lentari? Where the hell is that? I may not be a geography buff, but I've never heard of that country. You?"

"No, I haven't." Sarah suddenly stopped walking. "Wait. What were the names of the king and queen again?"

"Ummm, I'm pretty sure he said 'Cree Entoo and Nigh Kuhlay'. Maybe he said 'Kallay'. I don't know. Why?"

"Hon, give me the journal."

Steve pulled the journal from his pocket and passed it to his wife. Sarah opened it to the first page and gasped.

"Whoa! Look! Remember that inscription we couldn't read? Look at it now!"

Steve came up behind his wife and looked over her shoulder at the journal. In an elegant hand were the following words:

Return to R'Tal whenever ye or yer friends would like to visit– Kri'Entu & Ny'Callé

"What the hell? This just magically appears in English now?"

Sarah smirked at her husband. "Magically, huh?"

Steve grunted, electing not to comment.

Sarah pointed at the names. "Look! Kree Entoo and Nigh Calay. Do you know what this means?"

"I'll say! R'Tal! That's where the king and queen live. Hon, I think 'Nayan' refers to the queen! That means that my grandparents knew the king and queen!" Steve thought a moment. "I would say this confirms our theory. Since their names are in my grandparents' journal, and there appears to be an open invitation to return, then clearly they have come here before and obviously had a way to return home." He grabbed Sarah's shoulders. "Honey, this is our proof!"

Sarah was clapping her hands excitedly. "Oh, YES!! Just what I wanted to hear! Okay, so the plan is now to get to R'Tal. We need to seek an audience with the king and queen. They have got to be able to get us home."

Encouraged, they hurried back to the enchanted road and headed east once more. As they rounded a gentle bend in the path, neither husband nor wife noticed a faint shimmering over the road.

Sarah was excited. "Hon, let me see that journal again. Yes, see? The entry makes it sound like your grandparents were either highly respected or else held positions of high status in the court. Might make sense why they were always gone. Maybe they had important work here."

"I can buy that, I guess. But to prevent them from coming back home to spend time with us? That would suggest that the king and queen are a couple of hard-asses."

"I'm just saying that there is obviously more going on here than we originally thought, so I think we ought to hold judgment until we get all the facts, 'k?"

Steve nodded. "That's fair."

Another hour passed by, finding Steve and Sarah in high spirits. That came to a screeching halt, however, when the path they had been following unexpectedly vanished, leaving them in the middle of an open glade. Without realizing it, they had wandered well away from the river. No signs of their enchanted path or the mighty river they had been following were anywhere to be found.

"Ummm, what just happened here? Where the hell did the path go?" Steve was looking around worriedly.

Having been lectured very firmly by Kornal about straying from the path, neither Steve nor Sarah had taken a step in any direction.

"The path is right where ye left it, miscreant. About three leagues back."

The voice sounded harsh and mean, and meant business. It belonged to a small, wiry man wearing rags and brandishing a wicked-looking dagger. He pointed it at Steve.

"I must say that no one has fallen for my path trick in quite some time."

Sarah moved closer to Steve and whispered, "What do we do?"

"Play it safe. Don't provoke him."

The thief was looking them over. "So what do I have here? Yer money pouches. Toss 'em over. Now."

Steve stepped forward. "I know you won't believe this, but we don't have any money. We are just a couple of travelers, on our way to Donlari. We don't have anything of value."

The brazen thief walked over to Steve, brandishing his knife. "Aye, right you are. I do not believe ye. Toss over that pack. Turn out yer pockets."

Steve reluctantly handed the pack to the thief, who snatched it out of his hand. He upended the contents on the ground, kicking around the packages of dried meat and several small leather pouches.

"So ye are playing games with me. Ye are hiding yer money. Not smart. Hand it over now and ye just might walk away from this."

It was then that the bandit caught sight of Sarah's purse. "I'd be passing that over, girl. Ye don' want to be trying anything stupid."

Sarah was stuck. She really didn't want to give the thief her purse, but she didn't want Steve to attempt anything heroic, either. It wasn't worth it. Oh, wait! The gold grif and the jorii were in her change purse! If the jorii was as powerful as Kornal said it was, it would be catastrophic to give it to someone like this! What was she going to do?

Before she could decide, however, the thief made the decision for her. Quick as a fox, he leaned forward and snatched the purse off of her shoulder. After a couple of quick fumbles with the zipper, the contents of her purse joined the contents of their pack on the ground.

The robber saw the shiny metal cylinder of her lipstick and snatched that off the ground, tucking it into an inside pocket. Her car keys, work keys, and package of Juicy Fruit were swept aside. The thief found her smaller change purse, opened it, and dumped the contents on the ground as well. Sarah held her breath. Maybe he wouldn't find them! Wait a minute. Where were they? Sarah peered at the ground. Both the small sphere and the gold coin were nowhere to be found.

The bandit shouted with triumph as he eyed the small pile of change on the ground. He grabbed a double handful of American coins and thrust it into another pocket.

"I knew ye were not empty-handed. Not very smart, hiding 'em with the lady." He then pulled out a bundle of rope and tied both Steve and Sarah's hands together. Throwing their possessions back into the pack, the wily thief then made Steve hoist the pack onto his back and carry it along with them.

For several hours they marched in silence as their captor led them through thick brambles of dry, scratchy brush. They were following a trail all right, Steve noted, but this clearly wasn't an enchanted one. They were forced to wade through several small, shallow streams until they finally came upon a clearing which had a small cottage in serious need of repairs.

The diminutive thief led them inside the foul-smelling hut, pushing them into the far recesses of the shanty to what appeared to be a trap door in the floor. Turning around, he leered evilly at his prizes.

"It ain't that cozy, but I guarantee ye will be safe and sound." The thief pulled back the locking bracket and opened his cellar door. "Naught but stone walls. Ye will not be escaping from there, rest assured." He pushed Steve and Sarah down the stairs.

Sarah had tears in her eyes. "What are you going to do with us? Why are you doing this?"

"The two of ye will fetch a handsome price as slaves. Preparations must be made. I should not be gone for more than a couple o' days."

"You can at least leave us food and water," Steve demanded.

"Ye can have yer pack, and that be all ye get."

With that, the cellar door was closed with a loud bang. The locking bracket was shoved back through, and the last thing they heard was the laugh of their captor.

Chapter 4 – Prisoners

The root cellar stunk of moldy earth. There was several empty burlap sacks scattered throughout their prison, along with a couple of empty, wooden crates. Several rotting bales of straw were strewn against the far, northern wall. What little light there was came through several small chinks in the stones of the foundation of the house.

Sarah and Steve were standing in the center of the room. The tiny bit of light they had was beginning to fade. Dusk was settling in. Steve was glancing around, trying to take in as much as possible before all the light vanished completely. He held Sarah close as she sobbed quietly into his shoulder.

"Hey, we'll be all right." Steve was speaking softly to her. "We'll get out of this."

"How? There's no one here to help us." She sniffed loudly. "We're lost on some unknown world where no one knows we're here, about to be sold into slavery. How the hell are we possibly going to be alright?"

"Where there's a will, there's a way. Mr. Hospitality there specifically said he wouldn't be back for at least two days. I sure as hell don't plan on being here when he returns."

With that Steve straightened up and started working feverishly on his bonds, trying to wriggle his wrists free. Sarah decided to look around for anything that might help her. While Steve struggled with his ropes Sarah started feeling around the straw strewn about the floor.

There's got to be something here that we can use, Sarah thought. A shard of glass, a sharp piece of metal, anything!

Sadly, the only things she discovered were a decaying lump of cheese, a few scraps of rope, and some shreds of burlap.

"So what happened?" Steve wondered. "We didn't wander off the road. How did we end up following some fake path?"

"He mentioned that he hasn't seen anyone fall for his 'path trick' in quite some time. Does that mean he somehow tricked us to follow a fork on the road?"

Steve shook his head. "We didn't come across any forks in the road. We would have remembered."

"Illusion. He had to have covered up the real path and projected an image of a different path that led away." Sarah looked at her husband, who was now trying to chew his way through the ropes. "That's the only thing I can think of."

Steve stopped chewing and smiled sheepishly at his wife. "Hey, we're newbies here. How were we supposed to know that that type of thing could even be done?"

"So now that we know he tricked us, how does that help us now?"

Steve sighed. "It doesn't. What it means is that we have to be extremely careful here. We could walk right into the den of some monster if we're not cautious."

Steve continued biting and chewing at his ropes. That bastard knew how to tie a knot, that's for certain. He wasn't sure what these ropes were made out of, but so far, they were resisting all his efforts of escaping. Maybe he could try loosening a couple of knots with his teeth instead. Hmm, that one looks like it's on top, maybe that one first.

Sarah, meanwhile, had found a small scrap of metal and was gently feeling its sides to see if any had a sharp enough edge to cut her ropes. Nope, doesn't feel like it. Smooth on all sides. Dammit! There had to be another scrap somewhere. If only these ropes weren't so tight, or else she had skinnier wrists.

Her knees were hurting after being on them for the last couple of minutes, so she started to stand, only to stumble and land back down on them. Hard.

"Ouch!!"

"Are you okay?" Steve hurried over to help his wife up. Sarah grabbed a hold of her husband's outstretched hands and hoisted herself up.

"Yeah, I think I was sitting on my foot. It fell asleep. I'm okay." Sarah flexed her arms, restoring some circulation back into her fingers. Was it her imagination? Did the ropes feel like they were loosening up a bit?

She looked over at Steve, who had resumed picking at his bound hands with his teeth. She decided to hold off mentioning anything just yet. After struggling for another moment or two, much to her surprise, her left arm came free. The ropes slid down her right arm and plopped onto the floor.

Steve, intent on making good his claim to earn his freedom, was still focusing on getting at least one knot untied.

Sarah walked over to her husband. "Can I give you a hand with that?" And without waiting for an answer, dove into the many knots holding Steve's hands tightly together.

"What the…" Steve blinked. "How did you get free? You were tied up just a couple of minutes ago."

"It must have been when I fell down. My ropes felt loose and I was able to pull an arm out."

"Way to go!!" Steve remained motionless while Sarah worked on the ropes. Her small, delicate fingers made short work of the hastily tied knots.

In just a matter of minutes, both former prisoners were rubbing their wrists, looking around in the fading light.

"Now, let me take a look at that door." Steve strode over to the ladder leading up. "There must be some way to get that thing open."

The rickety wooden ladder groaned under his weight as he ran his hands over the heavy wooden door fastened to the ceiling. The bolt to open the door, however, was on the other side.

Steve pondered for a moment. Well, maybe the hinges? No, that's not gonna work. I don't even see any hinges. Maybe I can move it.

He pressed his right shoulder against the trapdoor, braced his feet on the ladder, and heaved.

C-r-a-c-k!!

The wooden rung he was standing on gave way, dropping him unceremoniously down to the next rung, which didn't like having two hundred fifty pounds suddenly appearing on it either, so it broke as well, plummeting him down to the next rung and so on.

"Steve! Are you alright?" Sarah hurried over to where he was sprawled out on the floor. She tried fanning the air to get the dust out of her face. "What happened?"

Steve coughed and stood up. He brushed off his clothes and made an attempt at reclaiming some dignity. He scowled at the remains of the ladder.

"Piece of crap ladder. Damn thing is made out of twigs. No wonder it wouldn't hold."

"So now we can't reach the door." Sarah threw up her hands in frustration. "This is great. Just great! This just keeps getting better and better!!"

Steve knew he had to calm his wife down. Somehow. One can't project a sense of calm if one didn't feel calm himself. He took a deep breath.

"Okay, honey, look at it this way. The lock for that door is on the top-side. There isn't any way to get that thing open from down here. So we'll just have to find another way out."

Sarah bristled with anger. How can he remain so calm? Didn't he realize they were in a serious predicament?

"Another way out? How?? There are no more doors and in case you hadn't noticed, there are no windows, either."

Steve sat down on one of the wooden crates and motioned Sarah to join him. Reluctantly, she sat. She looked at her husband, her eyes filling.

"What are we gonna do? We're trapped in here!"

"First things first, let's calm down. That jerk said he wouldn't be back for at least two days. So that gives us some time to think."

"Time to think? About what? About not panicking?"

Steve took another deep breath and let it out slowly. "No, right now we need to start brainstorming. How can we get out of here? Can we use that jorii thingamajig?"

Sarah sadly shook her head. "It's not there. I put it, the crystal, and that gold coin in my change purse. When he took my purse, he upended everything on the ground. I didn't see it. And you've seen that change purse. It's small. They're gone."

"Where's your purse now? Maybe it just fell down into the bottom. That sort of thing happens all the time to you."

Sarah was losing patience. It was her favorite purse. She knew it a lot better than he did, and she knew *exactly* where the missing items were placed: the small change purse. Besides, she had watched as the contents were dumped to the ground. They were missing. Period.

Steve frowned as she scowled at him. If they weren't there, then what did that mean? They were robbed? Was that why Kornal and Nilhanu offered to give them what money they had? Did they figure that they could sell the jorii? No, wait. That couldn't be it. He had watched Sarah put the items from the safe back into her purse. Not only that, he didn't even remember any of their hosts so much as touching their marble. So if the robber didn't find it, then it must be somewhere in that purse.

"Honey, now please don't get mad, but would you mind if I looked?"

Sarah's glare could have initiated the next Ice Age.

"I'm NOT a moron. This is my purse. I know damn well it's not in there. Fine. Here. Don't believe me??"

Sarah pulled the pack over to her, yanked out her purse, and marched over to Steve. Without moving her eyes from his, she emptied the contents of her purse onto the crate. With a scowl, she reached down to pick up the small change purse.

Even in the diminishing light, Steve could tell that the jorii or the gold grif were not among the contents of the purse. He watched as Sarah started to unzip the small purse when she hefted the purse in her hand, squeezed lightly, and with a small scream, dropped it.

"What's the matter?" Anger aside, Steve was beside her in a flash. "Did something hurt you?"

"No! It's there!! I felt it in the purse!" Sarah bent down and retrieved the small pouch. "See? See the bulge? It's in there!"

She unzipped the purse and held it upside-down over her hand. Sure enough the grif, crystal disc, and the jorii all landed softly in her hand.

"What the hell? There's no way that guy could have missed that. I watched him go through it, too."

Sarah was poking and prodding at her change purse. It just wasn't big enough to hide something that size. Was there a flap or something that might have snagged it and prevented it from falling the first time? She poked several fingers in and felt around. Nope, the coin purse was of a simple design. No inside pockets, just the main zipper to prevent anything from escaping.

Steve was perplexed, and whenever he was presented with a problem that he couldn't figure out, he would start mumbling to himself.

"Maybe since it's ours, only we can see it. Maybe that's how possessions work here."

Sarah snorted. "If that was true, then Kornal and Nilhanu wouldn't have been able to see it."

"Good point. Okay, maybe jorii can only be used, and therefore seen, by people with a good heart."

"Unlikely, but if that was the case, what about the coin? It's their currency. He should have been able to see that."

Steve nodded. "Good point." He started to pace, another indicator that some serious synaptic misfiring was taking place. "What about protective magic? Maybe there is security-type magic that prevents these things from being stolen."

"That knew we were about to be robbed? I don't think so. He clearly said he wanted our money. Seemed very surprised when we didn't have any."

"Another good point. Hmmm."

Sarah watched as Steve continued to pace. She took her husband's hand as he passed her the next time, pulling him to a stop. "Hon, umm, what if it was us?"

Steve paused in mid-mumble to look at his wife. "Huh?"

"What if it was us? What if we did something to it?"

"Us? Do magic? Yeah, right. We aren't from around here. I don't think it's us."

"Kornal said that he had never met a human without some type of power."

"He also said that they didn't get that many visitors."

Sarah smiled. "Well played, dear."

He grinned back at her. "Wouldn't that be something, though? Having an ability to protect your valuables, without you even knowing we were doing it? If we could market that then our financial difficulties would be over."

"I think we do need to acknowledge, though, that something did happen to the jorii."

Steve thought a moment and then smacked his hand on his forehead.

"I've got it! What do you want to bet that that jorii thing, being magic, and strong magic at that, has some sort of built-in protection? And since it does, it probably was able to mask the disc and coin as well. Huh? Huh??" He playfully poked his wife in the ribs. "What do you think?"

Sarah considered. That scenario was actually plausible.

"I obviously don't know for certain if that's what happened, but I like that idea. A lot. If it can protect itself, then there has to be a way that we can use this thing to get us out of this predicament."

Steve hefted the jorii in his palm. "Okay, Mr. Marble, do your thing." He held the jorii up to the closed trapdoor. Nothing happened. He gestured wildly, swinging his arms back and forth across the trapdoor. Nothing.

"Maybe you need to be closer to it," Sarah suggested. "The door, I mean."

"Okay, I'll buy that. Let's see. I can use some of this stuff to get closer."

He dragged the moldy bales of straw directly under the door and placed several crates on it. Gently, ever so gently, he stood up on the crate and repeated his movements from before. The door remained fastened, and the jorii was still unchanged in his palm.

Since he was teetering precariously on his makeshift podium, he climbed down and glared at the door. Clenching the jorii tightly in his fist, he raised his arm and asked the door to open.

"Open sesame!"

Sarah burst out laughing.

"Open sesame? You gotta be kidding me! Did you really think that would work?"

"Hey, it was worth a shot," Steve grumbled. Another glare at the door. "Abracadabra! Hocus Pocus!"

"I have an idea."

"I'm all ears."

"Maybe it needs a spell."

"A spell? As in witches and wizards?"

Sarah held up her hands. "Hey, I'm just giving ideas here."

Steve chuckled to himself. A spell. Great. This ought to be a hoot. That means he needed to come up with some type of rhyme, right? Let's see. What could he use?

He took a breath and faced the door. With the jorii held tightly in his right hand he started to chant.

As visitors to this land, we wish to leave
We don't know what could be in store
So using the power of this jorii,
Blow away that mother freakin' door!

The door was unimpressed. Still locked, with nothing to even indicate that they were on the right track.

"I'm impressed!" Sarah gave him a high-five. "I thought you weren't good at rhyming!"

"I'm not. That just came to me. Besides, what are you complimenting me for? It didn't work. Stupid thing is still closed."

"Okay, let me try for a while."

Steve handed her the jorii. "It's all yours. I hope you have better luck."

"Maybe it has a mental trigger." Sarah concentrated on the spherical object in her hand, willing something to happen. Anything. No luck. She drew a picture of a door in her head that led to the outside world and tried to invoke the jorii into making that a reality.

Steve suddenly grabbed her hand. "Umm, I think I know what the problem is here."

"You do? What is it?"

"I just remembered what Nilhanu said about that thing. Remember? She said that a jorii enhances your jhorun to the point of being on the same level as the wizards. She didn't say that it created an ability, only that it enhanced what you already have. So if we don't have magic to begin with, how can it enhance what doesn't exist?"

Chalk one up to her husband. Now that he had brought it up she did remember Nilhanu mentioning the fact that a jorii only enhances the magic inside you. Well, so much for this thing helping them esca-wait. Then what had happened to the jorii? How did it hide itself from the would-be thief? Was it something that one of them did? Keeping this revelation to herself for the time being, she decided to practice on the marble in silence.

Marble. Sarah chuckled to herself. He had her doing it now. It's a jorii.

Sarah worked on the jorii well into the night. While Steve slept soundly (how does he do it??) next to her on the floor, she tried everything she could think of to activate her jhorun. Did she really have some magical ability lying dormant inside her? Could she walk through walls here if she tried hard enough?

She concentrated so hard, for so long, that her only accomplishment was to give herself a pounding headache. Admitting defeat, she snuggled next to her snoring husband. Being both mentally and physically exhausted, she dropped instantly off to sleep.

She was uncertain how long she slept, but at least she did sleep a few hours. Of that, she was certain. However, she could never sleep once the sun started to shine. She shifted her back a little. Why did her back hurt so much? Did she forget to turn down her Sleep Number bed? Why was there debris on the bed? Did the cats drag something up? Since her left arm felt pinned, she used her right arm to explore her surroundings. Damned if that didn't feel just like straw.

Her memory of last night came rushing back to her. She groaned. Damn. Not a dream. They were prisoners in some damn cellar with no way out.

The sun! Why was it so bright in here?? Sarah's eyes snapped open. Sunlight was streaming down from above. The trapdoor was open!

Sarah shook Steve awake. "Hon! Wake up! The door is open! We have to get out of here! The mugger might have come back early!"

"Wha'? Timezit?" Steve rubbed a hand over his face and tried to blink his eyes. They refused to open. "Did the alarm not go off? Damn thing." He started fumbling for the remote to the TV. In their household television, not coffee, woke them up.

Any other day Sarah might have found this amusing, but not now. She had to get him to wake up. Fast. She hadn't heard any movement from upstairs, yet, and she didn't want to take any chances.

"Steve, wake up! The door is open! I swear, if you're not awake in two seconds I'm going to pull every single arm hair off of both of your arms!"

"I'm up, I'm up. What's going on?" Steve used both hands to rub his eyes.

"Look! The door is open!"

He craned his head to look up. Sure enough, the trapdoor was open. In fact, he blinked a few times, the door was gone!

"What happened? When did that disappear?"

"Disappear?"

"Hon, the door isn't open, it's gone!"

Sarah peered at the opening. No door. She had assumed the door was open, leaning against the wall above, but that wasn't the case. In fact, by squinting her eyes she could see that the locking bar was still protruding over the sides, securing the nonexistent door in place.

Steve yawned, stretched, and stood up. So what had happened to the door? Maybe one of the attempts to invoke the jorii actually worked! But what? There's no way his "hocus pocus" attempts could have worked. So what else did they try? The arm gesturing, the scowling, the mental cursing. Hah! The spell! That cheesy rhyme he came up with. That had to be it!

"I got it! I think my spell must have worked! It obviously took a bit longer to kick in. That has to be it!"

Sarah was momentarily confused. "You cast a spell? You don't even know how to cast a spell. Oh, you mean the rhyme you made for the jorii?" She thought a moment. "Usually spells are instantaneous. I've never heard of a spell that had a delayed reaction."

"You're basing this on, what, television shows?"

"Don't be an ass. I clearly don't know for sure, but all references we've ever seen have always led us to believe that when a spell was cast, either it worked or it didn't. No gray area there."

Sarah glanced up and listened intently. "I don't hear him up there. No noise. Let's get out of here. We'll try and figure out what happened later. I just want to go."

"Agreed." He looked at his rickety platform. "How do you want to do this? I can go up first then pull you up, or I can give you a boost and then come up afterwards?"

"Why don't you give me a boost up? I'd rather have you helping me up than yanking my arms out of their sockets."

With Steve's help, she climbed up onto the platform of wooden crates and bales of straw. If she stretched way up on her tippy-toes, she could just reach the lip of the hole. If only she was a few more inches taller, she thought angrily.

Steve jumped up on the bales of straw. "I don't dare join you up on the crates. I don't think they'd hold both of us." He interlocked his fingers and held them out to his wife. "Put your foot here and get ready."

Sarah took a deep breath and steadied herself. She put her right foot into the basket Steve's hands had formed and braced herself. "Ready!"

Steve lifted, propelling Sarah straight up about four feet. It was more than enough to get leverage to brace herself and look around.

"Watch out for that bar!" Steve cautioned. The locking bar was still extended, presenting an unwelcome obstacle.

"Can you brace me for another couple of seconds?" Sarah asked.

"Sure. What're you doing?"

With Steve bracing her legs, she risked moving her right hand over to push the bar back out of the way.

"Good one!" Steve was grinning. "That would have left a mark, no doubt about it."

With Steve's help from below, and straining every muscle in her body, Sarah was able to pull herself up out of the cellar.

"You okay?" Steve called from below.

"Yeah, just trying to catch my breath."

"Here, take this!" Steve hoisted the pack up into the opening. Sarah took it and placed it next to her.

From below, Steve clambered onto the top of the wooden crates. Being a full ten inches taller than Sarah, he was easily able to grab the edge of the opening. However, upper-body strength was not one of his strong suits. With arms shaking more than saplings swaying in a hurricane, Steve finally pulled himself out of the cellar to lie next to Sarah.

"I swear, when we finally do make it home, I'm joining a damn gym."

Sarah laughed and sat up. "C'mon, let's get going. I want to get out of this place."

They both scrambled to their feet and made for the door. The sun was shining brightly outside, only a few wispy clouds were visible just above the western horizon. Now that they were not prisoners, they took a little time to look around.

The cottage was sitting in a small clearing with the forest surrounding them on all sides. A small fire pit had been dug about ten feet from the house. Used regularly, from the looks of the refuse scattered about. Several recent kills were still hanging upside down from a branch from the closest tree. Looks like large squirrels, Steve thought.

"We came from that direction, right?" He pointed northwest. A tiny, overgrown footpath ambled off in that general direction. "Do we head off that way and risk running into that guy on his way back? Or should we head in a different direction altogether?"

"Well, as much as I don't want to take the same path as that other guy did, I really don't want to go wandering through the forest blindly. It took us several hours to get from where we were captured to get here, and we're still ahead of when he told us he'd be back. I say we take this same path back and hope we can find the enchanted road."

"I'll go along with that. At any rate, we need to hurry and we need to be quiet. If for some reason he decides to come back early, I don't want him catching us off guard."

Steve opened the pack, took out several strips of dried meat, and handed one to Sarah. He bit off nearly half of the strip, hoisted the pack back onto his shoulder, grabbed Sarah's hand, and took off down the path at a healthy clip. It wasn't until they were well away from that run-down cottage that both of them were able to relax.

"I am SO glad to be out of that house!" Sarah bit off a piece of her meat. "I was starting to have serious doubts that we were not going to find a way out of that mess."

Steve had finally slowed their pace. A little. He wanted to put as much distance as possible between the house and themselves. Did Sarah just say something? She hated it when he didn't pay attention.

Something about doubts and messes. Doubts about getting out of the mess they were in? Well, Steve thought, I have a fifty-fifty shot at this.

"Yeah, me too. I'm so glad we're out of there." He waited, watching Sarah for the imminent danger signs.

"So what do you think happened in there? Where'd the trapdoor go to?"

Oh, thank God. Got it right for once.

"I still think that something we did, whether intentionally or unintentionally, made that door go away."

"Okay, but what?"

Steve shook his head. "I wish I knew. 'Cause whatever we apparently did, I'd like to learn how to do it again. That will definitely come in handy."

"I'm impressed! This coming from someone who had difficulty believing in magic yesterday. What convinced you?"

"Well, think about it." Steve counted off on his fingers. "First, the jorii, the crystal disc, and the coin that were in your purse up and vanished when the thief wanted to steal it. Second, all three items were back safely in your purse when you checked. And thirdly, that trapdoor flat-out disappeared. I think we would have heard someone remove it in the middle of the night."

"I was thinking that, too. I think one of our jhoruns manifested itself last night. I just don't know if it was yours or mine."

"Okay, let's find out. I tried using the jorii for a little bit. You took it so that you could try. I fell asleep. Honestly now, how long did you work on it?"

"Ummm, well, most the night if you want to know."

Steve stared at his wife in shock. "All night? You were up for practically the entire night trying to get that door open?"

Sarah grinned guiltily. "I really thought I could do it."

Steve had stopped walking and was holding his wife by the shoulders.

"Then it has to be you! You did something to that door. You made it go away. What did you do?"

"Clearly, if I knew that, then we wouldn't be having this discussion."

"The jorii disappeared from your purse. The door vanished as well."

"But the jorii came back! You're telling me that *I'm* responsible for making the jorii disappear so it wouldn't be discovered, then reappear when the coast is clear? Not to mention making that trapdoor completely disappear?"

Steve snapped his fingers. "I got it. It's triggered by fear, or maybe by some intense emotions. Has to be. That's the only common denominator I can think of in the two situations we've seen it work."

Sarah was silent, deep in thought. Steve continued.

"You were worried. You didn't want that jackass to find the jorii, or anything else, did you? So without realizing it, you made it disappear so that our friend back there couldn't find it."

Sarah was still silent. Was he right? Did she make those things disappear? But how? How could she have done something without realizing she did it? Could she test it? Is there some way to find out if she has a jhorun here in Lentari?

"Maybe you're right. Maybe something I inadvertently did caused those things to disappear." She took a deep breath. "Can we test this? I want to know if I did it, how I did it, and how to do it again."

"Yeah, sure. I want to know, too."

They stopped by one of the massive oak trees. Steve shrugged off the pack, reached in and pulled out his wife's purse.

"Okay, try this. You did it once, you should be able to do this again. Is the jorii still in the change purse?"

Sarah nodded.

"Okay, then, try to make it vanish again."

"How? How do I do that?"

"Well, just pretend that a whole gang of thieves are hot on our trail and are about to overtake us, and we know that the jorii can't fall into the hands of someone like that."

Sarah let out a nervous chuckle. "That shouldn't be too difficult to imagine. I'm already halfway there." She clenched her fists. "What do I do? Try and make a mental picture of the jorii vanishing?"

Steve shrugged helplessly. "I don't know. Ummm, that'd be a good first start."

Sarah conjured up a mental picture of the jorii sitting in her change purse. She imagined it disappearing, tried to imagine what the change purse would feel like empty. She looked at Steve. "Any luck?"

"With what?"

"I'm trying to make the freakin' thing disappear! See if it's gone!"

"Oh! Sorry, I'll check." Steve opened her purse, fetched out her change purse and felt it. "Nope, still there."

"Damn. Okay, how about..." Sarah brought up a picture of the jorii and imagined a hole appearing in her purse leading to who knows where. She pictured the jorii falling into the hole.

"What about now?"

Steve reached back into the purse and felt the small purse again.

"Nope, sorry. Remember, pretend you're in a serious dilemma and that you're scared."

"Scared. Got it." Sarah concentrated, imagining the thief was rapidly gaining on them, about to overtake them at any moment. She must not let the jorii fall into the wrong hands. She couldn't let it. Why, if it did, then who knows what would happen to this beautiful land and –

"What the hell?"

Sarah snapped back to the present and looked at her husband.

"What is it?"

"Your change purse. It's gone. I know I put it back in your purse."

"Are you serious? It worked??"

Steve's eyes widened to the size of dinner plates. "You did it! What did you do? What did you do differently from last time?"

"It's triggered by emotions! I really got into the moment there and pretended that he was about to find us. I knew that if it fell into the wrong hands then we'd be in deep crap."

Steve snorted. "Ain't that the truth." He reached inside the purse again. "Umm, how do you reverse it? Can you make it come back?"

Sarah considered. She hadn't thought of that. How does she make it come back? Obviously she knew that the thief wasn't closing in on them. She's relaxed now, isn't she? Why didn't it come back?

"Uh, I'm not sure. I just assumed that once I stopped thinking about it, and those intense feelings had passed, then things would revert back to normal."

He felt inside for the small purse again. It still hadn't reappeared. Better double-check. He pushed aside her brush, keys, emergency makeup kit. No, it doesn't appear that... Wait, there it was! He had just checked the far right of the purse. It wasn't there a second ago!

He pulled out the change purse triumphantly.

"It's back! Nicely done!"

"But why did it take so long to come back? Does the magic have to wear off or something?"

"Let's do this." Steve opened her purse, pulled out the tube of her lip balm, and held it in his open palm. He looked at Sarah. "Can you make this vanish?"

"My chapstick isn't as important as the jorii. I don't know."

"It's worth a try. Wouldn't you like to know if it'll work on non-essential stuff?"

Sarah concentrated, bringing back the feelings of pursuit, of being scared and not knowing if or when she'd be caught next. She didn't want her things to be found, not by that scumbag. As a matter of fact, nothing she owned would ever fall into his hands again if she had anything to say about –

The small circular tube that was sitting on Steve's palm vanished. As did the jorii, change purse, purse, and their pack, with all their supplies in it.

"Holy crap! I was just talking about the balm!"

Sarah didn't respond.

"Hey! Are you okay? Come on, snap out of it!"

Sarah gave a little jerk and her eyes snapped open.

"What happened?"

"Not only did you make the chapstick disappear, you made your purse and all of its contents vanish as well. Not to mention our pack."

"What?! I made it all disappear?"

"That you did! You must have really conjured up some scary feelings!"

"All I have to do is pretend that that mugger is behind us, coming after us. It's not hard to do. Only thing is," she paused a moment, "every time I think about it, it's like I'm back in that cellar again. I can still smell that dank odor, feel the straw under my feet."

Steve took her hand and pulled her close. "I won't let him touch you, honey. That's a promise."

Just like that, Steve was holding Sarah's chapstick again. Down by his feet, the pack materialized back into existence. The purse followed a moment later, both sitting on the ground as though they had been there all along.

"Whoa! That's cool!" Sarah picked up her purse and rifled through it. She pulled out her change purse and felt for the jorii. Yep, still there.

Steve was all smiles. "Do you realize what this means?? You have a magical power! That's so cool!"

Chapter 5 – Magic

This is so bizarre! I made it vanish! I actually made that thing disappear!" She giggled. Her gaze fell upon her husband. "What about you? If I can do this, what do you think you can do?"

"I have been asking myself that very question over and over. The problem is, I haven't noticed anything else happening that might explain what I might be able to do."

"Mmm, good point. I haven't noticed anything else that's odd, either."

"What did you do when you had that jorii last night? Maybe I should start working with it."

Sarah fished the small sphere out of her purse and handed it to her husband.

"The only thing I did was mentally focus on this thing and try to invoke something to happen. Of course, it didn't work as far as I could tell. I tried for hours last night. It might take even longer for something to happen that one of us notices. That's all we can do."

"I'm willing to try. Hell, I want a magical ability, too! How cool would that be? You have one. I want one!"

"Jeez, honey!" Sarah laughed. "How old are you again?"

Steve snorted. He took the jorii from Sarah and willed something to happen. Naturally, nothing did. He gripped the warm sphere tightly, concentrating furiously. He didn't know what to expect, only that *something* should happen. The jorii, however, refused to accommodate him.

Sarah stifled a smile. He looked so cute when he was frustrated. His brow was furrowed, eyes closed, mumbling feverishly to himself.

"Hon, I worked with it for hours, and even then nothing happened. With me, my emotions are the trigger. Apparently the stronger the emotion, the stronger the ability. Maybe you should try that."

Steve let out the breath he didn't realize he had been holding and unclenched his hands. Maybe she was right. Maybe he was going about this the wrong way. He had to relax. Letting his mind go blank, he tried to pretend he was scared, tried to believe he was being chased by that asshole thief. He felt himself grow angry as soon as he brought up a mental picture of their captor.

No, I don't want anger, Steve thought, and pushed it aside. I need to feel scared, terrified. So what am I scared of?

A Tyrannosaurus Rex. The thought popped into his head before he could even take a breath.

A dinosaur? A damn dinosaur?? What was he, five years old? Watching Jurassic Park did *not* cause nightmares, thank you very much. He knew they didn't exist here, and he knew that no matter how hard he tried, he wasn't going to be able to pretend there was a seven ton reptile chasing the two of them through the forest.

A small, timid voice spoke up in his head. *Maybe they do exist here.*

Steve snorted. Unless one shows up and starts chasing us, I'm not gonna believe one it. Dragons maybe. Dragons! Was he scared of dragons?

No, not really, the voice said. *You think they're cool, not scary.*

True, Steve agreed. Although if I ever do meet one face-to-face, I'll probably think otherwise.

Steve squared his shoulders and took a deep breath. It can't be this difficult. Think of something scary. Doesn't have to be realistic. Think! Concentrate! I can do this!

Sarah took his hands in hers, and gently pulled the jorii from him and put it back in her purse.

"Look, we just escaped from that cellar. We might run into that robber again on this trail. Let's get out of here, find the right trail and get as far away as possible. Then you can relax properly and I'll help you work on this, okay?"

Not really wanting to quit now, but wanting his wife's help even more, Steve nodded.

"You're right. We can work on this later. First and foremost, let's get the hell outta here and find that road."

Picking up the pack, they continued north.

Holding Sarah's hand and swinging it back and forth the way a couple of love-struck teenagers would, Steve was happy. They had been mugged and had been able to foil their mugger. They had been imprisoned and had managed to escape. Now here they were, on an alien world, making their way towards an enchanted path to find their way to the king and queen. This was the stuff of legend! Most people only dreamed about doing something like this, yet here they were, with magical powers even!

Steve smiled. His wife could make things disappear! Vanish completely! Not only that, she could bring them back! Did that mean the trapdoor had returned? It would have to be! That mugger was in for a major shock. He'll find the trapdoor closed and his prey missing. Wait. Sarah had pushed the locking bracket back out of the way, so it'll appear as though someone had deliberately set them free. He laughed quietly to himself. He would love to see the look on his face.

Steve looked at his wife. Sarah, inexplicably, could always tell when he was looking her way, so she met his look and smiled. Nothing was spoken. Nothing needed to be.

Content to walk silently with her husband, Sarah started checking out the local flora.

I wonder what the extent of her powers are, Steve mused to himself. What are her limits? Could she make something larger than a door disappear? And where did the door go to, exactly? She obviously moved it from one place to the other and then back again, so…

Moved it? That's it! It has to be! She teleported the jorii first, then the door! She simply chose to move those items from their starting positions to, um, to…

Steve shook his head. He really didn't have a clue as to where she sent those things. Clearly, though, Sarah was able to pull the items out of wherever she put them and return them to the starting point. If she could focus her energies and be able to direct where she was moving those things to, then that would be a formidable defense mechanism here in Lentari!

He thought about asking Sarah to continue to work on perfecting her newly acquired skills, but thought better of it. If she is willing to help him with his, then he can give her a hand with hers. We'll practice tonight, Steve promised himself.

Meanwhile, Sarah was trying to absorb as much as she could about the local plant life. How many opportunities would she get to check out what life was like on another world? Small, impossibly vivid purple flowers splashed with soft yellow streaks were the most abundant. They were growing on squat, green bushes that clumped together in groups of three or four.

A maroon cat-sized animal darted from tree to tree, chittering away raucously while watching the two bipedal creatures below. The two foreign beings weren't its prey, so it focused its attention elsewhere. It blended into the foliage and disappeared.

After a couple of hours of steady walking they came upon a clearing with a large pond. Or a really small lake.

"Do you remember passing this on the way in?" Steve asked his wife.

"Ummm, no, I don't," Sarah confessed, "but then again I wasn't really paying attention to any details. Too scared."

"True." Steve looked at the small path that skirted the edges of the lake. "Let's take a quick breather."

Sarah stretched her back, and then paused. She was hearing the soft, gurgling sounds of a brook. Maybe feeding the lake? She started exploring the immediate surroundings and found the small stream of clear water. A closer inspection confirmed that it was indeed flowing west, towards the lake.

"I found a small stream. Water looks good. I'm gonna take a drink."

"Say what? You don't know what might be in that water. Might have some foreign bacteria in it or something." Steve shook his head. "I'd rather you didn't."

"I'm hot, thirsty, sore, and willing to take the risk."

"Fine. But at least let me drink first so that…"

Sarah had already scooped up some water in her hand and drank. The water was cold, clear, and utterly refreshing. She felt the cool water flow all the way down her throat and well into her stomach. She must have been dehydrated, she thought. This was some good water! Eagerly she scooped more into her mouth.

About to protest until he saw Sarah take another drink, Steve abandoned all doubts, dropped to his knees, and started scooping out water for himself.

Finally sated, Sarah stood back up, water dripping from her chin. She wiped her mouth with the back of her arm. "Didn't realize how thirsty I was until I took a drink of that."

Steve straightened back up as well. After wiping his mouth, he nodded his head. "Wish I had a canteen of some sort. Oh, well."

Farther behind them, but gaining rapidly, their former captor, exploring a realm of anger he hadn't realized existed, was making good speed. He had taken a route that had led southeast from his lodge, when much to his surprise, had encountered acquaintances of his slaver contact. They had confirmed that the ship he was looking for was presently docked at a pier not half a days walk along the Wanlu River. Not known for his patience, he had immediately reversed course back to his home to retrieve his prizes, only to discover his birds had flown the coop.

So who had helped them to escape? Clearly someone had come onto his land. Somebody entered his house, found the hidden trapdoor, and opened it. Whoever it was will pay, of that he was certain. Maybe he'll just add the Good Samaritan to his growing collection of prizes to be sold into slavery.

With that reassuring thought in mind, he grabbed his only bow and a quiver full of arrows and tracked the couple to the small lake he frequented often. Ah! There they were! Did they actually think they could lose him? In his forest??

He crouched in silence and watched, hidden amongst the greenery. He watched as the stupid male open their pack, pull out one of the strips of dried meat and hand it to the female. The female tore the strip in two and handed half back to the male. It was so sickeningly sweet it made him nauseous.

The male out massed him, by more than twice, he reasoned. He's bound to cause trouble, perhaps even physically defeat him in a fight if it came to it. Did he really need the male? He could easily fetch a handsome price for the female. She was fetching, showing signs of fire and spunk. The male, he decided, had just become expendable.

He reached behind him to pull out his longbow. He fit an arrow to the string and pulled back as far as he was able. A typical longbow could fire an arrow well over three hundred meters. However, that was if the bow was pulled to full extension, and it took steady arms and constant strength. A pull of one hundred fifty to two hundred pounds was typical of a weapon of this type. The mugger, though, lacked the musculature in his arms to use the bow to its full capabilities. With shaking arms, he took aim at the man.

Hold up, they were embracing. He couldn't eliminate the male without harming the female. Oh, thank the gods! His arms could no longer maintain the strength required by his weapon. He released the tension and stretched his arms. He hadn't used his bow in a while. Making a mental note to practice more, he waited patiently.

Ah! The male has moved off! Here's his opportunity! He knocked an arrow to the bow and once again took aim at the male. The strain on his arms was unimaginable. They started to shake, and to his horror, he realized it was throwing him off balance. He took a step back. The twig he stepped on snapped loudly, breaking the silence in the glen.

Sarah's head jerked up, along with Steve's. She saw their former captor before he did, saw the imminent danger, and screamed. Long and loud. The thief, startled, swung his aim over to her, and without realizing it, released the arrow.

Time slowed to a crawl. Steve watched in horror as the arrow was released. He knew that Sarah was too far away for him to try and block it, but what could he do? He bunched his legs and leapt in Sarah's direction, hoping his futile, last ditch effort might somehow protect Sarah from the imminent death that had begun to streak towards her.

The concussion knocked both Steve and Sarah well into the lake. The flash of searing fire and heat instantly vaporized the arrow in mid-flight, reducing it to ash where it floated away in the breeze. Their former captor, now wearing nothing but a light dusting of ash in front, while the clothing covering his now retreating backside still remained intact, turned tail and ran for all he was worth. With nothing to keep the clothes in place, they caught on little bits of shrubbery, or flapped away in the breeze, and generally fell off. The bare-assed thief disappeared into the woods, stringing curses behind him as he ran. No prize was worth this.

Coughing and spluttering, Steve and Sarah surfaced.

"What the *hell* was that?" Steve coughed up water. Being thrown into the water unexpectedly was akin to getting a healthy dose of water up your nose and in your mouth. "Are you okay?"

Sarah coughed. "He blew us up? How'd he do that? What happened to the arrow? I saw him shoot an arrow at us!"

"Yeah, me, too. Better question is, what happened to him? I don't see him anywhere."

They stumbled out of the water and collapsed onto the shore. Steve rolled onto his back, continuing to cough up water while Sarah, also struggling to remove all the fluid from her lungs, scanned the shore, looking for some signs of their pursuer. Her gaze fell onto their pack and her purse, still sitting where she dropped it by the brook. Then she noticed that the trees and plant life in the "blast zone" (as she called it in her head) had all been deeply singed. The trees all bore black scorches, but only on their eastern sides. Nothing on the west, from the direction of their assailant. If the pack, which was on the ground, was still there, that could only mean that whatever detonated did so in the air, not on the ground. But to have the vegetation burned on their side, the east? But that could only mean…

"I think the blast came from our direction, and it happened in mid-air."

Steve looked behind him. "From the water? Why did it blow us into it then?"

Sarah's mouth closed with an audible snap. "Good one. Well, if it came from this direction, yet didn't come from behind us, then that would suggest that it came from us!"

"You mean you did something to protect yourself from that guy?" Steve was both proud and jealous at the same time. "That's awesome!!"

"Hon, I don't think it's me. I think it's you!"

"Me? I didn't do anything! Why do you say that?"

"Well, the only thing I did was scream. Nothing remarkable there. Can you remember if you did anything?"

Steve thought a moment. "It all happened so fast. I had actually stopped worrying about that guy. I let my guard down. I'm so sorry." Steve held his wife's hand. "I heard a snapping noise; I looked up to see what it was. I heard you scream, and I saw that guy point his bow at you instead of me. My heart stopped dead. I just knew I had to get in front of you to somehow block the arrow, but deep down I knew it just wasn't possible. You were too far away. I think I threw up my hands and the next thing I knew I was inhaling water."

"You gestured with your hands?"

"I wouldn't call it gesturing. More like helplessly flailing my arms."

"No you didn't. I remember now. You put up both arms as if to brace for some type of impact. Remember?"

Steve thought a moment. He did, in fact, remember putting his arms up in a defensive position, as if he'd be able to prevent the arrow from reaching its intended target.

"Well, maybe…"

"That's got to be it! You generated some type of blast that knocked us into the lake, out of harm's way. And," she eyed the vegetation, "it was a rather intense blast at that. It must have burned that arrow up completely!"

"Did it incinerate the thief, too? That's who I'd like to take out," Steve muttered.

Sarah walked around the clearing, noticing bits of fabric here and there. She bent to retrieve a fluttering piece of cloth and held it close to her face for inspection. Her eyes opened wide. The giggles started bubbling out of her until she was laughing so hard she had tears running down her face.

Steve, baffled at his wife's behavior, came up next to her and just stared at her.

"What's so funny? What are you holding?"

Sarah handed him the fabric. "This. This is a piece of his clothing. You can see it was once part of his trousers. The back side, if I'm not mistaken." She chortled again. "This leads me to conclude that the front half of his clothes were flash-burned. Look, you can see the singed edges here. This half of his clothes were burnt off him, and the rest just fell off. That means he's now running around buck naked!"

Steve held the fabric close to his face. Yes, he could see the burnt edges. He could even smell the burnt fibers. This piece of fabric had been burned recently, and it did match what the robber had been wearing. So that meant that he was indeed running around in the buff.

Whenever he started to heartily laugh, and then made some attempt to hold it in, Sarah had always told him that his laugh sounded more like a donkey's bray. That's what came out of him now as he pictured their former captor high-tailing it back to his place.

"That's too good to be true! Serves his ass right," Steve muttered, his mood quickly turning dark again. "Punk. I just wish I could have burned something else off besides his clothes."

"It was better than that," Sarah pointed out. "Do you really think he'll bother us now? He probably wouldn't touch us with a ten foot pole!"

Steve chuckled. "True. If that blast truly came from me, then I need to figure out what triggers it and how to bring it back and control it. That would be invaluable here."

They started putting their belongings back into their pack. Sarah repacked her purse (properly) and stowed it in the knapsack. Steve checked their food stores and with a shout, pulled out a large leather pouch he hadn't noticed before.

"If I didn't know better, I'd say that this is a bouda bag."

"A what?"

"A bouda bag. It's a leather bag used for holding water, I'm sure of it. At any rate, I'm going to fill it up at that spring."

"Is there any water already in it?"

Steve pulled the stopper out of the bag and squeezed. A small jet of water whooshed out of the bag and splashed him squarely in the face.

Sarah laughed. "Yep! Now that you've emptied it, maybe we should fill it back up again."

Steve ran his hand down his face, pushing the water off of him. Well, it did feel good. He hadn't realized he was this hot. Probably tasted good, too. He took a long drink and offered the bag to Sarah. She drank deeply as well and passed the bag back to Steve, who proceeded to fill it from the spring.

As Steve was placing the leather canteen back into the pack, Sarah, who had been standing off to the side, walked up to him and ran her hands down his back, feeling his clothes.

"Hon, you're dry! Completely! Even your hair is dry!"

"What?" Steve felt his shirt, pants, and then his hair. His clothes were dry already? How'd that happen so quickly?

Sarah extended her arms, palms facing Steve. "Do you feel how much heat you're generating right now? No wonder you're dry!"

"You always tell me that I'm warm. No big surprise there."

"Enough to dry clothes? A body generates heat, yes, and given enough time, will dry your clothes, but not in five minutes!" She stared at her husband. "What are you thinking? Right now?"

"Honestly? That I could go for a double bacon cheeseburger."

"Okay, before that. What were you thinking? Was it about that creep?"

"Yeah, I just wish I could have inflicted some pain to him for all that he's done to us. He tried to kill you. That sort of thing is hard to forget."

"So you were thinking about him, probably getting angry, right?"

Steve nodded. "What's your point?"

Sarah smiled. "We found your trigger. Anger. You get angry, you get hot. You get angry and protective, God forbid, and you blow away the surrounding vegetation."

"Anger? You think my trigger is anger?"

"Yes, I do. And the same the-stronger-the-emotion-the-stronger-the-magic bit is probably in place for you, too. The angrier you are, the more your jhorun will manifest itself."

Steve laughed as he thought about that. "Just so long as I don't turn green."

Sarah giggled.

"Do you mind if I test this? I'd like to think that I can control my anger. If I can find out what works and what doesn't, it'll make me feel a lot better."

Sarah looked at the nearby lake. "Test away. Better here where there's water than out in the middle of a forest where there isn't any."

"Oh, ha ha ha. Think I'm gonna burn down the forest, do you?"

Sarah turned and looked at the burnt trees.

"Okay, bad example."

He sat down on an overturned tree and started thinking. How do I start this, he thought. Anger. If I explode every time I get mad, then that isn't gonna work. I'm going to have to be able to rein in my emotions so I don't hurt anyone. Well, anyone that matters, that is. What can I start with?

His eyes started roaming the ground in front of him and alighted on a small branch that had broken off from one of the tree branches far above. He picked it up. Okay, this'll work. Let's start imagining that I know that the mugger is coming back. He obviously wants to harm us. Am I going to let him?

Steve gripped the branch tightly in his right hand, his left balling into a fist.

More than likely, that creep wanted to kill him because he probably would cause problems during the attempt at apprehending them again. Probably wanted Sarah for himself.

Wisps of smoke started to appear.

Standing quietly by the safety of the water's edge, Sarah said nothing. She was too far away to see the tiny tendrils of smoke appearing over Steve's hand.

The robber wanted to kill him and take his wife away, to make her a slave, to make her subservient to whoever "purchased" her. It was intolerable. Unthinkable! Not while he breathed! Not while he was able to fight, able to protect her, able to-

Now Sarah noticed the smoke. Where there's smoke, there's bound to be fire! Concern for her husband had her reaching for the lake water. She scooped up some water and paused.

"Steve! Whatever you're doing, stop! Snap out of it!" Sarah flung a double-handful of water in his direction. The few drops of water that made it to him hissed when they landed. Her husband didn't react. Oh, boy. More dire action was needed. Reaching into the pack she grabbed the bouda bag, uncorked it and gave a mighty squeeze angled in Steve's direction. The spray of water nailed him square in the face.

Steve jerked, looking over at Sarah. "Wha'? What happened? Why did you do that?" Wiping the water out of his eyes, Steve looked at the branch. No flames. "Something wrong?"

"I see smoke! Something is smoking over there!"

Steve looked at the branch in his right hand. No smoke there. He looked at his left. Smoke was indeed emanating from his clenched fist, which had turned a dark, mottled red.

"Well, would you get a load of that!" Steve opened his hand. More smoke was billowing from his hand. A detached part of his brain thought maybe he should be in pain, but nothing registered.

His hand was tingling, as though it fell asleep. Still no pain. Was his hand going to literally start combusting, right before his eyes? He eyed it, waiting. Luckily, no flames appeared. However, his skin was still an angry red.

"Okay, now what? How do I make it stop?" Sarah shrugged. She didn't know. Now what? Not really wanting his hand to burn, he rushed over to the lake and thrust it in. Steam hissed up from the water, coalescing around his face. After a minute or two, the clouds of vapor drifted away, and he pulled his hand out.

Sarah rushed up to him. "Are you hurt? Are you in pain? Let me see your hand."

Steve held up his left hand. It was back to being a healthy pink. He wiggled his fingers. No discomfort anywhere.

"Everything in good working order. But we have a problem. Scratch that. Lets back up a bit. First off, I'm thrilled that we know the nature of my jhorun. And I'm ecstatic that I was able to prevent that arrow from reaching you. However, what happens if there isn't water around? Why wouldn't it shut off by itself?"

"Well, maybe you didn't give it enough time. It might have reverted back to normal after a few minutes."

"I'd like to say that I didn't panic, but in my defense, for all I knew, it did look as though my hand was gonna catch fire."

"When your hand was all red like that, did it hurt? Could you have gone longer with your hand that hot?"

Steve thought back. "It didn't hurt at all. In fact, it felt all tingly, like when your hand goes to sleep. Something like that. But no pain, and I certainly couldn't feel any heat whatsoever."

With their gear all stowed back into the pack, Steve refilled their canteen (again) and proceeded on, heading northwest along the path. Sarah walked quickly in front, with Steve bringing up the rear. Since their adversary had caught them unaware for a second time, especially when he had vowed not let that happen again, Steve was now on high alert, constantly listening for any sounds of pursuit. The only thing he could hear, however, were he and Sarah's labored sound of breathing.

This was so *cool*! Talk about being straight out of the comic books! Now that he knew the nature of his jhorun, he wanted to do what any kid would want to do with a new toy: keep playing! He wanted to experiment! How strong did his anger have to be in order for it to manifest itself? Did he have to focus on a specific item? Was it only pertaining to anger? Could he summon the heat if he concentrated hard enough?

He had generated a flash of heat so intense that it burned trees and completely incinerated an arrow that was shot at them. The level of heat that was necessary to flash burn a speeding arrow was unimaginable to him. Scorch marks on the trees… Wouldn't that suggest fire as well? Where there's heat, there's fire, right? Did he generate fire? Could he actually summon fire?

That, Steve thought, was critical, need-to-know information! Wouldn't it be fantastic if, at just a whim, he could conjure a fireball out of thin air and hurl it at a bad guy? Think of the ways he could protect Sarah in this strange world! God forbid he encountered any other muggers now!

That was something he was going to practice until he had all the specifics down pat, Steve vowed to himself. How to activate, how to control the intensity, how to target different objects, and most importantly, how to turn his ability off. Without water present, he needed to be certain he wasn't going to harm Sarah in any way. That was critical.

So while the two of them tried to retrace their route back to the enchanted road, Steve mentally practiced summoning his jhorun. He focused his mental anger at passing rocks and twigs. He even picked up a small branch while Sarah was walking in front of him, but was unsuccessful in generating so much as one joule of heat out of himself.

Wait a minute. If he couldn't detect any heat coming from his hand, would he be able to tell if he was heating up? If his power was heat and/or fire, wouldn't he be immune to its effects? Wouldn't make much sense generating the heat if he couldn't handle it, would it? Wait a minute, what about his clothes? They weren't going to be able to insulate him against the heat, so they were liable to burn off.

Got it. No getting mad at himself. Wouldn't want to be running around out here in the buff, either.

But what is the key to activating this? How could he tap into his magic just a little bit without igniting everything in a fifty foot radius? He needed to be able to focus his energy, thus focusing the intensity of heat emanating from him. Once he had the intensity down, then he would work on his aim.

Clenching the twig tightly, Steve focused all his mental energy on the small piece of wood. He could clearly imagine it bursting into flame, rapidly reducing to ash. Only, he didn't want ash, he wanted the thing to burst into flames. Not scorching heat that would hurt anyone, just a little flame.

He looked over at Sarah, still walking along the path ahead of him. His mood instantly softened. There was his one true love, his soul mate. The bond that he shared with Sarah couldn't be described with just mere words. He would do anything for her, and that included dying, if the need arose. She was his inspiration. He needed to master this skill. Since they needed to find a suitable place to camp for the night, he needed to master it quickly. He eyed the twig and ordered it to ignite.

Much to his amazement, the small twig burst into flame. He stopped dead in his tracks and watched the twig burn.

Sarah, alerted to Steve's absence, looked behind her. She saw her husband holding a burning twig. He was just staring at it, holding it this way and that, admiring it from different angles.

"What happened? Did you just make that fire appear?"

Steve nodded. "I essentially ordered it to burn. And it burned."

Sarah clapped her hands. "Good job! Did you focus your anger on it?"

"No, I didn't. Hon, I don't think anger is my trigger."

"Really? Why do you say that? What is it, then?"

"I tried getting angry," Steve explained, "only that wasn't working. Wanna know what I did?"

"Absolutely!"

"For a lack of a better word, its chivalry, or a sense of protection. I think about you, protecting you, making certain you're safe, and I can sense this, uh, presence, if you will. Like something is about to happen. I think at that time my jhorun is ready to emerge, and I just have to tell it what to do."

Sarah blinked. Was this her husband? Since when did he become so damn good at interpreting his emotions? They only had just taken their "swim" in the lake about an hour ago. How could he have figured out so much in so little time? Was he right about his magic?

"I'm impressed! How did you figure it out? Are you sure you're right?"

"I can try to do it again, to see if I'm right."

Sarah looked at the (still) burning branch. The flickering flames had just about worked its way down to his hand.

"You're about to get burned."

Steve nodded. "I know. I want to know if fire will burn me here."

"And you're willing to risk a burn?"

"Ordinarily, no. But since I can't feel any heat whatsoever, I figured it was worth a shot."

"No heat? Nothing? It doesn't hurt?"

Steve watched as the flames completely engulfed the twig, and consequently, his hand. The fire danced between his fingers, tickling his skin. This was the coolest thing ever! The flames didn't have any effect on him at all! No heat and no pain!

"Nothing." He twisted his arm around so he could watch the flames from all angles. "I can't feel a thing."

"Can you turn it off?"

Steve looked at the burning stick. He imagined that the fire was there to do his bidding. The stick burned, it caught fire, mission accomplished. Sarah could be in danger if that fire isn't extinguished. Time to put it out.

The flames snuffed out, leaving the branch smoldering in his hand.

Sarah's jaw dropped. Holy cow! He did it! He put the fire out! Unbelievable! Her husband was now left holding a smoldering twig. Immense pride swelled within her.

"That's awesome! Way to go! I'm so impressed!!"

Steve was beaming. That had worked much better than he thought it would. He looked at the smoking stick. A nagging thought just occurred. Was he responsible for putting it out or did a gust of wind do the job for him? Better see if he can ignite it again. He concentrated, conjuring up his protective feelings for his wife once more. He eyed the stick again, ordering it to flame up. The smoldering stick ignited instantly, blazing brightly in his hand.

Sarah, in the process of reaching out to touch Steve's hand, jerked back. "What happened? Did you do that?"

"Yeah, sorry, I just needed to know if I could do it again. I thought maybe a breeze might have blown it out the first time, so I need to be certain it was me who put it out."

"Put it out, would you?"

Once the flames had been extinguished, Sarah gingerly touched her husband's hand. His skin was warm to the touch, but not overly hot. She felt his forehead. Again, warm to the touch, but nothing alarming.

"Anything feel warmer than it should?" Steve asked.

"Your skin's a little warm, like you've been in the sun for a couple of hours, but other than that, no."

Steve dropped the burnt stick and rubbed it out on the ground. Only when he had ground it thoroughly in the dirt did he move on. Taking Sarah's hand, they continued north.

"You didn't answer my question." Sarah pointed out. "How did you figure it out so quickly?"

Steve reached out and moved a low-lying branch out of the way for his wife. "Well, I was thinking about it, trying to use my anger, focusing it on anything. And I wasn't getting the slightest response. At that moment, I looked up and saw you. I started thinking that I really needed to master this skill of mine, 'cause we're gonna have to find a place to camp for the night, and I wanted to be able to use this ability to be able to protect you from anything that might happen. And that's when it happened."

"What? What happened?"

"As soon as I thought about protecting you, I started to feel a warm sensation spreading all throughout my body. My hand started to tingle, the one holding the stick. And somehow I knew, just knew, that something was about to happen. Like something was waiting to happen. Since the tingling wasn't unpleasant, and it only appeared when I thought of you, I figured it might be my jhorun. So, since I wanted to practice on the twig, I ordered it to burn. And what do you know? It started to burn."

Sarah was silent as she absorbed this latest bit of information. Her love for her husband, and his love for her, is causing this sense of protection? His sense of chivalry is what triggers his magic? She didn't know how to react to that, other than to feel flattered beyond all belief.

"Um, I'm speechless, honey, I really am. Your feelings for me, your desire to make sure I'm safe, that's the trigger?"

"Yes," Steve said. "I'm positive."

Sarah flung her arms around her husband and hugged him hard. "That's so sweet! I love you."

"Right back at you. As I live and breathe, no one is gonna touch you."

Still embracing Steve, she sighed against his chest. "Thank you."

Gently pushing her away, Steve started looking around. "Come on, let's find a place to camp for the night."

He took Sarah's hand and explored around the trail. About thirty paces east they discovered another one of the massive trees had fallen. Actually, it looked like it had been pushed over, completely uprooted from the ground. Steve didn't want to know what it took to push one of those huge trees over. Whoever was responsible for maintenance on these trails apparently had their hands full.

Taking off his pack, he set it down, leaning it against the trunk. While Sarah rooted around in the pack for some more dried meat, Steve set about making a camp fire. Fortunately, there were quite a few stones scattered here and there that were suitable for making a decent hearth. Moving about a dozen stones over to the trees, and arranging them in a ring, Steve scouted around looking for firewood.

After a suitable pile of wood had been collected, Steve fished through it, looking for smaller pieces to be used as kindling. The larger pieces would be put on later, once the fire was going.

"What are you doing? What's wrong with those pieces of wood?" Sarah was gesturing at the thicker pieces.

"Well, I need kindling to get it going," Steve explained. "May not have been the best Boy Scout in the world, but I do know at least that."

Sarah snorted, trying not to laugh. "This coming from the person that can probably make rocks burn."

Steve froze. She was right. What did he need with kindling? He could make the largest pieces of wood burn, regardless of type, size, or dryness. He laughed, and dropped the small sticks he had been holding.

"Got me on that one." He placed the sticks inside his ring of rocks. "Ready?"

Sarah was backing up a little. "Go easy on it. Start small."

"Think small, think small…" Steve thought of Sarah and her need to be warm and safe tonight. He looked at the wood pile and imagined the central log in the hearth burning. Wisps of smoke appeared. Heat waves shimmered over the hearth. He thought of Sarah again, warming herself next to the fire. He glared at the log, daring it to not burn.

The log instantly burst into flames. The fire crackled merrily as it spread from log to log. In just seconds, the fire was burning steadily, casting warmth and light amongst the darkening surroundings.

"I can get used to this! Good job, hon!" Sarah gave him a hug. "You're not even warm. You're getting much better at this!"

"I still need practice. It should have lit the first time."

"The first time? What do you mean?"

"I tried to ignite it once, and I saw smoke appear. Just a little. Then I thought of you again and concentrated a little harder, and I pretty much dared it to not work. And it worked!"

Sarah looked at their steadily burning fire. Could he put out a fire that large? Should she have him try? She really hoped they would never be in a situation where they would need to know that, but better safe than sorry, right?

"Honey, put this fire out. Right now. Pretend it's an emergency."

Steve glanced up from rummaging through the pack. "Serious?"

"Yes, do it now. Quickly. I'll tell you why in just a sec."

"Ummm, okay." Steve looked at the fire. He didn't know why Sarah wanted the fire extinguished, but she definitely had a reason. Not questioning her logic (for now), he brought up his feelings of protectiveness and extended them to the fire. *Extinguish yourself.*

As a candle poofs out when someone blows on it, so did their campfire. With a soft whoosh, the fire went out.

Steve was concerned. "Alright, why did I just do that? Did you hear something?"

Sarah took gently took his hand and patted it reassuringly. "I'm sorry. I just needed to know if we had to leave here quickly whether you could put out a fire larger than the branch you had lit earlier. And you could. Thank you. I didn't mean to scare you."

Steve exhaled, loudly. "Well, you did. Damn. Whew, don't do that again!" He took several deep breaths to try and calm his nerves. His heart was racing! Expecting the worst, he had called up his jhorun again, and it was standing by, ready to lend him aid. Instead of quelling the sensation, he directed his energy towards the hearth again and ordered the fire to reappear. The smoldering campfire was instantly blazing merrily once again.

"Wow, did I do that to you?"

Steve nodded.

Sarah looked contrite. She was definitely going to have to be more careful. She had watched Steve give just the merest glance at the hearth and the fire was roaring once more.

"Hon, I think…"

"Sweetie, we need to work…"

Again, neither one heard what the other said.

Sarah smiled. "You first."

"Sorry. I was just saying, I really need to work on controlling this. I don't want to lose control and ignite something that shouldn't be ignited. Know what I mean?"

Sarah laughed. "I was just going to say the same thing. Actually, I think we should both practice. You're much more in tune with your jhorun than I am with mine."

"I'd be more than happy to help out. Not sure how I can help though, but I'm willing to try."

They set about making themselves a comfortable place to sleep for the night. Sarah found several large plant (fern, maybe?) fronds and put those down for ground cover. Taking several of the larger ones, she held it up, feeling the texture and thickness. This might work to keep them warm at night.

"Whatcha doin'?" Steve had come up behind her and was peering over her shoulder.

"I'm thinking we might be able to get a few more of these things to snuggle up under tonight."

Steve looked at the frond. It was about four feet long by three feet wide with curved green and black stripes running the length of the frond, much like zebra stripes. It also had a light aromatic fragrance emanating from it. Steve held it up to his nose and sniffed lightly. Almost like citrus. Odd. Citrus and pine. Great. He'll dream about dusting furniture tonight.

Settling down near the fire, they said nothing for a few moments. After all, it had been a day for some incredible firsts, the most important was learning that the two of them had developed magical abilities while they were here. Apparently Kornal's record remained unbroken, namely every person he had ever met had some type of jhorun simply because jhorun was a part of every human here, whether native or not. So –

Sarah sat bolt upright. The fire in the hearth flared up suddenly, as if feeding on an unknown source of pure oxygen. She reached out to put a comforting hand on her husband's shoulder. "Sorry, relax. I just thought of something."

The fire settled back down to its normal intensity.

"What's up?" Steve asked.

"Your grandparents!"

"What about them?"

"They came here, too, right? Just like us."

"I would say that's a given."

"What do you suppose was the nature of their jhorun?"

Steve bit into one of the fruitcake-looking things Nilhanu had packed for them and chewed thoughtfully.

"Never thought of that. Maybe they had really powerful jhoruns, and liked using them so much they kept coming back here. Hey, it's a possibility, right?"

Steve broke off part of his fruitcake and held it out for his wife. Sarah reluctantly accepted the offering and took a tentative bite. "It's not bad. I could totally make this better."

Sarah loved to cook and experiment with recipes, a skill her husband thoroughly enjoyed.

"I don't think I'll ever look at fruitcake the same way again, though." She picked the husk of some type of berry out of her teeth.

Steve, mouth full of cake, said, "I wonder what they were. Wonder if they were strong. Do you think ours are considered strong?"

"I don't have any idea. It's hard to say what's considered important here. On one hand, one might consider being able to find a hard-to-see fish in the river unimportant. But as I said earlier, it enabled Kornal to provide food for both he and his wife. How do you classify that? Weak or important?"

Steve took a drink from the bouda bag. "I would think it'd be considered weak."

"Why? Because he can only find fish in the water?"

"Well, yeah. Don't you think?"

"No, I don't. It might be considered useless, and Kornal found a way to make it useful. Just like Nilhanu discovered she could enhance plant-life. Minor to everyone else, but major to them."

"Okay, I get it. So what we consider lame, they might consider important. So how do we know?"

Sarah sighed. "Until we find someone else we can talk to, we don't."

Steve threw another couple of logs on the fire. He didn't want it going out anytime soon. He paused. Could he make a fire burn when there wasn't anything to burn? Best to experiment with that notion at another time.

"Tired?"

Sarah stirred against his side. "Not in the slightest. You?"

"Nope. I should be, but I have too many things running through my head at the moment."

"Me, too. Care to help me work on my jhorun?"

"Sure. What can I do?"

"We need something I can experiment on. Let me see." She grabbed her purse and rifled through it. What could she use? Her lip balm again? Maybe her keys? Just about everything in her purse would suffice.

Steve reached over her to grab a small, smooth stone from the ground. He presented it to her. "Here, use this."

Sarah took the rock and studied it.

"Think you can make this vanish? It doesn't belong to us and it's about as insignificant as it gets. What do you think?"

Sarah concentrated, invoking her jhorun. Now that the surrounding environment had settled down for the night, the only sounds to be heard were soft chirps of what she believed to be nocturnal insects. The stars had come out, and without the ambience of city lights to impede the sky, they were out in force. Countless thousands of twinkles of light peeked down from above, imbuing Sarah with a sense of calm she had seldom felt before. Delving inside herself, she searched for any signs of foreign sensations. Steve had likened the feeling to having an arm or a leg fall asleep and starting to awaken. Is that what she should be looking for?

Try as she might, she just couldn't remember if she had felt any types of tingly sensations before. But one thing she could do was vividly recall the feelings of pursuit, of being locked in that cellar. Well, it was a place to start.

Reliving the past experiences with their former captor, Sarah once again slipped into the role of her past self, imagining with relative ease the disturbing feelings of being pursued, of being helpless. She began to recollect that miserable night locked in the cellar when she paused.

What was that? Something felt different. Her pulse rate had increased, her breathing becoming shallow. What was happening? Was this her jhorun? No, she decided, just nerves. Then again, her fingers had started to tingle. Just a little bit. More curious than concerned, she waited, wanting to see if it was nerves or her imagination.

The tingling spread slowly from her fingertips, through her hands, and up her arms. She hesitated. Would it spread any farther? Hmm, doesn't feel like it. Just her arms and hands then.

She opened her eyes and looked at her husband. "I think I'm ready."

Steve, scouring the area for more items to experiment on, hurried back to her side. "You sure? Can you feel anything?"

"Yeah, it feels like my arms have goosebumps on them, yet I'm not cold, and I clearly don't have any goosebumps anywhere." She sat down on the nearest log and tentatively stretched her arms, not wanting to disturb the new sensations she was experiencing. Fortunately, the tingles were there to stay. At least for now, she mused.

"You have the tingly feelings, too?"

"Yes, I do. It feels really weird. But I see what you mean, it feels like there's another presence in the area. Like something is about to happen. Is that what it felt like for you?"

"Almost exactly the same. Okay, let's experiment. Try the stone."

Sarah looked at the worn stone in her hand, willing it to disappear. The stone abruptly vanished. Elation coursed through her, and then slowly abated. Something didn't feel right this time. What she just did only felt half right. What was missing?

"What's the matter? Why are you frowning? It worked! The stone vanished."

"Something isn't right. It doesn't feel right."

"What doesn't feel right? The way you did it?"

"Kinda, like I'm missing a step. I just don't know like what."

"So you feel unsettled?"

Sarah nodded.

"Bring it back. See if you feel better when it's back."

The stone blinked back into existence in Sarah's outstretched hand.

Steve looked at his wife. She was smiling now. "Feeling better?"

"Yes, much. That was it. I must be doing something wrong or else I'm always going to feel like something is off every time I make an object disappear."

Steve considered. "Hon, what if you're just not doing it right?"

Sarah shot him a dark look. "You handle the fires, and I'll handle the, uh, teleportation of…" She smacked her forehead. "That's it!"

"Okay, I'm lost. What's it?"

"Teleportation! I think that's what I'm doing! I'm moving something from one place to the other!"

Steve mulled that over for a moment or two. Slowly he nodded his head.

"I can agree with that. Okay, if you move something from point A to point B, where are you moving it to?"

Sarah thought a moment then jumped up into his arms, hugging him tightly. "That's it! I swear that's it!"

"Alright, you keep saying that. What's it? What are you talking about?"

"This feeling of doing this wrong. I think I know what I where I messed up."

"Really? What, then?"

"When I made that stone disappear, I ordered it to disappear, like I gave it a mental command to vanish. Going under the assumption that I am moving stuff around, then I would need to tell it where to go, right?"

"You mean like a destination?"

"Exactly! I think that's why I'm feeling unsettled."

"Ok, try it. Try to move something and then specify where you want it moved to."

Sarah looked down at the smooth stone in her hand. She then started looking around for a suitable place to move the rock to. Her eyes lit on her husband.

"Hon, hold out your hand."

Steve stretched out his right arm, hand open, palm facing up. Sarah glanced down at the rock and gave it a command: *I want you to move from here*, and she glanced up to Steve's hand, *to there*.

The rock obligingly vanished from Sarah's hand only to reappear moments later in Steve's. He was so surprised that he dropped the rock on the ground.

"Holy shit!"

Sarah was shocked as well. She hadn't expected it to work that easily and that quickly. The stone had literally vanished from her hand only to appear moments later in Steve's! That was a serious thrill! What else could she experiment on? She cast her gaze around their makeshift campsite, looking for suitable objects. There, a small stick on the ground. Sarah's brow furrowed as she ordered the stick to move over next to the hearth. However, it remained in place. Confused, she again ordered the stick to move. Again, the stick refused to cooperate. What's wrong? Why isn't it working? Wait, did she really have an exact location in mind when she ordered the stick to move? She looked over to the hearth and chose a spot next to Steve's collection of firewood. There will do.

Just like that, the stick vanished and reappeared right next to the pile of firewood.

"Just learned something important," Sarah said.

"What? Did something happen?"

"You could say that. I just tried to move a small stick over to the hearth."

Steve glanced at the hearth. "Okay, so what happened? It didn't work?"

"Not at first. It didn't work until I chose a destination point. No, wait," Sarah said. "That's not right. It didn't work until I knew exactly where it would end up. I had to be able to visualize exactly where it was going to go."

"So unless you could visualize in your head where you wanted it to go, it won't work? Wait, that can't be right. You made those other things disappear."

"Good point. Maybe since I'm specifically trying to move it from one place to another I have to have a destination in mind so that I know exactly where it's going, what it looks like, etc."

Steve pulled Sarah back over to the fire and they both sat down.

"So you're saying if your intent is to teleport it then you need to know exactly where you're sending it to. No guessing, is that it?"

Sarah nodded. "I think so. If I'm just trying to make it vanish, then I can do that, but if my intent is otherwise, then it won't work."

Steve smiled and pulled Sarah close. "Think you can get a handle on it? Work out the nuances?"

"I sure am going to try. I'd like to get to the point where if I see an arrow speeding towards us, that I can make it vanish, or maybe put it right in the path of the archer firing at us."

"Hey, there's a thought! That'd be cool!"

"Me being responsible for someone dying is cool?"

"That's not what I meant. Sorry. I mean that if it comes to that, you'd be able to protect yourself and me as well."

"Protect…" Sarah mumbled. "I wonder."

"What? You wonder what?"

"I think my trigger is protection as well."

"I thought it was fear."

"Yeah, so did I, only the more I think about it, the more it makes sense. Think about it." She took Steve's hands in hers. "When we were threatened by the mugger, I wanted to prevent our stuff, namely the jorii, from falling into his hands. That wasn't fear. It was self preservation. I didn't want anything to happen to us, and that included all of our possessions."

"Can your trigger and mine be the same?"

"Clearly it can. There are probably a significant amount of people here, and you know as well as I do that there aren't that many individual emotions."

"True." Steve sighed deeply, stretching out on the soft grass. Moments later Sarah joined him. "Damn, it's pretty out." He looked up at the stars, trying to guess what constellations existed in this sky. "We need to get some sleep. I have a feeling that we are both gonna be feeling this tomorrow."

"Feeling what?"

"Sore. I don't know how people managed to get around before cars were invented."

Sarah giggled. "People have been managing to get around long before they domesticated animals or invented cars, so I'm sure we'll manage. Think anything will try to bother us tonight?"

Steve snuggled up next to Sarah. He threw a few of the large plant stems over the two of them, more to camouflage themselves than for warmth.

"I'm sure we'll be fine. At any rate, if something tries anything, we're a lot more prepared to defend ourselves now. Besides," Steve murmured, becoming groggier by the second, "I'll personally fricassee anyone's sorry ass if they get too close."

One of the burning logs split open. The sap inside started hissing and crackling, sending up erratic bursts of light that lit up their campsite for brief moments.

For once in her life, Sarah knew she wasn't going to be cold tonight. Not snuggled up next to this six foot three furnace. Wow, was he putting off the heat! Better than any electric blanket, that's for sure!

The pair fell asleep instantly. Whether it was Steve's final threat of the night, or just some much-needed good luck, they were undisturbed for the entire night.

Chapter 6 – Journal

Sarah awoke to the sounds of a crackling fire and the aroma of cooking food. Whatever it was, it smelled delicious! Wait a minute. Cooking? Here? Steve?? Both eyes shot open. There, spitted on a makeshift rotisserie over the fire, was a roasting fish. A rypo, Sarah corrected. Where the in the world did he get that? Better yet, where the hell was Steve?

She wandered over to the fire and rotated the fish so that it was cooking evenly. Baffled, she inspected the rypo. It was just now starting to blister, so her husband couldn't have been gone for more than a minute or two. Where did he get this? Back at the lake? That would be at least an hour's walk!

Steve arrived just then with a few more pieces of wood for the fire.

"Mornin'! How'd you sleep?"

"Amazingly well. I was really tired." Sarah turned the fish again. "Where did you get this? You must have caught it. Where? How??"

"It was an incredible bit of luck. I went back a bit to that small stream we passed last night. I wanted to get some more water. Thought it'd be a good idea before we started out again. This thing apparently made a wrong turn somewhere and was caught in a shallow part and was struggling to get back. Personally, I'm tired of fruitcake, so I thought some fresh fish would be good for breakfast."

Sarah just stared at her husband, senior computer tech, video game junkie, movie fanatic. He really didn't care for fish, didn't like to fish, and didn't even know how to clean a fish.

"So you caught this with your bare hands?"

Steve grinned. "Yep. Hard as hell."

"And you cleaned it yourself."

"Disgusting as hell."

"And you built this rotisserie thing to cook it."

"Ingenious as hell."

"But you hate fish. I can't even imagine you cleaning this thing."

"Stubborn as hell."

They breakfasted on roast rypo and fresh, cool water. It was quite excellent. Steve didn't even bother to trim the excess fat from his portion of fish, a fact that didn't go unnoticed by Sarah.

Together, they stowed their gear back into their pack, throwing the used palm fronds into a clump of bushes. She looked at the fire, still blazing away.

"Can you put that out? Or should we just put some dirt on it to make sure all the coals go out, too?"

"Hang on, let me see what I can do." Steve concentrated, invoking his jhorun and directing it towards the fire. Focusing his attention on the flickering flames and the hot coals, he mentally pulled the fire's energy inward, letting it consume him. The flames decreased in size until finally tapering out. The coals, glowing red from the constant heat, gradually darkened until no signs of warmth remained. Steve gingerly held his hand over the hearth, testing for signs of heat. Nothing. Smiling, Steve looked at his wife. Sarah, however, had her trademark skeptical look plastered on her face: one eyebrow raised in a true, Vulcan fashion.

"What?"

"How are you going to tell if that's warm when you can actually hold fire in your hand and not get burned?"

Steve's smug smile melted into a sheepish one. "Okay, you try. See if there's any heat. I don't feel anything."

Sarah held an open palm out to the fire. Nothing.

"I think we're ready to go. Nicely done, by the way."

Steve's smug grin was back. "Thanks!"

Travelling north, they again followed the small, winding path through the thick growth of the forest. Their moods were high as each contemplated the special power that had been quite literally dropped in their laps. Steve, more confident than he had been since arriving in Lentari, was on constant alert for any signs of pursuit. His eyes were continuously scanning the distant trees, checking for any signs of pursuit.

After two hours of solid walking they finally emerged from the forest to a very welcoming sight: the impressive Zylan river stretching from east to west as far as the eye could see. And there, running parallel to the mighty river was the enchanted road they had been so desperately searching for.

"Oh, score!!!" Steve let out a loud whoop of victory. "Is THAT a sight for sore eyes!"

Sarah sighed, relief flooding through her system, soothing her more than a glass of iced tea could ever do, and boy was she craving a glass of tea. Shading her eyes from the sun, she scanned up and down the road, looking for any forks that might have led them astray. Nothing.

This was indeed a good sign. Now that the road was again in sight, she wanted nothing more than to be standing square in the middle of it. She grabbed her husband's hand and pulled him behind her, practically breaking out in a run in order to get to the safety-enhanced road as soon as possible. Once on it, she finally released his hand and turned to face him.

"Are you okay?" Steve could only imagine how relieved his wife must be to be back on the path. He hadn't registered one word of complaint as he was drug along behind his wife during her urgent dash to the enchanted road.

"Just very glad to be right here. Very, very glad." She sighed again.

"Tell you what, the way I see it, that village Kornal spoke of should be close. Let's see if we can find a place to stay for the night."

"And how do we pay for it?"

"We have the grif."

"What if it's not enough?"

"Then we'll figure something out. Come on." It was his turn to take her hand and pull her down the road.

In high spirits, the two visitors journeyed east, adopting a hurried pace. Steve glanced up, noting the position of the sun. It was directly overhead, placing the time somewhere around noon. If they kept due east at a respectable pace, then he figured they should be able to reach the village of Donlari just before sunset. He had every intention of procuring a room for the night with a bed and decent provisions. And, he was fairly confident that his single gold grif would be more than adequate to cover the cost of the room plus the supplies.

Walking silently hand-in-hand, both observed the immense slow-moving river. They could just make out a boat of some sort with what looked like cargo and supplies on it, gently drifting downriver.

The Zylan river, running parallel to the road they were on, was the main method of transportation for the Lentarian people when it came to moving supplies from the western region of the kingdom to the east. Citizens used the wide, calm river to transport crops, manufactured goods, livestock, etc, to the main capital city, R'Tal.

Steve looked at the smooth, glass-like texture of the river and wondered if they might be able to make a raft of some sort so they wouldn't have to walk. He rapidly nixed that idea. The river simply wasn't flowing that fast. Besides, he wouldn't trust any raft he was capable of making to be seaworthy.

True to his earlier estimate, just as the sun was about to dip below the horizon, two weary Americans beheld the village of Donlari as it was preparing to settle down for the night. Not wasting any time, Steve walked straight over to the first person he saw, a local who was busy packing his wares into his cart.

Steve cleared his throat. "Pardon me, can you tell me where we can find the nearest inn?"

The merchant glanced up, noticing a potential sale. "Good evening, travelers! What might I be able to do for ye? Have ye an interest in fine crockery?" He hastily pulled a few choice pots from his cart and proffered them to Sarah. "Ye will not find a finer made pot in these parts, let me assure ye."

Steve gave his best amiable smile. "Not today, thanks. Can you point us to the closest inn? Is there one in this village?"

The merchant noted the strange affliction to the way they spoke, but he had heard far stranger. Nodding, he pointed towards a street still packed with people. "Ye will find several here in this village. The closest is just down that alley. Follow the alley until it dead-ends, then turn right. Ye cannot miss it. Thacken Lodge. Ye will do no better in Donlari."

"Thank you."

The merchant nodded, dragging his cart away, disappearing into the crowds of people. Steve shifted the pack to his other shoulder to give his aching right shoulder a break.

"Come on," Steve took her hand. "Let's go. I don't want to be caught out here when it gets dark."

Thacken Lodge was a large, three story stone and mortar structure with several chimneys poking out of the top of the thickly thatched roof. Dark smoke was billowing out of one of the chimneys as cheerful lights and music beckoned to the two of them from the open double doors. Giving Sarah a brave smile, he ducked into the inn, his wife following closely on his heels. Navigating around the bustling patrons, Steve glanced around, noticing the huge vaulted ceiling with the exposed rafters, the roaring fire in the huge hearth, and running along the entire length of the far wall, a large wooden counter. The medieval equivalent of a bar? Several patrons were seated at various spots along the counter. Figuring the large man behind the bar to be the owner, he headed in that direction.

Sarah blinked her eyes, waiting for them to adjust. The atmosphere felt warm and welcoming to her, albeit a tad on the dirty side. There was a crackling fire in the hearth against the far wall. Sounds of banging pots and general laughter came from a room to the right of the roaring fire. The kitchen maybe? Scents of burnt meat wafted lazily about. Numerous scarred tables and benches were scattered across the room. Many were empty, so she reasoned the lodge had to have at least a few vacancies.

Steve finally made it to the counter and caught the proprietor's attention. The burly overweight man ambled in his direction, wiping his hands on a worn, greasy apron. "What can I do for ye?"

"We need provisions, and a room for the night. Do you have any available?"

The owner of the lodge scratched his beard with a huge hand. "I s'pose ye are one of Rhenyon's men? Still irks me why I must give away m' best rooms fer free."

"Umm, I'm not with Rhenyon, whoever that is. I just need food and lodging for the night. I can-"

The owner leaned precariously over the bar, studying Steve intently. He then noticed Sarah behind him, watching closely.

"Good news, indeed. But can ye pay?"

"Well," Steve stammered, "I have a-"

The owner cut him off. "Can ye perform some type of service in exchange?"

The rusty wheels upstairs ground into motion. "I can probably help out with cooking. I seem to have the ability to heat things up." He looked at the large man in front of them and smiled. "Rapidly."

The man's jaw hit the counter. One would have thought that the stranger had just announced that he had slept with his daughter. "Speak ye the truth? Can ye affect large cauldrons or are ye limited to small objects?"

Now he was in for it. He hadn't expected the innkeeper to actually entertain his notion of helping in the kitchen. Did they have a shortage of cooks in this tavern? Steve shrugged his shoulders and smiled. "I haven't noticed any size limitations, if that's what you're wondering. Umm, do you actually need some help in the kitchen?"

Their new friend ran his hands through his thick, black hair.

"Ye might have heard me before. Rhenyon is the captain of the royal guards. He and most of his men will be staying here tonight and are due to arrive at any moment. The king's soldiers get free lodging wherever they go, and I have to have enough food ready when they arrive, which I do. But I was given no notice this time, and the food has not yet been prepared. My wife can cook for that many, but it takes time to prepare that much food. So," he tapped his meaty finger on Steve's chest, "help my wife get that food ready in time, and the two of ye may stay the night with a meal. We have an accord, yes?"

Steve's grin ran from ear to ear. "Deal." He offered his arm, which was grasped in return. He turned to Sarah. "Can you watch the pack? Seems I have a little cooking to do." He turned back to the barkeep. "Umm, sir, can my wife sit at one of the tables and wait for me? We've been travelling all day. I know she's tired."

"Call me Thack. As for yer wife, not a problem. Better yet..." He whistled shrilly. A small, skinny boy of perhaps ten years darted out from one of the back rooms. "Ellis, take the lady and her things up to a room. See that she has what she needs."

The boy took the pack easily on his shoulder and gestured for Sarah to follow.

"Go on up. I'll join you as soon as I can."

"I'll go up and get us settled. Then I'll be back. I'll bet I can help out, too."

"Hon, don't start. Just go up and rest."

"Nothing doing. We're in this together. Besides, I don't want to be alone up there."

Thacken, who had heard the entire argument, shook his head. If another person was willing to help his wife out, no one would catch him arguing.

"Okay, fine. But try to rest a little, will you? Join me when you can." He kissed his wife tenderly and watched as she disappeared up the stairs.

He clapped his hands together. "Okay, show me where I can find the kitchen."

Thacken whistled again, loud and shrill. "Bolli, come out here for a moment, will ye?"

A harassed, middle aged woman wearing a brown apron appeared in one of the doorways.

"Thack, what is it? I have not the time for these interruptions. There's much work to be done an' I don' see ye doing it!!"

"This is..." Thacken looked at Steve.

"My name is Steve."

"Steve. He will be assisting ye while ye are cooking for Rhenyon and his men."

"A man? In my kitchen? Are ye daft? This is not the time for jokes, Thack."

Steve spoke up. "Believe it or not, ma'am, I think I can help you out. I have a knack for making things hot. Really hot really fast."

"Do ye now? Unless ye can somehow manage to heat up three cauldrons at the same time, ye would just be in my way."

Steve smiled. "As a matter of fact, I believe I can."

Bolli's eyes widened. She studied Steve a moment. "Changed my mind, I have. If ye can do what ye say ye can do, then ye just became our guest of honor. This way, hurry!"

Bolli guided Steve into the back of the kitchen where three enormous metal pots were sitting against the back wall. Two were full of what looked like stew, and the third was being prepped. She had clearly been interrupted in the middle of finishing the final cauldron.

"So what can ye do? How do ye plan on heating all three?"

Steve looked around. "Where can we put these things that won't be affected by intense heat?"

Bolli gestured to a section of the wall where a series of metal hooks were protruding from the stone. "Ye can put the pots there. I typically do not prepare this much food at one time, but I had Thack install extra hooks in case I ever needed to."

"Will it hold the weight of the cauldron and the food?"

"Thacken fastened those hooks into solid stone. They are going nowhere, trust me."

Grunting and straining, Steve hung two of the full pots on their hooks in the huge hearth. After Bolli finished preparing the third, he (with Bolli's help) hung it next to the other two.

Stretching her back, Bolli eyed her assistant. "Now what?"

Steve gently guided Thacken's wife away from the enormous metal pots.

"To make sure I get this right, I'm going to heat just one cauldron first. Keep an eye on the contents. I'll start increasing the heat, and it's going to cook. Fast. If it starts getting too hot too fast, let me know, okay? Once it looks good, we'll start on the other two. Sound good?"

Growing cautious, Bolli nodded.

Steve took in a deep breath, and let it out slowly, trying to calm himself. He searched within for his jhorun. It was definitely getting easier to find. The tingles appeared instantly this time, almost eager to do their part. Steve eyed the first pot and ordered it to start getting hot.

In a matter of moments the aroma of cooking meat instantly filled his nostrils, making him realize just how hungry he was. A slight sizzling sound had also started within the pot. Baffled, Bolli approached her first cauldron and carefully leaned over to peer inside. Being skeptical by nature, she tentatively held a hand over the pot to ascertain the pot's temp, but had to snatch her hand away lest she be given a burn. She didn't know how this stranger was doing it, but he was! Her first cauldron was already cooking! She pulled out a large wooden spoon and stirred the contents. Pieces of meat floated to the surface of her stew. She also noticed that a few chunks of meat were beginning to char.

"Can ye lessen the heat some? The meat has started to burn."

Steve nodded, pulling back in some of the heat from the pot. With the temperature now at a comfortable range, she indicated she was ready to get pots two and three going. Steve looked them over. Within seconds, all three pots were glowing a soft red. He was startled to discover that if his attention diverted to anything else, his jhorun receded on its own accord. Slowly, ever so slowly, it started to cool off. Luckily, it was easy to tell when the well-used cauldrons started to fade from red back to black.

Sarah, following her nose, finally wandered into the kitchen and saw Bolli moving from pot to pot, giving the contents of each pot a thorough stirring. She also noted that all three pots had a warm, soft reddish color on the bottom. From Steve's jhorun? It had to be. No flames whatsoever! She was impressed!

Steve glanced over at her and smiled. Instantly, two of the three pots lost their reddish glow. Sarah noticed and gestured for Steve to look. His head whipped around, saw the problem, and restored the proper amount of heat.

"This is incredible!" Bolli kept saying, going from pot to pot. "Ye will have the entire feast cooked in the time it takes me to make the fire! I can not thank ye enough!"

Thacken poked his head into the kitchen. "Rhenyon and his troops have arrived. His men have practically filled every table we have. How soon before -" and he saw the three pots hanging in a row over the hearth, no fire present, yet glowing red. Even standing where he was, he could feel the heat emanating from the large pots and smell the enticing aroma of his wife's cooking. "By the wizards! They are cooking! It smells great! Ye did it! Thank ye, Steve! Ye have saved my wife and I hours of work! Go rest. I'll send two plates of food up. Ye both look dead tired."

"Thank you, Thacken. Bolli, I'm glad I could help." He gestured to the pots. "Once I leave, they'll start to cool down. It might take it a bit, but they will start cooling off."

"I'll have proper fires started by then. Thank ye, Steve. I'll have Thack send up a bottle of our finest wine. Rest well!"

Following Sarah back out into the great room, he was amazed to discover that practically all the tables were full of soldiers, and more kept streaming in. Giving the weary soldiers a wide berth, Sarah led him to the far stairs where he followed her up.

Their room was small and homey, with a padded mattress in the corner. The bedding was folded neatly (Bolli's influence, Sarah presumed) on the corner of the bed. A small fireplace was situated directly across from the divan, with the small window open wide to allow the fresh night air to enter. It also appeared that the window served double duty as the air outtake for the fire, as there were signs of black soot on the window frame and on the glass itself.

"Want the window open?"

Sarah nodded. "Yes, please. The air smells so fresh here. No evidence of industrialization. We ought to bottle it and sell it on eBay!" She giggled and looked at the fireplace. "Can you light the fire?"

"Are you asking me if I can or if I will?"

"I know you can, silly, I want you to light the fire, please."

Steve looked at the fireplace, and within seconds the logs instantly erupted into flames. Warmth flooded into the room, chasing out the cold bite of the night air. Steve leaned up and pulled the windows to within an inch of being closed.

"If it gets too smoky, let me know. I can open it some more."

"Thanks." Sarah sank down onto the bed and kicked her shoes off. "I don't think," she began, "that my feet have ever been this sore. But you know what? I don't care. I'm actually having a good time!"

"I'm glad you are." Steve joined her on the bed. "So what did you think of my culinary abilities down there?"

"I wanted to ask you about that. What possessed you to volunteer for that? I thought you were going to use that grif to pay for the room?"

"So did I. Thacken didn't give me a chance to offer it. His abruptness caught me off guard, and he mistook that hesitation as us not having any means of paying for the room."

"So you offered to cook instead? I'm impressed!"

"You clearly didn't hear the whole conversation, did you?"

"I thought I did, but, ummm, clearly I didn't." Sarah laughed. "What'd I miss? It was kinda noisy in there."

"He wanted to know if I could do any service that would be the equivalent of paying our way. So I said that I could heat things up. Rapidly."

Sarah snorted. "That's the understatement of the century."

"You would have thought I just informed him I could turn lead into gold. He told me about those soldiers arriving any moment, and he hadn't been properly notified, so his poor wife was struggling to get all the food ready."

"And you just happened to have the ability they needed to rapidly cook everything." Sarah nodded. "That's thinking quickly on your feet. Good job!"

There was a soft knock on the door. Steve opened it to reveal Ellis, holding a large tray with several steaming bowls of the same dish Steve had helped cook earlier, a round loaf of bread, a bottle of wine, and several glasses. Steve took the tray from the boy, thanked him, and sent him on his way.

"Looks good!" Sarah said. "What'd we get?"

"Let's see," Steve put the tray down by the bed. "We have some bowls of stew, loaf of bread, and some wine. They didn't send any water, though." He picked up the bottle and eyed it. The contents swished around as he rotated it, looking for some clue on how it might taste. Unsurprisingly, no label.

"It's what we were given. Supposed to be the finest here. Let's not insult our hosts, okay?"

Steve sighed, uncorked the bottle, and poured a glass for each of them. It looked to be some type of merlot. He hoped it wasn't too strong. Gingerly, he took a sip. Mmmm, not bad! He didn't ever recall red wine tasting like this! The sweet, fruity liquid was light and fragrant, with a light aftertaste of… Steve smacked his lips. What was it? Some type of flower? Spice? Lavender, or maybe rosemary? Whatever it was, he realized he was so grateful to quench his thirst that he didn't care if it tasted like raw sewage. Eagerly, he gulped more down.

"Whoa there, bucko," Sarah cautioned. "Go easy on that stuff. We don't know what's in this, and it might be more potent that the wines we are used to. And since you don't drink wine, I'd just as soon not have a drunk, human flamethrower in the same room. Know what I mean?"

Steve snorted, spraying flecks of wine onto the piece of bread he was about to take a bite of.

"Is that what you think of me? A human flame thrower?" Steve paused to let that sink in. That characteristic smug grin of his appeared on his face. "Yeah, I can live with that."

Sarah rolled her eyes. "You're just a big kid, do you know that?"

Mouth full of stew, Steve nodded. "With pride!"

Comfortably sated, Steve pulled the bedding over the mattress and invited Sarah to stretch out alongside him.

"Let me get something first." She walked over to the pack, fished around inside for a moment, then pulled out the leather journal.

Stretching out next to her husband on the bed, she held the journal up questioningly.

"Whatcha doin'?" Steve noticed the journal. "Are you looking for something?"

"Remember when we talked briefly about your grandparents? We were curious about what their jhoruns might be. I want to see if it's mentioned anywhere in here. Do you mind if I read this?"

"By all means. Help yourself."

"Let's see," she opened the journal, "here's the opening inscription, which changed from that foreign language to something we can read. We'll get into that later. But for now, let's see what we have." She skimmed the first couple of pages. "Nothing much, just talking about New Year's dinner they had, here's an entry about some old book that Simon," Sarah looked up questioningly at her husband. "Simon. Just to be clear, that is the name of your grandfather, right?"

Steve nodded.

"Apparently he was working on repairing some old book. Doesn't mention if it was rare, or where it was from."

"Find that entry from before, with that Volan person."

Sarah started flipping through the pages. "Okay, let's see. I think it was roughly halfway through, closer to… Ah! Here it is. Volan's journey. Let's see, that was an entry for April of 2008. I'll read the whole entry:

April 3rd, 2008

It's our first day of this visit. The Kri'yans have granted us leave to discover the location of the manuscript. Several years of steady, relentless questioning has apparently finally convinced them to grant us permission to access the Archives.

On day 3, we uncovered a reference to a distant family member that lived on the sea. What we found incredible was that there were references to a small island off the western coast which was allegedly rumored to resemble a griffin cub in flight. There have been only a few villages that have been along the western sea, and of those, only one remains: Capily. As it happens, there are several small islands nearby. We were very surprised to learn that no one had ever investigated the western coast. So the following day, we journeyed to the coast via their royal highness' personal marjihn.

We explored all along the sea from the village's most northern point to the most southern, all the while keeping the village in our sights. It wasn't until Grace went to refill her canteen from one of the freshwater streams that she discovered the ruins of a house tucked away in the forest.

Poking around in the ruins we discovered that the forest had, unfortunately, decimated anything that might have at one time helped us. After a brief search in Capily, we located the town scribe and told him we were on official business.

"Official business?" Steve interrupted. "Sounds like they were definitely in league with the king and queen, don't you think?"
"I do. Let me finish."
"Sorry."

Lucky for us, the scribe was a very knowledgeable, organized person and had records dating back several hundred years. Spending a day or so in his company helped us learn all we needed to know about that quaint, seaside village. It was only a matter of time before several documents were uncovered that helped us track down the name of the family that had lived in the ruins of that small house and how long it had been vacant.

The house had belonged to a man named Kahrill. He had married a local girl and moved into her family's house in the village, thus abandoning his ancestral home. Once again, our new-found friend came to our rescue. The scribe searched his records and identified a great-great-granddaughter that was still living in the same house. Apparently living in the family home from birth to death is a common occurrence in this village. The woman was very cooperative, letting us search through her great-great-grandmother's things.

There, sitting inside a dusty, dirty trunk in the cellar of this small, thatched house we finally located the manuscript, there in Capily. I'm anxious to start reading about Volan's legendary travels, but Grace would like to return. The Nayan is also eager to see the manuscript, and I believe Grace would like to share the discovery with her.

"I wonder who this Volan person is, then?"
"Would you stop interrupting! Sheesh!"
"Sorry."

We've contacted the Nayan. She's ecstatic the manuscript has finally been found and we can once and for all read about how the Bakkian was originally discovered. You would think that if this Bakkian is as important as everyone says it is, then more references should exist.

I'm grateful of the confidence that was placed in Grace and I, yet I can't help feeling a little worn out. Now that this task has been completed, I'm looking forward to some rest. We've earned it. Kri'Entu himself told me that there has never been a more dedicated, diligent set of official biographers than us.

This being the seventh successful task we've accomplished, we're going to ask for an extended period of time. I know Grace would like to return.

"'Grace would like to return'? That suggests that he'd much rather stay there than come back."

"Seven successful tasks? How long do you think that they have been coming here?"

Steve scratched his chin. "I wonder how they first got there? I mean, we got here because of them. I wonder how they learned how to get here?"

"Well, what if those doors were in that house long before your grandparents bought it?"

"Kinda cold, don't you think?"

Sarah paused. "What? What's cold?"

"Before they 'bought it'? Come on, you know the doors were there before they passed away. They had to be using them. It's a question of how long before their deaths."

"Before they *bought* the *house*," Sarah clarified. "I didn't mean before they bit the big one, but whether those doors were always there. Did your grandparents build that house? That's the question I'd be asking right about now."

"Well, remind me to look it up once we get back."

Sarah flipped through the next couple of pages, scanning the entries. Was there anything in here that could help us out? She was about ready to turn the page when a familiar word caught her eye.

"Jhorun! They talk about jhoruns in this entry!"

"Let's hear what it says."

Sarah passed him the journal. "Your turn."

Steve took the journal and started to read.

September 25th, 2008

The castle has finally quieted down. With the journeys of Volan finally disclosed, all anyone can talk about is who, or what, the Nohrin are. Who they are, where they are from, why they have not appeared yet, and most important of all, what their jhoruns might be. I can't even imagine the jhoruns required to fulfill the Bakkian.

I've seen the levels of the wizards of R'Tal, and it makes mine seem miniscule.

"Hah! There, did you hear that? They did have jhoruns! I knew it!"

"Keep reading! I want to hear what they were!"

And it doesn't even work all the time. I have to concentrate so hard I give myself headaches, and even then the pen doesn't write fluidly like it should. The parchment that Grace conjures suffices for our work, but it would have been nice to have something stronger.

"Question." Steve said. "Doesn't that sound like our jhoruns are more powerful?"

"Well, ordinarily, I wouldn't say so, but it's hard to refute that. Your grandfather could make a pen move? Like having it transcribe for them? And your grandmother conjured the paper for him to use?"

"I'll say it. Those jhoruns sound pretty wimpy to me."

"It sounds convenient. Those two jhoruns go together really well, don't you think? Keep reading, will you?"

Steve returned to the journal.

I really shouldn't complain. It's taken thirty years to become trustworthy in the Kri'yans eyes, and even longer to earn our jhoruns. I'm grateful Shardwyn is a powerful wizard.

Steve's jaw clanged noisily on the ground as his mouth fell open.

"Say what? At least thirty years? And they were given those jhoruns??"

"But, but..." Sarah sputtered. "They should have had their own! Thirty years! Couldn't they figure out how to access their own jhoruns?"

"Thirty years." Steve repeated. "If they had jhoruns, they would have figured out how to make them work. What if they didn't have them?"

Sarah considered. "Well, if they didn't have them, why do we? Are we just smarter than they were and figured out how to use them whereas they didn't?"

Steve shook his head. "We have only been here a few days. And we already know what it takes to make our jhoruns work. We might not have all the nuances down, but we have a decent idea on what it can and can't do. I think you're right. I don't think they had jhoruns on their own."

Pointing to the book, Sarah indicated to Steve that she'd like him to continue reading.

October 16th, 2008

We've received our eighth quest. Discover the identities of the Nohrin and facilitate their arrival in any way we can with the full support of the court of R'Tal.

I would say that we've been escalated again in their eyes to give us this much responsibility. The king and queen clearly are disturbed that the Nohrin haven't arrived yet. They are utterly convinced that their son, Kre'Mikal, is in mortal danger. His highness is only seven years old, and hasn't a clue to the danger his parents believe him to be in.

I can't say that I'm convinced the danger exists, but clearly everyone here believes it to be real. The foreign kingdom of Ylani has always been Lentari's greatest rival, and would love to cause strife for their peace-loving neighbors. But would Ylani really make such a bold statement of war by trying to kidnap the young prince?

The entire kingdom is rife with unease. I do not think it would take much for civil unrest to escalate out of hand. Everyone here loves their King and Queen, and the little boy Prince. If a rival kingdom were to somehow get their hands on that little boy, this kingdom will declare war faster than a griffin can snare a wiht.

So now we've been tasked with finding the identities of the Nohrin. The Bakkian clearly states that the royal family will be challenged, and that the little Prince will not truly be safe until he is in their care. So who are they? What magic do they possess that can out-perform the wizards of R'Tal? Where do they come from? How can we possibly ascertain the origins of people mentioned in a four hundred year-old reference?

Steve whistled. "A four hundred year-old reference? I wouldn't want to have to track down these people, either." He gestured to the journal. "That was two years ago. I wonder when these Nohrin guys showed up?"

Sarah looked thoughtful. "Even if they did, I wouldn't want to be the king or queen. How can you be certain that the people who arrived and claimed to be these Nohrin people were in fact who they claimed to be?"

"Good point. They probably came up with a test of some sort."

Sarah took the journal from Steve. "If these people showed up, I'll bet there would be some mention in here, don't you think?"

"Good one. Skim through and see what the next entries say."

"Let's see." Sarah scanned the next couple of pages. "Here's an entry, dated early the next year. No progress made. Ummm, next we have an entry from the summer of 2009, still no progress. Looks like your grandfather is getting very nervous. Apparently the king and queen are getting restless."

Getting defensive, Steve snorted. "How can they expect them to track down these people if the only clues they have are from four hundred years ago? I wouldn't know where to start, believe me. Sounds like the Homework Assignment from hell."

"Actually," Sarah said, reading the next entry, "It looks like the king and queen were worried, but not frustrated. This entry says that the queen has been continually reassuring them, telling them to not give up hope. Looks like your grandfather was being incredibly hard on himself. I guess he took his job seriously." She looked up from the journal and met her husband's eyes. "Sound like anyone we know?"

Steve hmmphed at her, indicating for her to continue.

"Let's see, the next couple of entries are all from 2009, and all of them pretty much say the same thing. They aren't having any luck identifying who the Nohrin are. The first entry from 2010 mentions that the king and queen have granted them an extended leave of absence so that they can then focus all of their energies into their task when they return. Says here that the king is figuring they are working too hard and need to rest."

Sarah quietly closed the journal. "Hon, that's the last entry."

Steve paled. That meant his grandparents died during their "vacation" and would therefore be unable to complete their last quest.

Sarah took his hand. "Are you okay?"

"Yeah, it's just spooky to hear about what they were doing before they died. And apparently, they were on some important mission to find several people who could supposedly protect the little prince."

There came a sudden knocking on the door. Both occupants quickly sat up on the bed. Steve made it to the door first and opened it. There stood a soldier, clearly a high ranking one due to the way he carried himself. His uniform was a deep, scarlet color with a jeweled sword sheathed on his hip. Several daggers were visible in various locations along his belt.

Behind the soldier was the innkeeper, nervously twisting his apron in his large, beefy hands.

Steve's demeanor quickly shifted to neutral. "Hello. Is there something I can do for you?"

The soldier's eyes narrowed, noting the different manner in which the foreigner spoke. He raised his right hand, dismissing the owner of the inn.

"May I enter?" Without waiting for a response, he strode purposely into the room and faced the occupants.

"I am Rhenyon, captain of the Royal Guards. Who are ye? And more importantly, where are ye from? Mr. Thacken told me a man, ye, I presume, was able to heat three rather large cauldrons effortlessly using naught but his jhorun. Did he speak the truth?"

Sarah had silently positioned herself behind her husband. Just in case. She was pretty sure her husband would keep his head and not do anything foolish. However, she had also personally witnessed what he was capable of.

Steve met the captain's stare.

"Good evening. My name is Steve. This is my wife, Sarah. And as you can probably figure out, no, we're not from around here."

Not sensing any danger from either one of the strangers, the soldier relaxed his posture.

"The lady of the inn tells me that she had help preparing for my arrival. She was very appreciative of the strange man and his powerful abilities." Rhenyon held Steve's gaze. "Care to explain the nature of that ability?"

"Long story short, I can apparently control heat and fire."

Rhenyon's eyebrows shot up. "Ye have control over one of the elements? Speak ye the truth??"

"I don't know if I'd call it that, but yeah, I do appear to have control over fire. Why? What's the big deal?"

"Demonstrate this, if ye please."

Steve glanced over to the fire in the fireplace.

Poof!

The fire went out, leaving red-hot coals glowing brightly in the flame's absence. Steve counted to ten, and then re-ignited it.

Rhenyon cocked his head, staring at the newcomers. He was silent for a few minutes as he contemplated what to do.

Sarah peaked around her husband to look at the soldier.

"Is there a problem? Why do you look as though you were just given some bad news? We aren't a threat, if that's what you're wondering."

Rhenyon met her eyes. "It's not often that we see someone with an elemental jhorun, milady. I wanted to see for myself if that were the case." He studied the two of them. "What are yer intentions? Why are ye here?"

Steve elbowed his wife aside and faced Rhenyon head-on.

"We're just looking to return home. But in order to do so, we need the help of your king and queen. So we're on our way to R'Tal to seek an audience."

Rhenyon nodded, pleased. "Then I wish ye well with yer journey." He unbuckled one of his daggers and handed it to Steve. "Take this. My crest is on the hilt. If ye are stopped by any of my soldiers, show them this. Ye will be able to travel throughout the kingdom unmolested."

Startled by this unexpected turn of events, Steve took the dagger, momentarily at a loss for words. "Ummm, thanks." He ran his hand along the hilt, admiring the workmanship. "Is this necessary? Are we apt to run into troubles with your soldiers?"

Rhenyon shrugged. "Two foreigners who are unfamiliar with our customs. My soldiers are trained to ask questions." He eyed the couple. "At least, they should."

The captain extended his right forearm. Without even thinking, Steve grasped the proffered arm and gave it a friendly shake.

"Good journey to ye, then," the soldier said.

"Thanks."

Rhenyon turned and left the room. When the door finally closed behind him, Steve let out the breath he hadn't realized he'd been holding. He looked at Sarah.

"What the hell was that all about?"

Sarah spread her hands. "Don't ask me. Did we do something wrong? Maybe you shouldn't have used your jhorun to heat those cauldrons up. Apparently you have a really unique ability."

"If they knew about yours, they'd say the same thing. But you're right, we really should use caution. I don't want any more surprise visits from any type of soldier." He thumped his chest to get the blood flowing. "That scared the crap out of me." He turned to his wife and cracked a smile. "Couldn't help but notice that you moved directly behind me."

"And be in the line of fire if it came to that? No thank you." Sarah put her arms around him. "Besides, I know that you really don't want to hurt anyone, unless they pose a serious threat."

Steve paused. "Do you think that Thacken turned us in or something?"

Sarah shook her head. "I don't think so. He seems nice, as does his wife. Rhenyon probably offered up his thanks to the owner of the inn for being ready for him on such short notice, and then Thack mentioned that he had help. I don't think there was any harm done."

Steve hefted the jeweled dagger. "So why in the world did he give us this? Don't you think that it's a bit odd? I really don't think he's worried about his men. I think he had some other motive in mind."

Sarah took the dagger and ran her fingers over the crest. It was of a stationary griffin, clasping some type of tree branch in his beak. A broadsword and a crossbow rested nearby. This was not some rudimentary dagger. The craftsmanship that went into the creation of this weapon was truly masterful. So why would he willingly part with it? What was his motive?

Confused, tired, and oddly enough, in high spirits, husband and wife fell instantly asleep. The fire in the hearth slowly died down until nothing but coals remained. Sarah, unconsciously noting the absence of the fire, snuggled closer.

Only a little while later, Sarah had awakened, drenched with sweat. When had their room turned into an oven anyway? Propping herself up on her elbow, she looked over the sleeping form of her husband to glare at the small hearth. Only a few coals were still glowing red. That couldn't be it. What was going on? Steve rolled suddenly until he was flat on his back, his snores threatening to shake the dust of the rafters. The blast of heat had her gasping. Was he having a bad dream? If she didn't do something quickly, this room was going to become a sauna. Nudging him gently in the ribs, she told him to roll over. There, that did it. She could feel the heat diminishing, like someone turning off a space heater. That was so much better!

Cooler, and much more comfortable, Sarah fell asleep.

Chapter 7 – R'Tal

Thacken Lodge was still and quiet. It was about an hour before sunrise and the lady of the house was already stirring. Bolli was gathering her fire-making materials to get the hearth lit again as her oaf of a husband had failed to properly bank it from last night. Naturally, it had gone out.

Several floors above, in the farthest room away from the main hall, Steve's eyes snapped open. Something had just jolted him out of a sound sleep. Had he heard something? Had he detected some type of movement in the room? With all his senses on high alert, he lay motionless next to Sarah. She, however, was still sound asleep.

He rubbed his eyes. Sarah was a much lighter sleeper than he was, so since she didn't wake up, then maybe he had just imagined it. That had to be it. If Sarah wasn't concerned then he wasn't concerned. Feeling the matter settled, he closed his eyes.

He had just started to doze off when he felt a sharp tingle, but only for a split second. What was that? Fully awake again, he waited to see if it would happen again. Sure enough, a minute or two later he felt the sharp tingle again, and just as quickly as it appeared, it vanished. The sensation was reminiscent of getting a charley horse. Not the actual charley horse but the sensations that lead up to getting one. What was going on?

His jhorun started to awaken, sending his awareness to other areas of the lodge. His attention felt drawn down to the main hall. No, he corrected, that didn't quite feel right. A room off of the main hall? Was it the kitchen? That was it. What's going on in the kitchen?

The sharp tingle returned a third time, lasted a moment or two longer than the others, and then vanished. Curiosity piqued, he quietly got out of bed, dressed, and exited the room. With as much stealth as the creaky wooden floor would allow, he descended the stairs down to the main hall. All was quiet and dark, although he did hear some movement coming from the back of the inn. Someone was moving around, cursing softly.

Steve went up to the doorway and looked in to see Bolli angrily poking at one of her cooking hearths and attempting to coax a spark out of her nodule of flint. Throwing her stones down with disgust, she looked up and yelped with surprise.

"For the love of all that is good and blessed!!" Bolli had slapped a hand over her heart. "Ye scared ten years right off me life! Steve, make noise, knock on the door, something!"

"Sorry! Man alive, Bolli, I'm sorry. I heard noises, and I came to investigate. I didn't mean to scare you. Are you okay? Can I give you a hand with something?"

"This fire is not cooperating. I cannot keep the spark burning. I tried using dried naka dung, I even tried my old fire starting sticks. Nothing. It burns for a moment, then before it can catch, a gust of wind blows it out. Damn all the winds and their makers." She eyed Steve. "Ye can heat cauldrons. Can ye start fires?"

Steve gently, but firmly, guided Bolli back away from the hearth moments before it blazed up, burning merrily as though it had been burning the entire night.

Bolli visibly relaxed and even started to smile. "That be the second time you have come to my rescue. I will not forget it. As soon as I get breakfast cooking I will send up some up for ye and yer wife. Probably be in an hour or two." She tossed a few more logs onto the fire. "All Thack had to do was bank the fire," Bolli muttered in disgust. "Think he could remember to do that one simple task?" She looked at Steve and smiled. "Get some more sleep. I can take it from here." She escorted him to the main hall and gently pushed him up the stairs.

As Steve ascended, a sudden realization occurred. Were those sharp tingles Bolli's attempts at starting a fire? Did that mean he could sense fire when he couldn't even see it?

Try it now, the ever-present voice in his head said.

Activating his jhorun, he cast his awareness about. Standing motionless, he felt his jhorun being gently pulled downwards and off to the left. Straight to the kitchen, he presumed. Interesting! He also felt a small piece of his awareness being drawn to a room off the second floor. Apparently one of the soldiers had a fire going in their small hearth.

Easing the door to their room open, he slipped back inside. It didn't appear that Sarah had so much as moved an inch. Good. Looks like he had managed to avoid disturbing her. Undressing, he slipped back into bed. Sighing, he stretched out and felt himself becoming drowsy.

"So where were you?" came the voice out of the dark.

Smiling, Steve propped himself up on his elbow. "Should have known that wouldn't have worked. I went down to the kitchen."

"You did? Why? Were you hungry or something?"

"Would you believe that Bolli's attempts at making a fire woke me up?"

"Really? I didn't hear anything. Was she making a lot of noise?"

"Nope, no noise. I *felt* it. A sharper tingling than the jhorun. But much shorter and more brief."

Sarah considered, digesting this most recent bit of news regarding Steve's jhorun. He could now detect the presence of other fires in the area? Did that mean since he could start fires so easily that any other attempts to create a fire alerted him?

"What do you think it means?" Sarah asked him. "Someone tried to make a fire and it woke you up?"

"That's it, in a nutshell. What I'm supposed to learn from that I have no idea. What I can tell you is that I can actually sense other fires in this place. Like right now, for instance." Steve paused a moment. "Bolli has the fire I started for her going good, and in fact," he sent his jhorun down to the main floor to investigate, "she has started another fire from that one. It's in the same room, but how close together, I can't tell."

Amazement flooded Sarah. That was so cool! How was he doing it? He was able to determine that there were two fires were burning in the kitchen? How was he learning to control his abilities so quickly?

"Anyway," Steve continued, "I'm sorry I woke you up. On the bright side, Bolli is going to send some food up to us as soon as it's cooked. I thought that was nice of her."

Nodding, Sarah said, "That is nice of her." She looked at Steve, who was hoping to get another hour or so of sleep. Not today, dear. "I'm getting up. I want to clean myself up, and I want to try to wash our clothes. I have an idea."

Steve dozed off and on as Sarah washed, then took handfuls of the powdered soap, the pitcher of water, and the basin, and slowly and methodically washed their clothes. Once finished, she wrung as much water as she could out of them before waking up her snoring husband. Again.

"Okay, hon, your turn. I need you to dry these." She handed the soggy pile of clothes to her husband. Seeing him rubbing his eyes, and clearly not quite awake, she plopped them down on his lap.

"Damn!" Fully awake, Steve held up the wet clothes. "What happened? Did you wash these already?"

"You fell asleep. I'll let that slide for now. I've washed them. You get to dry them."

"Dry them." Steve repeated, chuckling. "I think I can handle that."

Ten minutes later, dressed in their clean, dry clothes, they were ready for the knock on the door. The same small serving boy again delivered a tray of food and drink. Without asking permission, Ellis silently moved over to the far wall and retrieved the dishes from last night's dinner, quietly shutting the door behind him.

"Doesn't say much, but he's efficient as hell." Steve eyed the bottle on the new tray. "Are you kidding me? Wine for breakfast? Maybe they should consider joining Alcoholics Anonymous."

Sarah opened the bottle and sniffed the contents. "Smells non-alcoholic. I think you're in luck."

Breakfasted, refreshed, and with their pack repacked, they made their way down the hall to pay their respects to Thacken and his wife. The burly proprietor was chatting with a soldier when he spotted his new friends.

"Steve. Sarah. Slept well, did ye?"

"We did, thanks," Sarah answered. "We sure do appreciate the food you sent up. Both times actually."

"Good deeds are rewarded in this house, I can assure ye. Bolli is busy in the back, but she told me what ye did for her early this morning, Steve. She made this for the two of ye." He held out several tightly wrapped packages of varying sizes. "This should see you to R'Tal. Good journey to the both of ye. Thanks again for yer help."

Steve grasped his arm with his, giving a friendly shake. "You're welcome. Please convey our thanks to your wife." He hefted the wrapped packages. "This was very thoughtful of her."

"If ye come by this way again, stop by t' say hello, will ye?"

"We will," Sarah assured him.

Stepping out into the bright daylight, Steve hoisted the pack on his back and looked around. The village was just starting to awaken. Local merchants were already setting up their carts to display their wares to passing onlookers. Taking Sarah's hand, he guided them through the maze of clay pottery, bolts of fabric, and carts of various fruit and produce.

"Do you know where you're going?" Sarah asked.

"Yep. That way." Steve pointed past the swarm of merchants. "We're heading towards the river." Gesturing in the direction of all the eager salesmen, he chuckled. “Don’t look ‘em in the eye, don’t smile at ‘em, and maybe we’ll get through with our lives.”

Sarah laughed. “I wish I had some of the local currency. I’d love to buy a few things. You know, support the local economy.”

One merchant, a silversmith, overheard her remark and quickly selected a green crystal pendant on a silver chain. Catching Sarah’s eye, he handed her the necklace. “A pretty necklace for a pretty lady!”

Sarah smiled warmly at the salesman. “Thank you, sir, but I cannot pay at this time. Another time perhaps.” She moved to return the necklace.

The jewelry was gently pushed back into her hands. “Take it. Wear it with pride. If ye be asked who made it, tell them Kahtro o’ Donlari, finest silversmith this side o’ the Zylan River! Can ye do that for me? An’ ye can, then the necklace belongs to ye.”

The generous merchant was rewarded with one of Sarah’s million dollar smiles. She slid the chain over her neck and admired the pendant. The cabochon was of the purest green, shining brilliantly in the sun. She showed her new jewelry to Steve. “This is beautiful. A truly masterful work. Kahtro of Donlari, I’ll tell everyone I see about the amazing silversmith who can make such beautiful things.”

The merchant flushed with pride. “That is all I ask, milady.”

Once they were out of earshot, Steve looked at Sarah. “Keep flashing those pearly whites. We can probably get all kinds of cool stuff here.”

She playfully smacked his arm. “I’m not looking for any freebies here. These merchants need to make a living. I’m halfway tempted to buy something and cash in this grif.”

“And how do you know you won’t be hosed by some greedy salesman?”

“True. I guess we really don’t know how much our grif will buy. We could be cheated and not know it.”

The activity in the street steadily increased until husband and wife were forced to walk one in front of the other, with Steve forging a path through the bustling throng of people. Villagers had come from all around to barter for various goods; housewives browsed for the freshest produce, farmers inspected new tools, and small children shrieked with delight as they ran from cart to cart.

A small skirmish broke out as one child tried to snatch a shiny trinket from a cart laden with rings and necklaces. Unfortunately for the would-be thief, the owner of the tiny shop, having years of experience with street rats, had been watching this particular little monster since he had started eyeing potential marks. The hand snaked out and grabbed the medallion, but the shop owner was quicker. Shaking the youngster by the arm, drawing him up and away from his prized wares, he forcefully snatched the jewelry back from the bawling brat. Flinging the crying child away from his cart, he turned to discover that four more necklaces had been pilfered, thanks to the rest of the brat's gang.

They could still hear the curses from the merchant as they finally reached the outskirts of the village and approached the steadily flowing river. Once there, they stepped back onto the enchanted road and continued east towards the Lentarian capital city of R'Tal.

As they walked, they continued to pass merchants and villagers alike, all who smiled at them and tipped their caps. There were even a few passing soldiers who nodded in their direction, preventing Steve from having to present the captain's dagger.

This is a nice place to live, Sarah thought; a much simpler way of life exists here. The people here are friendly, courteous. Citizens of this kingdom, whom they didn't know, had taken them in for the night. For the entire night! How many people would do that in her neighborhood back home? The village they just left clearly had a strong economy, with merchants coming far and wide to trade their goods. Law and order seemed to be well established, so clearly the king and queen were doing a good job governing their people. She was starting to see why her husband's grandparents spent so much time here as opposed to their own world.

"Penny for your thoughts," Steve said.

"Honestly? That I could see why your grandparents spent a lot of time here. All appearances suggest that this is a peaceful kingdom. The people are friendly. And the king and queen here had given them positions with responsibility. They must have felt important here."

Steve frowned. "I still think family should come first, but then again, I can see your point. To tell the truth, this wouldn't be a bad place to live."

Not being accustomed to using one's legs as the main method of transportation, the predicted one day journey to R'Tal, Steve recalculated, was going to end up taking them a day and a half. Disheartened, he started looking for a suitable place to camp for the night. His legs were on fire and he had developed a stitch in his side, but was determined to not let Sarah see how much he was in discomfort. Sarah, on the other hand, was starting to come in to her traveling legs. She was walking at a steady pace, had regulated her breathing, and was generally fine. Being the astute observer that she was, she had noted Steve's labored breathing and an overall decrease in his pace. Time to find a place to rest for the night.

With the sun setting, and dusk starting to set in, they came upon a small clearing surrounded by large oak trees. Without knowing what the other was thinking, both simultaneously decided they were done traveling for the day. Grinning at each other, Steve took off the pack and leaned it against the closest tree. Stretching his back, he looked up at the darkening sky.

"I don't know about you, but I'm beat."

Sarah gestured at some nearby stones. "If you make me a fire I'll see about heating up whatever it is that Bolli left us."

Steve grunted. "Deal."

Minutes later, with the fire blazing, Sarah sorted through the various packages given to her by the innkeeper's wife. She carefully unwrapped a package that appeared to be a dried brick of something. Studying the solidified substance closely, she discovered dried vegetables and chunks of meat. It was soup! She could fix this. She just needed to add some water and heat it up. Retrieving the small sauce pot given to them by Nilhanu, she added some water from the river and was ready to drop in the brick of soup when she abruptly stopped and stared at the clear water swishing around in the pan.

Noting Sarah's sudden cessation of movement, Steve glanced her way. Walking over, he looked in the pot.

"What's the matter?"

"What if there are germs and bacteria and stuff in this water? I don't want to make us sick using contaminated river water. I mean," she hesitated, "animals could have, you know, pooped in this water."

Steve started to laugh out loud but sobered as he thought about it. Coming to a decision, he gently took the pot from his wife and started heating the water. It only took about ten seconds to bring it to a full boil. Maintaining the heat for a minute or so, he then pulled his jhorun back, allowing the pot to cool. Once it was safe enough to touch, he returned it to his wife.

"There you go. All sterilized."

Smiling warmly at her husband, she gingerly felt the pot and its handle before taking it back. Perfectly cool to the touch. Hoping it was the right amount of water, she dropped in the block of dried soup. She moved to put the pot on the fire when she discovered the next problem: there wasn't any way to heat the pot without having to place it directly on the fire. Not only that, there wasn't even a flat surface to balance the pot on. What was she supposed to do? Continuously hold the pot over the fire? Thinking back to watching some of those outdoor cooking shows she was fond of, she tried to remember those that had been cooked by campfire. If memory served, there was usually some type of contraption that held the pot safely over the fire. She looked back to her husband, raising an eyebrow in the process. Noting Steve's inquiring look, she held up the pot and looked at the fire. Steve wandered over.

"How the hell did people in medieval times not starve?" Steve peered around the fire, looking for a place to put the pot. He sighed. "Oh, well, what the hell." He ignited his right hand and held it under the pot. Within moments, their dinner was cooking, right in his hand. Humming to himself, he watched as the solid thing in the pot broke up. It was clumping in the middle, not really mixing too well with the water.

"Hey, do you have something to stir this with?"

"Nilhanu gave me a wooden spoon. Don't move."

He furrowed his brow. Don't move? What was that supposed to mean? He wasn't going anywhere. Suddenly, a wooden spoon materialized in his left hand, which was hooked in his jeans pocket. His left hand instinctively grabbed it before it fell. He grinned.

"That's cool! You've been practicing?"

"Yes, I have. That one was actually a test. I knew that spoon was in the pack, but I didn't know exactly where. I just ordered it to move to your hand. And it worked!!"

Steve's smile was unmistakable. Without knowing for certain that she could use her jhorun in that manner, she attempted anyway, and voila! She must have been practicing that demonstration for a while now.

"How long have you been working on that little move?"

"Honestly, about five minutes." Steve's jaw dropped. Sarah continued. "You mentioned that you needed something to stir the soup with. I knew we had the spoon, and didn't feel like digging through the pack to get it. So I thought I'd give it a try."

Steve smiled again, pride for his wife emanating from every pore he had.

"But I have been practicing on other things. For instance, I'm pretty sure I can do this. Watch this." Sarah closed her eyes and was silent for a few seconds.

Steve waited. Nothing was happening.

"What are you doing?"

Sarah opened her eyes, glancing down at her feet. Letting out a small squeal of delight, she picked up a little piece of something at her feet. She presented it to her husband, placing the little bit of metal in his hand. He studied it for a few minutes.

"And this is what exactly?"

Sarah clapped her hands. "That's the piece of metal I found in that cellar where we were held prisoner. I thought might help us escape, but didn't have any sharp edges."

"As in when we were prisoners in that smelly cellar?"

Sarah nodded. Steve's mouth fell open in disbelief. That meant that thing she was holding came all the way from that thief's shabby little house! How far away was that, anyway? Steve thought for a moment. He really didn't have any idea how far they had traveled, but still, Sarah's most recent feat of accomplishment was very impressive.

"How'd you know you could do it?"

She shrugged. "I'm not too sure. It was something that I felt, something that I knew I could do. I thought about those last moments we were in that cellar, and I knew that little piece of metal was still likely to be there."

"But you didn't know exactly where it was!" Steve pointed out. "How could you transport something if you didn't know if it was still there?" He paused, still struggling to understand how Sarah was able to pull that piece of metal out of thin air. Clearly her mastery over her jhorun was increasing, developing new techniques to bend her jhorun to her will. Wondering what else she might be able to do, he started scouting around their makeshift campsite, looking for small items to experiment on.

Sarah knew that she had to nip this in the bud. She was tired, hungry, and desperate for a back rub. As eager as she was to discover what else her jhorun might be able to do, she wanted to be able to relax more.

"Hon, come on, let this go for now, okay? We can both practice later. How's the soup coming?"

"The what?" He glanced down into the pot he was still holding. "Oh yeah, the soup." Hastily stirring the contents and reapplying the heat he had let lapse, the soup thickened, releasing the enticing aroma of seasoned meat, veggies, and who knew what else. Either way, it was smelling pretty damn good.

Banking the fire to last well through the night, Steve and Sarah snuggled close together. Looking up at the twinkling stars, Steve counted no fewer than ten shooting stars within just a couple of minutes. Always having an interest in astronomy, he started looking carefully at the clusters of stars, searching for any similarities to the night sky he was accustomed to. Was that Ursus Major? Nope, not unless the Big Dipper had expanded its basin from four anchor stars to nine. The shape was close, though.

He looked to the west, watching as the last colors of the sunset drained from the sky. There was a group of stars there that looked vaguely familiar. Must be those three prominent belt stars, reminding him of one of the most recognizable constellations from his world, namely the constellation of Orion. However, try as he may, he couldn't identify any constellations in the sky.

Sarah was snoring softly into his shoulder. Determined to stay awake long enough to ascertain nothing threatening was in the area, Steve decided to count all the bright stars he could see in the sky. Counting stars being akin to counting sheep, he was out before he reached the count of ten.

Morning came much too quickly for Steve's liking. There were no snooze buttons on any alarm clocks. No curtains to pull closed to block out the light. Nestled together under several large fronds, Steve and Sarah slept like the dead. However, as soon as the sun awoke, so did Sarah. Which meant, naturally, so did Steve. He was famous for sleeping through just about anything. If WWIII ever happened, Steve would be able sleep right through it. Not Sarah. If the sun woke her up, then she couldn't sleep. And if she couldn't sleep, was it fair that her husband could? So she woke him up with a friendly poke in the ribs, which turned into a friendly jab, which became a hard shake on the shoulder.

"Wake up! The sun is shining and the birds are singing. Let's get something to eat and get going. I want to make it to R'Tal today."

Steve groaned and tried to burrow into the ground. How did she do it? How could she wake up and within ten seconds be fully awake and ready to start the day? Yawning profusely, he sat up and looked around. His back protested loudly, unhappy with the sleeping arrangements. Slowly he got to his feet, stretching the kinks out of his back.

"How'd you sleep? I slept great! I didn't toss or turn at all. I did get a little cold, though," Sarah said, busy preparing some breakfast for the two of them, "but all I had to do was scoot a little closer to you, and presto, problem solved." She looked at Steve and held out the pot. "Can you heat this up for me, please?"

Steve glanced in her direction, looked at the pot, and had it simmering in just under a minute. He reckoned he could have heated it faster, but he didn't want to burn the- what was she cooking, anyway?

"Whatcha got in there?"

"Bundle number two. It appears to be some type of thickened gruel. Before you thumb your nose at me, I just want to say that I think it smells pretty good."

He wandered over and sniffed the contents.

"It smells great. Can't wait to have some."

Sarah studied her husband. No trace of sarcasm, no hints of disdain. Does he not know what gruel is?

"It might taste rather plain, but at least its breakfast."

Taking his bowl of steaming porridge, he sat down near their former campfire and waited for Sarah to join him. Once she sat down, they both ate in silence, with Sarah waiting for Steve's disparaging remarks about the quality of food. When none were forthcoming, Sarah watched him for a few moments more. He was truly enjoying it, continuing to eat spoonful after spoonful of the thick glop.

"You actually like it?"

Steve paused with his spoon halfway to his mouth. He glanced at her. "You don't? It tastes just like oatmeal. Reminds me of my grandmother. Just wish I had a little brown sugar to put on it."

"Okay, what's with you? You don't put up a fuss with the stew last night, and you're not having any problems with this stuff. I'll admit it, it's bland. I don't really care for it too much. Since when did you stop being so picky?"

"Since it's clear that the food we're used to eating can't be acquired here," Steve explained. "I keep hoping we'll cross the next bend and I'll see a burger joint, but I know we won't. I know I'm a pain when it comes to eating new stuff, and I'm determined not to do it here. We have food, it might not be the best, but I'm damn grateful it's there."

Sarah closed her mouth with an audible snap. This wasn't the husband she was used to dealing with. Pleased beyond words, Sarah finished her morning meal and set about helping her husband dismantle their campsite.

Steve hoisted the pack (how, exactly, was it getting heavier?) onto his shoulder and took Sarah's hand. "What do you say we go find this king and queen and find a way home?"

"Now you're talking."

As the day progressed, the landscape gradually changed from flat, empty plains to grassy knolls covered with yellow and white flowers. The road they were following sometimes went directly over the mounds, but mostly it snaked amongst them, weaving about, sometimes appearing to reverse course and head the other way.

Chatting amicably about how quickly they would be able to return home, they rounded the last knoll and approached the seemingly endless coastline of the Great Sea of Koralis.

Sarah whistled. "Kornal mentioned we'd hit the sea sooner or later."

Hooking a thumb in the direction of the water, Steve looked at his wife. "That's a sea? Damn! Look at the size of that sucker! Looks more like an ocean to me."

Sarah inhaled, testing the air. "Freshwater. That's got to be the largest freshwater sea I've ever seen. Glad we don't have to cross it."

The road they had been travelling on dead-ended abruptly. Sarah and Steve eyed their choices: left, heading north to the mountains, or south, towards an open prairie devoid of any trees or hills.

Steve looked towards the empty prairie and grunted. Sucker was flat as a pancake. "That way, right?"

Sarah shook her head. "Nope. We head north, towards the mountains."

"You sure?"

"Positive. Not only that, it's the way Kornal told us to go. Besides," she continued, "don't you remember the carving on the doors?"

Steve nodded.

"The castle in that carving was in the northeast."

"You think that carving depicted Lentari?"

"You don't? It had the mountains, forest, valley, sea, and castle. So far, we're four out of five here."

Steve had to admit it made sense. He hadn't really given much thought to those mammoth doors from his grandparent's master suite lately. Was that really only three days ago?

Walking together, they watched the rhythmic undulation of the waves cresting on the beach. Steve would have preferred to walk along the coast seeing how the road they were traveling on had started to veer away from the enormous body of water.

The terrain became rocky, and eventually started to ascend. Thousands of years earlier, the small tectonic plate that ran under the kingdom of Lentari was pushed upwards by the much larger plate running adjacent to it, creating the extensive Bohani Mountains to the north, and the Selekai Mountains to the south. With relentless erosion from the Sea of Koralis, a gradually sloping plateau had formed that had created Lentari's curved eastern coast. The northern road followed the rising highland, at times coming right up against the vertical dropoff.

Proceeding north, they started encountering other travelers. A squad of soldiers came up on horseback from behind. Paying no attention to the two strangely dressed peasants standing well out of the way, they continued to head towards R'Tal, laughing and joking amongst themselves all the way.

They passed an old peasant walking slowly alongside his donkey powered cart, laden with firewood. He smiled at Steve and tipped his hat to Sarah. It was the smile that prompted Sarah to ask the friendly villager for directions.

"Excuse me, sir, is this the way to R'Tal?"

The wizened man nodded his head. "Aye, that it is. Just around that bend up there ye will find an outcropping of rock where ye will be able to see for leagues in every direction. Ye will be able to see the castle from there."

Smiling again, Sarah patted the donkey and thanked the villager. Hand in hand, they walked around the bend and stopped dead in their tracks. The old man was right. The ledge of rock extended some twenty feet out over empty space and gave an excellent view of the lay of the land, with the shores of Lake Koralis forming a gentle crescent curve off in the distance. And there, some five or so leagues distant, Steve could see the capital city of R'Tal, with the castle situated up against the base of the heavily forested Bohani Mountains and also jutting up against the far edge of the great sea. Steve even saw the turret that in their carved representation had the key-shaped window.

"Is that cool or what?"

Sarah was ecstatic. There was the castle! An actual kings-and-queens-live-there castle! What history must exist within those walls? Who was the architect? When was it built? A thousand questions sprang to her mind as she gazed upon the castle and the surrounding countryside. From her vantage point she could make out hundreds of thatched cottages within the perimeter walls, with hundreds more dotting the green valley south of the capital.

"Think we can make that before sunset?"

Steve looked at the distant castle and then looked up, judging the position of the sun in the sky. Not quite overhead yet. Good. If they picked up the pace, then they could probably make it with time to spare.

"We're going to have to double-time it," Sarah observed, still staring at the distant castle. "I'm guessing that's, what, ten miles or so away? If we pick up the pace, we should be able to do it. Don't you think?"

Steve wasn't sure if he could maintain a walking pace that fast, but he was certainly ready to try. Following closely behind his wife, he sighed with relief as their pace automatically increased due to the gradual declining slope. They had finally reached the apex of their climb and had started downhill.

Two hours later they were better than halfway to the castle. Progress was good. Steve, being much more accustomed to walking downhill than uphill, was walking as fast as he thought Sarah could handle. Sarah, on the other hand, already much more acclimatized to walking than her husband, was easily maintaining the increase in velocity.

Trying to keep his mind off of his tired legs and aching back, Steve did what he always did when travelling with Sarah: he quizzed her on some pointless movie trivia. In this manner, they had completely missed exits on freeways, ended up in wrong cities, missed turnoffs, landed on wrong streets, etc. Submerged in a world of Star Wars trivia, Steve later figured this lack of attention to the immediate surroundings accounted for what was about to happen.

The vegetation was also starting to pick back up, with small clumps of shrubs starting to appear, and a lone tree here and there. The first clump of large oak trees they came across drew them both up short. Camped by the copse of trees was the group of soldiers that had passed them earlier, resting their horses and having their midday meal.

In unison, all soldiers stopped eating and talking and looked with astonishment as two peasants in strange clothing boldly walked right into their camp. As one, they all turned to look at their lieutenant who was in the process of taking a bite out of a piece of meat skewered on his dagger.

"Hoo-boy," Steve muttered. "Umm, sorry to disturb you. We'll just leave you people alone."

"Methinks not, peasant," the lieutenant said, rising to his feet. "Who are ye and what business do ye have here? Where are ye from?" The soldier slowly walked around husband and wife. "What manner of attire are ye wearing?"

Sarah had once again surreptitiously moved behind her husband. Steve took a deep breath.

"Uh, we are visitors to this kingdom, on our way to seek an audience with the king and queen. As a matter of fact, we already met the captain of the royal guards. Maybe you know him? His name was Rhenyon. He gave me this." The act of reaching under his jacket to fumble for the jewel-encrusted dagger attached to his belt had every soldier in the clearing jumping to their feet. Swords were unsheathed and two soldiers took aim with bow and arrow.

"Whoa, hang on a sec there, guys. You don't want to do that." Steve raised both arms, hands open, palms up. "We really don't want any trouble. Look. On my belt. See the dagger?" He rotated slowly in place, lifting up his jacket to expose the dagger to everyone present. "You can take it out, if you prefer."

The lieutenant, with his sword drawn, looked at the stranger's belt. Was that one of the captain's personal daggers? Wizards be damned! He reached out and pulled the knife out of its sheath. Yes, it was. There was his crest. How did two foreigners acquire this?

"Explain yourselves, strangers. How came ye by this dagger?"

Steve relayed the events of the previous night, explaining how he had encountered the captain at Thacken Lodge.

The soldier nodded thoughtfully. Luckily, the story corresponded with what he knew of the captain's trek across the kingdom, seeking signs of the Scribes.

"The captain gave this to ye? Did ye tell him yer intentions to seek an audience with their majesties?"

"We did, yes. That's when he gave us that."

"Curious, I am, to find out why he gave ye that, but it is not my business. Go then, be on yer way." He handed the dagger back to the wary peasant who had to unclench his fists. As he took the dagger, the soldier couldn't help but notice the stranger's hands and face. Was he feverish? His face was flushed, and parts of his hands had turned an ugly, mottled red. If he caught some type of sickness from this dim-witted peasant, dagger or not, there will be hell to pay.

"Gladly, sir. You people have a nice day."

With that, Steve pulled Sarah along behind them and practically ran down the path, away from the group of soldiers. Once they were out of earshot, Sarah had to pull her arm out of Steve's grip, as he was intent on putting as much distance as possible between Sarah and those men.

Finally slamming on the brakes, she spun Steve around until he was looking her directly in the eye.

"Steve, you have to let go. Now!!"

Alarmed and annoyed, Steve released his wife's arm. "What is it? What's the matter?"

She held up her forearm, with the beginnings of a slight burn on her arm. Steve was horrified.

"Did I do that? Oh, man! I'm sorry!"

"It's okay. It feels rather like a sunburn. It stings a little, but I'm okay. You were nervous, it's understandable."

Steve wasn't about to let it drop. His wife was in pain, and he was directly responsible. He had to get her to the safety of the castle and see about getting some type of ointment for her arm.

"I'm so sorry. We'll get some help and I'll get some type of medication for it. Something like that has gotta exist there."

"Honey, it's trivial right now. Let's just get going, okay?"

With sunset now about an hour away, the weary travelers walked up to the outer garrison of the castle. A soldier wearing a maroon uniform stepped up to them.

"Greetings, strangers. What business have ye in R'Tal?"

Thankful to encounter a soldier more prone to ask questions than in drawing steel, Steve yet again presented the dagger. This time he didn't even have to take it off his belt.

Tired, hungry, and not wanting to mince words, Steve summed up their situation. "My wife and I seek an audience with the king and queen. This dagger belongs to Rhenyon. He sent us here."

Being highly trained not to ask too many questions once the proper credentials had been supplied, no matter how bizarre, the gatekeeper stepped aside and waved them through.

Working their way through the many streets, always angling towards the high turreted fortress they could see in the distance, Steve and Sarah made it to the castle just in time to see the guards preparing to raise the heavy wooden drawbridge for the night.

"Wait, wait up!" Steve called out. "We need to get inside."

The three guards that were retreating into the castle stopped to look back across the moat. One stepped forward.

"State your business."

"We seek an audience with the king." Again, he presented the dagger. Again, they were waved across. "I can see why Rhenyon gave us this thing now," he muttered to Sarah once they had entered the castle interior. Together, they turned to watch as the drawbridge was raised. Both jumped as the massive wooden structure thumped forcefully up against the stones of the castle. "So, what now, brown cow?"

Sarah laughed. "Well, when in doubt, we get some directions." Looking around, she walked up to the closest person she could find, a woman roughly her own age that was pushing a cart of clean linens. "Excuse me, ma'am, can you help us?"

The servant girl, startled to be addressed, paused and looked at the newcomers. "Yes? Can I help ye?"

"We seek an audience with the king and queen. I know it's late, but can you tell us where we might find them? Or maybe get a message to them?"

The servant girl blinked in surprise. Two strangely dressed foreigners were in front of her, openly inquiring about the whereabouts of the Kri'yans? Should this be reported to the guards? As a loyal servant to the crown, she directed them towards the Great Hall, while rushing off to find someone in authority.

Gently navigating their way through throngs of castle personnel that all appeared to have somewhere important to go, Steve and Sarah finally beheld the castle's Great Hall, receiving room for ambassadors, emissaries, and visiting kings and queens. There, against the far wall to the right of a massive hearth were the gilded thrones of their royal majesties, Kri'Entu and Ny'Callé.

With no one to say otherwise, Steve slowly walked up to the pair of golden thrones, running his hands along the carved surface. Upon closer inspection, the thrones appeared to be hand carved with designs, symbols he was not familiar with. Squatting down on his haunches, he was unsurprised to discover that the strange runes on both chairs matched the symbols on the portal door frames back home. Sarah came up behind him.

"I don't think you should be doing that, do you? The people here might consider it offensive if two non-Lentarians are caught messing with the thrones of their king and queen."

"Non-Lentarians?"

Steve and Sarah both whirled around. The voice was soft, kind, and fortunately, non-threatening. The lady, Steve judged, looked to be in her early thirties, wearing a simple but elegant grey floor-length gown lined with green silk on the inner sleeves. A pair of emeralds dangled from her ears, with several silver bracelets clinking softly on her left arm. Her long brown hair was pulled back into a braid that extended halfway down her back. She had to be the wife of a nobleman, Steve figured.

"Non-Lentarians?" she repeated. "Did I hear ye correctly?"

Taking a deep breath, Steve met the lady's eyes. "Yes, ma'am. You heard correctly, we are not from this kingdom. If you ask me where we're from, I doubt you'd believe me."

Looking at the two fidgeting people in front of her, the mystery lady smiled. Although, Steve thought, the smile did appear rather guarded.

"Do not let that concern ye. I would know how two foreigners came to be in this castle. So," she clasped her hands together and sat in a nearby seat. "Let us begin with yer names." Waiting patiently, she stared expectantly at her captivated audience of two.

Bemused by the odd nature on how this conversation was playing out, Steve and Sarah could only stare at the seated woman that was studying them, waiting patiently for an answer.

"Ummm, okay, my name is Steve, and this is my wife, Sarah."

Those intimidating brown eyes shifted to his wife and held her gaze.

Sarah gave a small wave and a quiet "hello".

"We come from, um, a far away land and are just looking for a way home. We were told that the king and queen would be able to help us find some way to do that."

The soft voice spoke again. "Find some way?" she asked. "That implies that the two of ye do not know how to return home. What is the name of yer kingdom?"

"Our land is called America. And no, you wouldn't have heard of it," Steve said, before their interviewer could ask where that particular kingdom was.

"I see. Would ye be from the Land of Idaho in the Kingdom of America, then?"

Shock registered in both of their eyes. How? How does she know where they're from? There's no way she could know that! Steve and Sarah looked at each other. What do they say now?

The lady in gray simply held her hand up, surprising both Steve and Sarah into silence. Clapping her hands three times, a servant girl, the same from the corridor before, appeared out of the shadows of the room.

"Please ask my husband to join me here."

The girl nodded, and disappeared back into the shadows.

Sarah looked at the lady in gray, realization finally dawning on her. "You're the queen, aren't you?"

Smiling, Ny'Callé nodded her head. "The two of ye intrigue me. I would hear yer story, but we will wait for my husband."

A few minutes later, Kri'Entu entered the Hall, striding up to his wife. He gave her a small smile and a nod before looking at the two strangers. The king appeared to be about five years older than his wife. His temples were graying, but his demeanor was energetic, seeming to electrify the room with his presence. There was a scrambling in the background as all the soldiers keeping a silent vigil snapped to attention.

"Steve, Sarah, I present my husband, Entu, King of Lentari."

The king nodded, measuring up Steve as a potential opponent. He and the stranger shared many physical traits with one another, Kri'Entu decided. They were the same height and roughly the same mass. Could this actually be who he thought it was? If so, then that means…

"So ye are from the Land of Idaho? Kingdom of America? Are ye kin to the Scribes?"

"Are you talking about my grandparents? Simon and Grace? Is that who you're referring to?"

The queen inhaled sharply. "Yer grandparents? They are safe then? We have not had any word from them for many fortnights."

Steve's gaze fell, and the Kri'yans knew the answer before he could speak.

As gently as she could, the queen asked what had happened. Relaying all that he knew about the accident, omitting anything that the Lentarians wouldn't understand, Steve told them about his grandparents' unfortunate demise.

The king spoke up. “We are truly sorry for yer loss. Yer grandparents were respected members of our court.” He looked at his wife and shook his head. “I would not have thought to look at the kin of our Scribes for the answer.”

Steve looked from the king to the queen. “The answer to what?”

The queen suddenly came to life and leapt forward to embrace them both in a hug, as though they had known each other all their lives.

“We are so thankful ye are finally here! I had suspected and hoped that I was looking at the Nohrin when I first saw the two of ye.”

In unison, the two Americans said, “The what?”

Kri’Entu smiled, clapping Steve on the back. “It is an ancient word. In the archaic tongue, it translates to ‘The Protectors.’”

Chapter 8 – Prophecy

Staring straight at the smiling king and queen, Steve slowly started patting himself down, trying to remember which pocket he had stuffed his grandfather's journal into. Finally discovering the small book tucked away in his front jacket pock, he pulled out the leather diary and held it out for Sarah to take.

"Find that entry."

"What entry?"

"The one that talked about those "Nohrin" people. There were several that mentioned them. Any one will do."

"You want to read about that now?"

"Yes, I do."

Scowling, Sarah flipped open the leather book and found one of the entries. "Okay, I have it here. Now what?"

"Excuse me," Kri'Entu interrupted, gesturing at the book Sarah held. "What book is that? There are only several true references to the Bakkian and the Nohrin, and that is *not* one of them."

Gesturing to the diary, Steve said, "That's the journal that my grandfather kept. We found it in his house after we learned we inherited it. In my land, when a person dies, his effects, namely his property, goes to his family."

"Yes, yes, I understand," the king said impatiently. "About the Nohrin, what is mentioned?"

Not liking the king's tone one bit, Sarah shoved the journal into her husband's hands. Reading from the entry that she had found, he skimmed until he found the first occurrence of the word 'Nohrin'.

"It says here that they, my grandparents, had been tasked with identifying who the Nohrin are and helping facilitate their arrival."

"Yes," Kri'Entu said, stroking his chin, "I do remember assigning that task. It was actually at my wife's suggestion."

As one, Steve and Sarah looked at the queen.

"The Scribes were very eager to please," Ny'Callé explained. "It was my observation that they craved responsibility, a sense of purpose. Perhaps they felt they could not acquire this on yer world."

"Perhaps," Steve agreed. To his shock and horror, he heard himself start babbling. "I just wish they would have taken a further interest in their own family. I didn't even know them." He looked into the queen's compassionate brown eyes. Why did it feel as though he could confide his deepest, darkest secrets to her and not worry about it ever being disclosed to anyone? He actually felt compelled to keep talking. "Believe it or not, you actually know them better than I do, or better than anyone in my family does."

Sarah also felt the pull, the desire to convey nothing but honesty with their majesties. Well, she didn't really feel the desire to confide with the king, just the queen. Wait a moment. Was this the queen's jhorun then? Or some aspect of it?

Taking the initiative to steer the conversation towards that which she was dying to know, Sarah said, "The diary mentioned it took thirty years for them to get their jhoruns. Did they over exaggerate or was that the truth?"

Curious, Steve turned to his wife. What was she playing at? She knew full well the answer to that. Then he started nodding. She must want to hear it from their mouths. That had to be it.

The Nayan spoke first. "Yer grandparents, Steve, were first approached by Entu's father, Fallun. After he observed a demonstration given by yer grandfather restoring an ancient text, he was asked to restore many of the tomes in our library that were woefully unpreserved. Demonstrating extreme proficiency, Kri'Fallun bestowed unto them their first task."

"To which they accomplished readily and skillfully," Kri'Entu helpfully added.

"Once they earned the king's trust, he gave them more tasks, with increasing responsibility. We started referring to them as 'The Scribes', a term given to them with affection."

"It was not until many years had passed," Kri'Entu interjected, "that we began to entertain the notion of presenting the Scribes with their own jhoruns."

"Ye have to understand, Steve," the queen continued, "that to give an outsider a jhorun was unheard of. Kri'Fallun was strongly against it. It wasn't until my husband ascended the throne did he make the first exception in the history of our kingdom."

"My grandparents were the first ones without a jhorun to ever receive one?"

Kri'Entu nodded. "They were. I thought it best to reward them with a strong, practical jhorun, but, as I was informed later, it was quite difficult to gift someone with one. Our wizard, Shardwyn, had a very, very difficult time accomplishing it.

Steve scoffed. “You call being able to make a pen write on its own accord strong?”

“Steve!” Sarah scolded. “Don’t be an ass.”

The queen swallowed a chuckle.

“Fear not, lass, it takes more than that to raise my ire. Besides,” Kri’Entu said, waving his hand dismissively, “he is quite correct. I wanted something stronger, but that is what Shardwyn was able to give them. As I said, it is damn near impossible to gift a jhorun to a person.”

“So you’re telling me,” Steve said slowly, “that you people think we’re the ‘Nohrin’? That we’re going to be babysitters to your son? You don’t even know us!”

“It has long been predicted,” Ny’Callé began, as though she were lecturing a group of school children, “that there will come a time when the whole kingdom will be in danger. A child will be born with a special mark upon them, and that they must be kept safe at all times. My son, Mikal, has a mark just below his right shoulder, on the back of his arm. It resembles a griffin with one foreleg raised.”

“The mark looks like a griffin?”

“It is a griffin,” Kri’Entu declared. “The same mark that is on the Bakkian itself. Our son must be the one.”

“Does ‘Bakkian’ also mean ‘prophecy’ in this ancient language of yours?” Sarah asked.

“Aye,” Callé nodded, “it does. Does the journal mention that as well?”

“A few times,” Sarah said. “Simon didn’t really mention what it was, though. Only that the prophecy in its entirety would finally be revealed. I just think you’re mistaken. We can’t possibly be the Nohrin.”

“And why not?” Kri’Entu asked. “Ye are non-Lentarian. Yer jhoruns are - wait. What are yer jhoruns?”

Steve smiled. “I heard it called by your own captain of the guard as being an ‘elemental’ jhorun. I can… What?”

Both the king and queen had given a small jerk, a fact that did not go unnoticed by both of their guests.

“Ye have power over one of the elements?” Callé whispered.

Steve stared at the queen. “You’re the second person to do that to me. What’s the big deal? I know it’s an elemental jhorun, but I figure it can’t be that rare, can it?”

“Which element do ye have control over?”

“Um, well, if you want to know the truth, it’s fire.”

Both the king and queen gasped. This news was far better than any could have guessed or hoped for. One of the Nohrin was a fire thrower! What better protection could they ask for?

Callé laid her hand over his. “Steve, listen to me. The elemental jhoruns are the rarest of all, and the most powerful. Earth, air, water, and fire. And of these, fire is the most potent, the rarest of the rare. There have been no fire throwers for nearly two centuries!” She paused a moment to try and calm her nerves.

Steve was panicking. The Kri’yans were acting as though he had just transformed lead into gold! It was just a jhorun. So it might be stronger than most, but could it really be that rare? Take the king, for example. His jhorun… What was his jhorun, anyway? Did he say?

“If you don’t mind me asking, what jhoruns do the two of you have?”

Still speechless, his mind forging ahead faster than a Bohani mountain dragon in flight, Kri’Entu opened his mouth, only no sounds were forthcoming. Ny’Callé stepped in for her husband to answer.

“My husband’s jhorun is classified as a ‘wyverie’, which is rare, but not nearly as rare, or strong, as an elemental.”

Sarah was unfamiliar with the word that the Nayan had uttered. What had she said? A ‘why vurry’? What was that?

Seeing confusion on their guests’ faces, the queen explained. “A wyverie is a person that is immune to dragons. No dragons would do him harm, even if they wanted to.”

Steve’s jaw clanged noisily on the ground. “Dragons! Really? Does that mean he can control them? Has he ever ridden one? What are they like up close? Do all of them fly? I have always wondered if there were land-bound dragons as well. Do they -”

Sarah cut him off. “I’m sorry about my husband. He has always loved dragons. They exist only in our imaginations in our world.”

Kri’Entu finally spoke. “There is no need to apologize. In the order ye asked, Steve, the answers are: no, no, intimidating, no, and there are.”

“My own jhorun,” the queen continued, ignoring Steve’s outburst and her husband’s answers to the aforementioned outburst, “is veracity.”

Sarah blinked. “Truth? Your jhorun makes you tell the truth?”

Smiling, the queen shook her head. “I have the ability to cause others, in my presence, to speak the truth.”

Steve was amazed. So that was why he had felt compelled to tell the queen all those things about his past and his family. That was a very powerful jhorun and a valuable one at that, considering her status.

The Nayan looked at Sarah. "Did ye mention what jhorun ye possess or did I miss it?"

Sarah shook her head. "You didn't miss it as I haven't mentioned it to anyone yet. I'm still learning to control mine. Steve has more control over his than I do. Mine appears to be teleportation."

Kri'Entu whistled. "A fire thrower and a teleporter. The Bakkian could not have predicted a stronger pair of jhoruns to protect our son."

Steve held up his hands in protest. "Now wait, just wait a damn minute. You haven't even asked if we're willing to take on the role of these Nohrin. You don't know us, and we're certainly not prepared to take care of a kid, let alone yours."

"There is no need. The Bakkian is unfolding right before our very eyes. Ye see, tension has been rising in the north, with Ylani," the king explained. "The threat of physical harm to our son is greater than ever. Even abduction is a strong likelihood. As ye can imagine, I will do everything in my power to prevent that. So as elements of the Bakkian began to appear right before my very eyes, I had begun to wonder if it was time for the Nohrin to appear. Much to my delight, two foreigners appeared in our midst."

Steve snorted. "The two of us appeared because there's some damn portal in my grandparents house that we accidentally activated, and now we're here. I doubt very much we have anything to do with this ancient prophecy of yours."

The Kri'yans looked at each other and smiled, saying nothing.

Steve was literally at a loss for words. How could he make them understand? They were American, not Lentarian. There's no way the two of them could be mixed up in this. Struggling to come up with some other avenue to argue, Sarah stepped in.

"Maybe you could tell us about this prophecy. Can we hear it? If this concerns us, as you believe it does, don't you think it would be prudent to let those affected hear it for themselves?"

Already liking this foreign woman immensely, Callé put a restraining hand on her husband's arm. Kri'Entu appeared poised to argue as well, and she was getting a headache. With each of them desiring to steer their husbands away from imminent hostilities, the queen met Steve's gaze and silenced him without saying a word.

"Ye have no doubt travelled a great distance today, and probably have been doing so since arriving in our kingdom, of that I am certain. Have ye supped yet? Perhaps the two of ye would like to rest. We have much to discuss." Without waiting for an answer, she looked at her husband. The king nodded. He had not fathomed this aspect of the prophecy, namely that the Nohrin would blindly stumble into their midst and be completely unaware of their own destinies. It was a lot to digest. Best to give them a while to come to terms with their newfound responsibilities.

"Tristan."

A tall, bald soldier standing so quietly he was practically invisible in the shadows, stepped forward immediately. He bowed.

"Sir."

"Please escort the Nohrin, er, our new guests to a suitable chamber."

"Aye, sir." The soldier bowed once more and held out an arm, directing them out of the Great Hall.

"If ye feel up to it," Ny'Callé called out after them, "return in an hour's time. I am sure the two of ye will have many questions."

"Ain't that the truth," Steve muttered.

The husband was very direct, not masking his emotions well at all, Callé mused. This was someone she could trust her son with. "We will talk later, I promise ye, Steve. Ye deserve to know everything, and ye will."

Following the soldier from the Great Hall, they walked silently through the castle, passing bustling kitchen maids, servants, and soldiers patrolling the halls. Ascending a large spiral staircase, they came upon a wide hall with large archways, lit by torches on either side. Each archway had a large, wooden door recessed into the wall. Leading them past the first dozen or so doors, they finally came to the end of the hall. Two torches were lit, illuminating a large portico and an even larger wooden door.

Tristan opened the door for them and gestured for them to go inside.

"This will be yer quarters for the duration of yer stay in the castle. I will have some provisions sent up. Once ye are ready, ring the bell," he indicated a rope hanging down from the ceiling in a corner on the far wall, "and I will return to escort the two of ye back to the Great Hall. For the record," he added, "I am very glad the two of ye are finally here."

With that, he gently closed the door, leaving the two utterly baffled Americans staring at each other.

"Okay, what the hell just happened here?" Steve demanded. "We just became babysitters, didn't we?"

Sarah walked over to the closest seat, a large plush green couch, and sank down onto it. The surreal moment still hadn't passed for her, ever since being informed that she was one of the Nohrin, the royal babysitters it would seem. How? How could they be the ones from that prophecy? It was by sheer accident that they stumbled across the portal to Lentari, wasn't it?

Moments later, Steve joined her on the couch. There was so much going through his head that he didn't even know where to begin. Clearly these people have made a serious mistake. How could they, who hadn't even been here a week, be the people from this centuries old prophecy? This had to be nipped in the bud, and done so rapidly.

Staring straight ahead, Sarah sighed heavily. "So what do you think about all this?"

"That they're all off their rocker. Just because we happen to be outsiders does not mean we fit this prophecy thing. They have clearly made a mistake. Plain and simple."

"But what about your jhorun? If what they say is true, then you have a super strong, super rare jhorun! I can see how the king and queen might see that as being the perfect jhorun to compliment the responsibilities of caring for their son."

"Are you telling me that you're buying in to all this? You believe we're the people from this prophecy?"

Sarah leaned back, staring up at the ceiling, which happened to be display a very masterful fresco depicting several groups of griffins in flight. Admiring the handiwork, she slowly surveyed the room, taking in the tastefulness of the decorations, the carvings, and the paintings. The fireplace appeared to have carved marble figurines decorating the mantel. The three windows in the room (suite?) had thick, dark green drapes drawn across, thus allowing as much privacy as was possible. In the far corner sat a plush chair, also dark green, next to several bookcases full of old tomes. Rising up off the couch, she wandered over to the bookcases to see what types of books they contained. Books on history, care for exotic creatures, and the like met her eye. There, next to the chair, was the rope Tristan had referenced before. Must be the medieval equivalent of a telephone, she mused.

"Well?" Steve prompted.

"What does this room tell you?" Sarah's hand swept the surrounding area. "Do you think that we're in a simple guest quarters or do you think we just might be in the best room of the castle?"

"What does that have to do with anything?"

"It tells me that they truly believe we're the Nohrin. They believe we're here to protect their son. And I have to tell you," Sarah admitted, "I actually think that we are." Seeing her husband's shocked look, she took his hands in hers. "Listen to me. Look at the facts. We have powerful jhorun. We're outsiders, and once we figure out how to get back home, who best to care for this boy than us? We can take him to a completely different world!"

The final piece of the puzzle slid into place. She was right. They alone in this kingdom could offer this endangered child the best level of protection. They could keep him safely on their world where nobody from this one could touch him.

He sighed deeply. Sarah angled her head to study his expression. *Yes, it looks like we finally have some comprehension in there.*

How was it possible, Steve wondered, that it could be foretold several hundred years ago that they would be here in this place? More magic, he presumed. If he had the magical ability to control fire, then it's feasible that someone might have the ability to predict the future, see premonitions, etc. He sighed again.

Sarah smiled at the man she loved more than anyone else. "Tell you what, let's have something to eat, freshen up, and see what the king and queen have to say, okay?"

He nodded. "I don't feel that hungry. But-" he held up a hand as Sarah took a breath, "let's have something to eat and then we can go down and chat with them. The only real thing I want to know is how the hell to get home."

An hour later, the two of them were ready to confront the Kri'yans once more, so Sarah tugged on the rope. She cocked her head, expecting to hear some type of sound. Nothing. In less than five seconds, there was a curt knock. Walking over to the entrance to their room, she opened the door to reveal Tristan smiling at them. Had he been waiting out there all this time? Could he have heard anything that they had talked about? As discreetly as possible, she ran her fingers over the door. Very solid. No eavesdropping here.

Steve rose from the couch. "We're ready to see the king and queen."

"Excellent," came the crisp, clear tone of his voice. "If ye would follow me, please."

This time, the efficient solder took them to a richly decorated chamber away from the Great Hall, and away from prying eyes and ears.

"Where are we?" Steve asked.

"We are in the Antechamber. There is protective magic all throughout this room, so ye may talk freely. Oh, I should mention to the two of ye that this room is enchanted against virtually all jhorun."

Steve stared at the soldier. "Why did you tell us that? Do you think we'll try to hurt someone?"

"I mention it only to warn ye, friend. If ye try to use yer jhorun, and nothing happens, then ye will know why."

Steve visibly relaxed. "Oh, my misunderstanding then. Sorry."

Tristan left the room, closing the doors behind them. Steve and Sarah looked at each other.

"Think our jhoruns will work here?" she whispered to him.

"I'd like to try," Steve whispered back, eyeing the burning logs in the hearth.

At that moment Kri'Entu and Ny'Callé entered the room. "Steve, Sarah, ye appear much more relaxed than when we parted." The king gestured to four plush chairs set in a circle by the fire. "Please, sit, rest. We have much to talk about."

The queen looked at her two guests. Steve wasn't fidgeting, or rolling his eyes, or showing any signs of the skepticism that he had demonstrated from their previous meeting. He and his wife must have had a long talk.

As the king talked with Steve, chatting about what his world was like, Callé observed her future babysitters. They were completely at ease with one another. They were holding hands! Clearly these two get along well together. The perfect Nohrin.

Sarah felt as though she was being watched. She glanced over to the queen and met her eyes. The queen smiled at her. Feeling nothing but kindness emanating from the refreshingly direct queen, Sarah felt herself trusting her more and more. When the men paused in their conversation about wildlife native to the kingdom, the queen took the opportunity to ask a question she was dying to know.

"Sarah, do ye have any children?"

Sarah shook her head. "No, we don't. We're thinking about having a few, but nothing yet."

Suddenly finding his seat uncomfortable, Steve fidgeted, and attempted to steer the conversation to a different subject.

"Is it true that this room blocks all magic?"

The king nodded. "Only a very select few have jhoruns strong enough to resist the protective enchantments cast upon this chamber." Recognizing the stubborn streak in Steve's eyes, the king smiled. "Feel free, my friend."

Sarah shook her head. Nothing but a big kid at heart.

Steve glanced at the hearth. Extending his jhorun to the blazing fire, he pulled all the tingling energy inward. The flames extinguished with a soft 'poof'.

Steve was grinning from ear to ear. "Cool!"

The Kri'yans were also smiling. They hadn't mentioned that if they weren't the Nohrin then their jhoruns would have been unable to defeat the Antechamber's restrictive charms.

"Try yours."

Thinking of what she could teleport into the chamber, she remembered her lip balm in her purse back in their quarters. She held out her left hand. The balm materialized instantly in her palm. She uncapped it, applied a small amount to her dry lips and sent the small tube back to her purse.

Queen Callé laughed. "Now that is a jhorun I would love immensely!"

Sarah grinned. Here was someone she could easily become friends with. The queen had an easy-going, comforting personality that exuded openness and honesty.

"I'm still learning the nuances of it," Sarah confessed. "Steve seems to have more control over his jhorun than I do with mine. I'm still practicing, though."

In a hushed, conspiratorial tone, the queen leaned forward and spoke to Sarah. "One might think honesty is a good jhorun to have, but how often do ye want yer husband to tell ye that a dress chosen for a certain occasion is unflattering?"

Sarah stifled a giggle. "He does that to you?"

Smiling, the queen nodded. "My jhorun is one of the more powerful manifestations of veracity. It is difficult to suppress. Not impossible," she added quickly, as Sarah looked ready to ask a couple of questions, "but difficult. Therefore I let my jhorun be active at all times." She looked at her husband who was deep in conversation with the foreign man. "I just have to be careful which questions I ask."

Interested, Sarah leaned further towards the queen. Sensing a shared female moment of mirth, Callé conspiratorially leaned towards her as well. In hushed tones, she whispered to the queen, "how does your husband feel about telling you the truth about everything? Some women would view that as the perfect marriage!"

Suppressing the urge to laugh out loud, the queen risked a glance at her husband. "Entu has said on more than one occasion that it is difficult to handle at times. So he has to choose what he says, too. The truth can be said many ways, and some ways are less dangerous than others."

Sarah giggled. "I never thought of it that way."

"He is very skilled in word play. He can still say the truth to me and yet convey another meaning entirely. I am still amazed at how he can do it."

Steve, noting the huddled conversation Sarah and the queen were having, shook his head. Unbelievable. She did it again.

Kri'Entu, noting Steve's astonished stare, glanced over at the women. What was this? His wife had only just met this woman a few hours before, and yet now they were acting like they have known each other all their lives!

"I don't know how she does it," Steve murmured. "We haven't been in this kingdom that long and yet she can instantly bond with any woman here and become their best friend."

Stroking his beard thoughtfully, Entu smiled at the two gossiping women.

Sensing they were being watched, as one, the women turned to the men. The queen and Sarah both raised an eyebrow. Since both were within the peripheral vision of the other, each noted that the other did the same thing. As if on cue, both smiled.

"Sorry to interrupt," Steve began, "but I need to ask the million dollar question now."

Sarah nodded, indicating for him to proceed.

"Your majesties, in my grandparent's house on my world, there is a really large door carved with a representation of this kingdom." Seeing no acknowledgement from either king or queen, Steve continued. "In their safe was a big green crystal key. It fit into a keyhole shaped window of the castle on the door. Sarah turned the key, and presto, we had an instant portal to Lentari."

"He incorporated the portal into the decor. I must admit I was curious about that," Kri'Entu murmured.

Steve jerked in his chair. "So you've heard of this type of portal then?"

The king nodded. "It is the main method of transportation between great distances in Lentari. There are only a few portals, so they are reserved for official use only. We tasked Shardwyn with finding a suitable method of returning the Scribes to their home world. He contacted the best craftsman of portal keys that ever lived. Well, the only maker of portal keys."

Elation surged through Steve. "Yes! So you have another portal here! Beautiful! So you can send us home then? We figured that's how we can best protect your son, taking him to our world."

The king and queen stared at each other in shock. Of course! It was so clear now! The Nohrin would hide their son on a world where no harm would befall him. No one from their kingdom, nor any others for that matter, would be able to find him!

"Is there a portal here, in this castle, then?" Sarah asked hopefully.

"Aye," Kri'Entu answered slowly, as realization sank in that his son would soon be leaving. Taking a deep breath, he faced the two Nohrin. "Ye only need yer key to activate the portal."

The queen watched as Sarah's face fell, her eyes filling with tears. "Yer key is not with ye, is it?" she asked softly.

Both Sarah and Steve slowly shook their heads.

Turning to her husband, Callé asked the obvious question.

"If they do not have the key, how does the portal work then?"

The king shook his head. "Without the key, our portal cannot tune in on the receiving portal. So it would not work."

Sarah, on the verge of tears, looked to her husband for solace. Steve, however, wasn't ready to give up.

"Okay, so we don't have the key. Can't we get another one? I mean, there's got to be some way to replace a missing key, isn't there?"

"I had not thought of it that way," the king confessed. "No one has lost one before. Ye will have to seek out Maelnar."

"And he is?"

"The dwarf who crafted your key."

"How do you know he's the one who made it?"

"Because," Entu explained, "Maelnar is the Strathos, the maker of keys. He is the only maker of portal keys and has lived for hundreds of years, with every indication of living for hundreds more."

"Is this Maelnar person easy to find? Please tell me he's here in the castle."

"Unfortunately, no, I am sorry. His clan lives in the Bohani Mountains far to the north. I last met Maelnar when I was but a boy. I have not seen him since. He's very reclusive." Seeing the Nohrin's faces fall yet again, the queen spoke up.

"Fear not, we will find him. We will send out word immediately to ascertain his present whereabouts. The dwarves govern themselves, so we can not order Maelnar to reveal himself. But they are our allies. They should at least be able to point us in the right direction."

Clapping his hands, the king summoned Tristan into the room once again. "Send word immediately. We need to locate the dwarf Maelnar. He should be in the vicinity of the Bohani Mountains. Go now."

"Sir." Tristan bowed, leaving the room as silently as he had entered.

"How long do you think that will take?" Steve asked.

"Truthfully, I am not certain," Kri'Entu admitted. "We can only wait. There is no sense in wandering all over those mountains until we have an idea which area to search."

"So what do we do now?" Steve wanted to know.

The queen spoke. "I think now we should talk about the Bakkian. Would ye care to hear about it?"

Scooting his chair closer to his wife's, Steve nodded.

The king rose, went to his private desk in the far corner of the room, turned, and faced the stone wall behind it. Reaching out with his right hand, he gently pushed in one of the stones. There was a soft click, and a section of the wall slid aside, revealing a large cavity within the wall. Sitting within the cavity was a larger version of the griffin safe that Steve and Sarah had become very familiar with. The griffin on this safe started the musical humming as the king approached. As before, the griffin raised its leg, and the king pushed the button.

Reaching inside the hidden compartment, the king withdrew a small, rusted chest. As he turned to walk back to his guests seated before the fire, the compartment within the safe closed with a snap, and the griffin stepped back onto the button, hiding it from sight. Even the wall slid smoothly closed, Steve noted.

Kri'Entu set the chest on the small table before the two Nohrin and gently pushed it towards them. He couldn't hide his smile as a very skeptical Steve glanced down at the rusted chest.

"What's this?"

The king smiled. "That, my friend, is the Bakkian."

"That??"

The king nodded.

Reaching slowly out to the chest, Steve undid the latch and gently opened the coffer. Leaning forward together, Steve and Sarah peered into the small, deteriorating container. Sitting inside was a crystalline object resembling a small shield, about the mass of a clenched fist. The crystal had a symbol embossed onto the surface, depicting some type of animal. Steve nodded, recognizing the image now: it was a picture of a griffin with one foreleg raised. Was this the mark that the young prince had upon his shoulder? Clearly the griffins held some type of unknown importance here.

Sarah sat back and studied the king and queen. "I thought this prophecy would be in a book, or on a scroll, or something. That journal mentioned a four hundred year old document."

"My grandparents said they found some manuscript last year. It's mentioned in their journal. Once it was found, the journal said the entire kingdom could read the Bakkian in its entirety."

"Ah, the manuscript." Kri'Entu nodded. "It chronicles past attempts to locate the Bakkian."

"So who found it, then?"

"A knight who lived hundreds of years ago. Went by the name of Volan."

"Was wondering who that was," Steve muttered.

"So what are we supposed to do with that?" Sarah asked, pointing to the crystal shield.

"Pick it up," the queen suggested.

Sarah eyed the small, crystal shield. "What will happen if we do?"

"No harm will come to ye, I promise," the queen assured them. "The Bakkian will only reveal itself to those involved with its prophecy."

More curious than cautious, Steve stared at the object. "And how does it do that?"

"Ye only have to touch it."

Sarah looked to her husband to take the initiative. Correctly interpreting her glance, he shrugged. Reaching in with his right hand, he took the crystal object out of the box.

Surprised by the weight of the thing, Steve hefted it in his hand. Unlike the jorii, this object didn't appear to be generating any heat. Quite the contrary, it was cool to the touch. He held it up to his face, studying it closely. Was this carved out of a single piece of crystal?

Cool! These guys really had a knack for working with precious stones.

Holding the Bakkian out in front of him, Steve looked questioningly at the Kri'yans. "So what do I do? How do I open it?"

Kri'Entu stared at the strangely quiescent piece of crystal. What was wrong? Why wasn't it working? The spell should have been activated once contact was made. Were they not the Nohrin?

At that moment Sarah leaned over her husband's shoulder and ran her fingers along the raised image of the griffin embossed onto the surface. Suddenly there was a flash of golden light, illuminating the entire Antechamber. Finding themselves unable to let go of the crystal shield, Steve and Sarah watched with amazement as several seams appeared on the surface of the crystal. The center, which had the griffin on it, parted right down the middle and swung open. An iridescent golden light escaped from the heart of the crystal shield, bathing both husband and wife with an eerie glow. A soft female voice started to speak:

Many years from now, it will come to pass,
A child will come, born unto class.
The mark of the Gryph, found upon his arm,
Indicates to all: protect from harm.

Into Their care the Marked will be placed,
Fending off challengers who must be faced.
Advice and guidance, given to the boy,
His life will be filled with love and joy.

Power over an elemental, one will possess,
Which will it be? No one can guess.
The second will be cunning and clever.
Hesitate to protect their charge? Never.

An' this child grows to man
Peace will spread throughout the land.
However, if the Marked happen to fail,
Then the darkness will prevail.

As the darkness rises in the north,
This child must go forth.
Stand ye not in his path,

Seek ye not the Protector's wrath.

Wait for the Guardians to arrive on this soil,
Their coming rejoiced, avoiding turmoil.
Who are these people with the strong jhorun?
They are the Protectors, the fêted Nohrin!

The shimmering light withdrew inside, reverting back into an unblemished crystal once more.

Sarah's mouth was gaping open. "Okay, I can see how that might pertain to the two of us."

Steve snorted. "'Seek ye not the protector's wrath'? What's that supposed to mean?"

"Well, you can get a temper if you're provoked."

Steve harrumphed. "What's the 'darkness' refer to?"

Kri'Entu tapped his fingers absentmindedly on his chair as he held a silent conversation with the queen. She nodded to the two of them.

Go on, her eyes said. *They need to know.*

How much do I tell them? his eyes inquired.

Everything, was the response.

Knowing that some type of communication was going on between the two silent monarchs, Steve and Sarah nervously eyed each other, waiting for them to finish.

Taking a deep breath, the king faced his two guests.

"There have been disturbing reports coming from the north," the king explained. "A dark wizard from Ylani has found a way to steal jhorun."

"Say what? How?"

"No one knows. They have captured three of our spies and returned them to us, their jhoruns stripped away from each of them."

"Can't your wizard replace the stolen jhorun?" Steve asked.

The queen sadly shook her head. "He has been secluded in his workshop working diligently on a remedy. Thus far, no luck."

"Maybe their jhorun will return in time," Sarah suggested.

"The first spy was returned to us over three years ago."

Steve whistled. "I take it losing your jhorun is a bad thing?" Seeing his wife's horrified look, Steve hastily added, "No offense to your majesties. We have lived the majority of our lives without jhoruns, so I don't know how you people would react to losing one."

The king held up a hand and stared hard at Steve. "I said stolen, not lost. Our spies reported seeing this dark wizard wielding their own jhoruns against them."

"How does your son fit in to this?" Steve asked.

"Mikal restored them," Kri'Entu said simply.

"What?" Steve exclaimed. "How?"

"The closest we can approximate," Ny'Callé said, "is that Mikal's ability, his jhorun, is enhancement. It was quite by accident that we discovered this."

"Indeed," the king agreed. "We had consulted Shardwyn several times about Mikal's lack of a jhorun. Ye see, a Lentarian child's jhorun first manifests itself around their fourth birthday. We did not discover what jhorun our son had until last year."

"What happened?" Sarah wanted to know. "How did you find out?"

"Mikal was curious about the land to the north, so he was talking to one of the people who had their jhoruns taken from them. Tristan. Ye met him before."

Both Sarah and Steve nodded.

"While talking with Tristan," the king continued, "Mikal evidently asked what type of jhorun he had that the wizard stole from him. Tristan told him what his jhorun was, which was being able to temporarily summon small daggers. Since at that time Mikal did not know the nature of his jhorun, he wished Tristan could have his jhorun back so that he could see a demonstration. At that moment, for a span of a few seconds, Tristan was able to conjure a small dagger."

"Is it fully restored now?"

The king nodded. "Tristan reported that after that initial conversation with my son, his jhorun was fully regenerated in about three months."

Steve stood up and started to pace. "So, let me get this straight. This dark wizard guy, he finds some way to steal the jhorun from a Lentarian."

The Kri'yans nodded.

"And your son has the ability to restore it. My question is," Steve paused a moment, "does he restore the jhorun so that both the original person and the wizard have it as well? Or does your son somehow restore the jhorun to the original person, thus stealing it back from this bad wizard?"

The queen spoke. "I do not know how he does it, but he is actually taking them back from the dark wizard."

Sarah leaned forward. "Are you sure?"

"Quite sure," the king said darkly. "There have been five attacks upon him. Since he is protected by the strongest jhorun at our disposal here in the castle, I believe it will only be a matter of time before they try a more daring scheme to lure him out of the castle."

"I'll take that as a big ten-four," Steve muttered.

The king stared matter-of-factly at Steve. "Will the two of ye protect our son for us?"

Sarah moved to stand next to her husband. He took her hand in his. Addressing the king, Steve nodded. "Your majesties, we will do all we can to keep him safe. You have our word."

Chapter 9 – Protectors

With tears of gratitude in her eyes, the queen rose and faced both of the newly appointed Nohrin. She couldn't help it. She embraced Sarah in a tight hug. "I, we, thank the two of ye. A thousand times over."

The king stood up and extended his arm. Steve grasped it.

"Ye honor us with yer courage."

Grinning sheepishly, Steve shrugged.

Releasing Sarah, the queen caught Steve's arm as he tried to sneak by her and pulled him into a hug as well.

Patting her awkwardly on the back, Steve plastered a smile on his face and waited to be released.

"Tristan." The king was staring at the darkened corner of the Antechamber.

Tristan appeared yet again out of the shadows. When had he returned, anyway?

"Sire.

"Please escort Kre'Mikal here."

"At once, sire." Tristan melted back into the shadows, and from the far reaches of the chamber they heard a door open and then close. A servant girl then materialized out of the shadows, a different one this time, holding a large platter with four goblets on it. She stopped by each person in turn. Both Steve and the king each took a goblet. Sarah and the queen declined with a smile.

"So," Steve said, absently patting his pockets, "your son's jhorun is enhancement. So he can pretty much do the same thing as a jorii, right?"

The king was in the process of raising his goblet to his lips to take a drink when he froze. "How are ye aware of the jorii?"

"Because we happen to have one with us," Sarah explained. "When we were going through his grandparent's house, we found their safe."

"The same type as yours," Steve said, hooking a thumb over his shoulder in the direction of the fake stone wall.

"Did ye find a large quantity of jorii in their possession?" the king asked carefully.

Steve nodded. "Yep, a whole sack full of them. We didn't learn about what they were until we met up with the first people we saw here. They hadn't seen one of them before, either."

"Speaking of which," Sarah interrupted, "we need to send word back to them to let them know we arrived safely. They were a tremendous help and we wouldn't have made it this far without them."

"I will send word immediately," the king assured them. "Who are they?"

"A young man by the name of Kornal, and his wife-"

"Nilhanu," the king finished for her. "He has the ability to find a certain species of fish, and if I am not mistaken, his wife's ability is the enhancement of local pontal."

Sarah was amazed. The king not only knew of them but also knew what their jhoruns were? Maybe there weren't that many people here in this kingdom after all.

"Do you know them personally?" Steve wanted to know.

"I do not, but I do make it my business to be apprised of all types of jhorun in Lentari." The king walked over to a map that was stretched across his desk. Steve joined him a few moments later.

Staring down at the map, the king tapped his fingers on a dot. Was that a village? Curious Steve leaned over to see for himself. "This is Avin," the king explained. "A small village nestled in the southern region of Bohrra Forest. I believe your friends live maybe a day's journey east." The king looked up then. "Is this where ye first came into our kingdom?"

"Ummm, I think it was further west. The portal dropped us in the middle of the forest, and if I remember right, we walked for half an hour before we found this really big waterfall."

The king studied the map. "I know the one. It is here," indicating an area close to the village. "Had ye walked west, ye would have encountered the village in less than a day."

"Figures," Steve muttered. "I choose a direction to go, and naturally if we would have gone the other way, we would have found help sooner." He sighed. "Oh well, I'm glad we went the way that we did."

"As are we," the king was tapping his fingers on his desk. "Steve, Sarah, may I make a request?"

Both Nohrin nodded their heads. "Sure," Sarah said. "What can we do for you?"

"Allow me to hold on to the jorii. It is highly coveted here. I will rest easier knowing that it is properly secured."

"With pleasure." Sarah held out her right hand. The sphere materialized on her open palm. She passed it to the king. "It's all yours. Is that why there's a whole sack full of these things in the safe on our world? So no one here would be tempted to steal them?"

"Aye, it is," the king agreed. "I have enough to deal with right now, and the last thing I need is for word to go out that an unprotected jorii exists here in the castle."

Inspired by this recent explanation, Steve asked Sarah to retrieve the crystal disc for him. Sarah pulled it out of thin air and handed the crystal nonagon to her husband. Holding the sparkling disc, Steve turned to the king.

"Okay, what's this, then? There's a small sack of these in their safe as well."

The king smiled, taking the proffered object. "This is called a mimet. Shardwyn gave a large number of these to the Scribes." He smiled again, as he recalled the memory of Steve's grandparents being given the crystals by the canny wizard. "Using this disc, ye can store yer jhorun to be used at a later time." Seeing Steve's quizzical expression, the king explained even further. "Jhorun will regenerate once it is used. As an example, assume ye are preparing to go on a journey. Ye start storing jhorun in these discs. Yer jhorun regenerates. By the time ye go on yer journey, ye have several times more jhorun at yer disposal."

The king returned the disc to Steve, who turned it this way and that, admiring the workmanship. "How does it work? How do I put jhorun into it and how do I pull it back out?"

"I will show ye. Hold the disc in yer hand. Now, focus yer jhorun, yer energy, on the disc. In yer case, try to make it burn."

Looking down at the disc, Steve ignited his left hand. The disc was now warm to the touch. Curious to know if the disc's power level was related to the warmth it exuded, Steve sent a brutal blast of power down to the crystal. Nope, the degree of heat that the disc was generating remained the same.

"Handy!" He extinguished his hand and held the crystal up to the light.

"I have a question," Sarah began. "If Steve charges that thing up, can anyone use the stored jhorun in it or is it accessible only to him?"

"Only those who store jhorun in it are able to draw from it."

Sarah smiled sheepishly. "It was worth a shot."

"So how do you get the jhorun back once it's in there?" Steve wanted to know.

"Go over to the hearth and try it out."

Steve grumbled all the way. "Everyone instantly assumes I'm gonna burn the place down. Great, just great."

Sarah decided that the painting closest to her was fascinating and pointedly stared at it, lips quivering as she fought desperately not to laugh. The queen also looked away as she stifled a bad case of the giggles.

Grasping the crystal disc tightly in his hand, Steve sent his jhorun down to investigate. He discovered a large quantity of his jhorun, all bottled up, clamoring to be released. So how does he tap into the stored jhorun?

Steve turned the disc over and over in his hands, his jhorun mentally probing the disc. He could feel the extra power, but it felt like it was locked in another room. What's containing it?

Growing tired of mentally probing the disc, Steve finally decided to pull the energy he felt within the disc inward, as though he was extinguishing a campfire. Without any restraints in place, all the jhorun decided to come out and say hello at the same time.

The fireball blasted Steve onto his butt, catching him completely unaware and consequently burning a large hole in his shirt. Fortunately, the fireball burned itself out before it hit the ceiling. Deep rumblings reverberated throughout the floor.

"Omigod!" Sarah rushed forward. "Are you okay?"

Steve sat up, looking down at his now exposed gut. Gingerly he felt his eyebrows. Good. Still there. He huffed out a muffled apology and just shook his head. Callé, taking her cue from Sarah, now pretended the tapestries on the walls held the Secret of Life and therefore studied them meticulously while she waited to see if Steve was injured or not.

Kri'Entu, already noting the lack of damage to the Antechamber, had laughter dancing behind his eyes. Doing his best to not smirk too much, he leaned down and gave Steve an arm up. "Are ye well?"

Looking down at his chest, with his white belly on display to the world, Steve couldn't help but laugh. "Learn something new everyday, dontcha?"

With tears streaming down her eyes, Sarah was able to compose herself long enough to ask if he was burned.

"No, not really. I don't feel any pain." Puzzled, he looked at his wife. Eyes narrowing as she laughed inwardly, he frowned. "Why did my shirt burn? I just figured my clothes would be immune to my jhorun."

"There are probably limits," the king suggested. "Caught unaware, ye were, and the mimet had a bit of a charge, adding its energy to yer existing jhorun."

"Everything happened so fast you did not have time to react," Callé reasoned. "It could have been worse, ye know."

Steve's ears turned bright red as he blushed crimson at the thought.

A guard stepped out of the shadows and offered him a green tunic. Skeptical on whether it would fit, Steve pulled the soft shirt over his head, smoothing the edges, tugging here and there to assure himself of a comfortable fit. Not bad, he mused, not bad at all. Nice, light material. Smiling, he turned to the soldier, who had melted back into the shadows.

Admiring his new shirt, Steve turned to the king. "How did that guy happen to have a shirt in my size available?"

The Kri'yans smiled. "Actually, that was Shardwyn's doing. He advised us to have a spare tunic ready for this evening."

"He knew I was going to do that? That's cool! I can't wait to meet the guy!"

In high spirits, Steve wandered back to the map on Kri'Entu's desk. Studying the parchment closely, he tried to memorize all the features, hoping to impress Sarah at a later date.

"Allow me to show ye the lay of the land lest ye are not familiar with it." Entu gestured to the country above his own. "The kingdom of Ylani lies directly to our north. So are the Bohanis. Those mountains are home to our allies, the dwarves. They are also home to the dragons."

He pointed to the icon of a castle bordering a tremendous body of water.

"Now, this is where we are, if ye were wondering. This," he pointed to the mountain range bordering the northern boundaries of the kingdom, "are obviously the Bohanis. The dwarves have strongholds here, here, here, and here," indicating various points along the mountain range. "Those are just the ones that we know about. There are two dwarven cities, and I have been to each, but I could not begin to tell you where they are in relation to this map as both are subterranean. I do not know which is Maelnar's home. Now here," he pointed to a lake at the very top of the map, "this is Lake Raehón. The majority of the dragon lairs can be found near this lake, but there are many that are scattered throughout the mountains as well."

Steve pointed to a small dot southwest of the lake.

"Is this a village? How do those people survive with dragons all around? I was told that they are very dangerous and aren't to be messed with."

"There is a truce in effect with the villagers. I have spoken with the dragons in the area, and they have agreed to not prey upon the livestock they might find there provided the villagers stop harassing them."

Steve couldn't help it. He laughed out loud. "How can someone possibly harass a dragon? Couldn't the dragon, you know, eat the villager?"

The king nodded solemnly. "Aye, that they could. And they have. But get enough villagers together and they could drive off the prey the dragon feeds on. They have been trying to drive the dragons out of their territory, but the dragons are fiercely territorial. It has taken many months of negotiations, but I finally have managed to stop the villagers from bickering. Also, I am presently in negotiations with the lord of the dragons, hoping to forge an alliance with them."

"If he's successful," Ny'Callé added, "it'll be the first time in our history when both men and dragons co-existed peacefully."

"Do dragons actually talk?" Steve asked incredulously.

"Some do, aye. The problem is that the dragon's instinct is to chomp first, see if anyone is still alive, then maybe ask a question or two. They have a deep seated mistrust in all humans."

"So your jhorun allows you to talk to a dragon and not get eaten?" Steve asked. "Did you find one that was willing to listen? I bet they aren't a very patient species."

Kri'Entu smiled. Steve's enthusiasm was contagious. Here was someone he could converse with about his favorite subject: dragons. He would have to see about arranging a meeting with Kahvel, liaison to the dragon lord.

Kahvel was a full-grown golden dragon roughly thirty meters in length from nose to tail, with a wingspan of more than twenty meters. Due to his size, whenever Kahvel visited, he had to remain in the northern orchard for the duration of his stay. Kri'Entu had commissioned an underground cavern to be constructed solely for dragon use, a move unprecedented in R'Tal's history. Never once has any human monarch ever made an effort to accommodate any dragon.

It was a move that the king hoped would foster good will for future relations.

Kri'Entu thought for a moment. Kahvel has been absent for days now. He's due for a visit soon. Steve, in the meantime, hadn't stopped asking questions about dragons. Focusing his attention back on the conversation, he listened to the next set of questions.

"Have there been any wars between dragons and men? What about riders? Has anyone ever ridden a dragon?"

The king laughed. "There have been several throughout the course of our history. None were very pleasant, I can assure ye. As for riders, there may have been," to which Steve perked up, "but nothing is known for certain, as no one has ever returned to tell the tale. I only heard of one villager from Capily who said he was going to be the first to tame and ride a dragon. I am told he was successful in getting onto the dragon's back, however, the dragon noticed half a moment later."

"Ummm, dare I ask what happened next?"

"Let's just say that dragons have very supple necks."

Steve winced. There was a fate he wouldn't wish on his worst enemy.

One of the side doors opened and Tristan entered the room, followed closely by a young boy. He had a slim build, dark black hair, and impossibly vivid blue eyes. The boy went over to his parents and gazed at the two strangers intently.

"Who are they?"

"Mikal, this is –"

"They are the Nohrin, are they not?"

Both the king and queen jerked visibly in their chairs. What was this? How much did their son know? Thus far, the king had believed that they had kept heir son blissfully ignorant of the Bakkian, and more importantly, of the danger he was in. How much had he picked up?

Looking at the bright-eyed boy sizing him up, Steve walked over and extended his arm.

"Steve. Steve Miller. Pleased to meet you. This is my wife, Sarah."

Sarah walked up and also greeted their new charge. "Hello, Mikal. Nice to meet you."

"Nice to meet the two of ye, too," Mikal answered automatically, having had his manners drilled into him relentlessly from parents and tutors alike.

"Son, where did you hear about the Nohrin?" the king wanted to know. "I know this is one subject we have not discussed at all."

The boy looked to the ground and shuffled his feet. "Father, I am not stupid." His bright blue eyes looked up at his parents. "It's all my friends talk about. 'When are you going to get your new babysitters', or 'have they found you a nanny yet?' It is very embarrassing."

"Which friends spoke of the Nohrin? Be specific."

"Entu!" Callé scolded. "Do not ask our son to tattle on his friends!" Sighing, she pulled her son over to her. "Listen carefully, Mikal. Ye are in grave danger. There are bad people out there that want to take ye from us and probably kill ye."

With a horrified look on his face, Mikal whipped his head around to stare at the two strangers standing before him.

"No, not them," the queen hastily corrected, "they are here to protect. We wanted ye to meet them in person so ye can see for yourself that there is nothing to fear from them."

Taking a deep breath to try and calm his pounding heart, Mikal looked at the two foreigners suspiciously. If these were the people everyone was talking about, then he figured they should have some powerful jhorun, right?

Mikal walked over to woman with the friendly eyes. "So what jhorun do ye have?"

Sarah squatted down to his eye-level. "Tell you what, I can show you, if you'd like."

The young boy nodded his head enthusiastically. He enjoyed seeing other people's abilities since his wasn't able to manifest itself physically.

Standing up, Sarah looked around the room for a suitable object. Not finding many small knick-knacks, she looked at the queen. She had several rings on her fingers. Maybe one of those.

"Pardon me," she motioned to the queen, "could I borrow one of your rings?"

Having an idea of what Sarah was about to do, Callé smiled, slipping off one of her small silver rings. She handed it to Sarah, who in turn, handed it to the prince.

"Here, put this in your pocket, okay?"

Puzzled, Mikal took the ring and looked at his mother. The queen nodded her head, encouraging her son to do as he was bid. Tucking the ring into his inside jacket pocket, he looked at Sarah again.

"So what are ye going to do?"

Sarah held out her hand. Something was glinting in it. Baffled, Mikal leaned forward to see what was there. Whatever it was, it was small and shiny. Equally curious, the king discreetly leaned forward for a better view. Once the boy saw the silver ring back in Sarah's hand his eyes flew open and he instinctively felt his inside pocket. It was gone! But she hadn't moved! How did she get the ring back?

Sarah grinned. "Care to try again to see if you can hold on to the ring?"

Determination had him snatching the ring out of her outstretched palm and returning it back into his pocket. Still feeling the circular bit of metal through his jacket, he backed well away from the smiling woman. When he had retreated far enough away to assure himself that there wasn't any possible way for her to get it back when he was somehow not looking, he finally dropped both hands to his sides. What was this? She was smiling again. She's holding out her hand! The ring! It was back in her hand! How was this possible? Again his hands flew to his inside pocket. Once more the ring was gone!

"How are ye doing that?" Mikal inquired, still feeling his empty pocket. That was so cool!

"Do you have anything else in your pockets? Anything at all?"

Mikal started patting himself down, looking for anything else he might have. Wait, there was something in his other inside pocket. He started to withdraw a crude slingshot when he remembered that his father had confiscated it several days ago. One disturbing little kitchen incident where a stone had 'accidentally' been discharged at a suit of armor, knocking it off its perch and onto a fully laden table, had marked his favorite weapon as illegal. It wasn't his fault that Rhenyon and his men just happened to be sitting in the line of fire. How was he supposed to know that custard would cause armor to rust so quickly?

The king's interest had been piqued. What did his son have that he didn't want them to know about? He glanced at his wife. *Find out.*

"What do ye have there, Mikal?"

Trying to fight the urge to tell his mother what he didn't want her to know, he felt his pocket. It was empty! What the-? His nervous eyes flicked to the strange woman's. She winked at him. Relief flooded into him like cool rain washing over someone dying of thirst.

"Nothing mother, really."

Callé looked at Sarah, who had her back to her. Sarah was still facing her son, with both arms clasped behind her back. Clutched in both of her hands was his prized slingshot. The queen stifled the laugh that wanted so desperately to escape from her mouth. She looked over at her husband. He, too, had also noticed the slingshot. His eyes narrowed, but he didn't want to betray her to their son. He allowed himself to be 'duped' in his son's eyes. Just this once, anyway. If it helped their son bond with his new guardians, then so be it.

Liking this strange woman more than he cared to admit, and wanting to focus everyone's attention on something besides himself, the young prince turned to the other Nohrin. "What is yer jhorun? Can ye do something as cool as that?"

"Mikal!" the queen exclaimed. "Manners!"

Resigned to seeing an example of some boring and mundane jhorun, he gasped aloud as the burning torch on the far wall went out with a poof, the flames flying into Steve's outstretched right hand. He was a fire thrower! If only he could have such a power!

Without thinking about what he was doing, Mikal moved over to view the pyrotechnical presentation a bit closer. Mesmerized by the dancing flames intertwined through Steve's fingers, he reached up to touch it for himself. As always, Steve, grinning at his wife for his brilliant display of his abilities, wasn't paying attention.

Several things all happened at once: Sarah let out a yell; the king leapt to his feet to try and intercept his son; the queen cried out a warning; and finally, Steve's head whipped around in time to see and feel Mikal grab his flaming hand. He instantly extinguished the flames and grabbed the boy's hand, inspecting for damage.

"Sorry, kid! Really! Are you okay? I wasn't paying attention."

The queen made it to her son first. "Mikal, let me see yer hand."

"Mother, what is the big deal? I am fine!" Mikal pulled his hand away from his worried mother.

The king arrived at his wife's side. "Ye are uninjured? Give me yer hand."

"I am fine, father. Really."

The king fixed him with a stare. "Yer hand. Now."

Sighing inwardly, the prince presented his hand for his father's inspection. The king snatched it and forcibly pulled him forward, twisting his hand this way and that.

"Ow! That hurts!"

The queen gently pulled her son's arm out of Entu's grasp and inspected it herself. His skin was warm to the touch, but no burns anywhere. She herself had felt the heat emanating from Steve. How could he not be burned? She eyed the nervous Nohrin fidgeting from foot to foot.

"Ye neglected to mention that ye would not harm those that came into physical contact with ye. Mikal should be burned, and burned seriously. I felt the heat coming from yer skin." She turned back to her son. "Did ye not feel anything?"

"Well, his hand was a little warm, but mom, it was on fire, ye know."

The king frowned. "Do ye typically grab a hold of something that's on fire?"

Mikal stared at his father. He looked at his mother. She, too, was frowning at him. Were his parents really this slow?

"Mother, father, please. If he is truly one of my 'protectors'," the prince rolled his eyes as he said this, "then it would not make much sense if he could defend me with his jhorun, but then burn me alive in the process, would it?"

Both the king and queen, along with the newly appointed Nohrin, stared at the boy in shock.

Sarah turned to her husband. "Did you know you wouldn't burn him?"

Steve shook his head. "I didn't even see him. I had no idea. I thought he was burned."

The king stepped forward. "Test this. I need to know if this is true or not."

Steve stepped backwards a few paces, just to be safe. His right hand ignited once again. He watched the red flames dancing along his fingers, but he also noted that Sarah was wincing. In fact, all had taken a step or two back from him. Too hot? Looking at his hand, he ordered his jhorun to decrease the temperature. The flames, still dancing through his fingers, switched from red to blue. He looked to Sarah to judge the temp. She nodded. Good. He turned to the king and held out his hand.

Cautiously, the king reached out to poke a finger at Steve's burning hand. It was warm, as if from strenuous exercise, but nothing he couldn't tolerate. He made a motion to grasp the hand. "May I?"

"Be my guest." Steve took the king's hand in his.

The king watched as the flickering blue flames completely enveloped his hand. "Minor heat," the king reported. "There is no discomfort at all."

A sudden thought occurred to the queen. "Steve, can ye increase the heat some? Just a little," she added hastily, as the king stared at her with shocked eyes.

"Let me know the instant it becomes too warm, okay?"

The king nodded.

Slowly, Steve increased the intensity of his flames. Watching the king's eyes for discomfort, he was directed to keep proceeding. Steve increased the temperature of his blazing hand a few more notches. Still, the king was unaffected. The flames were back to being red.

By this time, the other three occupants of the room had backed well away from the both of them. Beads of sweat were starting to form on Sarah's brow.

"Okay, hon," Sarah called out, "I think that's enough."

Steve extinguished his hand and automatically pulled the king's hand up to his eyes, rotating it around to ascertain for himself that his new sleeping arrangements would not be in the dungeon. Fortunately, he couldn't see any damage. Suddenly aware of the fact that he was holding a man's hand, and the hand of the reigning king at that, he released it as though he had just discovered he had been holding on to a scorpion.

Smiling, the king checked his hand for himself. No pain, no discomfort, no marks. Excellent!

"I didn't know I could do that," Steve confessed. "I never really tried."

The queen walked over to one of the many bookcases in the Antechamber, selected a book, and brought it to Steve.

"Would ye repeat the experiment, but this time, hold this." She handed him the book.

"Ummm, okay, this is a book. It'll burn in a flash."

Sarah shook her head. "That's the point of the test, dear. Let's see if you can ignite your hand and not the book."

Mikal snorted and tried to disguise it as a cough.

"Oh. Duh." He grinned sheepishly at his wife. "Right. Here we go."

Passing the book over to his left hand, he ignited his right. Willing his jhorun to lower the heat as much as possible, his right hand took the book from his left. The tome was swallowed by the flickering flames.

"I think it's burning," Steve observed.

"How can you tell?" Sarah asked.

"If it was burning," Mikal pointed out, "the book would be turning black, right?" Making what he hoped was an impressive display of courage, he walked over to the fire thrower and took the book from him.

The thick volume was sitting unscathed in the boy's hands. He looked at his parents, whose mouths were open in shock. He shrugged. "Well, now we know, right?" He handed the book back to Steve, who took it with his burning hand without even thinking.

Amazed, Steve looked at the book, and even opened it. The dancing flames made it rather difficult to read, but it was possible. The book contained what looked like descriptions of tariffs and taxes, and how they should be applied to the different citizens of the kingdom. He snorted. No wonder the queen selected this one. Probably doesn't care if it gets burned.

Catching Steve's eye, the queen winked at him.

Sarah turned to the king. "Can you give him something he can burn? I want to see if he can only burn things he's not holding."

Liking how the woman's mind worked, the king walked over to the hearth and selected a piece of kindling from the wood bin. He handed it to Steve.

"Burn this."

Handing the book to the king, Steve walked over to the hearth and studied the burning fire. "I'll restore it in just a sec, okay?"

The king nodded.

The flames in the fireplace went out with a soft whoosh. He held the kindling in his favored right hand and ignited the flames. He studied the thin piece of wood. *Okay, sucker, burn.* Suddenly red flames were mixing with the soft blue flames of his hand. The stick started to darken. Looking over his shoulder to verify no one was close, Steve focused on the burning piece of wood and sent a strong order to his jhorun: *I want this stick burned to ash. Now.*

With a flash of fire, the piece of kindling shriveled to a charred remnant of its former self. Seconds later, it crumbled into ash. Extinguishing the fire, he clapped his hands together, sending the last bits of ash into the hearth.

"How was that?"

The king was smiling. "Impressive. Very impressive."

"That was awesome!" Sarah grinned at him. "That stick crumbled like those cartoon cigarettes do when they burn up suddenly."

Mikal approached timidly, having seen what his new 'protectors' were capable of doing. No more eye-rolling here!

Sarah yawned suddenly. A long, drawn-out yawn that had her slapping her hands over her mouth.

"I am so sorry."

"Nay, ye and yer husband have nothing to be sorry for. The two of ye had a long journey thus far. Go, rest now. We will talk more on the morrow."

"Thank you, your majesties," Steve said. He looked at Mikal, still staring at him with those bright, blue eyes. "Until tomorrow, sport." He looked back at the hearth. The fire blazed back up as though nothing had transpired.

Sarah leaned close to the boy, whispering, "Don't move for about ten seconds. I'll put your slingshot back." And in a louder voice, "Nice to meet you Mikal. See you tomorrow!"

Mikal grinned up at her. "Nice to meet you, too. Good night!"

As Sarah turned to follow Steve out of the room, she restored the slingshot back to its rightful owner, but not before hearing the queen ask her son what he thought of his new guardians.

"For old people, they are pretty cool."

After Tristan escorted them back to their quarters (again), Steve collapsed onto the bed. Moments later he had sprung back up when he realized he had just laid on something lumpy. What was this?

"What's the matter?"

"Did you know this was here?"

"Did I know what was here?"

Steve held up several piles of clothes. He unfolded a dark green doublet, with a pair of khaki trousers underneath. He held them up to himself. Damn, looks like they'd fit! Sarah looked at the second pile of clothes. There were several other folded doublets, all green, with several more pairs of trousers. All fitted for Steve.

"Apparently you get a new wardrobe," Sarah commented.

"What about you?" Steve asked. Before she could respond, he caught sight of a couple of doors that were slightly ajar on the far wall. Walking over to the doors he pulled them open, revealing a large, walk-in closet with no fewer than twenty gowns in it. All in various shades of green. And, if he wasn't mistaken, all would fit Sarah perfectly. Grinning that smug smile of his, Steve glanced over at his wife. She was busy inspecting one of his new doublets when Steve cleared his throat. Looking up at him, and then following his gaze into the closet, she stared open-mouthed at her new wardrobe selections.

"Who-o-a-a! Look at that! Where did those all come from?"

"I'd say from our gracious hosts. Guess we get to dress the part tomorrow." Steve cracked another smile. "When in Rome, do as the Romans do, right?"

Looking at his many reflections as they passed numerous mirrors on their way to the Great Hall, Steve couldn't help but feel as though he was one of Robin Hood's merry men. Dark green tunic, khaki trousers, and brown leather boots. All he needed to complete the picture was a hat. With a big feather. He chuckled. At least the material was comfortable and lightweight. Sarah was incredibly fetching in her floor-length gown. As with his new clothes, her dress was a lightweight material as well, with several swirl-type gold designs on the bodice. He wanted to inspect the designs a bit closer, but that sort of thing could wait. Don't want to give off the wrong impression amongst their new friends.

Together, they walked into the Great Hall (without Tristan's help – Sarah had watched him intently the last couple of times they had been escorted from their room) and looked around. There were general murmurings everywhere as people conversed with one another over what today's activities would bring, whether the weather would hold for the harvesting of the crops, and so on.

Sarah selected an empty table off to the side and sat down. Steve sat down at the other side and looked around.

Noting that the Nohrin were finally sitting, Tristan caught the eye of the head of the kitchen staff. The soldier looked pointedly at the young couple then back at the king's chef. Several other servants gathered behind her. *Is that them?* Her eyes asked. Tristan nodded. *Yes, take care of them.*

The king's personal chef selected her most efficient server, a young peasant woman, and whispered instructions to her. The girl darted off at once to the table where Steve and Sarah sat.

"So, I wonder how we go about getting something to-"

At this time the servant girl arrived. She introduced herself as Julia, and very politely inquired what they would like for breakfast. Certain that a glass of cranberry juice and a bagel with cream cheese were out of the question, Sarah went with their waitress' opinion. "Julia, what do you like to have for breakfast?"

Surprised to have her opinion asked of her, Julia paused a moment as she thought about it. "I like to have a glass or two of tara juice, with a chedra." Julia smiled. "Maybe two."

Steve leaned forward. "What's a chedra? What's in it?"

"Bread and cheese, mostly."

"Is tara some type of a berry?" Sarah wanted to know.

"Aye, they are small red berries that grow in the southern valley."

"Okay, then, I'll have a glass of tara juice and I'll try one of those chedras. Thanks Julia."

Uncertain whether or not these chedras would actually fill him up, Steve hesitated. Sarah, knowing her husband well, spoke up. "My husband would like something heartier. What would you suggest? What do the soldiers usually have in the morning?"

Certain she would be reprimanded if she suggested gruel and sausage for the famous Nohrin, Julia looked quickly over to her supervisor. Watching intently, the chef was ready with her response: G*ive them whatever they want.*

At that moment, Mikal came running up to them and joined them at their table.

"Good morning to ye!" he said to his newfound comrade-at-arms. "And to ye," he added to Steve.

"Mornin' kiddo!"

"Good morning, Mikal," Sarah said. She looked at the bright boy before them, an idea occurring to her. "Listen, we could use your help."

"Sure, anything!" Eager to please, his enthusiastic response made them both smile.

"My husband was wondering what to have for breakfast. We don't know what's good here, and he usually has a large breakfast. What do you think he'd like?"

Mikal thought a moment, and then looked at Julia. "Bring him some sheppard pie. I bet he'd like that."

Doing his best to act as nonchalant as possible, Steve inquired what was in it, knowing full well what was in the Irish version he was familiar with.

"It's a pastry type of thing," Mikal explained. "It has meat, some cheese, and-"

Steve slapped him on the back. "Sold!" He looked at Julia. "I'll have some of that sheppard pie." Deciding to risk the tara juice, he also ordered a glass.

Mikal, wanting to impress his new friends, also ordered the sheppard pie with a glass of tara juice.

Across the Great Hall, the queen stood, watching silently. Her precious son was laughing and having his morning meal with his new protectors. They were getting along spectacularly, she mused. Her husband came up behind her.

"What are ye doing?"

Putting her fingers to her lips, she shushed him and pointed to where their son sat, eating his breakfast.

"Mikal has taken to them very fast. They are quite good with children."

"So tell me about your jhorun," Steve said amiably to Mikal, as they walked outside into the fresh air. "We heard something about you enhancing other peoples' jhorun. How does that work?"

"My jhorun is so lame that even a troll would laugh," Mikal said miserably. For the umpteenth time he wished his jhorun was something different. "I can make someone's jhorun stronger." He eyed Steve. "Want me to enhance yer jhorun to try it out?" Another pyrotechnical demonstration would be an awesome way to brighten the day!

"I'll take a rain check on that," Steve muttered. "It'd be my luck that I'd blow up half the castle. As curious as I am to give that a try, I still have to learn how to control mine better. I'm still learning new things all the time."

"Like what?" the boy wanted to know.

"For instance, last night. I thought for certain I had burned you. I didn't realize I wouldn't burn something I was touching if I didn't want it to. Makes me wonder what else I can do and not know it." Steve looked down at his new shadow. "Does that make sense to you?"

"Sure, by the time people here are *yer* age, they already have their jhoruns figured out."

Sarah stifled a giggle. Steve glanced over to his wife. "Find that funny, do you? Snot."

Wanting to change the subject before Mikal started asking more questions, Steve asked if their young friend might be able to show them around.

"I am under orders not to leave the castle without an armed escort," Mikal complained, "but that does not mean I can not show ye around the perimeter. Not much to see. It's rather dreary."

Sarah laughed. "Says you! You live in a castle! In our world, there aren't many castles around. We'd love to learn more about this one. I have a good friend back home, Lia, that absolutely loves castles. I want to be able to tell her as much as I can remember when I see her next."

"Alright, follow me then." He walked over to the moat and started walking along the water's edge. "Bredo lives in there. He's nice."

"Did you say a burrito lives in there?" Steve asked, certain he had heard that wrong.

"Bredo is the serpent that guards the moat."

"A snake? How big?"

"The largest I have ever laid eyes on. Ye do not want to go in there." Mikal laughed. "A villager lost several bolgers in there once. Bredo got 'em before they made it out. Wish I could have seen it."

Making a mental note to not take a dip in the moat, Steve walked on, following his wife and their new friend. A sudden thought had him calling out to their small tour guide.

"Hey Mikal!"

Mikal glanced behind him and slowed his pace so Steve could catch up.

"Your father mentioned something about making an area specifically for use by dragons."

Mikal nodded. He knew of the large area in the northern orchard. "Why do ye want to see that? It is boring."

"Steve is fascinated by dragons," Sarah explained. "If it were up to him he'd seek out the closest one and hop on its back."

Mikal turned to give Steve an appraising stare. "Ye want to ride a dragon? Ye would not last long."

"So I've heard," Steve said. "I'd just like to see one."

Walking alongside the young prince, Mikal started telling them all kinds of stories. Stories about adventures he and his friends had undertaken. All of his stories had the same theme: tales on how he was unjustly grounded for numerous happenings he really didn't have a part in. They also learned that Mikal was extremely dissatisfied with his jhorun. Apparently it wasn't considered very cool to have a jhorun that couldn't physically manifest itself. "What fun is that?" he muttered darkly.

"I think it's a very practical and powerful jhorun," Sarah said quickly. "Being able to boost the strength of anyone's jhorun must be incredibly useful."

"Ye sound just like my mother," Mikal accused.

"Sounds like your mom is pretty smart, huh?"

Mikal snorted. "She's smart for a grown-up." Remembering Sarah's help from the night before, he looked over at the foreign woman. "Thanks again for hiding my slingshot for me. Had mom or dad caught me with that it would have been confiscated until I was old enough to marry. How did ye do that, anyway?"

"My jhorun is teleportation," Sarah said. "Like yours, my jhorun won't manifest itself either."

"Teleportation? So ye can move things around?" He mulled that over a moment. "So that's how ye kept getting the ring back without taking it out of my pocket."

Sarah nodded.

They continued walking for another ten minutes, moving well past the outer castle garrison. Large fruit trees had been planted about three meters apart in rows of ten, of what type Sarah couldn't say. She studied the heavily laden trees. She then stooped down to the ground to pick up one of the half-rotten fruits, rotating it in her hand. This one resembled a fat purple pear. She held it out to Mikal.

"What type of fruit is this?"

Mikal glanced over at her. "That is a jansa." He pointed to the next grove of trees, with a round, yellowish citrus-type of fruit hanging from the branches. "Those are sidah. And those are loken," gesturing to what looked like elongated red bananas in the next grove over. "The best tasting are the sidah. I do not care for loken. Jansa is also good, but messy."

Leaving the grove of loken trees behind, the trio came upon the recently created dragon lair. Steve was unimpressed. He wasn't sure what he was expecting, only that he figured there should be more than what they found. Bare, rocky terrain with a few large trees in the distance met his eyes. The only vegetation dotting the landscape was small, chalky green bushes that were trying to grow in the stony earth. The one odd thing, though, was that there was an enormous mounded section of earth that was swelling gently upwards, as if an underground giant was pushing straight up.

Looking around, Steve was discouraged. It's rather sparse, he thought. You'd think the king could have done better than this for the dragons.

That thought vanished from his head as they approached a mound of rocks and discovered it to be an opening to a vast tunnel angling steeply downhill. Steve's mouth opened in shock. Look at the size of this tunnel! Two semis could drive side-by-side down this thing with room to spare. How big are these dragons anyway?

"What's down there? Think we can take a look?"

"My father hollowed out a large cavern down there," Mikal explained. "That's why the ground here looks like someone is pushing up from below."

"The mound is the roof of the cavern?" Steve whistled. That must be some cavern! He guesstimated it to be roughly three thousand meters square.

Sarah turned to Steve. "I don't want to go down there. It looks really dark. Can we look at another time?"

Looking longingly at the dark tunnel before them, he shrugged and turned to go.

Suddenly four men wearing dark clothing came boiling out of the depths of the cavern. Sarah screamed a warning, grabbed Mikal, and held him close.

"Grab 'em! Quickly now!" the leader barked to the henchman closest to Steve. Before he even realized what was happening, a thug had him in a bone-splitting bear hug. Thick, muscled arms held him firmly in place. "As long as ye have him close, he cannot harm ye!"

With Steve incapacitated, the two remaining thugs menacingly approached Sarah, who had shoved Mikal behind her.

In a surprisingly calm voice, Steve addressed his assailant. "You have one chance, buddy, to let go and haul ass outta here."

Laughing heartily, the leader of the motley gang turned back to his victim. "Gag that scum, now!" He returned his attention to the two thugs who were approaching Sarah and Mikal.

"Will ye hurry up? We need to get out of here! Just kill the woman and grab the prince. Go!"

In one swift, fluid motion a goon had an arrow fitted to his bowstring. He pulled back and took aim at Sarah. But before the arrow could be released, it vanished, the bow following shortly thereafter. Dropping his now empty arms down to his side, the dimwitted thug looked to his boss for the next set of instructions.

Their leader, however, never got a chance to say a word, for in that moment, high-pitched screams pierced the air. The thug restraining Steve had just discovered he was holding a six foot three, white-hot poker. While Steve's clothing remained unaffected by the sudden appearance of the searing heat, his unfortunate assailant's apparel instantly burst into flames. Tattered bits of flaming cloth fluttered off the wailing thug, who desperately tried rolling on the ground to extinguish himself. Not making any headway, he then sprinted the ten or so meters to dive into the northern tip of the moat. Unfortunately for him, the largest serpent in captivity was waiting.

Snarling in anger, the leader leapt towards Steve, intending to do him in as quickly as possible.

Intense hatred permeated Steve's body, causing his jhorun to also seethe in anger. Realizing his jhorun was clamoring to be released, Steve flung out his arm, palm facing out, as though he was performing a traffic stop. A jet of pure fire erupted from his hand and hit the approaching mercenary square in the chest. Clothing incinerated in a flash. Screaming in pain, the engulfed man threw himself into the moat as well. Liking cooked food just as well as raw, Bredo flicked his tongue in the direction of his barbecued snack and hurried to retrieve it before it sank all the way to the bottom.

Behind them, back inside the castle, Steve could hear soldiers talking and laughing with one another, completely oblivious to their predicament. Sarah and Mikal were in danger. He needed some help and he needed it now. Raising his left hand, he shot three jets of fire straight up. That should get someone's attention, Steve thought. Now to deal with these last two goons. There was no way in hell he was going to let anyone so much as lay a finger on his wife or the young prince. Scowling, Steve turned to face his two remaining opponents.

One man lunged for the cowering boy hiding behind Sarah. In the blink of an eye, she and Mikal vanished. Steve gasped with astonishment. Did she just teleport Mikal and herself? Beautiful timing! He could only hope that Sarah had somehow managed to teleport them far out of harm's way.

The remaining members of the crew that had been hired to kidnap the crown prince stared in disbelief from their hiding place along edge of the forest. This was just supposed to be a simple snatch and grab! Nothing was going as planned. Their fool of a leader just got himself fried to a crisp. And, to top it all off, the prince had managed to escape. Silently motioning to the seven other mercenaries standing beside him, one fast thinking kidnapper whispered a new set of instructions to his mates. "We might have lost the prince, but we cannot go back empty-handed." He gestured to the tall foreigner with his back to them. "We have to grab that scum, now!"

The rest of the band stared at their new (self-appointed) leader with incredulity. "Did ye not see what he did to the others? What good are we against that?"

The goon glared at his companions. "Do ye want to return without anything to show for our troubles and face *him*? We might have a chance of living through this if we gift him with a fire thrower. Now, move!" He leapt out into the clearing and fit an arrow to his bow, running as fast and as silently as possible, his gang right on his heels. Their only hope was if they could somehow incapacitate this powerful new enemy before he even realized what was happening to him.

In the Great Hall, the king was seeing to matters of the state, as this was the designated time of month to listen to, and resolve, complaints from villagers, soldiers, farmers, etc.

Kri'Entu sat back on his throne in exasperation, his head throbbing mercilessly. These two bickering farmers each claimed they were responsible for the remarkable harvest that the other was fortunate enough to have had this year. Each, naturally, wanted a significant share of his neighbor's profits. Getting irritated with the pettiness of these two squabbling farmers, Kri'Entu began to explain how each were now going to give equal shares of their prized crops to the other when Sarah and Mikal suddenly materialized in their midst, stumbling to the ground.

The king leapt to his feet. "Mikal? Sarah? Are ye alright? What happened?"

Sarah made it to her feet first. "Your majesty, we were attacked! North of the castle at that underground dragon lair you made! Please, Steve is still out there, all by himself!!"

"Attacked?" Surprise registered on his face first, only to be quickly replaced by anger. "Sound the alarm! Captain!"

Rhenyon, who had been interviewing new recruits near the back of the Hall, wasted no time. Startled by the sudden intrusion of two people appearing out of thin air, he had leapt to his feet. He was pleased to see the woman from the inn, but mortified to learn that yet another attack had occurred, especially while he was on duty. He sprinted out of the Great Hall, all the while shouting for his men. "To the northern orchards! On the double!!" Every soldier he encountered had to scramble to keep up.

At that moment, a massive explosion sounded, rattling windows, causing several coats of arms to fall from their mounts on the wall. The floor rumbled beneath their feet.

The king locked his gaze on Sarah. "What was that? Was that yer husband?"

Sarah nodded. "It happened once before, when we were attacked. I'll tell you about it later, I promise. Please, we have to help!"

The king, along with practically all the rest of the castle personnel, ran to a side door Sarah hadn't noticed before. Mikal moved to follow his father when the king looked back, saw his son following, and instructed several guards to secure him in the Antechamber. Without waiting to hear Mikal's protests, they ran to catch up with the rest of the castle staff all rushing to make it outside. Sarah was following the king, weaving in and out of the multitudes of people that kept appearing in their way.

Still rumbling, the cloud of smoke generated from the explosion rose higher into the air, twisting and turning. The tower bells were ringing, sounding the general alarm. A second explosion suddenly ripped through the air, with a second large plume of dark black smoke rising angrily up into the sky to join the first. The second blast had been more powerful than the first, with the concussion forcing Sarah to stumble to the closest building and crouch in the doorway. The king joined her moments later. Together they waited for the rumbling to pass. Concern for her husband had her releasing her grip on the wooden door frame after about ten seconds. She sprinted towards the northern gate. She had to know if her husband was alright. But before she could race towards the gate, she felt a strong hand clamp around her wrist.

Gripping Sarah's arm tightly, the king grabbed the first soldier within his reach and pushed him towards her.

"Escort her back inside, now." He snagged a second soldier and shoved him towards the first. "Ye are with him. Go."

Finding herself with an escort on either arm, Sarah started her own protest, but was cut off by a glare from the king.

It took five minutes of running at a flat-out sprint before Rhenyon and his men arrived in the northern orchards. All the soldiers drew to a sudden halt as they finally emerged from the groves of fruit trees and observed the carnage before them. Several of the trees unlucky enough to have been within range were now blackened. Three men, clothed in charred, tattered rags, were lying face down on the burnt ground. Blackened bows and scarred remains of arrows, leather armor, and clothing lay strewn about.

Pacing back and forth behind the survivors of the attack, both hands still ignited, was Steve. Seeing that his reinforcements had finally arrived, Steve stopped walking and stared hard at the captain. "I remember you. Rhenyon, right? Just the person I wanted to see. You can take it from here. I have to go. Mikal and my wife disappeared on me. Literally. I have to find out if they're okay."

Rhenyon held up his hands. "They are fine. They appeared suddenly in the Great Hall. She told us what happened." He looked down at the terrified men who refused even to look up. "What happened here? Are ye alright?" The captain gave him a quick once over. He was unable to approach any closer due to the immense heat pouring off the Nohrin. "Do ye think ye might be able to tone it down some?"

Suddenly aware that his hands were still burning, he snuffed them both out. The temperature in the vicinity instantly started to drop. Steve took a deep breath.

"Sorry, I'm a little rattled, but I'm okay. Can't say the same thing for these guys. Sons of bitches tried to kill us and take Mikal."

Rhenyon's eyes widened. "Here? This close to the castle??" He swore under his breath. "Aye, we will take it from here." He gestured to several of his men, and within seconds, all three prisoners were trussed up so tightly that they could barely breathe. "Was it just these three, then?"

"There were more, but Bredo there took care of 'em for us."

Rhenyon frowned, looking over at the moat. The earth had been disturbed by the water's edge, as though someone took a swim but frantically tried to pull themselves out. "Why would they jump in there? Everyone knows not to go jumping into our moat."

"Well, they'd jump in willingly if they were on fire."

Rhenyon disguised his chuckle with a discreet clearing of the throat. "How many were there all together?"

Steve thought a moment. "I'd say at least a dozen. The first four came out of the dragon tunnel there, and then when they were unsuccessful in snatching Mikal, a bunch more came from the forest over there, where those three trees look like they are growing together as one."

Rhenyon instantly dispatched ten men to investigate. At that moment, two squadrons of fully armored knights on horseback appeared, with the king snapping out orders from the front of the procession.

"One squadron in reconnaissance. Disperse throughout the forest. If anyone or anything is found, report it instantly. All others," indicating the remaining group of horsemen, "secure the perimeter."

The soldiers instantly obeyed. Half galloped into the forest, vanishing amongst the heavily wooded trees. The second squadron immediately spread out, forming an armored circle around the scene of the battle.

The king dismounted, joining the two of them moments later. Rhenyon straightened as he approached. Kri'Entu glared down at the three tightly trussed up men. "What happened here? Are these three involved?"

"Directly," Steve said. "This one," he nudged the one in the center, "drew his bow on Sarah with the intent to kill her. This one," he indicated the bound man on the right, "tried to draw his sword on me. And him," he nudged the last man, tied up on the left, "he came out of the forest. His group must have been backup or something."

The king stared open-mouthed at the captives. Never once have they been able to take any prisoners from one of these types of attacks. Now they had three!

"I assume, then, that the remaining men escaped into the forest?"

"No, your majesty, they did not."

The king raised an eyebrow. He looked left, then right. No bodies. He didn't see anyone else other than these three. "What happened to them then? Were you forced to dispatch them?"

Taking several more deep breaths to try and calm his already pounding nerves, Steve relayed the events that had only happened to him moments before.

With his wife and the prince safely out of the picture, Steve had turned to focus his attention on the two goons that remained. It was the sense of something not being right that had him turning to look behind him. To his dismay, more men had appeared at the forest's edge and were running at breakneck speed towards him. This second group, however, clearly had more sinister intentions in mind. As he had turned to evaluate the threat level of his newest set of problems, he discovered that most of them had their bows out and were in the process of fitting arrows to their strings. One man was even preparing to fire!

In that split second as he saw the arrow released, he recalled that he had once before conjured up a blast that had incinerated an arrow in mid-flight. He didn't know how he did it then, and he sure as hell didn't know how to do it now.

Not liking arrows fired at them, Steve's jhorun took the decision-making process out of his hands.

The blast of fire caught the arrow en route to its target, vaporizing it into ash, as well as igniting the rest of the arrows waiting to be released. Anything combustible was flash-burned, reduced to ash in mere seconds. Strings snapped; bows were reduced to charred husks. The approaching ruffians were all thrown backwards onto the ground. Hard.

Momentarily stunned, the advancing thugs regained their feet and quickly realized that only bows and arrows had been destroyed. Seeing his comrades shocked expressions, their new leader drew his sword, motioning to his dimwitted fellows to follow suit. Swords were unsheathed as the gang, as one, rushed to overtake their pyrotechnical adversary. All they had to do was reach him before he figured out what to do next.

They didn't make it.

The second explosion caught the advancing group dead center. About half of them managed to dive to the ground just before impact. The others weren't so fortunate, becoming human torches on contact. Screaming in pain, the unlucky men dove into the moat to put themselves out. The resident moat monster, already having been alerted to the mayhem happening nearby, was waiting. Two of the remaining survivors elected to reverse course and high-tail it back to the forest.

Oh no you don't, Steve thought angrily. *That won't save your sorry asses.* His jhorun tingled, gaining in strength, as if calling for reinforcements. Suddenly his right hand blazed so brightly that it actually stung. Reacting as though he had just been bitten by an insect, Steve shook it. It didn't help. The shaking became more violent. So did the intensity of the sting. Without knowing how or why, Steve suddenly knew what he had to do. Pretending he was throwing the first pitch at a baseball game, Steve cocked his right arm back and let fly with his imaginary pitch.

The ball of fire that erupted was the size of a basketball. It streaked towards the two retreating men.

Sensing something amiss, one of the men looked behind him, only to discover a raging orb of death rushing headlong towards them.

He barely had time to shout a warning to his mate.

"Look out!"

The other saw what was happening and both took off, heading in different directions. The racing globe of fire separated itself equally into two smaller spheres and smoothly went after each fleeing man. Screaming hysterically, the mercenaries frantically dodged this way and that, hoping to elude their ever approaching fate.

The two fireballs struck their targets in as many heartbeats. Right on their butts. With their backsides flaming brighter than any torch, they ran for the moat to throw themselves in.

Bredo, having the time of his life, kept snapping up morsels as they kept appearing.

"Ye could not ask for a better fate for those men," Rhenyon muttered, when Steve had finished.

Suddenly remembering what it was that was bothering him, Steve grabbed the king's wrist. "Sir, I need to talk to you. Now." Kri'Entu, startled to be addressed in such a manner, agreed.

"Walk with me."

"I think we'll need Rhenyon, too."

Without breaking stride, the king looked over at his captain. "Join us."

Instantly complying, Rhenyon joined the group. The three men moved out of earshot of everyone else. The king turned to Steve.

"What is it? If ye are worried about Sarah, she is safe and secure in the castle."

"That's not what's bothering me, sir." Taking a deep breath, he thought about how to phrase what he was about to say. Better to just spit it out. "The leader of these guys actually said to his men that they had to grab me quickly. I think he said something about holding me closely because I can't burn anything next to me."

The king inhaled sharply. "Are ye sure?" Steve nodded. "But that means…" the king trailed off as the implication set in.

Rhenyon looked at his king. "That means what, yer majesty?"

Lowering his voice, he looked at the captain. "We conducted an experiment in the Antechamber last night. Just the queen, myself, Mikal, Steve, and his wife, Sarah. No one else." He took a breath. "At first, it appeared that anything Steve was holding would be unaffected by his jhorun and therefore would not burn, but was later proved false. Someone else was in that chamber, witnessed that part of the experiment, and then clearly left before the experiment was concluded. Whoever that was relayed what they had heard to a third party, and somehow that information ended up with those three men. My question is who? Who could it have been?"

Rhenyon stiffened. "There were three guards on duty that night in the Antechamber. I can vouch for all."

Steve held up a hand. Catching the king's eye, who nodded, he said, "Ummm, I believe there was another person in the Antechamber beside us and the soldiers."

Both king and captain stared at him, and in unison, asked, "Who?"

"The servant girl. Remember her? She came in to offer us drinks. You and I took a cup, the ladies didn't. Anyone have any idea how long she might have stuck around?"

Rhenyon started scowling again, pacing around Kri'Entu and Steve. "We need to contact the kitchen staff immediately and find out who was on duty last night. I will have the truth out of that harlot or she will hang."

Kri'Entu looked at his trusted friend. "Ye really think that girl is knowingly and willingly supplying confidential information to a Ylani spy?"

"I'll bet you she's sleeping with someone," Steve suggested, "and that person is using her for information, willingly or not."

"Regardless of who she's sharing her bed with," Rhenyon spat, "she should not be divulging any information she overhears to anyone else. Especially in royal matters."

The king nodded sagely. "I agree. I will leave this problem in yer hands then."

"Aye, I will resolve this, fear not. As for these three," Rhenyon gave a not-so-gentle kick to one of the bound men, "I will find out who they are working for and what their intentions are. Leave it to me."

Turning, the king took Steve's arm and guided him back into the castle, going straight to the Great Hall where Sarah was pacing. She had just sat down when they emerged into the cavernous room.

"Steve!" She ran over to him and flung her arms around him, hugging him hard. "Are you okay? I was so worried about you!"

"I'm okay. Really."

"What happened? How did you escape?"

Steve scoffed. "Escape? Didn't have to."

Comprehension flooded into her as she realized just what her husband had meant by that. "Did you have to, er, I mean, did you-"

"If you're asking whether or not I killed them," Steve interrupted, "then no. Umm, not directly."

"Not directly? What does that mean?"

"Let's just say I gave them some motivation to jump into the moat."

Mikal jumped up, letting out a joyous whoop. "Bredo got 'em, did he not? Alright Bredo!"

"What about you?" Steve asked. "You actually teleported yourself didn't you? Mikal, too!"

Sarah smiled. "I've been thinking about that. I don't know how I did it. I've been trying to recreate the circumstances, but I apparently am not doing something right."

"How did you know you could do it then?"

"I really didn't," Sarah confessed. "I wasn't even trying. Everything happened so quickly. I knew I had to get Mikal to safety, and I knew you could take care of yourself. So I grabbed him and thought of getting some help. Suddenly we were here. The king was here, too, and even that soldier from the inn. Did you see him?"

Steve nodded.

"After I told them we were attacked by the dragon cavern that Rhenyon fellow bolted outside, with every soldier I could see chasing after him. Then we heard the explosion. Honestly, I'm surprised no one was killed. It was loud. The floor was shaking, and things fell off the walls."

Steve grinned. He knew his first blast was strong, but they felt it all the way in the castle? Cool!

"The purpose of the first blast was to eliminate the arrow." He explained that, as before at the small lake, he saw an arrow being released. This time at him. He told her how he believed the purpose of the blast was to incapacitate his opponents, but not to harm.

"Did you do that specifically?" Sarah wanted to know.

"I wish I could say that I did. I'd rather have done the job with one blast and not two. What if I would have missed someone?"

Ny'Callé entered the Great Hall and rushed over to her son and her husband. "Is everyone alright? Mikal, are ye unharmed?"

"He is fine," Kri'Entu assured his wife. "It would seem that our Nohrin have arrived in the nick of time. It pains me to say this, but we have to get Mikal out of here. Tristan."

Tristan appeared. "Sir."

"Locate Maelnar. I hereby authorize you to use whatever means necessary. Use whatever personnel you require. Now."

The soldier gave a curt bow. "Consider it done, sir."

True to his word, Rhenyon identified the hapless maid who had been relaying information to the Ylani spy. While the servant's employment was terminated, the spy slipped away unseen, much to the captain's frustrations.

The days passed with still no word as to the present whereabouts of the dwarf craftsman, Maelnar. The king, having received a response of 'location unknown' from the dwarves, expanded the search to include all of Lentari. Messengers were sent to the coastal village of Capily, the mountainous village of Avin, and it wasn't until they sent messengers to the extreme northern village of Verdayn that they received their first glimmer of news.

Mikal came running into the Great Hall to find his guardians sitting down for their midday meal.

"Steve! Sarah! We have news!"

Steve looked up from his plate of steaming phedras, cousin to their breakfast brethren. The luncheon variety contained seasoned meat, steamed veggies, and some type of red root. He had to keep telling himself it was just a chicken pot pie and they typically didn't include beets. He hated beets.

Mikal was practically jumping up and down with excitement, anxious to share the news with his friends.

"You appear to be bursting at the seams," Steve observed, smiling at their charge. "What's up, Mikal? What's the news?"

"We heard back from the messengers sent to Verdayn!"

"Okay, with you so far."

Sarah smacked her husband on the arm. "Does someone there know where Maelnar is?"

"According to some old villager, he passed through Verdayn about ten years ago!"

Steve snorted. "Ten year old news is good news?"

"I guess. Father was really excited. He said that an old man remembered trading with a really good dwarf blacksmith who mentioned that he was on his way to Borahgg."

"Bo-rug?" Steve briefly wondered just how badly he had mangled that pronunciation. "Where's that? I don't remember your father mentioning that one."

Mikal rocked back and forth on his heels, bursting with his secret. "That is the point! There are only two known dwarven cities. This makes number three!"

Sarah nodded. "Okay, so there are three dwarf cities. After ten years, how do you know that's where he still is?"

"Father is positive that's where he's at. Why, he did not say." Mikal suddenly snapped his fingers. "He did want to talk with the two of ye."

Steve, working on getting as big a bite of phedra on his fork as possible, paused. "He wants to see us? Now?"

"Aye, right now. I forgot to tell ye."

As they walked to the Antechamber, Steve began noticing a subtle change in the general populace of the castle. Instead of everyone ignoring them, or else pretending that they didn't exist, servants, kitchen staff, even soldiers were now starting to smile, tip a hat, or even give a small nod of recognition in their direction.

They had just exited the Great Hall, walking through the large, vaulted corridor that took them to various rooms in the southern wing of the castle, when, as they were approaching the outer door to the Antechamber, several soldiers leapt to attention at their approach.

The four guards, two on either side of the door, all nodded. One even grasped the handle and pulled open the door. "Nohrin. His majesty is waiting for you."

Sarah beamed at him. "Thank you."

Deciding his messenger duties were fulfilled, Mikal ambled off, hoping to find one of his friends before he was given another assignment. Entering the Antechamber, they found the king seated at his desk. He looked up as they entered. He shook his head.

"Allow me to venture a guess. My son just asked ye to come in here, correct?"

Confused, Sarah and Steve nodded.

The king sat back, sighing. "I asked him to bring ye here close to an hour ago."

He couldn't help it. Steve chuckled. The king's tired eyes swiveled over to his. "Sorry, no disrespect intended. Boys will be boys."

"Indeed. As he may or may not have told ye, we have a lead as to where Maelnar might be."

Steve nodded. "Borug, wherever that is. Another dwarf city?"

Kri'Entu nodded. "Aye. Borahgg, a previously unknown dwarven city." He rose from his desk and walked to a section of wall that had the map of his kingdom tacked up on it. Small colored markers were now dotted all over. He gestured to the northern Bohani Mountains. Red markers were scattered across every inch of the entire mountain range, with a few yellow mixed in. He started tapping the various markers.

"Red signifies where we have already searched. Yellow is where we are presently searching. And here," he tapped a small, southern section of Lake Raehón, "ye will notice there are no markers. And there is a reason for that. That area is known to be heavily populated by dragons. It is here that I believe contains an entrance to the dwarven realm. This is where the two of ye need to go."

Sarah paled. Dragons! They had to traverse through dragon territory?

Steve cleared his throat. "With all due respect, your majesty, I seem to recall you mentioning that you weren't too sure where to start looking for the dwarves. What makes you think that's the right area? If we're gonna go into dragon territory, I think we ought to be damn certain we're going in the right direction."

With a gleam in his eye, the king smiled. "Come with me."

The king led them out the northern gate, continuing past the moat. With as much finesse as a fully armored phalanx of troops could attain, their armored shadow fell in step behind them.

"Where are we going?" Puzzled, Steve looked around. "There's nothing out here."

Turning to gaze at Steve while he walked, the king smiled again. "Ye wanted to know how I know where to look for the dwarves. It is quite simple, really. I should have thought of it years ago. Ye ask a resident of the area."

With that, they stopped at the familiar mound of rocks in the midst of the northern orchard.

Steve stared at the entrance to the great underground cavern.

"Are you telling me –" He didn't get to finish his question.

Small tremors could now be felt, growing steadily stronger, and coming in short bursts: thud… Thud… THUD… **THUD**.

Steve's mouth opened in shock. Sarah scooted behind her husband. The tremors were coming from inside the hollowed out cavern below the orchard, which meant...

Twin blasts of smoke erupted from the tunnel, causing all but Kri'Entu to jump back in terror. The tremors in the ground grew to an intensity strong enough to throw both Steve and Sarah off balance. More smoke was emitting from the tunnel mouth, as well as discreetly placed vents in the cavern ceiling, making it appear as though there was mist floating up from the ground.

The dragon finally emerged into the sunlight, giving Steve his long anticipated first look at an actual live dragon. Kahvel was a prime example of his species. He massed about ten tons, had a wingspan of seventy-five feet from tip to tip, and was an iridescent golden color. His claws alone, Steve figured, were at least two feet long. It would be a very foolish human, indeed, who tried to slay a dragon.

Kahvel took a deep breath and rustled his wings. There was the human he was familiar with, along with two other humans who were holding their ground, a male standing in front of a female.

"Kri'Entu," the dragon acknowledged, the bass of his deep voice being felt by all present. Kahvel gracefully lowered his head down to inspect the two humans who didn't flee. "Who are these two? I do not recall smelling them before."

Kri'Entu turned to the Nohrin. "Steve, Sarah, may I present the dragon liaison, Kahvel." The king turned back to the dragon. "Kahvel, allow me to introduce the Nohrin. This is Steve, and his wife, Sarah."

Two intelligent, reptilian eyes stared at the small female before shifting to the male. "Are ye not afraid, human?"

Steve was ecstatic. The dragon could speak! It was intelligent! "Call me Steve," he corrected, "and I'm very pleased to meet you."

With a rustling of scales, Kahvel raised his head back up to his normal range, all the while maintaining eye contact. He grunted, snorting out a small puff of smoke from each slitted nostril. He eyed the small human king. "This? This is the famed Nohrin that ye speak of, Kri'Entu? How could something so small be capable of generating the amount of fire and heat that ye have been talking about?"

Bemused, Steve grinned. He was really starting to like this dragon. There was a small voice in the back of his brain that was screaming at him, insisting he should be afraid. He just simply wasn't. Looking up at the dragon, he ignited both hands.

"It is my general understanding," Kahvel observed, "that humans are not supposed to burn."

"Who said anything about humans burning?" Grinning like a school kid, Steve raised both arms, palms out, and took aim at a tree, one of the blackened remains of a casualty from his last excursion to this orchard. Twin jets of fire shot from his outstretched arms, enveloping the already blackened tree in flames, reducing it to ash in mere seconds. Pulling his jhorun back, both hands poofed out. He smiled up at the dragon.

Nodding appreciatively, Kahvel sited the next blackened tree. His mouth opened slightly as he gently blew the tree a kiss. The resulting jet of fire had the tree instantly reduced to ash where it fluttered away with the wind before the tree could even break apart and fall to the ground.

Human and dragon stared at one another, each appreciating the other's abilities. "That was a helluva lot hotter than I can get," Steve said, impressed. "I don't know if I could ever reach that temp. That tree blew away before it had a chance to fall. That's so cool!"

Deep growls emanated from the depths of the dragon, which had started to gently sway from side to side. Tendrils of smoke escaped from his nostrils as the dragon rocked back and forth.

He's laughing, Steve thought. An intelligent dragon with a sense of humor!

Giving a final snort, sending more smoke up into the air, Kahvel once again stretched his neck down so that he was at eye-level with the human fire thrower.

"Ye damn me with faint praise, human. Steve. Ye will do."

"I will do for what?"

Kri'Entu appeared at his side. In a hushed tone, he said, "I will explain later."

"Are we to begin tomorrow, then?" the dragon asked, his voice rumbling out across the orchard.

The king nodded. "Aye."

"So be it." The dragon lowered his head a final time to scrutinize the two humans. "Be ready at sunrise."

With that, the massive dragon retreated back into his temporary lair under the orchard.

Steve raised a hand. "Um, excuse me, what about sunrise tomorrow? Does something happen tomorrow morning?"

Again, the king nodded. "Aye. Your quest to find Maelnar starts tomorrow. We must make haste." The king paused, lowering his voice considerably. "I fear another attack on my son."

Chapter 10 – Allies

Returning to the Great Hall, the queen smiled at them, letting her gaze linger on Steve. "So tell me, what do ye think of Kahvel? Impressive, is he not? To think there are much larger dragons than he still amazes me."

Sarah raised her hand. "Pardon me, but did you say he is a small dragon? How big do they get?" She looked quickly over at her husband who was chatting with the king. "Never mind, scratch that." She took a deep breath. "We're leaving tomorrow to find Maelnar?"

The queen nodded.

"Do we get some sort of guide? We don't know the way, and I personally don't want to get lost."

Callé put a reassuring hand on her arm. "Aye, Sarah, ye will. In fact, ye just met him."

Sarah gasped aloud. "The dragon? We're going to be travelling alongside that dragon??"

"Aye."

"Just the two of us? Alone?!"

"One other will accompany ye. Who that is, I do not think my husband has decided. Many have already volunteered to go."

Sarah was dumbfounded. "There are actually people who would willingly volunteer to travel with a dragon?"

Callé shook her head. "If ye must know, the dragon is the deterrent. Dragons have been a known threat to our welfare for so long that it has been hard to break the stereotypical attitudes that people have towards them. Everyone would much rather travel with the Nohrin."

"Us? Why?"

"Ye are the famous Nohrin! To travel with the two of ye guarantees themselves a place in our history books!"

The king, Rhenyon, and a strangely quiescent Steve joined them. "Consider it an honor, Steve," the king was saying. "Ye have been deemed worthy by Kahvel. A dragon has the same feelings toward men that we have towards them. They do not trust us, as they are not trusted by men. To allow men to accompany them is a feat unprecedented in our history."

"So in just a matter of a few minutes, he decided he liked me?"

"Aye, that he did."

Sarah spoke up. "I just don't think travelling alone with a dragon is such a hot idea." She looked at her husband. "Sorry, no pun intended."

Steve grinned.

"Fear not, Sarah, for you will not be alone. Rhenyon here will be accompanying the two of ye tomorrow. He will speak on behalf of R'Tal should the need arise."

Rhenyon smiled at the two of them. "I am glad I was chosen for this honor. I will serve ye well."

Steve held out his arm. Rhenyon grasped it. "Glad you're here, buddy. Can't think of a better person to have with us for this little excursion."

Suddenly realizing he had some unfinished business with the captain of the royal guards, Steve unbuckled his belt and slid the jeweled dagger off to hand to the newest member of their party.

"I believe this is yours. Thanks for loaning it to us. Sorry it took so long to get back to you. Forgot about it until just now."

Rhenyon took the dagger, sliding it out of the sheath, gazing at it with unrestrained affection. "I am glad to have this back. This has been in my family for many generations."

"Thanks for trusting me with it."

Later, after they had finished their evening meal, both had elected to retire to their quarters early so they could rest prior to their departure the following day. However, as they were preparing to leave, Mikal called to them from across the Hall.

"Steve, Sarah! Wait!"

Steve paused, allowing Mikal to catch up. "Hey there, sport! What's up?"

Becoming accustomed to Steve's familiar monikers, Mikal grinned. "My father was wondering if you would come to the Antechamber."

Both Steve and Sarah hesitated. "Right now?" Sarah asked.

Mikal nodded.

"Did he just now send you?" Steve wanted to know.

"Aye, I just came from there. I think he wants to wish ye luck for yer journey tomorrow."

"Oh, okay."

They turned to follow their young friend back to the enchanted Antechamber, only to discover that the king was clearly in the middle of some type of meeting. Several people they didn't recognize stopped in mid-sentence to turn and stare at them. Sarah blinked. The closest person to her was incredibly short, with a thick, braided beard. The other was a thin, middle-aged man with short, steel-gray hair. Why did Mikal have them come here now? Clearly his father was busy with other matters. She stared at the short, stocky figure that was standing closest to her. In fact, she blinked a few times more, if she wasn't mistaken, this was a dwarf! His long, braided beard was tucked into a belt that had several small tools hanging from it. The dwarf studied the two humans intently.

"I beg your pardon," Steve said, as an uncomfortable silence began, "but your son asked us to come here. You're busy. We'll come back at a different time."

The king held up a hand. "Not at all. I asked the two of ye here."

Awkwardly, Steve and Sarah approached the strangers who were staring unabashedly at them.

The king walked over to them. The visitors followed. "Steve, Sarah, may I present Quisen, of the Kla Renhn clan."

The dwarf nodded.

"And may I introduce our resident wizard, Shardwyn."

The thin man jumped forward to excitedly pump Steve's hand. "Pleasure to meet ye, m'boy. Great things I have heard about ye! Are ye really a fire thrower? That is simply amazing! To think that outsiders can have that much power without -"

"Later, Shardwyn," the king murmured, "there will be more than enough time at a later date."

"Of course, yer majesty, of course."

"Now. Steve, Sarah, I asked ye here for a reason. The two of ye will be heading out on a long journey tomorrow."

They both nodded.

"It is customary in our land that when someone goes off on a long journey to send gifts with them. Quisen and his people volunteered their services. Let me just say that they have outdone themselves."

Steve held up a hand. "Wait a moment. You're a dwarf?"

Quisen nodded.

"Then can you tell us where to find Maelnar?"

Quisen shook his head. "With regret, lad, I cannot. My clan lives far to the south, deep in the heart of the Selekais. I know naught of Maelnar but legends of his skill."

"Oh, okay. I didn't know there was more than one dwarf clan."

"There are far more that ye would think, human."

"Getting back on track," the king interrupted, "Quisen, go ahead."

Turning, the dwarf retrieved his bundle of gifts that he had placed next to the hearth. Untying the straps, he withdrew a white shirt. He handed it to Sarah.

"This is the finest armor our craftsmen can make. The threads are of pure bryl, our strongest metal. Ye will find it as light as a feather."

Sarah took the shirt and felt the texture. It felt like silk! This was armor? It looked as though a simple thorn would be capable of ripping it to shreds.

Sensing Sarah's thoughts, Quisen took the shirt, laid it on the floor, and with a yell, struck it a mighty blow from an ax that was on his belt. Not the slightest mark could be found on the shirt.

"That's remarkable! Thank you so much!"

He turned to Steve, who was admiring Sarah's gift. The dwarf handed him a package next. Opening it, Steve discovered a pair of leather gauntlets. He fit one to his right hand. Flexing his fingers, he was pleased to see a perfect fit.

"These gauntlets," the dwarf began, "are also made of bryl. They will protect your hands from all types of injuries. Observe."

Quisen turned to a slab of stone that had been brought in for this very occasion. Donning the other gauntlet, the dwarf punched the stone. With a resounding crack, the stone broke in two. Pleased, he returned the gauntlet to Steve.

"It's made of the same material as that shirt? Looks like leather! Thank you! I will treasure this always!"

"The gauntlets were indeed crafted to resemble leather. We thought it best to disguise their true nature, lad, lest ye run afoul of thieves."

"Absolutely perfect. Many thanks, Quisen of the southern mountain dwarves!"

The dwarf bowed and stepped aside.

Shardwyn stepped up. "Guess it's my turn, is it not?" He chuckled and slapped Steve heartily on the back. "Thought long and hard, I did." He reached behind one of the chairs to retrieve his parcel. "I personally think," he continued, as he opened his bundle, "that this is one of my finest achievements. But then again," he winked at Sarah, "I am biased. Here we go."

He handed the separately wrapped packages to the two of them.

"Go on, go on, open 'em!"

Chuckling to himself, Steve couldn't recall ever having a more misguided preconception of what a wizard would look like or how he'd behave. He acted like, well, like how he could see himself behaving when he hit that age. He chuckled again. Best not to bring that up.

He took his package and unwrapped it, revealing… a billy club? There was also some type of harness there with small pouches sewn into the straps. He checked to see what Sarah's held. Hers was some type of a medallion with a big, fat purple crystal sitting in the middle of it. He removed the wrappings from his 'club', picked it up and glanced at the wizard. What was he supposed to do with this? Sneak up on an adversary and thump them on the head?

Shardwyn noted his quizzical expression and started laughing. Big, fat tears rolled down his wrinkled face as he tried to control himself. Still chuckling, he wiped his eyes with his beard.

"I am very sorry, but ye should have seen the look on your face! Priceless!" He snorted out a few more chuckles.

Sighing inwardly, the king yet again steered the wizard back on track.

"Disguise, m'boy! It is in disguise! Just like Quisen here, I decided to make it look undesirable! Who'd want to steal that? Hoo hoo! My best work ever!"

Hefting it in his hand, he looked at the (still) laughing sorcerer. "So what does it do, then?"

"I will show ye, I will, and ye will see how clever this is! This is the 'nohrstaf', named in yer honor!" He took the club from Steve and then faced the dwarf, who had been watching with rapt attention. "If ye would be so kind, sir Quisen, as to approach with yer ax in hand. Go on, come at me!"

"And what will happen?" Quisen hesitantly asked. Tales of the quirky wizard have been told as far south as his beloved Selekais. He cautiously pulled his ax off of his belt.

"No harm will befall ye, trust me! Come at me!"

The dwarf approached the wizard, waving his ax from side to side. Suddenly, Shardwyn was holding a sword. Stunned, the dwarf retreated, putting his ax away. The sword vanished, and the club returned. Amazed, he again drew his ax and made a downward striking motion towards the cackling wizard. He stopped the descent of his ax lest it hit the shield that had appeared.

"That is truly amazing, wizard," the dwarf admitted. "I would know how ye came about crafting that weapon."

"A wizard never tells his secrets!"

Sighing, the dwarf returned to his spot by the hearth.

Sarah took her medallion out of the box and admired it. It had a large amethyst centered in a silver and gold setting, but it looked tarnished! Was it supposed to look that way? Must be in disguise, too, she mused.

"What does this do?" she asked the wizard.

"That is the strongest protective charm I have created thus far in my life!" Shardwyn said proudly. "While ye wear that ye will be immune to any jhorun. However, if ye are physically attacked, then it will be ineffective. Very important to remember that, miss."

"Will ye demonstrate the medallion's charms please?" the king asked.

"Thought ye would never ask!" Shardwyn gleefully rubbed his hands together. "Let's see, who can we get to attack the lady?" The wizard's crafty eyes alighted on Steve. "Perfect! Fire off a blast at yer wife and watch what happens!"

Steve snorted. "I don't think so."

Sarah shoved the medallion into her husband's hands. "Nuh uh, no way. You're not going to make me the guinea pig."

"Here, let's do this." Steve took the medallion from Sarah and placed it around his neck. "Okay, use me. Someone try to do something to me."

In the blink of an eye, Shardwyn had summoned an intense, frigid blast of air and fired it straight at Steve's chest. Within moments, a ten foot tall block of ice had completely enveloped him, hiding him from sight.

Sarah rushed to the mini-iceberg. "Omigod! Honey, are you okay? Say something!"

Steve's muffled voice could barely be heard through the thick ice. "This is freakin' cool!"

Sarah scowled at the grinning wizard. "Okay, you put him in there. Get him out!"

Shardwyn had just raised his arms when Steve's faint voice sounded again.

"Move back! I can get out of this."

Rivulets of streaming water poured off the block of ice, creating pools of water on the floor. In a matter of a few seconds, the ice had rapidly melted right before their eyes.

"See?" Shardwyn was cackling triumphantly. "Not a hair on his head has been harmed!"

"From his own jhorun keeping him warm or from the medallion?" the king wanted to know.

The wizard's mouth closed with a snap.

"I have a better idea." Kri'Entu turned to address the shadows on the far wall. "Tristan."

The tall, quiet soldier materialized next to the king's side.

"Sir."

"Use yer daggers. Try to attack Sir Steve."

Tristan didn't even blink an eye. A dagger appeared in his hand as he faced the fire thrower. A split second later, the knife had been thrown straight at the dumbstruck Nohrin.

Steve blinked. One moment Tristan had been standing right before him. The next, a flash of green light had temporarily blinded him. When the spots finally cleared from his vision, he could see the dagger lying on the ground in front of him. Tristan was just regaining his feet from his hasty journey across the Antechamber.

Sarah was giving the fallen soldier a hand up.

"Are you okay? That was a nasty tumble you took."

"I am fine. I have taken worse."

"I would say that was a successful test," Steve observed, removing the medallion from his neck and returning it to his wife.

Quisen was staring at the medallion with unabashed curiosity. Seeing that the dwarf wanted a closer look, Sarah took off the pendant and handed it to him.

Surprise spread over his features as the dwarf was handed the prized medallion. His respect for these two trusting humans increased by several notches as he held the medallion up close to his face, inspecting it this way and that. He gently prodded the metal, applying pressure to one end, then the other. With a soft click, a hidden compartment on the back of the medallion appeared, exposing a tiny vial. With a triumphant grunt, the dwarf held up the medallion.

"Hah! I thought as much."

"Ye are good, dwarf," Shardwyn admitted, "Ye found that very quickly. That is a vial of kaormac juice. Just one drop will heal practically any wound."

The dwarf grunted his approval, tucking the precious vial back into the compartment. He returned the pendant to Sarah, who placed it back around her neck.

"Thank you, Shardwyn, this means a lot to me. I don't think I'll ever take it off."

The wizard beamed with pleasure. "One more thing, Sir Steve. Ye will notice the nohrstaf harness has pouches on it?"

Steve pulled the harness out and inspected the pouches sewn into the straps. He opened one to reveal a mimet, the nine-sided crystal disc.

"Ye are familiar with a mimet?"

Steve nodded. "Yes, actually the king here told me what they were and even demonstrated their use for me. Trust me, I won't forget what it can do." He absent-mindedly ran his hands down the front of his tunic.

Sarah smiled, and had to look away. The king smiled as well, noting her behavior.

"Excellent, m'boy, excellent! Start charging them now. Incredibly handy, those things! Never know when you will need 'em!"

The king clapped his hands together. "So! The two of ye will start yer journey tomorrow morning. Rhenyon will meet the two of ye out by the southern moat just before sunrise. Ye need your rest. Go now, for ye have a long day ahead of ye. Good journey to ye."

Both Steve and Sarah bowed before the king. "Thank you, your majesty."

Husband and wife slept fitfully. Clearly they were anxious to start their journey the following morning. Steve couldn't get the fantastic notion of travelling with a dragon out of his head while Sarah fretted about not being able to locate the dwarf key maker. Realizing that the other was already awake, both decided to give up trying to fall asleep, opting instead for an early start. However, a stealthy departure wasn't to be had.

Standing at the entrance to the Great Hall, both stared in disbelief at the pandemonium before them. Cooks were scrambling to prepare food, servants were busy wiping down tables, and pages were hastily polishing numerous pieces of armor. Squires then fastened those pieces to stationary men holding their arms aloft.

"Did we miss something?" Steve inquired, looking about. "Why are so many people awake? This has got to be super early."

They would have made it down even earlier, but Steve ran into a little trouble trying to don the custom norhstaf holder. It consisted of a metal plate designed to fit into the small of the back with several small, elastic loops embedded into it to allow the weapon to be easily removed and deployed. The problem came, however, from the four straps sticking out of all four corners that required his arms to slip into the harness just so, buckling securely into place below his right arm. Fortunately, once the brains of the outfit figured out where each strap went, she was able to tighten the harness snugly with no possibility of losing the unique weapon.

Outfitted in a pair of khaki trousers and a loose-fitting green doublet, Steve escorted his wife into the heart of the mayhem. Sarah, wearing comfortable travelling clothes consisting of a long-sleeve forest green top and grey leggings (she utterly refused to wear a dress), fingered the medallion around her neck, reassured by its presence. Were all these people awake because of them? The sun hadn't even come up, and yet it appeared as though the entire castle had been awake for hours.

They rushed through their breakfast, both eager to commence this latest undertaking. The sooner they located this maker of keys, the sooner they could return home.

Not surprisingly, they were met outside by the Kri'yans, including a young boy who was using every trick in his arsenal to persuade his parents to allow him to join the troupe. Mikal's parents, however, were unmoved by his performance. Silencing his son with a disapproving look, the king greeted the new arrivals.

"I do envy the two of ye the journey ye are about to undertake."

Steve met the queen's gaze before he faced the king. "I have to be honest. I'm nervous about all of this. I'm starting to think that maybe we should have a few more members to this party. Like, say, your whole army."

The king gave Steve a paternal pat on the shoulder. "I spoke with Rhenyon last night and we agreed to send a small contingent of men along. Five were selected to join yer group."

Both of the Nohrin were nodding appreciatively. Sarah's eyes were drawn to the queen. Callé was smiling at her.

Did you suggest this?

The queen nodded.

Thank you.

The queen nodded again. *It's the least I could do.*

Rhenyon looked up as the clamoring began and grew in intensity. What the blazes was this? People were literally streaming out of the castle, angling straight for them. Was the entire castle now accompanying them on this quest?

"Ye have got to be kidding me," one of his men muttered under his breath.

"Apparently they wish to see us off," another soldier murmured.

Muted laughter sounded from all directions. Rhenyon turned to face his men.

"So much for an inconspicuous start." He sighed heavily. He had not slept well last night, either. Visions of dragons and belching fire kept interrupting his dreams, so he had figured he might as well abandon his futile attempts at getting some rest and opt for yet another check of their gear and supplies.

The captain surveyed the throng of people all heading straight towards them. At the front were the newly famous Nohrin, along with the king and queen. Congratulating himself yet again for being the first person to "discover" the identities of the Nohrin, he nodded his head at the tall foreigner as Steve gave him a two finger salute. He had been quite impressed with how the stranger had handled himself with the ruffians that had attacked them earlier. Personally, he reflected, had someone attacked he and his wife, and he had a jhorun as powerful as Steve's, there wouldn't have been any survivors. Yet the resourceful fire thrower had managed to incapacitate three of them. Three!

It had only taken about an hour to crack the three thugs. All of them were more than willing to divulge every detail they could remember, no matter how minute, about their failed plan to kidnap the young prince. However, none of them had been privy to more than just the absolute facts on what they needed to accomplish. None knew who had hired them, only that they had been hired by proxy, and their employer was a powerful man that was feared by everyone in their village. And that was the seaside Ylani village of Arlan.

He surveyed the five men he had chosen, the best of the castle militia. All were loyal to the crown and all were good in a fight. Pheron, his first lieutenant, had an extremely useful jhorun: nocturnal vision. Another lieutenant, Rhein, had a useful jhorun as well: daminalis. More specifically, he could make just about any small creature his familiar for a short period of time. The other three were fairly mediocre: one could persuade pontal to accelerate its growing cycle, a fact that the soldier desperately wanted to keep under wraps; another had the ability to always know which way was north, and the last soldier could actually polish metal to a shine just by touching it once. Needless to say one could not stare directly at him while he was fully dressed for battle in the direct sunlight.

Steve nodded at the five soldiers, all shifting their weight from leg to leg, impatient to leave.

"Mornin'. Where do we meet Kahvel at?"

"Far past the outskirts of the city," Rhenyon answered. "Steve, Sarah, may I present the other members of our group. This is lieutenant Pheron, lieutenant Rhein, Jalen, Kern, and Darius." Each soldier nodded as they were introduced.

The Kri'yans approached. The king grasped Steve's arm and gave a friendly shake. "Good luck to all of ye. Godspeed. May all of ye stay safe."

The queen took Sarah's hands. "I will have it ready just before midday. Good luck to ye."

"Thank you."

Much to Steve's embarrassment, everyone started applauding as they moved off through the southern gate, making their way towards the orchards. The echoes of their cheering could still be heard long after the castle was lost from sight.

"So what was that all about with the queen?" Steve asked. "What will be ready by midday?"

"Oh, just a little experiment she thought of that we're going to try."

"Well? What is it? Can't you tell me?"

"I don't want to say anything until I know for certain it'll work."

Steve grinned. "Fine. Be cryptic. I don't care. It's not like I'm curious or anything."

"Good. Thanks, honey."

"Okay, I'm curious," Steve confessed. "You're going to try something with your jhorun, aren't you?"

Sarah nodded.

"Just tell me!"

The only response he received was a smack on his arm.

The sun was nearing its zenith as the travelers finally left the capital city behind. The northwestern tip of Anakash Forest was visible several leagues away. In the meantime, however, an open expanse of grassy plains was before them, and their tour guide was nowhere in sight.

Rhein turned to the captain. "The dragon was supposed to meet us hours ago. No signs yet. Do we keep going?"

Rhenyon stroked his goatee thoughtfully. "I do not wish to delay any further." He glanced up, noting that the sun was practically overhead. "We will need to stop shortly for the midday meal. But I would like to at least make it to the forest's edge before we do."

"Aye, sir, we keep moving," Pheron said, overhearing. "The dragon will just have to catch up."

The deep bass rumbled directly behind them.

"Catch up? To bipeds? Methinks not."

Steve whirled around, along with Sarah and the rest of the company. Standing directly behind them was the enormous gold dragon, staring down at them. If Steve didn't know any better, he'd say that the dragon was actually smirking!

"How did you get there without us hearing you?" Sarah asked. "A creature your size would have surely made some type of noise."

"Not only did I manage to arrive unnoticed," Kahvel growled, "I did so before ye passed that last farm and have been following yer noisy progress. No doubt that masked my approach."

"Ye were following us?" Rhenyon asked, incredulous.

"Aye."

"That's amazing, Kahvel," Steve said. "How are you able to move without making a sound?"

"I have my ways, human," was the cryptic response.

Rhenyon and his men moved on, angling for a point in the distance where the forest appeared to be the thickest. While they conversed amongst themselves, Steve purposely held back, until he was walking next to the dragon. Sarah also slowed her pace to stay even with her husband.

"Is it true," Steve began, addressing the dragon, "that most dragons would never willingly associate themselves with men?"

The dragon looked down at the tiny biped. "Aye, that is correct, human. Yer kind and mine are a poor mix."

"So why go on this journey with us then? Couldn't you have just pointed us in the right direction and not trouble yourself with this? I mean," he gestured up into the sky, "wouldn't you rather be flying?"

"If I did not accompany ye, then ye would not survive traversing through the far north," the dragon answered.

"Isn't it easier for you to fly instead of walk?"

"Whether I fly or walk, it makes no difference for me. I agreed to escort ye through the domain of my brethren, and escort ye I will."

"Has anyone ever ridden a dragon?"

Kahvel snorted. "By that, I assume to mean has a human ever ridden on the back of a dragon? No. Not in my lifetime."

"Do you think that –"

"No, human," the dragon interrupted, "it will not happen. And do not attempt it."

"I- I wouldn't dare," Steve sputtered. "Well, honestly, I can't say I haven't thought about it," he admitted, "but I would never attempt it without permission."

"Ye do not have it," the dragon confirmed.

Sarah sighed, shaking her head. Even with a dragon this close, and warning him not to try, the thought had still infiltrated that one-track mind of his.

Those large golden orbs focused on Sarah. "Ye have an opinion, human female?"

Steeling herself, she turned to the dragon. "I will be honest, Kahvel, you intimidate me. I'm nervous walking this close to a creature that my own husband is fascinated with. To tell the truth, I'm worried he'll do something foolish."

"Hon!" Steve protested. "Do something foolish? Give me some credit, will you?"

"Credit? Fine. Answer me this, honestly. You've thought about what it'd be like, riding on his back, haven't you? Even after his warning, right?"

She looked at her husband's surprised face.

"Told you. Case closed."

"What human has not thought of riding on a dragon's back?" Kahvel asked. "Do not chide him for wanting what every human in this kingdom has desired their entire lives."

Dumbfounded, she again turned to Kahvel. "Are you taking sides here?" She waggled a finger at the huge dragon. "You may be bigger than me and able to turn me into a french fry, but don't even *think* about taking his side."

Kahvel snorted again, sending plumes of smoke high up into the air. The dragon's massive head turned to the diminutive human walking next to him. "Yer female, yer problem."

"Thanks a lot," Steve grumbled.

"My point," Sarah continued, casting a scolding look at the towering dragon, "is that my husband here will completely ignore his own personal safety if it's something that really captures his attention or fascination. I just don't want him going up to a strange dragon and start asking it questions because that's what he's used to, with you."

"I will make a pact with ye, human female," Kahvel began.

"Her name is Sarah," Steve supplied helpfully.

"Sarah." The dragon paused again. "I will make a pact with ye, Sarah."

Warily, she eyed the massive dragon. "I'm listening."

"I will keep an eye on yer mate for ye. If any of my brethren approach, I will make certain that he does not approach them until I deem it safe."

"And what do you require of me?"

The deep voice answered one word. "Conversation."

"I'm sorry?"

"Converse with me, Sarah, and I will uphold my end of the pact."

"Why?"

"Ye do not understand. My brethren are solitary," the dragon explained. "They do not seek the company of others, whereas I, myself, am naturally inquisitive about other cultures."

"You're curious about us! You want to learn about our world, don't you?"

The dragon nodded. "Aye, I do. How often will the chance arise to study a completely foreign culture?"

"Interesting."

"Excuse me, don't I have a say in this?"

She turned to her husband and made those distinctive shushing motions that every man was familiar with.

"That is the nature of our pact, Sarah," the dragon continued. "Do we have an accord?"

She beamed her smile at the dragon, all traces of nervousness vanishing. "We have an accord, Kahvel."

Satisfied, the dragon moved off in search of some unlucky prey for lunch. Steve caught his wife's arm, spinning her around.

"Okay, what was that all about? I don't need a babysitter."

Not wanting to create a scene there in the glade where everyone had stopped for their midday meal, she decided to invoke her secret weapon: Bambi eyes.

"Honey, this will make me feel better. Isn't that worth it?"

Steve sighed, rolling his eyes inward. She just had to hit him with that argument, to which he wasn't allowed, as a married man, to refute. So be it. Now he had a dragon looking out for him. As he thought about it, though, he couldn't stop the smile spreading from one ear to the other. He had a dragon for a guardian! An actual flesh and blood dragon was watching out for him!

Selecting a patch of grass that was partly shaded from the sun, Sarah sat down, pulling her husband down with her. Steve shrugged off his pack, stretching his back. Seems just like yesterday that he was wearing this thing, on the run from their kidnapper and hoping to make it to R'Tal as soon as possible. How long had they been here now, anyway? Steve was pondering the answer to that when Sarah gently prodded his shoulder.

"Hon, you're zoning. You okay?"

"Yeah, I was just wondering how long we've been here. I mean, what about home? My parents are going to wonder why I haven't called. Your parents, too. Aren't you concerned?"

"Can we do anything about it right this second?"

"Well, no."

"The way I see it," Sarah continued, "is that we are doing everything we can possibly be doing to get home. So why worry about something we have no control over?"

"What about our jobs?"

"What about them? Can we call in sick from here? Besides, aren't you the one who wanted to relocate to Coeur d'Alene? Start your own business? As for my bosses," Sarah said slowly, "they will be more concerned with my safety than anything. We're going to have some explaining to do when we get home, that's for sure. So until we do, I refuse to worry about it."

With that, she leaned up against the large shade tree and steadied her breathing. Moments later she closed her eyes, holding out her hands as though offering some type of prayer.

"What are you doing?"

"Quiet. Don't interrupt."

Intrigued, Steve watched as Sarah took another breath. Suddenly she was holding a large, heavy burlap pack.

"Oooof! Hon, help!"

Steve rushed forward to snatch the pack out of her hands. Whatever was in it weighed a ton. What was in this thing anyway? Curious, he made to untie the opening flap to peer inside but Sarah smacked his hands away.

"What are you doing? This is my surprise!"

"But, but- what is it? Is this the experiment of yours you were talking about with the queen?"

Smiling, Sarah nodded, rising to her feet. She took the bag from her husband and walked over to where Rhenyon sat, ready to pull out some of his travel rations: dried strips of meat and a small flask of water. He looked up as Sarah approached.

"Good day, Lady Sarah. What have ye got there?"

"Lady Sarah," she repeated, smiling. "I like the sounds of that. Anyway, this is for you." She handed the heavy pack over to the puzzled captain.

Rising to his feet, Rhenyon opened the pack and gave an exclamation of surprise.

"Wizards be damned! Where did this come from? I did not see ye or Steve carrying this!"

Rhenyon pushed back the flap and started pulling out tightly wrapped packages of food and three flasks of wine. The rest of his men were instantly on their feet, their bland provisions long forgotten. They each took a package and carefully unwrapped it, revealing two phedras each, still warm, some type of steamed vegetable, and, as Steve unwrapped his, one of those fat purple pears. Cups were produced, and the flasks were passed around, everyone filling their cups.

"You teleported that from the castle, did ye not?" Rhenyon took a big bite of one of his phedras. "I had not taken into consideration yer remarkable jhorun."

"It's actually something the queen thought of," Sarah explained. "I had asked her what I might be able to do that could be considered useful, and she wanted to know how much I could teleport at a time. I told her I truthfully didn't know, so she said that she'd have a pack of food all ready to go on the bed in our quarters. All I had to do was conjure the bag here. When we're finished, I'll send it back, where it will be filled and ready for the next time."

All the soldiers stopped eating and stared at her with awe, including her husband.

"Ye can keep providing provisions such as these?" one soldier asked, incredulously. He glanced at his captain. "I can get used to that."

"Would ye prefer if Lady Sarah accompanied us on all of our missions, Jalen?"

"Do ye want me to answer that, sir?"

Laughing, Rhenyon slapped the soldier on the back. "Ye will get soft eating like this all the time. Still, as long as it is readily available." He took another healthy bite of his phedra. Chewing thoughtfully, he glanced westward, to the edge of the forest.

Following his gaze, Steve looked at the forest's edge as well. "We should be able to make that in a couple of hours, don't you think?"

"Aye. Easily."

Finishing their meal, the soldiers looked uneasily at each other as they held their meticulously clean dishes.

"Uh, sir, what are we to do with these?"

"I know what I am going to do," Rhenyon answered, passing his dishes to Kern, who grudgingly accepted them.

Sarah came to their rescue, collecting dishes from everyone and returning everything into the pack. Smiling, she walked up to Rhenyon, holding the pack away from her. Interpreting the gesture as a request to take the bag from her, Rhenyon moved to grab the dangling strap when his hand passed through empty air, the pack vanishing right before his eyes.

"Lady Sarah, we are in yer debt. Ye have made six new friends this day. Keep up that type of service, and ye will have those six friends for life."

Sarah gave the soldiers one of her winning smiles. "It's the least I can do."

"Lady Sarah."

"Many thanks, milady."

"I thank ye, Lady Sarah."

By the time she returned to Steve's side, she was all but glowing.

"You're going to come in handy," Steve assured her.

The men finished breaking their small camp and made for the trees in the distance. The terrain remained smooth and level with no one really showing any signs of fatigue. They were making considerable progress towards the edge of Anakash Forest when Steve noticed the absence of the dragon.

"Where's Kahvel? Isn't he supposed to be our guide?"

"Since he's our guide, he'll know how to find us," Rhenyon called from the front of the line. "I do not think we need to worry about him. He will catch up when he can."

"What if he can't find us?" Steve wanted to know.

"It is easy, human," the familiar deep voice answered. "Ye follow the noise."

Steve whirled around. Sure enough, the golden dragon had approached silently yet again. How did he keep doing that? They weren't making that much noise, were they?

"How long were you there this time, dragon?" Rhenyon wanted to know.

"Perhaps a quarter hour."

"You certainly know how to move about with stealth, Kahvel," Sarah remarked. "For someone your size, that's impressive."

Kahvel unfolded his wings to momentarily stretch them out, temporarily casting a huge shadow over the amazed soldiers. Folding them back across his back, the enormous dragon gave a small, curt nod of his head.

"If I do not wish to be heard when I move about," Kahvel explained, "then I do not. How else could I be following the likes of ye without my presence being known?"

"We're about to enter the forest there," Steve pointed out. "Anything we need to know?"

Kahvel blinked, staring at the small human. "Need to know, human? Hmmm." The dragon was silent for a moment as it considered. "Ye will be walking amongst trees. Ye might find a leaf or two strewn about the ground."

Several soldiers snickered.

"Anything of relevance," Steve said impatiently.

The dragon chuckled, tendrils of smoke dancing in the air above him.

"Nothing that I am aware of," the dragon said, still chuckling.

Anakash Forest encompassed the entire northern region of Lentari, stretching from the western ocean all the way to the Great Sea of Koralis. At times the forest was many hundreds of leagues wide. Fortunately, though, the smaller southeastern section of the forest that they were about to traverse was only about twenty-five leagues wide before it jutted up against the base of the Bohani Mountains. The path they were aiming for, which would lead them to the northern lake, Raehón, should be somewhere close to the mountains.

The first thing Steve noticed, as they passed into the forest, was how quiet it was inside. Was it supposed to be this way? Where were the animals? Where were the chirps of the birds? The rustling of insects and such?

"Is it supposed to be this quiet?" Steve asked in a hushed tone.

"This forest is ancient," Kahvel rumbled, breaking the silence. "These trees were around long before dragons and men walked the earth. They are just as alive as any of us. They have their own means to protect themselves." Kahvel angled his long neck up to scrutinize the towering tree closest to them. "Respect them."

All eight humans were staring at the trees with the same thought in mind: just what would happen if one of them did fell a tree? In response to their unspoken thought, a tree directly ahead of them groaned a little, as if a strong wind were blowing. Several branches swayed in the non-existent breeze.

"No felling any trees," Rhenyon ordered. "Use fallen branches only as long as we are in this forest. Understood?"

There were choruses of 'ayes' as the soldiers hastily agreed.

Progress was slow through the thick trees as the ground started to slope gently upwards. Gathering wood for the fire tonight shouldn't be difficult, Steve mused, as there were fallen branches and trees everywhere. He was helping Sarah over a huge fallen log when the dragon moved up behind them.

Waiting patiently for the humans to climb over the tiny tree, Kahvel took note of his surroundings. He didn't particularly care for this forest. Actually, come to think of it, he didn't care for forests in general. There was too much debris on the ground. Fallen leaves, dried brush, broken limbs and branches were everywhere. One snort and the whole ground would fast become a raging inferno.

The dragon sighed. Instead of enjoying the freedom of gliding through the air he had become a nursemaid to a group of humans. Sure, he had gone on the record as saying walking or flying made no difference. But when one was walking amongst ancient, weathered trees much larger than you, with the tops of the trees many feet above his head, it made him yearn for the open skies. Still, the dragon mused, it would not take much for him to punch an opening in the canopy far above and vacate the area rapidly, if the need arose.

Darkness was starting to settle in when they emerged into a large clearing. A small, fast moving brook ran from west to east. Rhenyon glanced behind, half-expecting to find the dragon gone, but no, Kahvel emerged from the clearing and instinctively looked up. In less than a second his wings had unfolded and he propelled himself into the air. The resulting downdraft knocked everyone present onto the soft grass.

"He could at least have given a warning," Rhenyon grumbled as he and his men regained their feet.

"He's probably claustrophobic," Sarah suggested, "not that he'd ever admit it."

"We will set up camp here," Rhenyon ordered. "Jalen. Kern. Recon, two leagues."

Nodding, both men disappeared back into the forest.

"Where'd they go?"

"I told them to investigate everything within two leagues of our camp," Rhenyon explained to Sarah as he pulled gear out of his pack. "I do not want any surprises in the middle of the night."

Rhein had gathered a double armful of firewood and was setting up a large hearth. He pulled his tinder kit from his pack and prepared to get the fire started.

"Whatcha doin'?"

The veteran soldier glanced up. The male half of the Nohrin was peering into his hearth.

"Can I help ye with something, sir?"

"Actually, I was thinking I could help you."

The soldier stared at him for a moment, and then his eyes travelled down to his right hand clutching his worn piece of flint. He chuckled. "Aye, I believe ye can. Can ye start this for me?"

"Step back," Steve ordered.

As soon as Rhein took a few cautious steps backward the fire blazed up, crackling merrily.

Rhenyon's other lieutenant walked up. Steve thought a moment, trying to remember his name.

"It is Pheron, Sir Steve," the soldier said.

"You're a mind reader?" Steve wanted to know.

"No, sir, but it is not difficult to tell that ye were doing yer damnedest to remember my name."

Smiling sheepishly, he grinned at the friendly soldier. "Sorry."

Waving a hand to dismiss Steve's apology, Pheron turned to scrutinize the fire. "Ye and yer wife are truly an asset. Yer making our lives easier, that is for certain."

At that moment, Sarah walked up, carrying the heavy pack again. She smiled brightly at her husband, and then flashed a smile at Pheron.

The tall lieutenant stepped forward to relieve the heavy pack from her. Rhenyon approached then, surveying the fire and the pack. "Jalen was right. I can get used to this."

As Pheron passed out the provisions, he grunted with surprise. Reaching deep into the bag, he pulled out a sealed envelope with the king's insignia on it.

"Captain, I think ye should see this."

Rhenyon was on his feet in a flash. "What? What do ye have there?"

"Looks like a message." He passed the sealed envelope to the captain.

Breaking the seal, Rhenyon withdrew the folded piece of parchment and read the single word on its surface:

Progress?

Rhenyon smiled. Here was yet another aspect of Lady Sarah's jhorun he had failed to see the potential of. Communication. They could easily keep in contact by sending messages back and forth within the pack of provisions. Only, he didn't have…

"I do not have quill or ink. How am I to respond?" Rhenyon started looking through his own pack to see if anything would suffice.

"No need sir," Rhein said, reaching into a side pocket of the pack. He pulled out several quills, a sheaf of blank parchment, and a small bottle of ink. "Looks like they thought of that already."

"The Queen," said both Rhenyon and Pheron, in unison.

Detailing their progress thus far, as well as identifying the location of their camp, Rhenyon composed his response, tucked the parchment back into the envelope, where it sealed itself. Steve blinked a few times. Did he see that right? The envelope actually sealed itself?

Seeing the look on Steve's face, Rhenyon held up the envelope. "Is there something that ye wanted to add? I can append the message."

"It sealed itself."

"Aye, envelopes do that."

"Not in my world they don't."

"They do here. No doubt if I witnessed ye actually having to seal an envelope in yer world, I would have the same expression on my face."

"Yeah, well…" Steve thought a moment. "Okay, good point."

Returning the empty pack to their quarters in R'Tal, Sarah and Steve stretched out in their tent, falling asleep instantly.

"He sure does snore, that one," Pheron noted, nodding in the direction of the Nohrin's tent. Rhenyon twisted where he was sitting on the ground to look in their direction.

"Aye, that he does. It is a wonder Lady Sarah gets any sleep at all. Still, I am very glad that the both of them are here."

"And I, too." Pheron patted his full stomach. "I cannot think of the last time when I was on a mission where I did not have to worry about running out of provisions, or what those provisions would be when we could find some."

Rhenyon nodded in agreement. Kern and Jalen arrived then, having been relieved by Rhein and the quiet soldier, Darius. Raising an eyebrow, the captain looked at the new arrivals. "Well?"

"Nothing but trees for leagues around. We scouted farther north, on the route we plan on taking tomorrow. Nothing that we cannot handle."

"And Lady Sarah?" Rhenyon asked. "Remember we travel with a lady."

"She will be fine," Kern assured them.

"Nevertheless," Rhenyon said, "ask Rhein to find a familiar and check the area."

"Already did, sir. He found a small bird that scouted around. It remained calm the entire time. Nothing troubling."

"Excellent. Get something to eat."

"Did Lady Sarah teleport anything from the castle?"

"Aye, she did. It's over there, next to my pack."

The two soldiers eagerly took their provisions and retired for the night.

Dawn came quickly. One would think that every living creature within ten leagues of their camp slept *very* well. Birds were singing, insects were constantly chirping, and several small squirrel-type creatures appeared to be playing a very noisy game of tag.

The soldiers were all up and had their gear stowed before Sarah could even poke her head out of their tent. Damn, these guys were good!

Yawning, and stretching her back at the same time, she left the tent as quietly as possible. She knew her husband hadn't slept well. He had tossed and turned , moving about restlessly for most the night. He was finally asleep, so she let him be. No sooner had she stepped around her tent to see what everyone else was up to when she was accosted by one of the soldiers.

"So what have ye got for us today, Lady Sarah?" the soldier eagerly asked.

"Well, I don't know. Let's find out. You know, I'm sorry, I don't remember your name. Was it Kern?"

The soldier nodded.

"Kern, will you help me? That pack is heavy. When it appears in my hands, grab it, will you?"

Eager to help one of the famous Nohrin, the soldier tensed, waiting to snatch the pack the instant it appeared. Holding out her arms, Sarah closed her eyes, picturing the bed in their quarters back at the castle. There, on the bed, was the pack. *I want that pack to move from there to here*, Sarah ordered. The pack appeared in her arms. Even before the weight could register or her back could file a complaint, Kern had leaned forward to snatch the heavy bag from Sarah's outstretched arms. She blinked. Wow, he's good!

Like a pack of bloodhounds converging on their prey, the soldiers materialized next to their companion, eager for their share. Kern became her assistant from that day forward, always eager to help with whatever she required.

As Kern was passing out the individual packages of food, he pulled out the final bundle and handed it to Rhenyon. The captain took his portion and started to walk away when he suddenly turned back.

"Is there anything else in there? Perhaps a message?"

Kern opened the mouth of the pack as far as it would go, leaning forward to get a better look. Sure enough, the message was there, sitting on the bottom. He handed it to Rhenyon, who opened it, reading the handwritten message in the neat scrawl of the king.

Desperately curious, but not wanting to appear too nosy, Pheron fidgeted from one leg to the other, a fact not lost on his attentive captain. How often have they been able to keep in frequent contact like this? Even the fastest methods of communication, by trained familiar, or by jhorun, could easily take several hours, maybe even a half day. He fidgeted again.

Having long completed reading the message, Rhenyon chose to read it again. Slowly. He kept no secrets from his men, and he wasn't about to start now. However, having seen examples of his lieutenant's impatience, he decided to read as slowly as possible. Nodding sagely, as though he was now privy to the darkest secrets known to men, Rhenyon finally straightened, tossing the message into the hearth. There, that's what he had been waiting for. His lieutenant had actually given a small jerk, as though he was going to go after it.

"Wizards be damned, lieutenant. Ye want to read it? Fine." He leaned over into the hearth to snatch the crumpled paper out before it caught fire. Smoothing it out, he turned it around so everyone could read it.

Excellent. Keep us posted as to your progress.

"Profound, no?"

Pheron snorted with disgust.

Kahvel arrived with a bone-jarring thud as he landed in the glade. The impact of his landing was so great that the entire camp shook, with several tents coming close to being uprooted from the ground.

With a mischievous smile, Rhenyon turned to their enormous companion.

"Ye call that a quiet approach, dragon?"

The supple neck twisted, two reptilian eyes fixing on those of the captain.

"I chose to land in this manner," the dragon explained. "Not everyone in this camp appears to be awake. Perhaps they are now." Kahvel extended his wings, stretching them out to their fullest potential, before folding them flat against his back.

"Yeah, roger that," Steve grumbled, coming out of his tent. "You scared the crap out of me." He eyed the dragon with mild distaste. Any creature that was an early riser, be it human or otherwise, had some serious medical condition that should be treated. Immediately.

Kahvel leaned down low, meeting Steve as close to his eye level as he could. "Ye appear to be a bright ray of sunshine this morning."

Several soldiers snickered. Steve grunted. Sleepily, he looked around, judging the activity level of the camp, which was being dismantled efficiently right before his eyes. Crap. No time to relax for a bit. Sarah came up to him and gave him a quick kiss.

"Good morning. I was trying to let you sleep. Sorry."

"That's okay, it's time to be moving on. What's for breakfast?"

While Steve was digging through his parcel of food, Sarah gently nudged his elbow, gesturing at the hearth. He glanced over.

The fire had been banked for the night, but still had managed to reduce itself to just mere coals. Its primary use completed, no one had bothered to rekindle it. Darius was unsuccessfully trying to coax the fire back to life. He was desperate for a hot cup of tea. The art of fire-making had always eluded him, he thought with disgust. He hastily reassembled his tinder kit and shoved it angrily back into his pack. He gripped the small iron kettle, ready to upend the contents into the fire when he felt the heat generating from it. What was this? Curious, he flipped open the lid to look inside. The liquid was just now coming to a boil. His tea was steeping beautifully, assailing his nostrils with the aromatic scents of herbs and spices. It was then that his eyes found Steve's. The Nohrin grinned at him and gave a small nod of his head before he walked off to help his wife disassemble their tent.

As everyone gathered once more in the clearing, about to resume their trek through the forest, the dragon's deep voice sounded.

"Proceed northwest. Yer destination lies roughly twenty leagues from here, as the dragon flies," Kahvel instructed. "There ye will find a clearing a little smaller than this one. I will meet ye there just before sunset."

"How do you know it's there?" Steve asked. "Do you really know this forest that well?"

"In actuality, no," the dragon confessed. "But that is where I settled last night. I departed just before sunrise."

The downdraft from the dragon's wings blasted them all to the ground yet again.

"Confounded dragon," Rhenyon muttered darkly, rising to his feet. "He did that on purpose. I swear it."

True to his word, the dragon was waiting for them as they stumbled wearily into the small clearing. Travelling twenty leagues in a day was tiring enough, but complicating matters was the amount of debris strewn about the forest floor as well as the lack of a path to follow. And, of course, they were journeying uphill.

"You people seriously need to invent cars," Steve panted, struggling to catch his breath while doing his best to ignore the painful stitch in his side.

The closest soldier glanced over. He had hardly broken a sweat.

"Kahrs, sir Steve?" Rhein asked, casting his jhorun about for a familiar. "What is that?"

"Let's just call them horseless carts."

"What is so special about a cart without a horse?"

"The cart can still move around," Steve clarified. "Without the horse."

Rhein's jaw dropped open. "No horses?" The soldier thought about that for a moment. "Then what pulls the cart around?"

Steve grinned. "Modern technology. As soon as you discover how to do it, you'll love it. Trust me."

Wearily, Sarah sank to the grass-covered ground and stretched her back. As she took in the lush forest meadow she was sitting in, she asked herself yet again why she insisted on carrying a portion of their supplies in a smaller pack. She looked over at her husband, who had shrugged off the large pack he had been carrying. Hadn't he insisted on carrying everything himself? Hadn't he put up a fight about letting her borrow the smaller pack from one of the soldiers? But she had been adamant about pulling her own weight on this expedition, and damn it, she was going to do just that. Sore back be damned. Glancing up to see what everyone else was doing, she saw that most had already erected their tents and were preparing to start a fire. No, she corrected, as she watched Pheron dump armfuls of firewood into the large stone ring he had assembled. They were getting the fire ready for their human firestarter.

After providing everyone with their evening meal, and Rhenyon had written up his nightly progress report, Sarah finally sat down next to her husband by the entrance to their tent.

"Long day, huh?" he commented, eyeing his wife. "How're you holding up?"

"I'm sore," Sarah admitted.

"Me, too. I don't think I've ever walked this much in my entire life."

"It must be a truly alien culture indeed," the familiar voice of the dragon rumbled, "to live in a society where one does not use their own faculties as the main method of locomotion."

Without saying a word, husband and wife looked at each other. As one, they stood up and walked around to the rear of their tent. The dragon had approached from behind and was now resting on the ground, front forelegs actually crossed, as it studied the two approaching humans.

"Okay," Sarah started, wondering how to best phrase her response. "I need you to visualize something, Kahvel. Imagine you live in a society where there are so many people living so close together that there isn't enough room for them unless they build upwards."

"The domiciles that humans typically live in? Not enough room for every human to have their own?"

"Right. You take one human's house, and then on top of that, you build another, and then another, and so on. Now imagine a very big, very tall structure whose sole purpose was to provide shelter for hundreds of humans."

The dragon was silent as it contemplated this.

"Now, once you can imagine a structure such as that, it shouldn't be too difficult to imagine hundreds of such structures, all providing a specialized service, whether its shelter, food, entertainment, and so forth. Are you with me so far?"

The dragon silently nodded.

"My world has many such communities. These communities are so well structured and organized that hundreds of thousands of people can all live fairly close to one another."

Content to listen to his wife discuss aspects of their society with the dragon, Steve sat down companionably next to Kahvel, who paid him no notice.

"If every one of these humans," Sarah continued, "each chose to have their own horse for transportation purposes, then there wouldn't be room for all of them, would there? So there are community services in place that facilitate the transportation of large numbers of humans from one point to the other."

"And ye reside in an area such as ye describe?" the dragon asked.

"Well, no," Sarah confessed, "our city isn't that large. But the same concept goes. We have our own vehicle to get us to where we have to go. And when we go on really long journeys, such as this, it is necessary for us to use these vehicles lest the journey take many times longer than necessary."

"You believe this journey is taking too long?"

"Not necessarily," Sarah said quickly. "The point I'm trying to make is that the people in my world are unused to walking long distances because there are alternatives in place so you don't have to walk that far."

"Strange world indeed," Kahvel commented, "where humans would choose not to use their own appendages to move them about."

"I wish I could show you some pictures, Kahvel," Sarah said. "You could see for yourself what I mean. Then you could see these structures are even taller than these trees. By many, many times."

Kahvel angled his head up to note the distance to the far-off treetops. "Impressive," the dragon growled. "I do believe I would like to see that for my own eyes. The images you describe are difficult to visualize. I will consider what ye have told me, Sarah."

The dragon moved off, choosing a location near the far edge of the meadow to curl up. Clamping the tip of his tail firmly in his teeth, his golden eyes closed.

Steve stared at the still form of the dragon. "Is he biting his own tail?"

"Sure looks like it, doesn't it?"

"Why's he doing that?"

"How would I know that?" Sarah playfully pushed him towards the sleeping dragon. "You want to know, you go wake him up and ask him."

"Thanks, I'm good."

They settled into a comfortable routine, with the soldiers leading the procession, and Steve and Sarah bringing up the rear. Sometimes the dragon accompanied them and other times he gave directions and met them at an agreed upon rendezvous point. Sarah kept everyone well fed and in continuous contact with the castle.

She is turning out to be more useful than I am, Steve glumly thought to himself. There had to be something else he could do to be helpful. However, every time he offered his assistance to Rhenyon or one of the soldiers, he was politely refused.

"Best to not get in the way," Sarah had told him. She was starting to detect traces of irritation from her husband, but there simply wasn't anything to be done. The soldiers definitely had the routine down pat, she mused. Two always detached themselves from the group to scout around the area, looking for any signs of danger. Recon, Sarah reminded herself. That's what Rhenyon called it. While the two soldiers scouted, er, recon'ed, uh, investigated the surroundings, two more soldiers unpacked the gear and setup tents. The fifth collected wood to make the fire. Well, collected wood so that her husband could start the fire.

They had just fallen asleep for the night when Sarah jolted awake. Was someone shouting? Steve's snoring had all but eliminated the possibility of hearing background noises, but something had woken her up. Wait, there it was again. Multiple shouts this time. Someone was yelling about their arms. Sarah listened intently. There, more shouts about arms. Someone broke an arm? To arms? Yes, that was it. Wait. Wasn't that an order to arm yourself?? Giving her snoring husband a not-so-gentle shove on the arm, she scrambled into her clothes.

"What is it? What's going on?" Steve unceremoniously tumbled off of the cot and onto the hard ground. He noted his wife hastily dressing. He decided he'd better do the same. "Who's shouting?"

Sarah was just finishing pulling her clothes on. "I don't know, but it can't be good. Come on." She patted the medallion under her shirt, verifying it was there. Comforted, she moved behind Steve, eager to know what was going on.

Dressed, Steve positioned himself to keep his wife behind him as he cautiously poked his head out of their tent. Not much to see, however. It was pitch black outside. Steve glanced at the low level of flames just peeking over the rim of the hearth. It had been properly banked, intending to keep a small fire burning all throughout the night. The level of light emanating from the small fire was far from adequate, Steve thought. A split second later it roared up to five times its previous size, casting its much needed light out in all directions.

Kern ran up to them. "Lady Sarah! Sir Steve! Return to your tent! Ye do not want to present a target of yerselves!"

Sarah clutched her husband's arm tightly. "What is it? Are we under attack?"

"Aye, under attack by a flock of griffins. They've been stirred up somethin' fierce."

Pheron appeared briefly, shouting orders. He glanced over at the blazing campfire and saw Kern gesturing wildly to the Nohrin. Good, he had stoked the fire. "Kern! Catch!" He tossed over several torches. "Light these and get over to the southern edge of this clearing on the double. Move it!"

Without a second thought, Steve turned to Sarah, kissed her tenderly, and looked her straight in the eyes. "Back in the tent. No arguing. You wearing your medallion? Good. If something happens, get yourself back to the castle. Don't fight me on this, okay?"

"What do you think you're going to be able to do? These are griffins!"

"From the sounds of things, they don't like fire. If that's the case, then they aren't gonna like me at all."

"Here, before you go," Sarah ran into the tent and pulled Steve's leather gauntlets out of their pack, along with his prized nohrstaf. "Put these on. Please, be careful, okay?"

Steve donned his gauntlets as Sarah helped him into the harness. Reaching back to verify the norhstaf was snugly in place, he kissed Sarah one more time. Feeling fairly armed, he took off, running as hard as he could towards all the commotion.

Pheron peered into the sky, trying to see from which direction these blasted creatures were coming from. Jalen was down, a nasty gash on his right leg immobilizing him. Rhein had sustained a crippling blow on his left arm, no doubt breaking it, but had still refused to abandon his companions. The lieutenant was able to see in the dark, thanks to his jhorun, but by the time he could shout out the locations of the griffins he could see, they had already moved off.

Suddenly a large dark object swished by him at an amazing speed. A white flash of pain erupted in his right shoulder, his sword flying off into the darkness. With his right arm disabled, his choices were becoming bleak.

"My sword! I lost my damn sword! Fall back! We cannot fight what we cannot see!" Where the hell was Kern? How long could it take to light several torches? Gingerly feeling his shoulder, he could feel a warm sensation slowly spreading outwards. Outstanding. Now he was bleeding. Profusely by the feel of it. He pushed the pain aside. No time to worry about that right now. He had to find his sword.

Suddenly half the clearing lit up as twin jets of fire appeared out of nowhere, streaking upwards. Several griffins squawked loudly, swerving erratically to avoid the dual pillars of flames.

"Everyone behind me! Now!" Shooting blindly, Steve shot jet after jet of fire into the air. Squinting up into the night sky, he couldn't see a thing. How was he supposed to hit a griffin if he couldn't even see one? He had to be able to see what he was fighting. Okay, think light, think light. Something bright.

Pheron waved his good arm to attract his attention.

"Sir Steve, over here! Jalen is down and cannot move!"

Still firing off blast after blast of flames into the sky, Steve ran over to Pheron, who was crouching on the ground. The other wounded soldiers all made for the protective circle Steve's pyrotechnical abilities had created. A shield. He could really use a shield right about now. Without realizing what he was doing, he stretched his right arm behind him to grasp the nohrstaf strapped to his back. Pulling it out of its harness, Steve gave the small club a quick shake.

"Come on, sucker, I need a shield. Do your thing!"

The staff stubbornly retained its "billy-club" shape. Several loud squawks from somewhere above him had his eyes snapping back to the sky. Annoyed at the crackpot magician for giving him an experimental weapon, he decided to jam the club back into its holder. Suddenly, Steve grunted with surprise as his right arm was forcefully yanked downwards. The club had become a large heavy shield that he could barely lift off the ground. What good was this supposed to be?

"Excellent, Sir Steve!" Rhein exclaimed, taking the shield from the Nohrin. The soldier hefted it easily as he stood over his fallen companion, shielding Jalen from the attacking griffins. Both hands now free, Steve turned his attention back to the sky.

Concentrating furiously, he focused his jhorun, ordering it to create light, and lots of it. As before, the tingles started intensifying, but this time in both hands. Just as he aimed both palms straight up, his hands flared, the ensuing fireball spiraling high up into the sky. As a result, the entire clearing was illuminated, albeit only for a few moments as his jumbo flare flew high into the air. Hah! There they were! Steve counted a half dozen of the mythological beasties all circling overhead, deftly weaving in and around the blasts of fire.

"I see you now, you lily-livered sons of bitches. Have a taste of this!" Adjusting his aim to deliberately graze the pinfeathers of the closest griffin, he watched with satisfaction as the attacking creature screeched in protest and retreated higher into the sky.

Continuously blasting jets of fire to illuminate the surrounding countryside, Steve was able to keep the circling griffins at bay. Every so often one would skirt the flames and try to attack one of the men who had fallen in behind him, but an intense blast was all it took to send the offending griffin retreating back up into the sky, squawking angrily. However, while he was able to keep the griffins in check, Steve discovered that he was unable to let his attention stray, for if it did, then the ever observant griffins would attack the moment his flames lessened. Man, they were fast!

For the first time, he started feeling the effects of his draining jhorun. He was expelling a tremendous amount of energy into the air as he was protecting his companions from harm. If he kept battling like this, he could see himself becoming depleted soon. Either he'll have to tone it down, or else frighten them away.

His jhorun apparently agreed. Steve felt the familiar sting coming from his right hand. Eyeing it, he watched as the 'chaser-fireball' formed, ready to be thrown. If he threw that, then that would mean…

"Alright, you guys, listen closely up there! I know you can hear me, and I know you can understand me." That was actually a bluff. He didn't know if they understood human-speech, but if a dragon could, then so could a griffin, right? "You guys are obviously pissed off at something. Rest assured, we didn't do anything."

Angry screeches sounded from above.

"Now, I hereby swear," Steve vowed, "that if you so much as try to attack us again, I'm gonna release this. See this?" He raised the fireball for all to see. "I let this go and at least one of you goes down, possibly more. You got that? I don't give a shit if you're species is 'protected' or not. I'm a non-Lentarian. What do I have to worry about?" He peered into the sky, barely discerning the circling shapes far above him. He hefted the chaser and tried one last time. "Don't make me use this! I don't want to, but I will!"

Several squawks filtered down from above as the irate griffins conversed amongst themselves. After several tense moments, there was a sudden silence as one of the creatures started circling lower and lower. Taking careful aim at the approaching griffin, Steve waited. This one was behaving differently, as if it was sizing him up as an opponent. It landed gracefully a safe distance away, folded its wings, and eyed Steve warily.

"Ye say ye are not responsible for destroying dozens of our nests?" The voice was high-pitched and somewhat nasally. "That ye know nothing of the torture our young suffered? Tell me why I should believe that, human."

First talking dragons, now talking griffins. Pushing his amazement aside, he faced the courageous griffin.

"Someone attacked your nests? Do you know who?"

"Aye. Human soldiers." Pointing a wing at the soldiers who were still assessing damage to themselves and to their gear, the griffin squawked angrily. "Them."

Signaling the griffin to wait a moment, Steve extinguished the chaser and called out to the closest soldier. "Darius, have you seen Rhenyon? I need him over here immediately."

The normally quiet soldier refused to take his eyes off the sky for more than a few seconds. He had had his back to Steve and therefore had not noticed the arrival of one of their attackers. "He was last seen tending Pheron, who was hit on his shoulder fairly badly."

"Take his place then. This is important. You have to get him over here. Now."

"Sir Steve, we are a little busy here. Can this wait?" His restless eyes darted back up into the night sky, looking for indications that the circling griffins were preparing to strike again.

"They aren't going to attack. At least not anytime soon." Steve looked back at the griffin, who nodded in agreement.

This human was different. Why, the griffin could not say. But it appeared as though he truly wanted to help. If this fire thrower had wanted them dead, then dead they would have been by now.

"And how can ye guarantee that we will not be attacked again? Ye cannot, can ye?"

"I cannot, true," Steve smiled, hooking a thumb over his shoulder. "But he can."

Darius' eyes opened wide as he observed the griffin waiting silently ten meters or so behind Steve.

"What-"

"We have a bigger problem. Go get Rhenyon."

"At once, sir." In a flash, Darius was gone.

Turning back to the griffin, Steve raised his hands in what he hoped was a universal sign of friendship. It was then that he noticed both hands were still lit. Hastily extinguishing them, he gave the griffin what he hoped was a friendly smile.

"Tell me, your young, were they hurt badly? I know of someone that could help, if you'd trust me."

The griffin stared at him. Slowly, he approached. Since when would a wizard care about what happened to one of his kind?

"How can ye help, human? What knowledge have ye about the physiology of a griffin?"

"Not a damn bit," Steve confessed, "but I don't have to. We have a vial of, um, some type of flower juice that is said to heal any wound."

The griffin blinked his eyes, surprised. "And ye would be willing to share some of this elixir to heal our cubs?"

"Yes, I would. Well, I know she would." At the quizzical cocking of the griffin's head, Steve explained even further. "My wife holds the vial. She disperses the elixir to those who need it."

Wanting desperately to believe this human, for his cub's sake, the griffin fought an internal war. All his instincts warned him not to trust humans, but his parental instincts won him over.

"An ye can, human, I would ask yer assistance. For my cub and for the others that have been injured."

Darius appeared then, with Rhenyon hot on his heels. The captain stared in amazement as he noticed the griffin waiting quietly a few meters off.

"Wizards be damned. Let us put an end to this once and…"

The griffin extended both wings and was poised to attack, or return to the air. Steve couldn't tell which.

"Rhenyon, wait." He hastily stepped between griffin and soldier. "He says that their nests were attacked, and their cubs were seriously hurt. He says that soldiers did it."

In the process of unsheathing his sword, the captain hesitated. "What soldiers? My soldiers? I think not, griffin."

"And if it's someone else, masquerading as Lentarian soldiers, hoping to stir up trouble? What then?"

That brought the captain up short.

"Aye, it is possible." Rhenyon conceded, turning to face the griffin. "I know it is none of our soldiers, griffin. We are stretched thin searching for a dwarf."

"I will accept for now that yer soldiers were not responsible," the griffin said. He craned his neck up and gave a long series of screeches and squawks. Within moments five other griffins were standing next to their spokesman, all eyeing the soldiers with distaste.

"Can you get the cubs here? I'm guessing you can bring them here faster than we can get to them."

"Aye, that we can." More squawks and high-pitched trills. Two of the griffins took flight immediately, disappearing into the night.

Steve turned to the confused captain of the guard. "Their cubs have been hurt and are being brought here. Several of you have also been hurt. Can someone go get Sarah for me? I really need her now. Make sure she still has her medallion on. Oh, and be sure to tell her that I'm fine. I don't want her freaking out."

"Darius, fetch Lady Sarah. On the double."

When he returned, a breathless Sarah ran over to Steve, hugging him hard.

"Are you okay?"

"I'm fine. A couple of the soldiers here could use some of that stuff in the vial. And we're going to be helping the griffins. Some of their cubs were injured earlier."

Sarah was appalled. "Their babies were attacked? That's horrible!" Her eyes opened wide, staring at the soldiers. "Tell me they didn't…"

"No, they didn't. But we're guessing it's someone posing as Lentarian soldiers looking to start trouble."

Sarah removed her pendant and activated the hidden switch. She took the small vial containing nectar of the rare kaormac orchid and removed the small crystal stopper. She surveyed the men before her.

"Alright now, who's hurt?"

She was directed to Pheron first, who had obtained a very deep gash across his right shoulder. His right arm also appeared to have been broken. The bleeding had yet to stop and was evident that the lieutenant was in serious pain. His eyes were glazed and he winced at every movement he was forced to make. Withdrawing the tiny dropper from within the vial, Sarah administered the smallest of drops to his wound. Right before her eyes, Pheron's skin sealed itself back together, torn muscles reattaching themselves, severed tendons becoming whole. The fracture in his right arm withdrew into itself until it was no more as well.

Pheron blinked. One second he was in immense pain, and the next? Nothing! It felt as though his wound was gone. What ointment was this? Gingerly, he prodded his right shoulder. No pain. Probing further, he couldn't provoke an ounce of protest from either shoulder or arm. Baffled, he sat up and pulled the bandages off of his chest. Flexing his right arm, he stared at Sarah.

"My shoulder and arm are healed? How can that be?"

Sarah smiled at the lieutenant. "Job security. Excuse me."

The newly appointed Director of Medical Services moved off in search of others that needed her help. Kneeling down in various spots, she administered aid to every soldier but Darius, who was uninjured.

Steve smiled as he watched his wife moved amongst the soldiers. If they weren't devoted to her before, they sure as hell were now! Out of the corner of his eye he noticed the griffin watching his wife applying more of the precious elixir.

"I'm sorry, I didn't think to ask. Have you been injured?"

The supple neck snapped around. "I am unharmed. We did sustain several injuries. One of our scouts had most of the feathers on his left wing burned. I presume that ye are responsible for that."

Sarah returned in time to hear the griffin mention one of his group was hurt.

"Which one? Who's hurt?"

The surprised griffins all eyed each other. Would they be willing to let this human female heal them? The griffin with the scorched feathers stepped forward. His left wing still stung, threatening to ground him until he had a chance to heal. If this human female could heal him, then he'd be more than willing to take the chance.

Sarah nervously approached the griffin, which was holding out his injured left wing. Feathers were darkened and scorched everywhere. A single, tiny drop restored them to their full luster. Squawking appreciatively, the healed griffin rejoined his fellows, only to be pushed aside as the others approached the human woman, presenting beaks, talons, wings, and so on.

Sarah had just finished healing the last of the company of griffins when a screech sounded in the distance. She instantly scooted behind Steve, waiting to see what was heading their way this time.

A group of twenty griffins landed, with a dozen or so holding spindly cubs in their beaks. She started towards them when the leader of the griffins spoke. "Do not approach yet, human female. Ye will more than likely be attacked. A moment, if ye please."

The griffin moved amongst his fellows, squawking and chirping, no doubt explaining that the female human will heal them if they allow it. Several times they heard indignant screeches. Finally, the injured griffin with the previously torched feathers squawked his own defense for the humans. The females finally relented, approaching tentatively with their young. Ever so cautiously, with no sudden movements, Sarah applied a tiny drop to each of the creatures that requested her services.

Thirty minutes later, the newly healed phalanx of griffins, with their cubs hovering close by, stretched their wings and forelegs, settling down in the clearing as far from the humans as possible.

Rhenyon sidled up to Steve. "What is this? Why are they not flying away?"

Steve shrugged. "I have no idea. I just figured they'd go about their business. Maybe something is wrong. I'll go ask."

Waving his arms finally got the attention of the head griffin, who decided to draw near the powerful human once more. With his newly healed cub in tow, the griffin approached.

"Human. What is it?"

"Everyone calls me Steve. What's your name?"

The griffin hesitated before answering. "Pheris."

"Pheris, is everything alright? We can't help but notice that you guys haven't flown away. Is there something we can do to help?"

"My fellow griffins are tired," Pheris explained. "We never had a chance to finish our hunt. Myself and a couple others are now forced to hunt at night."

"Do you typically hunt at night?"

The griffin shook his head no.

"So you and the others are hungry, is that it? You didn't finish your hunt?" The griffin wearily nodded. "Would you permit me to see if we can help out one more time?"

The griffin looked down at his cub, his eyes full of pride and concern. He looked back at the human.

"There are over thirty of us. How can ye hunt for numbers such as this?"

"How do you plan to? Besides, I never said I was going to hunt. But we should still be able to help. Wait here, we'll take care of this."

Running back to Rhenyon, who had overheard the entire conversation, he motioned for his wife to join him as well. The three of them huddled together.

"Exactly how do ye plan to provide meals for that many griffins?"

"I'm not, Rhenyon. Sarah is."

Sarah choked. "Me? I can't hunt!"

"You don't have to. I'm willing to bet that the castle has everything we need. Think you can teleport the supplies we need here?"

"I don't know where they keep that sort of thing! Why would you think that I could?"

"Just trust me. If I can get a pack full of meat back on the bed in our quarters, you could bring it here, right?"

"Well, yes, but how are you going to do that?"

"Get word to the king," Rhenyon answered. "He will do whatever he can to help. He is a strong advocate for fostering interspecies relations."

"I can only send things back and forth in that pack from our quarters," Sarah explained. "I don't think the king will be in our room."

Rhenyon thought a moment. "Can ye place a message on his desk in the Antechamber? That is where he would be right now. He does not retire until much later than this."

Sarah concentrated, bringing up a mental picture of the Antechamber and the king's desk. That's where the map was, she recollected. The king had given an overview about the kingdom of Lentari to Steve there. Yes, she could visualize that desk very clearly. She was sure she could drop a letter right on the desk, if that's where the king was.

"Yes, I believe I can do that."

After parchment and ink had been retrieved from their camp, Rhenyon hastily scratched out his request:

Sire, are ye there? If so, respond here on this parchment. Will wait a moment before retrieving – Rhenyon

He folded up the paper and handed it to Sarah. She took it, closed her eyes, and conjured up the image of the king's desk. In case he was leaning over the desk for any reason, she chose to drop the letter several feet over the surface of the desk and let it fall the remaining several feet. If he wasn't at the desk, but in the Antechamber, it should attract notice. The paper in her hand vanished. She looked at Rhenyon.

"Now what?"

"We shall give him a moment to notice it, read it, and write a response. Then you can bring it back here."

After giving the king about thirty seconds to respond to the message, Sarah retrieved the paper. She handed it to Rhenyon, who unfolded it at once. There, below his message, was the king's neat handwriting:

I am here. What is it?

Rhenyon composed his response:

Brokering deal with griffins. Crucial. Will explain later. Need ye to take the pack ye have been filling with food and fill it to the brim with raw meat. Put in same spot for Sarah to teleport. Will return it as soon as emptied. Will need to keep refilling until advised. Awaiting response.

He refolded the paper and handed it back to Sarah, who sent it to the king. After giving him a full minute, Sarah returned the parchment.

Acknowledged. Ready in ten minutes.

Rhenyon smiled. "Excellent." He took the pen and wrote back, *Understood, sir. Our thanks.*

"Be ready to teleport the pack," he said to Sarah. "But we will have to help ye with it. It will be full of meat, so will be very heavy."

"We'll be ready," Steve assured him.

In ten minutes time, standing in front of the skeptical griffins, Sarah teleported the pack into her arms, then toppled forward. It must have weighed over seventy pounds. Luckily, there was a ring of soldiers standing around her, all waiting to grab the pack the moment it appeared.

Kern and Pheron got to it first. They gently set the pack on the ground while Steve untied the drawstring opening and gestured for Pheris to come over. The skeptical griffin peered in the pack and squawked with surprise.

"How do you want us to do this? Just dump it out or would you like to take the pieces out and hand it out yourself?"

"This will not be enough, human, but I do thank ye. We will let the cubs feed, and if there is anything left over, we will eat what we can."

"Ummm, you don't understand. As soon as this is emptied, it'll be sent back to be refilled, where it'll then be brought back here. We can keep doing this until everyone has eaten their fill."

The griffin studied the fire thrower. "We are in yer debt, human." Several squawks had the griffins forming a line, much like you'd find at a buffet, with Pheris guiding them along.

It took two refills before the griffins were sated. It was Rhenyon who made the surprising next step.

"If ye like, all of ye are more than welcome to share the clearing with us. Ye can rest yerselves here before returning back to yer homes."

The griffin shook his head. "Appreciated, but we will return to the forest. On behalf of myself and my fellow griffins, I thank all of ye for yer kindness. It will not be forgotten."

In a massive flapping of wings, the griffins took to the air and disappeared into the blackness of the night.

Chapter 11 – Mountains

The following morning found everyone sitting together amidst their partially-dismantled camp. Steve's eyes travelled around his companions. Rhenyon's eyes were bloodshot. Pheron met his gaze and nodded his head. He was yawning constantly. Apparently no one had slept as well as he had.

Why wasn't anyone talking? Even when Sarah brought them their breakfast (still warm!) they had barely mumbled their thanks and sat back down, huddling together. Jalen and Rhein were nervously scanning the skies. Apparently they were expecting something to drop in unannounced. They weren't disappointed.

Making his daily appearance, Kahvel glided in from the north, touching down with a gentleness that was unbecoming for a creature of his size. No one even bothered to look up, let alone say a word of greeting.

Kahvel snorted. "Missed something, have I?"

"Where were you last night, dragon?" Rhenyon finally asked. "We could have used yer assistance."

"I take it that ye are referring to yer little skirmish with the griffins, are ye not?"

"If ye knew about it, why did ye not help?" Rhenyon got to his feet. "If not for Sir Steve, we would have been done for."

Kahvel leaned low, inspecting the soldier up close. "Ye sound like a man and smell like a man, yet ye whine like a human female not yet grown. Ye are still alive, are ye not?"

Rhenyon grunted. "No thanks to the likes of ye. Ye could have taken them out with one bite."

"The griffins were yer problem, not mine, human."

Trying to stave off open hostilities, Sarah stood up. "Rhenyon, I think what Kahvel is saying is that he couldn't do anything without creating a feud between dragons and griffins."

Rhenyon turned back to the large dragon. "Is that the truth, dragon?"

Kahvel nodded. "I believe I already said that."

As the soldiers stowed away the tents and gear, Kahvel approached Sarah and Steve.

"Held off a flock of griffins, did ye?"

Bursting with pride, Sarah turned to the huge dragon. "From what everyone told me, he held off a half dozen griffins by himself while those who were wounded could seek cover."

"So-"

"And," Sarah interrupted, "he managed to negotiate a truce between the soldiers and the griffins as well."

"Then-"

"To top it off," Sarah continued, steam-rolling right past the dragon, "he convinced the king to send food for the griffins, who had been interrupted in the middle of their hunt by their nests being attacked."

The massive dragon paused, waiting to see if the small human female was finished speaking.

"Well? What do you say to that?"

"Are ye finished then?"

Sarah smiled. "For now."

"Ye have done well, Steve." Kahvel's piercing gaze rested briefly on Sarah, before returning to Steve. "Ye did not dispatch any griffins?" Steve shook his head no. "Ye are to be commended. I could not say the same if I felt my mate threatened."

"I could have, very easily," Steve admitted, "but I didn't. Something didn't feel right. So I showed them that I could, and that's when they started listening. I'm just glad that one of them could understand me."

"Ye will find most species can understand one another," the dragon explained. "Whether or not they choose to reveal that information falls within their discretion."

By midday, the travelers finally spied the small, worn path leading northwest up into the mountains. Clutching the painful stitch in his side, Steve scowled as his eyes followed the path uphill.

Great, just great, he mused. Uphill. He hated anything uphill. Downhill hiking was just fine. This, however, was probably going to kill him.

Sensing her husband's thoughts, Sarah came up quietly behind him. "Just take it slow and easy," she advised, knowing full well that one of Steve's strengths was not travelling uphill.

"And if everyone else outpaces me?" Steve muttered darkly.

"Let's just see how it goes."

Steve grunted, his mood souring quickly. Fortunately for him, the pace adopted by the soldiers was a gentle one, with frequent breaks.

Unbeknownst to Steve, the soldier setting the pace out at the front of the procession was Pheron, who was deliberately going slow for Lady Sarah's sake. Heal a shoulder and get a devoted friend for life!

The Bohani Mountains were not what Steve had expected. He paused long enough to stoop down and scrape away at the ground. Aside from some loose pebbles, and a thin layer of gravel, there was no vegetation, no soil, just rock. Were all of these mountains as barren as this?

He was used to the peaks of northern Idaho, which were covered with evergreens, various wildflowers, and so on. Steve thought momentarily to the last experience he had exploring those woods. Squirrels had darted up and down the long trunks of the tall trees. Woodpeckers searched for food in the distance. The incessant chirping of insects sounded from all directions.

These mountains, however, were as barren as a prison cell and as quiet as a library on Sunday. The dwarves lived somewhere up there? Their cities were underground? Steve shook his head. He couldn't even begin to fathom the amount of manual labor necessary to bore through solid rock.

The pace was slower than Rhenyon would have liked, but at least it was progress. They had discovered a small mesa that had the remains of several campfires scattered about. Steve had sighed gratefully. Was this the equivalent of a rest area then?

"How long will we continue to follow this path?" Sarah asked.

Steve, taking a long swig of water from his leather canteen, snorted. "All the way, right?"

Sarah smiled, gently patting her husband's arm. "We're going into the heart of dragon territory. I seriously doubt a man-made road will take us within range of the dragons."

Pheron smiled, nodding his head. "Well spoken, Lady Sarah." Walking up to the female half of the Nohrin, the friendly lieutenant pulled out a folded piece of parchment: a smaller version of the map hanging in the Antechamber. Pointing to a spot just northwest of the boundary between forest and mountain, the soldier tapped a thin blue line.

"We are searching for this river," Pheron explained. "Its source originates high in these mountains. Now, we do not need to find the source, but if we travel upriver, it will take us to here," the lieutenant pointed to a small area devoid of hills and peaks just south of the lake. "This plateau is our destination. We believe the dwarven entrance lies somewhere around there."

"The entrance to the dwarven realm lies on a plateau?"

"Yes, milady."

"A plateau is flat. How can a door be on a plateau? I'd think it would be on a wall somewhere, and according to this map, there isn't any. Not unless we try here, west of the lake, or possibly the east, where the mountains start again."

Pheron was silent as he studied the map. The lady's logic was irrefutable. There could not be any doors there. Questioningly, he looked at the captain, who had overheard Sarah's remark. Rhenyon, in turn, stood and walked over to the map.

"The exact location of the dwarven entrance is unknown. The dwarves are said to be masters of illusion." The captain tapped the map, directly over the plateau. "The entrance is there. We have but to find it."

Finding the mountain stream did not prove to be an arduous task at all, nor was it difficult to follow it upstream. The river had done a wonderful job of burrowing into the rock, creating footholds everywhere. Countless years of erosion had created a naturally flat embankment on both sides of the fast moving river. In this manner, they were able to make close to ten leagues before they found a suitable place to camp for the night.

As the gear was unpacked and Sarah prepared to teleport the nightly provisions from R'Tal, Steve found himself giving Jalen a hand stocking wood for their nightly campfire. However, scraps of wood were scarce, and only a few pieces of driftwood could be found.

"Let us try searching over there, Sir Steve," Jalen suggested, pointing farther upstream. "There might be some wood up there."

Steve looked up at the dwindling daylight. "We have maybe fifteen more minutes before it's gonna start getting dark."

Following the sounds of splashing water, Steve and Jalen came upon a small waterfall.

"You check around here, I'll look up there," Steve instructed, climbing up the rocks to scout around the river upstream.

"Yes, sir."

If there were any branches or driftwood to be found beyond the waterfall, Steve wasn't able to find any. A splash of water and a curse announced the presence of his companion.

"Find anything down there?" Steve asked, turning around. A blinding flash of pain brought him to his knees. Spots appeared in his vision as he viciously fought off a growing sense of dizziness. The second blow knocked him forcefully to the ground. Steve blinked his eyes a few times, trying to ward off the darkness that was threatening to envelop him. He managed to make out a few blurry faces before finally slipping into unconsciousness.

"Has anyone seen Steve?"

"I have not, Lady Sarah." Kern gestured in Rhenyon's direction. "The captain will know where he is."

Smiling weakly, Sarah hurried to find the captain. This just wasn't like her husband. He would either be by her side at all times or else let her know what he was doing, especially in a situation such as this.

She found Rhenyon writing out his progress report on one of the blank pieces of parchment. He looked up as she approached. He nodded. "Lady Sarah."

"Have you seen Steve? I can't find him and it's not like him to wander off."

Rhenyon frowned. He quickly rose to his feet. One of the Nohrin was missing? Not good.

"All hands, report in."

Alarmed, all soldiers dropped what they were doing and snapped to attention.

"Pheron reporting in."

"Kern here."

"Darius reporting in."

"Rhein reporting in."

A pause. "Jalen?" Rhenyon called. "Report in, now!"

Another pause. "When was the last time anyone saw Jalen?"

"I saw him earlier, captain," Rhein reported, "I believe he was searching upriver for firewood."

Sarah and Rhenyon nervously eyed each other.

"That's the type of task that Steve would want to help with," Sarah said quietly to Rhenyon.

That did it. Rhenyon strapped on his sword. "Sir Steve is missing. Jalen is missing as well. Split up. Find them both. Signal if ye find anything, no matter how trivial."

The soldiers scrambled into their arms.

Sarah gently kissed him awake. The smell of bacon was in the air, along with the enticing aroma of fresh cinnamon rolls. Steve sighed.

He loved Sundays. Why was she bouncing on the bed, though? That's not like her. Maybe it was an earthquake? Semi driving past their house perhaps?

Reality came crashing down on him as he regained consciousness with a pounding headache. He was lying flat on his back in complete darkness. He also appeared to be in some type of cart that creaked and groaned over every rut in the road.

Gingerly he tried moving his arms. Tied. Legs? Tied as well. His eyes? Blindfolded. That explained the constant pressure over them. Was he in this cart by himself? Where were his captors? A soft whisper sounded nearby. Lying perfectly still, pretending to be asleep, he silently eavesdropped on his kidnappers.

"… s'posed to do if he wakes up?"

"The potion will keep him out for a few hours more. Be silent."

"Can we not give him another dose now?"

"Too much can kill him. He's too great a prize to risk it."

His blood boiled. Son of a *bitch*! Not again! Hell no! Time to get out of this predicament and cause of few of his own.

Focusing all his mental energies, Steve called upon his jhorun for a different type of task: burning something he couldn't see. Feeling the blindfold around his head, he stretched his neck silently from one side to the other, feeling the straps move slightly on his head.

There. Those straps by his ears. That'd be the perfect place to try.

Okay, Steve thought, addressing his jhorun, *you've been great so far. Done everything I've asked. I have another job for you. I want those straps to burn through. Just the straps.*

It only took a couple of moments before he could detect the scent of burnt leather. The pressure over his eyes lessened: the blindfold was loose. A quick jerk of his head had his vision restored. However, he still couldn't see anything. Damn. Nighttime. How long had he been out, anyway?

His eyes started adjusting to the absence of light, allowing him to see the faint outline of the cart he was laying in. As silently as possible, he twisted so that he could see the ropes binding his arms and legs. Hoping that no one was walking alongside the cart to smell what he was about to do, he focused his jhorun to produce a tiny pinprick of intense fire, and then caressed that red-hot dot along his bonds. His arms were free! Now, his legs. The ropes fell away, neatly sliced open. Making sure there wasn't any other ropes holding on to him, Steve contemplated his next course of action. Should he just jump out of the cart and yell surprise? Or should he maybe try to sneak out and make a break for it?

At that moment, the cart hit a series of ruts in the road, making quite a racket. Thinking quickly, he silently leapt out of the cart.

"Be careful, dolt! Do ye wish to wake him?"

Steve's angry voice came floating out of the darkness.

"And if he's already awake?"

Twin jets of fire illuminated the shocked faces of his captors, catching all by surprise. In that moment of illumination, Steve finally saw who he was dealing with. There were three of them, all dressed in dark tunics and trousers. One was leading the horse and cart, and the others had been picking their way down the mountain path. Down the path? Where the hell was he, anyway?

"Now, do not try anything rash, scum. There is no way ye can take out all three of us before one of us makes it to ye. Just put yer hands above yer head and ye might live through this."

Steve couldn't help it. It just came out of him. He laughed.

Nervously eyeing each other, the would-be captors watched helplessly as their victim held up his right hand, still ignited. A large fiery orb appeared. Using the light from his chaser, he observed his attackers. All had swords, but none were drawn. They had instead opted to fit arrows to their bows. And, all three bows simultaneously snapped as they burned to ash. While the startled men looked to one another to figure out what they should do next, Steve's gaze dropped to the closest man's scabbard, with his sword still in it. It only took a few seconds before it was glowing solid red. The man howled in pain, scrambling frantically to get the red-hot weapon off his belt. The other two men went through the same ordeal, all howling in pain as their swords literally melted in their scabbards.

"Would you like to rephrase that?" Steve casually asked, tossing the chaser from one hand to the other.

The man that had been holding on to the reins of the horse turned tail and ran, disappearing into the darkness. There was a frantic scrambling in the distance and then they heard a scream of despair as the fleeing mercenary ran right off the edge of the path, plummeting hundreds of feet to the valley floor below.

Eyeing the two nervous men, he hefted the chaser in his right hand. "I like to call this a 'chaser'," Steve casually explained. "What is a chaser, you might ask? Let me explain. If I hurl this, it'll give chase. No matter how fast you run, no matter where you try to hide, it will find its target. And not just one, but both of you. I've used them before. Trust me, I have no problem using it again."

"What do ye want?" The high-pitched voice came out as a nervous squeak.

"Who are you? Who do you work for?"

The two thugs shared a glance, and then both darted away, running as fast as possible. They had to put as much distance as they could between themselves and the fire thrower before he had a chance to react. However, before Steve could throw the chaser, both men discovered the sharp turn on the mountain road that their unfortunate friend had found, and as a result, both ran right off the edge, plunging to their deaths. Echoes of their screams bounced around the canyon walls for several minutes before finally fading away.

Standing in complete shock, Steve's hands snuffed themselves out. Now what was he supposed to do? His prisoners had fled before he had a chance to figure out where he was, effectively stranding him in the middle of nowhere in the middle of the night. He patted the horse on the head.

"I don't suppose you know how to get us out of here?"

Neighing in fright, the horse took off. The clattering of the receding cart eventually faded away until he was left standing by himself in the darkness.

"This is just great."

Sarah didn't think she had ever run this much in her entire life. She just couldn't seem to catch her breath, yet she wasn't about to stop now. To do so would mean she'd be left behind, and she wasn't about to let that happen.

The other four soldiers had each taken a different direction. They were to search for an hour, and then report back to the camp to compare notes. All had donned their full gear, anticipating the worst. But it was Rhein who proved the most useful. He had managed to stumble across a roosting owl, and after only a few moments, was able to calm the agitated bird to make her his familiar.

The owl took flight immediately, searching for anything out of the ordinary, any disturbances, or any other people on the move in the area. In less than thirty minutes, the owl had located the horse and cart. The frightened horse was finally apprehended when, exhausted, it had stopped to rest, its head drooping low to the ground. All Kern had to do was grab the reins. The tired horse even whinnied its appreciation to its new owners.

After finally securing the spooked animal, Kern gave an exclamation of surprise. By the light of the newly risen moon he was able to see what lay discarded in the wooden cart. Reaching inside, he retrieved the ropes that had previously held Steve captive.

"Lieutenant, someone was held prisoner here. Look, these ropes were cut!"

Rhein took the ropes, scrutinizing them closely while Kern fidgeted from his left foot to his right.

"Think they were used on Sir Steve?"

Rhein nodded.

"Aye, I do. See the ends of the rope? No fraying. All the ends are singed. These ropes were burned off."

"Do we search the area?"

"Nay, my owl found the horse running full speed." He patted the tired horse. "We do not know where he was coming from. Back to the camp. We have to rendezvous with the others."

"Ye found it where?" Rhenyon studied the cut ropes.

"About three leagues from here, due west. From which direction the horse was running, I cannot say."

Sarah held up a section of rope. "But these were burned off. That has got to mean it was done by Steve, right?"

Rhenyon nodded in agreement. "I have seen ropes burned off before, but in this case, I do not believe in coincidences. Sir Steve was bound, in that cart. He managed to free himself, of that we can be certain.

"What now?" Sarah wanted to know. "Do we search for him?"

"I am sorry, Lady Sarah, but it is too dangerous at night. We are close to several cliffs. We must wait for first light."

Tears filled Sarah's eyes. Please be okay, she silently thought to her husband. We'll find you.

The following morning, dawn came without preamble. Without any vegetation, trees, or the like, there weren't any creatures or insects to generate the typical morning cacophony he had become accustomed to. Whether it was sheer exhaustion or the lack of noise to wake him, Steve slept in longer than he probably should have.

Snoring loudly, Steve's back sent constant jolts of pain up and down his spine. The intensity of the pain finally penetrated his awareness and brought him agonizingly back to full consciousness. Stiffly, he rose to a sitting position. Looking around in bewilderment, taking in the unfamiliar surroundings, Steve had to give himself a full five minutes before the memories of the previous night came back to him.

Wincing with pain, he stood, rubbing his aching temples. His headache from the previous night was still with him, and now, thanks to his hours of sleeping on solid rock, his back wasn't too pleased with him, either. Groaning softly, he finally took stock of his location. He was standing on an open expanse of rock along a steep wall, with a small path continuing upwards. The path also bordered the mountain's edge, with the drop off plunging straight down for over two hundred feet.

Bewildered, Steve looked around. There were mountains surrounding him on all sides, and far below, a small valley. Stepping out onto the path he looked both down and then up the path. It was barely wide enough for a horse-drawn cart. Where had they been taking him? He sure as hell didn't want to keep going that way. Best to head the opposite direction. Maybe there was a branch in the path that would take him back to where he came from.

Steve paused. Did he really know which direction that was if he found another path to take? He shook his head. Nope. Not a clue. Maybe he could light a signal fire, or shoot off several jets of fire into the sky. Nope, bad idea. If he did that, then not only could he alert his friends, but it would also alert any undesirables in the area.

Steve thought back to last night. If memory served, while he was restrained in the cart he did recall a gentle, downwards pull, so if he wanted to head in the opposite direction that meant uphill, right? He sighed. Of course. Uphill. Should have known. Trudging slowly up the path, he reached the sharp bend which had been the downfall of his captors. Steve leaned over the edge and looked down. Should he feel bad? Absolutely not.

"Too bad, so sad, guys. Serves your asses right."

Did the horse and cart go over the edge, too? Man alive, he hoped not. Having grown up in southwestern Idaho with horses on his family's farm, he had a certain fondness for the four-legged animals, and wouldn't wish a horse any type of harm, no matter what its temperament was.

Following the bend in the path, he picked up the pace as much as he was able. He asked himself yet again if he really know where the hell he was going. Somewhere out in the open. Some place away from heights. He didn't really have a problem with heights, but falling from them? That he could do without.

By midday he was feeling better. His headache had dulled to a muted throb, but now his stomach was protesting angrily for being ignored. After several hours of walking he had finally reached the path's summit. He had to admit, it made for one hell of a view. It didn't do anything to dispel his uneasiness, however. Unfamiliar terrain spread out all about him, and directly ahead? The path, unfortunately, terminated at the beginning of a large, open mesa that was covered with tall grass that rose to his waist. Which way was north, anyway? He glanced up. Judging by his shadow he guessed it was just after noon, and that the sun was heading to his left, which meant north was straight through the grass.

As he walked, the nagging fear of being lost refused to go away. Was he making things worse by trying to figure out which way to go? Maybe he should stop and stay in one place, in case someone was looking for him.

A gentle breeze began to blow, causing the grass he was wading through to sway gently to the left. He had just started noticing the hypnotizing effect of the gently rocking grass when the wind started to pick up. What's going on? In just a matter of moments, the gentle breeze had rapidly increased to a gale force wind and was blowing so hard that the grass was blown flat against the ground. The wind was buffeting him so hard that he could barely stand. What now? Was a tornado heading this way?

Suddenly he was wrenched to the ground and darkness enveloped him. What the hell? Who put out the lights? The howling wind had also disappeared. The air became stuffy. Had he stumbled into a hole? Gingerly he felt around him. Solid, pebbled walls met his touch. The ground continued to tremble beneath his feet. He blindly explored in all directions. More pebbled walls, not only surrounding him, but also encompassing him from above and below as well. Nudging the textured wall one final time, Steve sighed loudly. Maybe it was a -

"Would ye kindly stop doing that?"

The voice came from nowhere and everywhere at the same time.

"Who's there? And doing what?"

"Stop moving about, human. That tickles."

A small chink of light appeared. Then bits of light appeared all around him as the walls about him separated. Steve gasped aloud. His "cage" was in fact a basket two hands made when they were cupped together. However, these were some massive hands! Not only that, he was soaring through the air! They were moving at such a tremendous rate of speed that the air was actually whistling through the huge fingers.

Holy crap, he thought excitedly, I've been snatched by a dragon! What is Kahvel doing? Wait. That hadn't sounded like the dragon he knew. Besides, wasn't Kahvel a gold dragon? This skin is green. Uh, oh. Looking up, he could see the heavily scaled belly of an enormous emerald-green dragon.

"I just want you to know that I probably taste really bad."

"Not if cooked properly," the dragon disagreed. "Be at ease. I have no intentions of eating ye."

"Where are you taking me?"

"To Kahvel."

Steve held his breath. "Are you friends with Kahvel?"

"Am I friend to Kahvel? Aye, ye might say that. I am his mate."

Steve plopped back down onto the massive palm in shock. A female dragon!

"So you're taking me to Kahvel, then? Has he been looking for me?"

"Aye, along with the rest of yer companions. Kahvel checked on them just after sunrise, and that's when he learned of yer disappearance. He enlisted my help. I just happened to find ye first."

"What's your name? Mine is Steve. Steve Miller."

"I am Pryllan."

Rhenyon and Sarah wearily trudged back to their camp to await the arrival of the others. They were the first to arrive for their fourth rendezvous since beginning their search for the missing Nohrin.

Sarah had been silent for the last two hours. Rhenyon sighed again. He had been trained in hand-to-hand combat, weaponry, falconry, horsemanship, and a slew of other useful skills. Consoling a distraught woman, however, was not one of them. He was determined to be optimistic, for Sarah's sake, but the longer they went without news, the more dismal Steve's future became. What was he going to tell the king?

Kern arrived just then, followed closely by Pheron. Rhenyon looked at both of his men and knew without asking for a report that they had been as unsuccessful as he had.

"With regrets, no signs, sir."

"Acknowledged. We wait for Rhein, and we keep searching."

Both soldiers nodded. Suddenly Pheron straightened.

"Captain, do ye hear that?"

Rhenyon stood still, listening intently. Someone was shouting! "Can ye identify the source?"

Kern pointed to a bluff fifty feet or so above them. Shading her eyes from the sun, Sarah could just make out Rhein's head. He was frantically gesturing while shouting about something.

"Gather yer gear," Rhenyon ordered. "We move in one minute. Lieutenant Rhein appears to have found something."

In a quarter of an hour they joined Rhein up on the outcropping of rock.

"What is it? What did ye find?"

"My familiar made contact with a raptor, who witnessed a disturbance about four leagues from here, due north."

Sarah held her breath. "Was it something to do with Steve?"

"The raptor observed a human walking through a small valley when a large, green dragon passed directly over him. When the dragon flew off, the human was gone."

"Omigod! A dragon has taken him?"

Rhenyon smiled, putting his hand on her shoulder. "Be at ease, Lady Sarah. Kahvel has his mate looking for him, too."

"So?"

"She is a green dragon."

"But what if it wasn't his mate?"

"When we find Kahvel, and he does not know anything about it, then we will panic. Until that time, we will assume his mate found yer husband first."

It was a surreal spectacle to behold: two dragons in such close proximity to a human. Pryllan's green tail was entwined around Kahvel's golden one. She complimented him well, Steve thought. Both dragons were conversing amongst themselves, completely ignoring the increasingly frustrated human who was trying nonchalantly to be noticed.

There were joyous shouts in the distance as Sarah and the soldiers appeared over the bluff. She ran into his arms, sobbing hysterically, while all the soldiers breathed a collective sigh of relief. Sir Steve had been returned to them, appearing to be unharmed.

Sarah finally disengaged herself from her husband. “Are you okay? What happened to you? I was so worried!”

“I’m okay. Minor headache, and a few aches and pains, but nothing significant.” He faced Rhenyon. “Where’s Jalen? I’d personally like to thank him for such a wonderful outing.”

Rhenyon paused. “Jalen is still missing. I figured he was involved after he did not return when ye were reported missing. I have already informed the castle. They will find him. But what happened to ye? Do ye remember?”

“Tell you all about it in a sec.” Steve turned to the green dragon. “Pryllan, thank you very much for the rescue. I owe you one, big-time.”

Pryllan lowered her long graceful neck down to meet Steve’s gaze. “Ye are welcome, human.” Raising her head back up, she looked at her mate. “Kahvel. Be safe.” Unfolding her wings, she took to the air and disappeared into the distant clouds.

Steve looked at the huge gold dragon. “Thank you very much for getting her involved. I don’t know how she managed to find me, but I’m damn glad she did.”

“Ye are welcome, human. Yer disappearance was hampering our progress, so ye had to be found quickly.”

“I don’t suppose you have anything to eat?”

The question caught Sarah off guard. When was the last time any of them had eaten? She hadn’t teleported dinner for last night or breakfast from this morning. She looked at Rhenyon, who was talking to his men.

“Excuse me, sorry to interrupt, but I have a question.”

“Yes, Lady Sarah.”

“Ummm, with all that has happened, I didn’t get you guys dinner last night nor any breakfast this morning.”

Rhenyon’s face went blank as he realized she was right.

“So my question is, what will the castle do if we miss a couple meals and you haven’t reported in?”

The captain’s eyes widened. “Wizards be damned! His Majesty will assume the worst and dispatch men to our last known location. Quickly, fetch the quill, ink, and some parchment!”

Rhenyon hastily wrote a progress report and handed it to Sarah, who sent it straight to the king's desk. She looked at the captain.

"How long before I check for a response?"

Rhenyon scuffed his foot on the ground. "Best to give him a few minutes so that I might be properly reprimanded."

A few minutes later, Rhenyon was reading the king's response. He had indeed dispatched several squadrons of troops which had just left the castle. They were called back. The king even went so far as to have the food pack filled with fresh food.

As they all ate, Steve relayed all that he could remember, from the time that he was thumped on the head to when he had discovered he had been snatched by a dragon.

"Sorry to have put you guys through all of that," Steve said. "What are you going to do about Jalen when you find him?"

"I have not decided. I will deal with that later. For all we know, he could have been one of those that went over the edge of the cliff. How well did ye see their faces?"

"Not well at all. I guess he could have been one of them."

Finishing their meal, Sarah returned the pack to the castle. Rhenyon gazed off into the distance.

"Do you see that ridge, maybe ten leagues distant?"

Both Sarah and Steve nodded.

"That ridge," Rhenyon explained, "is the southern border to the valley we are looking for, adjacent to Lake Raehón. We should be able to make that ridge by nightfall."

"I will see all of ye there, then." Kahvel unfolded his wings and took to the air.

There was a much more laid-back attitude amongst the camp that night. Rhein was cracking jokes. Kern told several stories, heroic tales of high adventure that his ancestors were allegedly a part of. Steve juggled three fireballs. Sarah even hid Rhenyon's prized daggers. The soldiers roared with laughter as their captain dumped the contents of his pack all over the ground, trying to determine what had happened to them, only to discover moments later they had mysteriously reappeared back on his belt.

Later, as they settled down for the night, both husband and wife snuggled close under the blanket.

"I am so glad you are back. Don't ever do that to me again."

"How did I know that I was going to get knocked on the head by one of our own?"

"Would you like me to get the vial and heal you? That's a nasty bump you have there."

"No, thanks, save it for the serious injuries. I can survive a lump on my head." As she started to protest, Steve kissed her. "I'll be okay. Hey, did you hear what Rhenyon said earlier?"

Recognizing her husband's attempts to steer attention away from himself, Sarah shook her head. "About making it to the lake tomorrow? Yes, I heard."

Steve sighed, becoming groggy. "I hope it isn't too hard to find."

"You think an entrance to the dwarven realm is going to be easy to find?"

Steve snorted.

"The entrance is somewhere around here? You're kidding, right?"

They were all standing at the beginning of a large valley that stretched some fifty leagues from west to east. Fortunately for them, it was only about twenty leagues to the lake, which they could just see in the distance. Large groups of boulders were scattered here and there. There was also a lack, Sarah noted, of any vertical objects that were flat enough for a door to be mounted on.

Kahvel arrived then, landing with the grace of a swan. He surveyed the quiet valley.

"There are a dozen or so dragons in the vicinity of this valley. We must be careful. And we must be quick. Ye do not want to be out here any longer than necessary."

"Any ideas on where to start?" Steve asked.

"To reveal the exact location of their realm would violate the oath we dragons have taken with the dwarves."

All seven people stared at the dragon in shock.

"Ye know the exact location of the entrance? How?"

"One of my brethren observed a group of them using their entrance. They are not the only ones who are skilled with illusion."

"So where is it, then?"

Kahvel snorted, looking north. "That way."

"Smart ass. Can you be more specific?"

Sarah smacked her husband on the arm. "He just said that he can't reveal the location. Weren't you listening?"

"What I can tell ye," the dragon rumbled, "is that ye need to go roughly nine hundred paces north, then about two hundred seventy five paces east."

"But – you just said that you couldn't say where it was?"

"That will put ye in the correct area," Kahvel explained. "I did not say where the exact entrance could be found. Ye have to find that yerselves."

"Are ye coming with us, dragon?" Rhenyon asked.

"I will accompany ye until ye find the way down. Then ye are on yer own."

"Understood. Ye have our thanks."

Kahvel nodded.

Setting out across the open valley, not much was spoken. No one wanted to draw attention to themselves, however, seven humans and a gold dragon were going to warrant a second look no matter what species you happened to be. Counting off the correct number of paces north and then east put them in the middle of a large group of individual boulders.

It was, Steve mused, as if a large giant tossed a handful of stones up in the air and let them fall wherever they pleased. He walked over to one rock and knocked on it. Solid stone.

"It has to be one of these stones," Sarah said, more to herself than anyone. "The dwarves are said to be masters of illusion. We just need to know which one, and then we'll figure out how to get into it."

"Aye, let us split up and investigate the stones to see if any of them stand out."

For the next hour, anyone passing by would have laughed out loud as the seven humans dispersed amongst the large stones, knocking in various places, and peering suspiciously at assorted bumps and cracks. However, all were exactly as they appeared to be: rocks.

"Nothing here," Steve called, after circling around his stone three times, knocking at various places.

"Same here," Sarah reported, inspecting her rock closely for hidden hinges or buttons.

"No luck here," Rhenyon reported, as did the other four soldiers.

"What if there was another way to activate the door?" Sarah asked. "Clearly we're missing something."

"Like what?" Steve wanted to know.

"Oh, I don't know. For instance, if the dwarves had some special type of metal in their axes, and they had to lay one of them on the stone for some hidden mechanism to work."

Pheron whistled. "Impressive, Lady Sarah. Ye would make an excellent strategist."

Leaning on his rock, Steve tried his hand at thinking outside the box. Here they were, standing amidst a bunch of large stones, and one of them possibly contained a hidden door. What other way could they try to make a fake rock open up?

"What about jhorun? Some type of jhorun might be needed."

Sarah smiled and kissed him on the cheek. "Good one! Maybe the presence of jhorun or else a specific type of jhorun might open them up. Everyone ought to try their jhoruns on it."

All the soldiers experimented with their abilities, hoping the stones would react in some fashion. Rhenyon gazed at the large rocks. He wasn't sure how to apply his woodworking jhorun to this situation, but was willing to try. Pretending the stone was wood, the captain started pressing various spots to see if he could shape the rock to his will. Being composed of solid rock and not wood, the rock naturally refused to cooperate. Pheron inspected his rock, and then the stone's neighbors with his nocturnal vision. Nothing. Rhein coaxed a medium-sized lizard out from under one of the stones and had it investigate the area. Nothing. Kern pulled out his sword and watched as it polished itself to a mirror shine, then angled the sword so that the reflected light shone upon the rocks. Nothing. Finally, Darius stepped up, sheepishly looking at his companions, and made the flowers in the area grow to twice their normal height. Picking a few, he laid them on his rock. Again, the rock ignored them.

"Everyone rotate," Sarah ordered. "Pick a different stone and try again."

Nothing. None of the large boulders were impressed with their attempts to gain entry to the realm below.

As one, the soldiers all turned to look at the Nohrin.

Steve snorted. "Don't look at me. I happen to think that if I try anything, I'd end up melting 'em. I'm sure I'd wind up on the dwarves shit list, and since I need them to do me a favor, I'd just as soon not do that."

Sarah stepped forward. "I could try mine. What should I do?"

"Ummm, I'm not sure. Pretend there's something in it and try to teleport it out."

"Are you sure you don't want to try yours?"

"And what? Melt the rock into lava? I don't even know if I could get it that hot."

Sarah faced the stones and started mentally probing them with her jhorun. The first stone she examined remained inert in her mind. No images, nothing. She tried the others. Same thing, except… She backtracked, returning to the fourth stone. Something felt different about this one.

Steve watched as his wife hesitated over one of the stones.

"What is it? Something wrong?"

"This stone feels different, almost as if it's alive. The others were just lifeless masses of rock. This one is tingling."

The soldiers all gathered around the stone, inspecting every square inch of its surface, looking for any indications on how to open it. Nothing.

"I think ye are right, Lady Sarah," Rhenyon commented. "I believe jhorun is the key to reveal the entrance. Try again."

Sarah relaxed, calming her mind and her jhorun. She thought of the stone before her and attempted to get an image of what the inside might look like. Instantly, a picture formed. Yes, this was the entrance! There were the stairs leading down! The rock had hinges so well hidden that they would never be found. An image of a complicated mechanism also formed, showing her the intricate workings of the latch that opened the stone. There! She focused in on a small weight hidden just inside the stone. That weight needed to move in order to trip the latch. But how do you make it move? Moving her hands over the stone, her left hand stopped at a point directly over the weight.

"Here. There's a small weight buried within the stone. It needs to be moved. I just don't know how to move it. It appears to be delicately balanced on a scale of some sort. Maybe if we could budge the rock some it might tip the weight."

All the soldiers went to the stone and on the count of three, bumped the rock as hard as they could. They may as well have tried to pick up Kahvel. The stone didn't budge.

"Let's try again," Steve suggested.

This time everyone (minus Sarah) gathered on one side of the rock and heaved. Still nothing.

Sarah brightened suddenly. "Hon, I have an idea."

"What?"

"Heat it. Stone can sometimes expand under pressure. Or maybe it might simply respond to fire. You're the only one who hasn't tried anything."

All five soldiers instantly backed well away from the stone.

"Fine."

Steve ignited a hand and placed it over the spot Sarah had indicated. Nothing. Warming up, he increased the heat by several notches. Still the rock ignored him. Cracking his knuckles, Steve ignited his other hand. Pressing down on the same spot as before, he sent an intense blast of fire deep into the stone. What was that? Was it his imagination? Did the stone just tremble?

"Whoa! I think it moved! Just a little. I think I need to go hotter."

At this, the rest of the group took refuge behind several of the large stones. Steve sent a brutal blast of heat down into the boulder and maintained the intense levels for at least ten seconds. The surface of the rock heated quickly, glowing red within seconds. And then they all heard it: an audible click. As smoothly as if it were on oiled hinges, the entire surface of the rock lifted away from the base, revealing a dark staircase descending deep into the earth.

"Jackpot!"

Chapter 12 – Entrance

Sarah peered down into the depths of the darkness. They had to go down there?? This wasn't her idea of a good time. She hoped someone had the presence of mind to bring a flashlight of some type.

"I don't suppose someone brought a torch, huh?"

"Torches would be good," Steve agreed.

"We do not have any torches, sir Steve," Kern observed.

Torches. Rhenyon cursed himself yet again. Torches would have been a wise addition.

"We could ask the king for some torches," Steve suggested. "Use the food bag."

Rhenyon scratched out his request and handed it to Sarah, who sent it to the king. Five minutes later each soldier was holding a fresh torch.

Just then the dragon's head snapped up, gazing off towards the lake. "Yer time here has just expired. Go. Several of my brethren approach. Ye must hurry!"

"Thanks for everything, Kahvel," Steve said, genuinely disappointed to see the dragon go. "I wish you could come with us. I hope to see you again."

Sarah stepped forward and laid a hand on the dragon's foreleg. "Thank you for keeping your end of the accord. I consider myself lucky to have a dragon as a friend."

Kahvel nodded, amazed to discover himself at a loss for words.

Rhenyon held out his torch to Steve. "Can ye light this for me?"

Steve flicked his gaze on the proffered torch, then to the other torches the soldiers were holding. Within moments all had been ignited.

Silently and cautiously, they descended down the stone staircase in single file. They had descended perhaps twenty steps when the gold dragon moved the "rock door" back into place, blocking off the sunlight from above.

"Now we find out if anyone is claustrophobic," Rhenyon observed. "Before I forget. Lady Sarah, if ye please."

Startled to be addressed, Sarah stepped forward. "Yes?"

"I need ye to vividly picture our last campsite in yer head. Can ye do that?"

Sarah brought up a mental image of their former campsite, even picturing the stones they had sat on, the hearth they had made. Yes, she could see it quite clearly. "I can do that. Do you need to send something there?"

"Hopefully not, but if the need arises, it is good to know that ye can."

Sarah blinked. That was a good idea. As they progressed down farther into the depths of the earth, she recalled each and every campsite that they had ever visited, figuring if she ever needed to attempt an emergency teleport jump, then she at least had several reference points.

Steve silently fingered the leather pouches fastened to the nohrstaf harness. He had managed to charge three of the crystals and sincerely hoped he wouldn't have to use them. Even with six torches providing light, the darkness still felt as though it was pressing in on him. It was so very tempting to simply ignite both hands and fire off a blast.

After half an hour of traveling down the steep, narrow steps, they emerged into an immense cavern. A steady drip could be heard from somewhere in the distance as drops of groundwater cascaded down several stalactites and fell to the ground. Having become accustomed to their voices being muffled by the small confines of the tunnel they were just in, several soldiers whistled in amazement. Echoes of their whistles bounced around the cavern until finally returning back to them multiplied tenfold.

Steve added his own whistle. "Look at the size of this place! It's gotta be the size of Fedex Field!"

"Fedicks field, sir Steve?"

"Uh, it's a really large, er, field where people in my land play, um, games with thousands and thousands of people watching from the sidelines."

"Where's the light coming from?" Sarah asked, noting that there was just enough light to illuminate the closest cavern wall. "I figured it'd be pitch black down here."

"Something must be glowing," Steve observed, inspecting the closest wall. "What that is, I can't tell."

Sarah turned to Rhenyon.

"Okay, so what's the plan? What do we do now?"

"We make contact with the dwarves, Lady Sarah," Rhenyon answered.

"How? How do we find them down here?"

"Truth be told, I am not certain," Rhenyon admitted. "I figured that they would have made contact by now. We are, after all, now in their realm."

In the flickering light provided by the torches, Rhenyon could see Pheron gazing around the cavern. At least one of them was able to see something.

"What do ye see, lieutenant?"

"On the far wall, directly opposite us," Pheron reported," are two openings that appear to be tunnels. There are numerous stalagmites scattered about, and quite a few stalactites that hang dangerously low."

"How low?"

"Dwarves would be fine. But even Lady Sarah would be unable to pass beneath one without stooping."

"We make for the tunnels," Rhenyon instructed. "Use caution. No wandering about here. Single file. Lieutenant Pheron, take lead."

Picking carefully amongst the large rock formations, they skirted about the circumference of the large cavern, moving towards the closest tunnel. When they finally peered into the small, dark opening, it was Kern who took lead. Holding his torch up high above his head, he entered the tunnel, continually casting looks behind him as if to verify that he wouldn't be alone.

"Problem, sir," Kern called out moments later from the front of the line.

"What is it?" Rhenyon called back.

"Dead end."

"Alright, we backtrack. Try the other tunnel."

However, tunnel two also provided the same results. It angled downward for about fifty paces and then it, too, abruptly terminated. Rhenyon peered closely at the wall. Countless marks from hammers and chisels scarred the surface.

"These tunnels are incomplete. Why would they leave unfinished work? Very undwarflike." The captain snorted with disgust. Once again they were forced to reverse course, returning back to the great cavern.

"They're testing us," Sarah whispered, barely audible. "They're making certain we're deemed worthy to enter their territory."

"What was that?" Steve didn't quite catch what his wife had said. Something about a test?

"This is a message from the dwarves."

"What is?" Steve looked around. "Where do you see a message?"

"The tunnels. They are telling us to not take things for granted," Sarah explained, raising her voice so that everyone could hear her. "The entrance is here. It's hidden. We have to find it."

There was a collective groan as the soldiers looked around them. Stone stalactites dipped down low from the ceiling, at times joining with their ground dwelling brethren forming numerous mineral columns all throughout the cavern. Unusual rock formations met their eyes wherever they looked. Where do they start?

"The entrance could be anywhere," Steve complained. "How do we find it?"

Rhenyon thought a moment. "If the entrance is truly here, then it will be concealed and more than likely disguised even better than the main entrance."

He started to pace.

"Now, it took the two of ye to both open the entrance, therefore it stands to reason that it will take more than that to open this other passageway."

Sarah nodded. Makes sense. She looked at her companions. So, the question was, who had to be the ones to do it?

"Let's see if we can find the entrance, and then we'll figure out how to open it."

Rhenyon was nodding, facing his troops. "As before, disperse. Look for anything out of the ordinary. Call out if ye see anything that stands out, understood?"

There were choruses of "ayes" as the soldiers moved out, inspecting rock formations and tapping stone pillars. Sarah started to move off when Steve grabbed her arm.

"What is it?"

Steve nodded in the direction of the two incomplete tunnels. "What do you want to bet it's in one of those things? You said it yourself. Don't take anything for granted."

Sarah peered into the first tunnel they checked. "That almost makes sense. Wouldn't that be the ultimate disguise? Waste hours and hours out here checking all these rock formations when what you were looking for would be right in there."

Together they moved into the first tunnel.

"Can you give me a little light?"

Two torches ignited instantly, casting their welcoming light around the confines of the rocky tunnel. Sarah eyed her husband's flaming hands.

"You really do come in useful around here, don't you?"

Steve grinned, giving his wife a small bow. "I do what I can, milady!"

Together they inspected the entire surface of the tunnel. Nothing but chipped and scarred rock met their eyes.

Not disgruntled in the slightest, Steve turned to his wife. "So we can't see it. Not surprising. Time to try the jhoruns. Do what you did last time. Try to imagine you're teleporting something from the other side."

Quietly, Sarah paced up and down the tunnel, running her hand along the curve of the walls. Nothing but lifeless masses of stone met her senses. Assuming she should expect a picture of some type to form in her mind, Sarah figured physical contact would be best. Therefore she skimmed her hand along the tunnel ceiling, and then the floor. Still nothing.

"No luck?"

"Not a bit. Let's try the other one."

Moving to the second tunnel, she repeated the process, only to be met with the same results as before. Sighing with exasperation, she finally dropped her arms to her sides. Together, they walked back into the main cavern. On the far wall they watched Darius systematically tapping various rocks, while Kern opted for the slower, but more methodical visual inspections.

"I guess we were wrong, honey."

Steve sighed. It was such a good guess. It would have made for a very clever ruse, hiding the actual entrance in one of the obvious tunnels. So why start two tunnels and not finish them, then? Wait. The ends of the tunnels… Did she check those?

"You checked the walls, ceilings, and floors. You checked the ends, right?"

Sarah froze, foot raised in mid-step. Of course she had, hadn't she? Wouldn't that have been the first part she would have checked? Problem was, she didn't remember checking the ends due to her husband pointing out various spots to try first. She looked at Steve, who had a smile on his face. His head gave a small, quick jerk back to the first passageway. Gloat all you want, dear, she thought ruefully, but if you hadn't distracted me, I would have checked those first. Plastering a smile on her face, she held out her hand, to which Steve snuffed out his to take it. They walked hand-in-hand back to the first tunnel they explored, not saying a word until they reached the end.

"Okay, do your thing."

Sarah ran her hands over the scuffs and scrapes of the unfinished tunnel wall. She once again tried to imagine there was something she wanted on the other side, waiting for an image to form. Nothing. Shaking her head, she turned to Steve.

"Sorry, nothing here."

"Let's check out the other one."

Retracing their steps to the second tunnel, Sarah again ran her hands over the rough surface of the stone. This time, though, she hesitated. A picture was starting to form.

"I knew it!" Steve was ecstatic. "What do you see?"

Sarah concentrated, willing the swirling images in her mind to focus. Every time she tried, the fuzzy shapes kept erratically jumping about.

"I can't get an image to focus. Something starts to form, but stays fuzzy. I don't know what else to do. It's like I'm not strong enough to - wait a minute. Hon, give me your hand."

Steve snuffed out his hand once more to take his wife's. The images in her mind had sharpened somewhat, but only marginally so. It hadn't been enough, however, for her to figure out what she was supposed to do.

"That helped, it really did. Only the picture is still fuzzy. I don't think we're strong enough. We need more people!"

"We need the others!"

"Rhenyon! Pheron! Anyone out there?" Steve called. "We have something!"

There was a clamoring out in the great cavern as a soldier poked his head into the tunnel. "What is it, sir Steve?"

"Darius, get the others. We found something!"

Within moments all the soldiers were crowding around husband and wife as Sarah explained what they had found.

"They hid the entrance to their domain in an unfinished tunnel. Genius." Rhenyon shook his head. "I would not have thought to look in here." He slapped Steve heartily on the back. "What do ye need of us?"

Steve held his and Sarah's clasped hands out before them. "Sarah can start to visualize something, but before she can see a clear picture, apparently the level of jhorun needs to be increased. I took her hand and it started to focus, but not enough. Everyone grab on."

Leaning in from every direction, the soldiers laid their right hand over the two joined hands, looking for all the world like a group of athletes ready to take on the opposing team.

Sarah closed her eyes and concentrated again. Yes! The images were coming into focus, giving her a clear picture of the entryway on the other side. Once again she saw stone steps angling down. She directed her jhorun to investigate, seeking out the mechanism to open the tunnel. However, try as she might, no additional images formed. Sarah sighed.

"What is it?"

"I've got a perfect view of the tunnel," Sarah explained, "but it's not giving me anything else to go off of. I have no idea what to do to open the door."

"If there are no locks," Rhenyon asked, "then that would suggest that there is nothing but a wall of stone between us and the entrance down, correct?"

Sarah nodded. "I have just one image. A very clear one, actually. The extra jhorun really helped."

"There's just a wall of stone preventing us from getting through to the other side?" Steve asked, eyeing the uneven stone wall.

"Yes, why?"

Steve held up one of his gauntlets. "Betcha I can get through that."

"I do not believe that is a good idea, sir Steve," Rhenyon advised, running his hands along the uneven surface. He knew of the Nohrin's enchanted gauntlets. "The dwarves would have found a way to prevent forced entry to their realm."

"Couldn't hurt to try, right?"

Sharing a quick glance with Sarah, Rhenyon smiled, holding out an arm in invitation.

Confident he would be able to punch his way through, Steve cocked his arm.

"Ready?"

Sarah shook her head. "Are you?"

Steve snorted, then punched forward. Figuring he wouldn't have to hit it that hard after witnessing Quisen's demonstration, Steve gave the wall a solid smack. Nothing happened. Annoyed, he struck harder. A dull, muted *whump* sounded.

"That didn't even sound right," Steve complained, ready to strike the wall again.

"As I told ye, sir Steve," Rhenyon explained, moving to prevent the fire thrower from throwing any more needless punches, "there are measures in place to prevent this very thing from happening."

"Then how do we get in?"

"I think I have it."

Steve looked at his wife. "What? What do we have to do?"

"The image I got before you tried to bash the wall down? It was much clearer than the picture I received on the surface when we were trying to open the entrance."

"So?"

"I think I know how to get us in."

"You do? How? Tell us!"

"The key to get through," she said slowly, "is me. I can do it. I think."

Understanding, Rhenyon smiled. "Ye have to teleport us through, Lady Sarah."

"Only problem is I've only teleported one person before, and that was by accident. I don't know exactly what I have to do. So you'd better give me a minute."

Steve hesitated. It did make sense. She had kept mentioning that the image she was seeing was very clear. And in order for her to teleport anything, then she had to clearly see the locations involved. He was silent, motioning the others to be quiet as well.

Sarah closed her eyes, focusing all her inner strength on the task she was about to undergo. With the image of the first step of the stairs leading down clearly pictured in her head, Sarah ordered her jhorun to move her physical body from here to there.

She gave a yelp of surprise as she was wrenched away from the tunnel. Her world tilted sideways as all her senses short-circuited, causing her to stumble. She fell solidly on her butt.

"Ouch!"

Scrambling to her feet, rubbing her delicate hind end, Sarah blinked and looked around. Complete darkness met her eyes. She couldn't see a thing! Didn't it work? Where was she? Taking several deep breaths, Sarah finally slowed her breathing down to take stock of her situation. If she was truly on the other side of the wall, then the first step down should be right about… She cast about with her right foot, searching for the step. There it was! She did it! She actually made it! No wonder it was dark. There weren't any torches on this side. She definitely needed Steve.

Back on the other side of the wall, Steve had watched with amazement as Sarah literally vanished right before his eyes. He didn't have any doubts that she'd be able to teleport herself to the other side. Apparently her jhorun worked very well the better you could imagine the locations involved. And, he knew Sarah had an excellent memory. What about coming back? She'd just have to picture the area she just left so… So in order to return back here, that meant nobody should move, lest they move into the space that she had just frequently vacated.

"That is amazing," Pheron remarked, starting to move forward. "I would love to have –"

"No! Wait!" Steve flung out his arm, thumping the soldier on his chest.

Pheron froze. "What is it?"

"Sarah has to make it back. Chances are she'll move back to the exact spot she vacated, so everyone must be in the exact same place when she comes back. No one moves until she appears."

Rhenyon was nodding. "Aye, makes sense. We wait for Lady Sarah's return. No one moves," the captain ordered.

From the other side of the wall, Sarah steadied herself, taking several deep breaths. Okay, here we go. Trying to calm her queasy stomach, she addressed her jhorun, giving them yet another command: *move me back to where I was*.

Another gut wrenching jolt and she stumbled into Rhenyon, who whirled to catch her before she received a nasty blow from the stone wall.

Steve caught her other arm and pulled her in for a hug. "You did it! Nice job!" He then saw his wife's ashen complexion and took her by the shoulders. "Hon, you okay? You're all pale."

Sarah put a hand on her stomach. "I know what I need to work on. There has to be an easier way to do that."

"What happened? Did you make it to the other side?"

Sarah nodded, still rubbing her queasy stomach. "Yes, I made it. I couldn't see much. No light. But that's not the part that concerns me."

Steve waited, not wanting to grill his wife, but desperately wanting more details.

After a moment of battling nausea, Sarah continued. "Imagine putting yourself in the pouch of a big slingshot, and then you're launched into the air. Now, once you're sailing through the air, imagine stopping rather abruptly, like you're flung into a large catcher's mitt. It feels rather like that."

"What is a 'sling-shot', Lady Sarah?" Kern asked.

"A device that loosely resembles a catapult in design," Steve offered.

The soldiers nervously eyed each other. They had to be shot out of a catapult?

Steve clapped his hands together. "All right! Who's first?"

"I will be the first," Rhenyon declared, stepping up to Sarah. "What do I have to do, milady?"

Sarah took his right arm in hers. "Just don't move and I'll try to do this as quickly as possible. Be warned. The sensation is quite a jolt to the system."

Rhenyon took a deep breath and nodded his head. Closing her eyes, Sarah concentrated, bringing back the image of the other tunnel.

In the blink of an eye, both woman and soldier vanished. Steve turned to Pheron.

"Do we have any water handy? If she's as pale as she was last time, some water would do her good."

Four soldiers instantly started patting themselves down, silently competing amongst themselves to be the first to present him with some water for Lady Sarah.

"Aye, have some of mine." Pheron ripped his own personal canteen off his belt and proffered it to Steve.

"Thanks." Steve looked at the soldier. "You moved. Where were you standing before?"

Pheron looked about, and then down at his feet. Without a word he moved about ten feet away. "I should be out of the way here. Ye moved as well, sir Steve."

Realizing that no one could remember if they were standing in the exact same spot, all decided to join Pheron. Steve decided to move as close as he dared, in case Sarah stumbled again. He didn't want to risk any unnecessary injuries.

Within moments Sarah popped back into existence, stumbling yet again. Steve jumped forward to catch her before she fell to her knees.

"Damn," Sarah muttered, "I can't seem to get those landings right."

"You're not looking as pale this time. Are you okay?"

Sarah nodded, taking deep gulps of air. "I'm not as nauseous this time. I'll take that as a good sign. But it's still a hell of a jolt."

It took about ten minutes, with short breaks in between jumps, for Sarah to transport everyone to the other side. Standing together in the flickering torch light, Sarah smiled weakly at her husband. Apparently she hadn't used this much of her jhorun at one time before. She looked and felt exhausted.

Correctly guessing what she was going through, Steve sidled up to his wife to walk with her as they descended further into the mountain.

"Feeling drained?"

Sarah could only nod. Steve felt along the harness holding his nohrstaf, and found a clasp to one of his mimet pouches. Silently slipping the crystal disc out of its holder, he pressed it into his wife's hand.

"What's this? One of those crystal charger thingies?"

"Yes, keep this with you. We'll start having you charge one up as well."

Getting irritated, she pushed it back at her husband. "It doesn't do me any good now. Let's worry about it tom-" she stopped in mid-sentence to stare at the crystal disc.

Hearing Sarah abruptly stop, Steve turned back to face his wife again. What's with the strange look on her face?

"What's the matter? What's wrong?"

Detecting the note of alarm in Steve's voice, Rhenyon froze midstep, causing a comical pileup of soldiers running into one another. Before any of his men could protest, he held up a hand, silencing them instantly.

Sarah was still staring at the crystalline object in her hand. Why was it warm? She'd felt them before, and she always recalled them being cool to the touch. She looked at her husband, concern clearly showing in his face.

"This is warm," she explained. "The last one I felt was cool. Are they supposed to be like that?"

"It's warm to the touch when charged. But it only works for the person who charged it, so you shouldn't be able to tell. That one should be empty." He retrieved another mimet, handing it to Sarah. She took this second disc with her other hand. She shook her head. This one was cool, the way it's supposed to be.

"Okay, this one is cool and the other is still warm. Why is that?"

Baffled, Steve withdrew a third mimet, one that he knew was charged. "What about this one? Hot or cold?"

Shifting both mimets to her left hand, she took the third with her right. "Warm," she reported.

"Let me see those three."

Taking back the three mimets, he sent his jhorun down to investigate. *Look, but don't touch*, he ordered.

He felt the power emanating from two of the discs, and nothing from the third. Holding the inert disc, he handed the two active discs to his wife.

"Hot or cold?"

Sarah took the mimets. "Hot. Both of them."

He handed the inert disc over.

"Cold," she instantly informed him.

"You can tell which mimet is charged? Try to draw power from one of the hot ones. Slowly and gently."

Handing two of the discs back to her husband, she sent her tiring jhorun down to investigate the disc and discovered a large reservoir of foreign, but friendly, jhorun. I wonder how I can pull it out, Sarah asked herself. Extending a mental invitation to the foreign jhorun to join hers, she instantly felt her body go warm as the mimet released a steady stream of power to mix with her own. In moments her jhorun was restored, invigorating her as only a couple of Red Bulls could. Her paleness vanished, as did her fatigue of mind. She handed the spent disc back to her husband.

"I didn't know I could do that."

"That makes two of us. You used my jhorun in this thing. Shardwyn said that wasn't possible!"

"I'm glad he was wrong. This feels great!"

Smiling and shaking his head, Rhenyon started to descend the stairs once more. As husband and wife brought up the rear, chatting animatedly back and forth about the possibility of charging as many mimets as possible, Pheron suddenly stopped, causing Sarah to walk right into the back of him.

"Ouch!" She smacked his shoulder. "Don't do that. I'm already sore enough."

"My apologies, milady," Pheron looked sheepish. "Do ye see that?"

Rubbing her sore forehead, Sarah looked around. "What?"

Pheron was rubbing his hands over a small section of the tunnel wall. "I believe we have found the source of the light down here. This rock is glowing."

Steve leaned in, peering closely at the textured surface of the rock.

"What part, specifically? I don't see anything."

"What is it, lieutenant?" Rhenyon came walking up. "Do ye see something?"

"Aye, sir, I do." He tapped the small section of rock. "This section of wall is glowing. Look. The light has been increasing the farther down we go. Coincidence?"

Rhenyon frowned, staring at the irrelevantly small section of the rock wall. With a grunt, he straightened, peering down farther into the tunnel. "I do not see what ye are referring to, lieutenant."

Pheron rolled his eyes and pulled Steve aside. "Can ye extinguish the torches?"

"Yeah, sure thing." Steve looked at the captain, who nodded. "Instant darkness coming right up."

Within moments the tunnel was plunged into a darkness so black that one wouldn't have been able to see their own hands waved mere inches in front of their face. Clutching Sarah's hand tightly Steve waited for his eyes to acclimatize. Yes, the tall soldier was correct. He could see a small, dim patch of violet light softly glowing on the wall. Running his hands over it, Steve whistled.

"Damn, Pheron, you saw this with the torches lit? I'm impressed. That sucker is faint."

"If ye like that, sir Steve," Pheron pointed in the other direction, forgetting that the fire thrower would be unable to see him, "then check that out down there."

Turning to look further down the passageway he could just make out the outlines of the tunnel walls. In fact, he could see for quite a ways down the tunnel's length before the faint light was swallowed by the darkness.

"Ooo, pretty!" Sarah's favorite color was purple.

"Everyone can see the light, right?" Pheron moved around his stationary comrades. "Why do we not use this natural light and save the torches?"

"I think not, lieutenant," Rhenyon stated. "Ye might be able to see just fine, but for the rest of us, it is damn dark. Sir Steve, light the torches, if ye please."

"Aye. Uh, I mean, right."

Steve ignited both hands and increased the intensity of his flames by a few notches so that the entire tunnel was illuminated. Once he had enough light to ensure he wouldn't ignite that which didn't wish to be ignited, he lit the torches, snuffing his hands out as the last torch sprang back to life.

Sighing inwardly, Sarah relaxed. She really didn't care for the dark, and had no desire to wander about using only the faint purple bioluminescence present on the walls as the only means of light. Maybe that's all the dwarves needed, she mused, but she was no dwarf. She wanted illumination and lots of it.

As the soldiers conversed amongst themselves ahead of them, Steve and Sarah pondered how to best make contact with the dwarves. Steve suggested making as much noise as possible, figuring that an excessive amount of disturbance would alert the dwarves to the presence of guests. Sarah argued, however, that the dwarves might be farther down, and to announce their location to everything within earshot might not be such a wise move.

"How do we know that there aren't other things living down here? Do you really want to take that chance."

Steve shook his head. "You have a point. So what do you think?"

"About how to make contact? We keep moving. Down. As long as we don't come across any side tunnels, we should be okay."

"Ye have already passed three, human."

The voice was gruff, with just the barest hints of a sneer.

Rhenyon froze in place, causing yet another pileup. "Who's there? Who speaks?"

There were shouts of surprise as soldiers were forcefully shoved aside by a stout, thick bearded dwarf dressed in dark leather armor. A heavy double-bladed axe was strapped across his back. Various tools were strung along his belt. Finally pushing his way past Rhenyon to take the lead, the dwarf turned to face the stunned group of humans.

"Are the lot of ye daft? What are ye doing here?"

"Who are ye, dwarf?" Rhenyon asked. "Where did ye come from? Ye say we missed three. Three what?"

"I am Breslin, of the Kla Guur clan." The dwarf bowed. "Ye ask what ye missed? Turns, dolt. Ye blundered by not one, nor two, but three. Why did ye not take the second, as ye were instructed?"

"We passed no other tunnels, dwarf," Rhenyon scowled, losing patience. "Nothing but a straight passageway from that large cavern to here."

"Obviously I must have been mistaken," the dwarf drawled. "Clearly I came in after ye and have been following silently behind. It is impossible to believe that I used a side tunnel that intersects this one."

Steve snorted. This was one sarcastic dwarf!

"Did ye not make a copy of the map as ye were instructed? How did ye expect to find yer way around down here?"

"Map? Instructions? There were none, I assure ye."

The dwarf paused, studying the human. Were all human men this stupid? He finally looked at the rest of the group. Four soldiers and a peasant couple returned his gaze.

"Did none of ye pay heed to the map?"

Sarah approached, looking down at the (clearly) befuddled dwarf. "Sir, I assure you, we encountered no map, let alone any instructions. Where was it?"

"As soon as the gate opened, the map would have illuminated on the opposite wall. Ye could not have missed it."

"Nothing lit up on any wall other than glowing moss," Pheron helpfully supplied.

"Impossible," Breslin scoffed. "The spell is triggered by the gate's movement. Map on one side, instructions on the other. Without both, ye can wander for years down here and not find anything. This," the dwarf swept his hand around in a circle to indicate their present location, "will eventually encircle the entire mountain range. That's well over nine hundred leagues, human."

Rhenyon held up a hand. "Wait. Did ye say the door opens?"

"Aye, that I did, lad. How else could ye have made it this far?"

The captain of the guard exchanged a glance with their resident teleporter. This was unexpected. Had they somehow bypassed the proper method to open the door by using Lady Sarah's abilities? Evidently this must be so.

"If ye are referring to that stone wall at the end of the second tunnel, then trust me, dwarf, it did not move."

"Eh? What was that?" The dwarf was certain he just caught the human telling a lie. If the door did not open, then there were enchantments in place to prevent any unwanted intruders. They would have been unable to breech the Barrier, so they must be telling lies. The Barrier had been successfully blocking unauthorized entry for centuries. "Then how did ye make it inside? Ye cannot have made it past the door without unlocking it."

"We didn't unlock it," Steve confirmed. "We teleported across."

Two beady black eyes stared at him, searching for the lie that he was certain must exist. "Ye could not have teleported," the dwarf insisted. "Enchantments have long been in place to prevent such actions."

"We're here, aren't we?" Steve grinned. Nothing like stating the obvious to prove a point. "That's how we got here. We teleported from the end of that tunnel to directly on the other side of the wall. Door. Gate. Whatever. If what you say is true, then no wonder we didn't see anything. Nothing was tripped by the door, 'cause the door didn't move."

"I cannot fathom how the likes of ye could defeat the Barrier, but that is not my concern. Let the Council ponder that one. Let us be off."

"Where are you taking us?" Sarah asked.

"The human king requested the location of the Strathos, did he not?"

"He's in Borahgg, we know."

Breslin turned to face the peasant. "And just how the ruddy hell did ye know that?"

"Ten years ago," Rhenyon answered, "the dwarf we are looking for passed through one of our villages. He traded with a few townsfolk for some food and supplies. He told one of them where he was headed."

The dwarf shook his head. "He always did have a big mouth."

Sarah gave a quick jolt. "Do you know Maelnar then?"

"Legends of his skill are widely known. Lesser known is his fondness for bragging about it."

Several soldiers snorted.

The dwarf's eyes quickly flicked to the soldiers. "Laugh it up, lads. We always do. Maelnar is a mystery, and that's no lie." The dwarf turned and pointed back the way they came. "That way. Follow me."

Pushing his way back to the other end of the group, Breslin took the lead position and started walking back up the passageway. He hadn't even bothered to check whether the humans were following.

Whistling merrily, the dwarf cheerfully began pointing out various formations, elaborating on the skills necessary to bore tunnels through solid rock. In thirty short minutes Steve and Sarah learned more about sedimentary rocks than the most talented geologist from their world.

Breslin slowed, allowing the others to catch up, before he finally stopped, staring intently at the wall before him. As the humans crowded close, Breslin unslung his axe and leaned on it, watching as the humans stared around with bewildered expressions.

"Why have we stopped? Is something wrong?"

The dwarf shook his head. "And that, human, is why ye have missed three intersections. This is the last one that ye passed."

Shocked, Rhenyon turned to the stone wall. Nothing but solid, unbroken stone met his eyes.

"Here? There is nothing here but stone!"

Steve approached, running his hands along the surface of the rock wall. As he neared the smug dwarf, his hand suddenly lost purchase, throwing him off balance. He stumbled towards the rock wall, fully expecting to receive a crack on the head at any moment. Fortunately several pairs of strong hands grabbed the back of his tunic and held him fast. Regaining his balance, Steve carefully felt the open space his hand told him was there, yet his eyes insisted wasn't.

Equally curious, Rhenyon and Pheron mirrored Steve's actions, running their hands along the surface and poking fingers at various places. Only when they were positioned just so, with the dwarf giving instructions, were they able to see the outline of the tunnel opening. The dwarves had created a truly masterful illusion, with the entrance of the second tunnel being well disguised with ingenious rockwork. The various strata and discolorations of the rock blended masterfully with the rock in the walls and floors of the second tunnel to achieve a perfect blending of color and texture.

Knowing full well that the tunnel branched there, Steve still had difficulty believing someone could be so skillful as to have been able to craft such an illusion. Gingerly, he walked into the tunnel, did an about-face, and looked back the way he had come. There, clear as day, was the opening with everyone staring in at him. He walked back out and faced the tunnel again. It had disappeared, presenting him with what appeared to be a blank wall.

"Now that is just freakin' cool!" Steve grinned at the dwarf, who grinned back. "Very impressive, Breslin."

With his smile hidden behind his thick beard, Breslin bowed. "I thank ye for the compliment."

Still smiling, Steve looked at his wife, who was leaning into the new tunnel to look around.

"No wonder we all missed it. Even standing in front of the tunnel entrance, I still can't see it. We would have been wandering for years down here."

Amazed and annoyed at himself for traipsing right by a "hidden" tunnel, Rhenyon was silent. He had heard stories glorifying the skill of the Bohani Mountain Dwarves, how they were masters of illusion, but this was a truly amazing feat. Looking down at the dwarf, who was clearly waiting for some type of acknowledgment from him, Rhenyon finally nodded.

"Yer brethren are truly masters of their work, dwarf. That is exquisite work."

Beaming with pride, the dwarf bowed again. His respect for this group of humans just shot several notches higher.

"This way, master soldier."

Leading them farther up into the tunnel, Breslin launched into the finer aspects of the art of blacksmithing, describing the type of metals best used for armor and the best way to spot precious gems buried in rock. He had just started to describe the types of stone diamonds were typically found in when he paused, stopping before another nondescript section of tunnel wall. All present, including the captain, had been holding their breath, waiting for the dwarf to finish his last train of thought. No such luck. The dwarf had now turned to face his charges again.

Rhenyon turned to look at the wall. He was still unable to spot any irregularities to indicate an opening of another tunnel. Breslin had been studying the human in charge.

"Can ye see it, human? This tunnel is used frequently, so it is bigger than the last."

"Bigger?" Steve stepped up again, moving to the left, then right, as he tried valiantly to see the outlines of the entrance. Being the most direct route to the subterranean dwarven city, it was naturally disguised better than the others. "I don't see anything this time."

"And ye will not," Breslin explained, "until I open the door."

Stepping up to the wall, the dwarf started softly knocking at various points along the surface. Pausing every few moments he would then move several feet away and start tapping the wall all over again.

"How the hell were we supposed to get in there?" Steve complained. "I mean, look at what he's doing. You're telling me that the instructions we should have been given instruct us to do exactly that? There's no way!"

The dwarf stopped his repetitive knocking and stared at Steve for several seconds before bursting out in loud guffaws. After much knee-slapping, Breslin moved to a completely different section of the wall and pushed. A large chunk of the wall slid smoothly out of place to reveal a well lit passageway behind. Light flooded into the tunnel to illuminate everyone's faces, including Steve's, who was scowling at the dwarf. Breslin wiped the last of the big, fat tears that were streaming from his face with his beard before finally apologizing to Steve.

"I am sorry, lad, but I could not help myself. We do not get many visitors down here."

"I can see why," Steve muttered under his breath.

After everyone had moved into the larger tunnel, Breslin moved the stone door back into place and with a soft chink, the tunnel was sealed, cutting off all access from the other side.

"You sure do take precautions about not being found," Sarah commented. "Can I ask why?"

"All dwarven tunnels used to be as open as ye saw with yer own eyes. Recent times have forced us to seal the direct routes into our city."

"Are you trying to keep someone out?"

"Ye could say that."

"Could you not ask them to leave in peace?"

"If we could, we would have, rest assured."

"Could ye not force them out?" Rhenyon asked.

"Again, if we could, we would have."

"Well, could you –"

"Forgive me lass, but it is not my place to say. There will be a time for yer questions later. Let us be off."

Three hours later they emerged into a cavern so immense that the far wall could not be seen, nor could they see the ceiling above them. The enormous cavern floor was several hundred feet below them as the tunnel had deposited them on an outcropping high up a subterranean mountain. It was at that moment that the first set of human eyes fell upon the previously unheard of dwarven city, Borahgg. The city itself was laid out in a perfect geometric circle, jutting up against an enormous black field to the west. Steve blinked. Black field? Squinting, he watched the field swaying from side to side. In fact, it appeared to be continually rolling, with the smaller folds coming closer to the city's edge, getting smaller as it approached. Wait! It's water! But that means… Steve's gaze followed the outline of the lake as it increased in size and disappeared in the distance. All that was water? Holy cow! The city bordered one of the largest lakes he's ever seen, and it was completely underground!

Sarah was gazing at the water as well, having come to the realization of what she was looking at much faster than her husband.

These people lived their whole lives underground without ever once observing the open sky! What was their source of light, anyway? Sarah looked around. Light just seemed to be everywhere. No source. Remarkable!

"Will wonders never cease," she breathed.

Tearing her eyes away from the hypnotic effects of the black lake, Sarah turned her gaze towards the city. From this vantage point she was able to see that the vast majority of the houses appeared to have a simple, thatched roof. It looked like it would have blown off in the slightest wind. Then again, what did you expect, she asked herself, when you lived in an area devoid of any type of precipitation. All one would need is a covering for privacy.

The dwellings were basic, rectangular in design. Yet they were larger than expected, with many having at least three chimneys. Were dwarven families large? Making a mental note to ask later, Sarah moved her gaze farther in, towards the center of the circular city. The houses started increasing in size as the stature of the occupant increased. Finally, near the center of the city, she could see large buildings set up in rows, facing each other. Hundreds of dwarves were moving about, all apparently having something to do.

"How many dwarves call this home?" Sarah asked.

"Perhaps a thousand."

"So where are we headed?"

Breslin gestured to the center of the city, indicating several large stone structures.

"Ye will find the Council there. But first," he unslung his axe again, "we need to announce our presence."

Moving over to a small, blue circular stone set into the ground just outside the tunnel entrance, Breslin held his axe upside down, with the blunt point above the axe head resting directly over the stone. Crack! The dwarf had lifted the axe and let if fall, with the point coming into contact with the glowing blue stone. Crack! The second blow sounded like an M-80 had gone off. CRACK! The third blow to the stone had the impact of several sticks of dynamite, with the shock wave resonating well up into the city, no doubt bouncing off the far walls of the great cavern.

Within moments hundreds of dwarves had appeared at the city's edge, all staring up at the mouth of the tunnel they had just vacated. The sounds of muffled conversation reached their ears as numerous hands were pointed in their direction. Ten dwarves, in full armor much like Breslin's, appeared before them. All had their axes in their hand and were staring hard at the humans, then, as one, all ten heads swiveled to glare at the dwarf who had led them into their midst.

"Breslin! What have ye done? Why 'ave ye brought humans here?"

"They seek the Strathos. They have requested an audience with the Council."

Still skeptical, the guards motioned the silent humans to follow them.

"Are you coming with us?" Steve asked.

"Aye, as far as I am able." Turning, the dwarf addressed the human soldiers. "Do not resist, and do not draw weapons. Ye are guests here. Do not abuse this honor."

Rhenyon nodded, turning to each of his men and repeating the order in case the soldiers needed to hear it from human lips instead of dwarven ones.

Walking slowly throughout the city, Steve felt as though he was being paraded by all the curious dwarves as though he was a prized prisoner of war. Many of them, well, the vast majority, Steve corrected, looked as though they had just been working at a forge, which he guessed was probably accurate. Many wore thick, protective aprons which had layers of soot, pieces of chipped stone, and small curls of metal sticking out at various places. Many were still gripping hammers and files in their hands as they stared with unabashed curiosity at the newcomers.

As they continued up the street Sarah leaned close to her husband.

"Where are the women? I don't see any. Do you think they might be someplace else?"

Overhearing the question, Breslin increased his pace until he was walking alongside the peasant woman.

"Why do ye ask that?" He looked up at the tall woman. "Ye could see just as many as I could. Dwarf women work just as hard as the men."

"I must have missed the women."

"That would be difficult, lass. They are hard to miss. They were wearing smocks."

Sarah's eyes opened wide as she realized she had, in fact, seen the dwarf women. They were the ones wearing aprons? Oh, good lord! Didn't they have beards?

Noting the look of abject confusion on her face, Pheron started chuckling softly to himself. Rhenyon had also overhead and was smiling as well.

By the time they finally reached the communal council chambers at the center of the city, word of their human guests had spread like wildfire. It was standing room only as their escorts pushed their way through to the head of the table. Nine elderly dwarves were all seated at the most beautiful table Sarah had laid eyes on. It appeared to be made of polished stone, but after nonchalantly running her hands over the smooth surface she could instantly tell that it wasn't stone, but petrified wood, adorned with inlaid gold and silver that had been delicately woven into the natural fibers of the wood.

One of the elders finally spoke, after an adequate time had elapsed for the human female to appreciate the expert craftsmanship of their revered table.

"I bid ye welcome, humans. Judging by the message we received from yer king, I presume that the lot of ye seek an audience with the Strathos. May I enquire as to the nature of this meeting? Our most gifted blacksmith prefers his privacy, and as such, we generally do not disturb him."

From the back of the room they heard a loud, derisive snort.

"Will ye please stop with the theatrics? They have come a long way to meet with the Strathos. Why, I cannot fathom."

The elder dwarf turned to address the corner of the room where the voice had originated.

"We have a right to inquire why humans would seek contact with the Strathos. We would also appreciate silence for these proceedings."

"Father, will ye please stop this charade? Humans are our allies. See what they want of ye."

"Breslin, for once, be quiet, will ye?"

Chapter 13 – Maelnar

"You?" Steve came close to sputtering. "You're Maelnar? You're this 'key maker' that we're supposed to find?" He angrily turned to Breslin, who was still scowling at his father. "Why didn't you say you were his son?"

"Ye did not ask, human."

All the dwarves were now laughing, clapping each other on the back. Apparently everyone in the room was in on the joke. Everyone but the humans, that is. Maelnar rose from his seat at the table to approach their guests.

"Ye were sent out to find me? I suppose then that ye will tell me what all this fuss is about. Why does the human king seek me out?"

"Is there someplace more private we can talk?" Rhenyon asked.

"Aye, through there." Maelnar pointed through an open doorway off the side of the chamber. Inside they found several cushions to which they each sat. Sarah sank blissfully down on her cushion, relieved to be off her aching feet. Noting the woman's actions, and correctly judging them all to be in need of refreshment, Maelnar caught the eye of an underling. The young dwarf nodded, slipping quietly out of the chamber.

Sitting down heavily on his cushion, the old dwarf began removing some of the ceremonial garb he had rushed to put on before their guests arrived. Most of it was solely for the purpose of impressing outsiders. Removing the three various, highly decorated robes he had been wearing, he tossed his staff aside, and systematically began pulling various implements off his belt.

"Confounded things do nothing but weigh you down. At my age, I do not need any extra weight on my belt." He patted his round belly. "If I want to increase my mass then I will indulge in more phedras at mealtimes." Smiling at Sarah, he winked. "I have a fondness for them, lass."

Sarah stifled a giggle. This was the celebrated key maker? Maelnar was not what she was expecting. A wizened little dwarf barely able to move, yes. A spritely fellow with lively eyes and a sense of humor? No.

"So. Tell me, why are ye here?"

"We are the Nohrin," Steve began. "We're here –"

"Are ye now?" Maelnar interrupted. "I have been wondering when the famed Nohrin would appear. Have one of ye an elemental jhorun then?"

Steve nodded, igniting his left hand as a demonstration.

"How did you know about the existence of the Nohrin?" Sarah asked. "Are you familiar with the Bakkian?"

"I should say so, lass. I created it."

"You made the prophecy?" Sarah was dumbfounded. "Then you must know why we're here."

"Nay, lass," Maelnar corrected, "I do not have the ability to prophesize. The Bakkian was a favor for a sorceress, the same who made the prediction. I simply crafted the vessel in which the prediction was held."

"Man alive, how old are you?" Steve wanted to know.

The dwarf snorted. "Much older than the likes of ye, lad."

"Okay, here it is in a nutshell." Steve paused, wondering how to best describe their situation. "You create portal keys, right?"

The old dwarf nodded, still smiling at Sarah.

"You created a green portal key for the Scribes, right?"

At this, the dwarf's eyes jumped over to Steve's. "Aye, that I did, lad. And a right royal pain that was. How do ye know the Scribes? Are they kin to ye?"

"The Scribes were my grandparents. They have passed away. On my world my wife and I inherited all that they had. We stumbled across this green crystal key, and we accidentally activated their portal, and presto, here we are. However, the key is still on our world."

Maelnar was in the midst of taking a large gulp of ale from the goblet set before him when he choked, sending it dribbling down his beard and onto his lap.

"Confound it. Damn goblet." He fixed Steve with a steely glare. "Ye lost the key to the Scribes' portal?"

"We didn't lose it," Steve clarified. "Why does everyone always assume that? We just went through the portal without having the key with us, so we can't get back home. Unless…"

The elderly dwarf scowled into his tankard. "Unless I create another key for ye, is that it?"

Sarah leaned forward. "Is that going to be a problem? Is it that difficult to create a duplicate key?"

"And what do you think, lass? The Scribes' home is on another world entirely. I was tasked with creating a key that would activate a portal on that world and link it to this one. Was it easy? Nay, it was single-handedly the most difficult task I have ever encountered."

Rhenyon leaned forward. "I realize it is difficult, but it is something that must be done. The king's son is being threatened by hostile enemies that want to do him harm. As of late there have been several abduction attempts. The Nohrin here will take the young prince to their world, out of harm's way."

The dwarf nodded slowly. "So the need for all the urgency becomes clear. The king seeks to protect his only son. Now that I can understand." Sighing heavily, he ran his gnarled hands through his thick hair. Leveling his gaze on the small group of humans, he singled out Steve. "This will not be easy, and will not be quick. The materials needed to craft the key are scattered far and wide. It will take me some time to collect them."

"Can we help?"

"Nay, ye do not know where the sensory crystals grow. We are much better equipped for this than the likes of ye." He sighed again, leaning back heavily on the wall. "This is bad timing, indeed. We have our own set of problems down here. In fact…" He eyed Steve appraisingly. "Ye are a fire thrower. Aye, that will do. That will do nicely. Very well. I have just set my price for doing this favor for ye."

Rhenyon sputtered. "Price? Ye dare to charge us for performing this task?"

Maelnar leaned forward, never breaking eye contact with the furious captain of the guard.

"Do not forget this, lad," he shook his finger at the soldier. "I am not under yer king's rule. I cooperate at my discretion. Ye ask that I undertake an enormous task. I therefore want a favor in return."

Sarah laid her arm on Rhenyon's. "That's fair. What do you ask of us?"

"We have a problem here that we are unable to resolve."

"Does it have anything to do with certain tunnels of yours having to be sealed?"

Maelnar fixed the human woman with a piercing glare. "It does indeed, lass. It most certainly does. How much do ye know?"

"Only what Breslin has told us," Rhenyon answered, starting to calm down.

At that moment, several dwarves appeared, instantly transforming the barren table before them into a sumptuous feast. Huge slabs of roast meat, fresh vegetables, pastries, wine, and beer were all brought before them.

"Ye must be famished," Maelnar said, indicating the heavily laden table. "Please, help yerselves to whatever ye like."

Rhenyon leaned forward, inspecting the offerings. Picking up an empty plate, and not entirely too certain of what he was about to eat, he selected a little of everything. Whatever he popped into his mouth melted on his tongue. Eagerly, he speared another piece of meat with his knife. Following their captain's leave, the rest of them, Steve and Sarah included, picked up empty plates and helped themselves.

At that moment a young dwarf set a plate of exotic looking fruit down in front of Sarah. Steve, who had been munching away on various pieces of meat, looked over the latest offerings and selected a fat, orange fruit. He waited a few moments to see if someone else would select one and show him how to eat it. Smiling inwardly, Rhein also selected a ghanje fruit and slowly sliced off the ends, peeling the skin back much like you would with a banana. Steve mimicked the soldier's actions and took a bite. Not bad. A little tart for his taste, but the fruit was large, so he sliced a few more pieces out of it and gave some to his wife.

Watching the proceedings with a smile on his face, Maelnar waited for everyone to finish selecting food before taking some for himself. Deliberately taking his time selecting several pieces of meat, as well as some of the fruit, he watched as all the humans eagerly consumed the meal before them.

Holding a piece of skewered meat on his small dagger, Steve opened his mouth to ask a question.

Instantly cutting him off, Sarah jumped in. "If he asks what type of meat, don't answer, okay? Better he doesn't know."

For the second time Maelnar spewed ale down his chest. Glaring at his goblet once more, he pulled his beard free from his belt to sop up his spilt drink. Chuckling more to himself than anyone else, he looked at Sarah. "That is the second time I have snorted my ale. I like ye, lass!"

The dwarf got to his feet to brush the rest of the dark liquid off his tunic. Wringing out his beard over a thick rug in front of the fire, he smoothed it back into place and re-tucked it into his belt. With a sigh, he sank back onto his cushion to study his guests.

"Ye have no doubt noticed," he began, "the size of this cavern. We stumbled across this place nearly two millennia ago. Most was already hollowed out, leaving us with a minimal amount of work to make it habitable. But what we were shocked to discover was that this is not a natural cavern. Something else had already cleared it out for us."

Intrigued, Rhenyon leaned forward. "Who, or what? Do they want to reclaim this space? If so, we are unable to get involved with what is clearly a dwarven affair."

"Nay, nothing like that, lad." The dwarf pulled out a long wooden pipe from inside his tunic and started packing tobacco into it. "The prior residents have long vacated the area, leaving behind numerous hollowed out caverns, tunnels, and so on. This cavern was the central junction point to their community. That is why this cavern is as large as it is."

"Are the past occupants and your present problem linked?"

Striking his flint repeatedly to get his pipe lit, Maelnar nodded. Steve leaned forward and held out his right arm, with a single flame lit on the tip of his right index finger. Nodding appreciatively, as though it was perfectly normal for a human to have a lit finger for which to light one's pipe, Maelnar puffed until his tobacco was lit. Inhaling deeply, he continued.

"Let me ask this of ye, before I continue any further." He blew a series of smoke rings into the air, each smaller than the previous one until he had what resembled a bulls-eye floating above the table. "Does the layout of this cavern and the many connecting passageways remind ye of anything?"

Steve nodded. "Reminds me of an anthill I once saw in school, one that had a clear sheet of glass on one side so that you could see the inner workings of the hill itself."

"And an 'ant' would be - ?"

"Oh, sorry, it's a bug. On my world they come in a variety of sizes, from tiny to about an inch long. Individually they are typically harmless, but where you find one you usually find several thousand more."

"Aye, that is an apt description."

Sarah straightened. "This is a huge anthill, isn't it? Some type of insect colony used to live here? Is that what you're telling us? And now they're back?"

"The guur that once called this home have been extinct for many thousands of years."

"What happened?" Rhenyon asked. "Have they somehow returned?"

The dwarf looked suddenly old. He took a deep breath.

"We have been able to determine that this cavern and the surrounding tunnels are many thousands of years old. Naturally we assumed they had long been vacant. And they have been." The dwarf fell silent.

"So what happened?" Steve prompted.

"One of our exploratory diggers came across a fossilized guur egg."

"And it hatched?" Steve whistled. "Talk about a long incubation period."

"Nay lad, I said it was fossilized," Maelnar corrected. "The egg was unable to hatch. It was petrified." Did this human not know the meaning of 'petrification'? "Therefore it was harmless."

"But clearly it did hatch, correct?" Rhenyon asked.

Maelnar nodded.

"How?"

"We dwarves typically do not have jhorun, and are quite proud of that fact," Maelnar explained. "Yet every generation one or two are born that are cursed with one. As it happens, this digger was one who, unfortunately, had a jhorun, and a unique one at that. He had the ability to restore a fossilized object. If ye found a piece of petrified wood, then he could restore it to a chunk of wood."

Sarah was nodding. "He restored the egg. So it hatched."

"Aye, lass, that he did. His actions may have been involuntary, but the damage had been done."

"How long ago did the egg hatch?" Pheron wanted to know.

"Perhaps two hundred years."

Rhenyon whistled. "So this ancient insect hatched. How was it able to procreate being the only one of its species left?"

"Because the egg hatched a female," the dwarf explained. "Without a male, she cannot lay viable eggs. However, a female guur can create drones by segmenting a part of itself off. Fortunately, the female can only undergo this metamorphosis no more than twice a month."

Steve whistled. "If this bug can produce, say, twenty-five drones a year, and it's been alive for two hundred years, then we're talking roughly five thousand bugs running around. How long do they live?"

"We do not know what their natural lifespan is, but we continually come across dead specimens deep in the tunnels. Without a live specimen to study, we are unable to say how long they live, only that some have been dying off. Either that or something else has been killing them and leaving their remains where they could be found. Personally, I believe they are dying of natural causes."

"Great. You're telling me that we have fewer than five thousand bugs." Steve rolled his eyes. "Sure, not a problem."

"We have led numerous attacks on them, trying to keep their numbers down. We estimate we have destroyed at least a thousand of their numbers."

"Leaving, what, at least four thousand? So you expect us to eradicate thousands of these bugs for you? Am I the only one who thinks this deal is a wee bit lop-sided?"

The dwarf smiled. "I know there are not that many. However, ye only need to dispatch one."

"The female?"

Maelnar smiled. "Aye. The female. She is the one that we cannot find because we have been unable to venture too deep into the tunnels."

"What about the rest of them?" Sarah asked.

"Without the female to keep the guur population up, the drones will eventually die off."

"These drones, they can't reproduce?"

Maelnar shook his head. "Nay, they cannot."

"Doesn't sound too bad," Steve began. "We just have to find –"

Sarah held up a hand. "I have a question."

"Yes, lass. Go ahead."

"Why couldn't you go deeper into the tunnels? Does something happen if you do?"

The dwarf sighed. "The guur have demonstrated signs of intelligence. They have led several of our scouting parties into traps designed to prevent them from retreating. If we go too deep, retreat no longer becomes an option. So we must be careful."

"So these things are smart, is that what you're trying to say? And when were you gonna tell us this?" Steve demanded.

"Fear not, lad, we will tell ye all we have learned about the guur."

"But they're smart!" Steve repeated, frowning into his tankard. He took a drink and leaned back on his cushion.

Not having any problems whatsoever about exterminating bugs, no matter what size they were, Sarah took her husband's hand.

"Is this going to bother you?"

"Here's the way I see it. These insects were believed to be extinct, and up until now, or whenever they showed up again, they were. Is that right?" He looked at the dwarf, who nodded. "Then," Steve rose from his sitting position and started to pace, "you're asking us, well, me, to send them straight back into extinction. How can you ask us to do that? Don't these things have a right to exist?"

Maelnar also rose to his feet, prompting the rest of the group to follow suit. "The guur," he began, "lived for many thousands of years. For unknown reasons they died out. If our digger had not touched that egg, we would not be having this discussion. These creatures had their chance, and now their time is over. If the guur are allowed to remain unchecked, then they will continue to kill us whenever they have the opportunity. Their numbers and their territory continue to grow each year."

"They have killed some of you?"

"Aye, lad, they have."

"How many?" Sarah wanted to know.

"Nearly three hundred over a span of several centuries, with the most recent just a few days ago. A digger broke through to a small cavern being excavated by a single guur. Before he could retreat, the guur attacked."

"One bug killed him? Are you serious? How big are these things?"

"Nearly three feet in length, from tip to tip."

Steve whistled. "Great. Bugs of nightmarish proportions."

Rhenyon approached, his men flanking him on either side. "How do we find these creatures?"

"We can tell ye where their lair is rumored to be, but I advise against a direct frontal attack. Their numbers are too great."

Pheron put a hand on his captain's shoulder. "I have an idea, sir, which might help us out here."

"I am all ears, lieutenant."

Pheron walked over to Steve, pointing to his harness. "How many of those power crystals do ye have, sir Steve?"

"I counted a while back. There are twenty five of them."

"May I see one, please?"

"Hot or cold?"

Remembering the encounter in the tunnel where Steve and his wife had experimented with the discs, he smiled. "Cold, please."

Retrieving an uncharged mimet, he passed the crystal disc to the lieutenant, who took it, clenching it tightly with his right hand. Concentrating furiously, Pheron was silent for several minutes as the other soldiers looked at each other, trying to figure out what he was doing.

The lieutenant finally opened his fist and looked at the mimet. He could feel a faint trace of his power within the disc. He handed it back to Steve. "Try to draw some of my jhorun out."

Suddenly understanding where Pheron was going with this, Rhenyon smiled, nodding his head in approval.

Looking down at the disc, Steve sent his jhorun to investigate. Sure enough, he could feel a faint sliver of power emanating from within the disc. Pulling the jhorun inward, he felt the unfamiliar power mix with his own.

"Yeah, I can do it," Steve confirmed.

"Excellent idea, lieutenant," Rhenyon said, clapping him on the back.

"What idea?"

"Steve," Sarah took his hand, "they are going to help you out. Since you're the best equipped to deal with these things, they are offering to charge up your mimets for you."

"Oh. Oh! Cool!" Steve took off his harness, opening pouches to withdraw all the mimets.

Dividing them up evenly into piles, Rhenyon handed three to each soldier, taking several for himself as well. "Start charging these things," he ordered his men. "We are going to give sir Steve as much power as we can should he need it."

Steve worriedly looked at his friends. "You're still gonna come with me, right?"

"Aye, sir Steve," Rhenyon confirmed. "Ye will not suffer this fate alone."

"How long does it take to charge this up to full capacity?" Rhein asked, studying a crystal disc intently.

"It takes me around four hours if I concentrate."

"And yer jhorun is much stronger than the rest of ours," Rhenyon observed. "It will probably be several days before they are all charged."

"May I make a suggestion then, lads?" Maelnar approached the group of humans. "Remain here for a few days. Be our guests. Charge yer crystals and we will tell ye all we know about the guur."

Rhenyon calculated it would take six days to charge all twenty five mimets, including an extra day for everyone to regenerate their own jhorun. In that time Sarah, Steve, and the others took the opportunity to explore the city of Borahgg, becoming acquainted with not only the huge variety of blacksmiths offering their wares but also with the people themselves. Every dwarf they encountered was very friendly and more than willing to demonstrate their specialties, whether it was silversmithing, the art of gold-plating chalices, crafting jeweled daggers, or any number of other variations.

Steve even learned the nuances of tempering steel used in the axes worn by practically all dwarves. The friendly proprietor had offered him the chance to put in a few blows. After whacking the red-hot piece of metal several times, and with his ears ringing, Steve handed the heavy hammer back to the smiling blacksmith. Picking up the unfinished shield, the shop owner studied the marks that Steve's blows had left. Nodding appreciatively, he invited the human to help him for the day, as he was far behind in his work.

As the dwarf went to retrieve a second smock for his new apprentice, Steve eyed his companions.

"What the hell? How the hell did this happen? Do I have a sign on me that says 'please put me to work'? Breslin, what are you staring at?"

The son of the Strathos was staring at Steve in open-mouthed shock. "Ye were invited to stay!"

"He must want some help. You'd think there'd be others he could ask. He's gonna regret choosing me, that's for sure."

"Ye do not understand, lad," Breslin whispered to Steve. "Master Kharus here apprenticed directly under my father. Do ye have any idea how many people would pay a king's fortune to study under him? Stay and ye might learn something."

Sarah gave him a fleeting hug. "Catch up with us when you can, alright?"

"Where will you be?"

"We have been invited to share the midday meal with the Council at the central plaza," Rhenyon answered. "Ye can meet up with us there."

Steve's new boss arrived just in time to catch the last bit of the conversation.

"Tha' be jus' fine, lads. I will have him back to ye in time for yer meal."

Grasping Steve by the arm, he steered the reluctant human into the heart of his workshop.

Still smiling at Steve's misfortune, Rhenyon led the rest of the group back into the street to continue exploring the city.

"So what can I do, Kharus? What would you like done?"

"Ye have demonstrated a remarkable knack for shaping the metal. Here," the dwarf plopped a long piece of unfinished steel on an anvil in front of him. "This will need to be heated, in the furnace there. Heat it as hot as ye can get it without melting it. Ye will need to fold the metal in half, much like ye would fold a piece of parchment."

"Okay, I can do that. You just need to fold this thing, that's it?"

"The more times ye do that, the stronger it becomes. I typically will fold the steel around a hundred times for a standard sword."

"A hundred times? Wow. Okay, I think I have it. Heat, fold, and then whack it flat. And then keep repeating."

The dwarf nodded.

Steve hefted the hammer. "I can handle this. Saw this on the Discovery Channel once."

"Eh? What was that?"

"Nothing."

"I will be over here if ye need anything." The master blacksmith watched as the ungainly human picked up the piece of steel, eyed the roaring furnace, and then looked back at the length of metal. What was this? The metal was heating in his hand! It's already glowing red! And he is not using any protection! Wizards be damned!

Seeing Kharus' amazed expression, Steve grinned. "I thought this was part of the reason why you wanted my help. Fire and heat don't really faze me too much."

In mere seconds the metal was hot enough to bend in half. Steve picked up a heavy hammer and pounded the bent blade flat. He smiled at the amazed dwarf, only now he noticed that his instructor was indicating the metal should be dropped into a large trough of water. Hissing angrily, the metal rapidly cooled. Understanding that he was tempering the metal as he went, Steve retrieved the steel and repeated the process.

He had lost count how many times he had heated the blade, folded it over, whacked it flat, cooled it, and started over. All he knew was that his arms were killing him. Seriously. When he made it back home he was joining a gym.

Kharus was smiling profusely as he kept an eye on his pupil. He had already managed to layer the metal well over sixty times. Ordinarily, that many layers would have taken him close to a week. This human would make a formidable blacksmith!

Time for the midday meal was approaching. Noting that the layer count was now well over a hundred, and his pupil was wheezing, the sympathetic teacher finally indicated it was time to wrap things up.

"Where do you want me to leave this?" Steve asked.

"Jus' drop it in the water there, lad."

Steam hissed as he dropped the hot blade back into the water for the umpteenth time. His arms, back, legs, hands, hell, every part of him protested angrily. He probably shouldn't have pushed himself so hard, but he was surprised to discover that he was actually enjoying his time as a blacksmith. He had actually crafted a very serviceable blade for a sword. It just needed a little shaping and sharpening. But other than that, it looked pretty good!

As Steve washed his hands and face in a basin near the back of the cottage, Kharus inspected his work.

"Impressive! Most impressive, indeed! Ye would make an admirable apprentice! I thank ye for yer help."

Steve shook the proffered arm. "You're welcome. Boss."

Kharus snorted, peeling off his smock. "Come, lad, I promised I would have ye back in time for the midday meal."

Together they walked to the center of town, angling for a large plaza near the Council chamber they first met Maelnar.

"Ah, there is yer lady, Steve. This is where we depart. I will see ye again, lad." And with that cryptic statement, the dwarf returned the way they had come.

"Welcome back!" Sarah stood up and gave her husband a hug. "Did you have a good time?" She took a closer look at him. Dark smudges of soot stained parts of his clothes. His hair was all matted, and he looked bone tired. "Are you okay? What did he have you do?"

"I'm a lot better than I look, I'm sure," Steve assured her. "There's a reason why we've never seen an overweight blacksmith." Standing a little straighter, he grinned at his wife. "I made a sword blade."

"Really? He showed you how to make a sword blade?"

Steve nodded. "It ain't easy. Gotta keep folding over the metal into layers. Over and over and over."

Sarah was nodding. "That's the same technique they use for making those Japanese katanas you're so fond of. The really nice, expensive ones."

"That's right. How'd you know that?"

"You're always filling my head with useless trivia. Since you've always been interested in swords, I get to hear all about it."

Steve laughed and gave his wife a kiss.

On the sixth day of their stay in Borahgg, Steve and Sarah were observing a weapon demonstration that Rhenyon and his men were participating in when a young dwarf came up behind Steve and gently tugged his tunic. Surprised, he and Sarah turned around and looked down at the 'underling' as they were called here.

"Yes?" Steve asked. "Can I help you?"

Keeping his eyes on the ground, the young dwarf child shyly delivered his message. "Master Kharus requests your presence at his workshop."

"Thank –"

The child darted off before Steve could properly thank him. Or her. He wasn't sure.

"– you. He better not want another day of work out of me," Steve grumbled. He had been guilted into returning to Kharus' shop to finish the blade the following day. Thankfully, he hadn't been asked to return since.

Scribbling their intentions on a small piece of paper, Sarah caught Darius' eye from across the arena. She held up the message. Quizzically, Darius cocked his head at her. Sarah held up her hand, palm facing up, and waited until the soldier mimicked her. As soon as he did, she sent the message to him. She mouthed instructions to the soldier. *Give it to Rhenyon.*

Understanding, Darius nudged his captain, handing the small slip of paper to him. Reading the message, Rhenyon glanced across the arena at the Nohrin. He nodded.

The familiar blast of heat welcomed them both back into Kharus' workshop as they stooped to walk through the door.

"Welcome back lad, lass." Kharus took off his smock and walked over to the far wall where numerous shields and swords were hanging. Bending down, he retrieved a large cloth covered bundle. Walking back to the humans, he started untying the strings holding the package closed.

"Thought ye might like to see how this turned out. I will say, this is the quickest I have ever assembled a sword."

Removing the last of the wrappings, he presented the golden hilt of a broadsword to his former apprentice. Gently taking the sword from the dwarf, Steve stared at the amazing craftsmanship of the hilt. The grip, or handle, of the sword was wrapped in tightly bound dark leather, while the pommel had several intricate designs carved into it. In fact, Steve held the sword closer, they looked like interlocking crescent moons. The guard was absolutely breathtaking. Kharus had carved a golden dragon in flight, using the wings as the bulk of the guard, with the dragon's tail entwined around the grip and coming to a point at the tip of the pommel. The dragon's eyes were sapphires, while the claws clutched a large emerald.

"Wow! That's gorgeous!" Sarah was standing up on her tiptoes to admire the dragon sword. "Are those real jewels? Unbelievable!" She turned to the glowing creator of the sword. "That is a true work of art. Whoever gets that sword will treasure it always, I have no doubt."

Steve unsheathed the sword, noting immediately that the surface had been polished and the blemishes from the repeated strikes from his hammer had been smoothed. Gently touching the edge of the sword he could tell that it was probably sharper than a surgeon's scalpel. He whistled in admiration.

"It turned out a lot nicer than I would have thought. Thanks for letting me see it before you give it to its new owner."

Kharus smiled. "I am looking at the new owner, sir Steve."

"I'm sorry?"

"Ye gave yer heart and soul into the making of this blade. That type of devotion does not go to a simple warrior. It was destined to be yer blade. And now it is."

Shocked speechless, Steve could only stare at his new sword. Smiling warmly at the dwarf, Sarah spoke up.

"Your skill and your generosity will never be forgotten. We are honored. Thank you."

Kharus nodded. "It is I who am honored. Use it well."

Steve, however, was still staring at the magnificent sword, and was unable to move or say anything. Chuckling to himself, Kharus picked up the scabbard and gently slid it back on the immobile blade, preventing the human from slicing off a toe in case he dropped it, which it looked as though he was ready to do.

Pulling her husband back out into the street, Sarah gently shook him.

"Hey, are you okay?"

"What? Yeah, sorry. I'm okay." He held up the tightly wrapped sword. "Look what he gave to me! I mean, I need to pay him something. I can't just accept this!"

"He wanted to give it to you. Which he did. Be thankful. Everything happens for a reason, right?"

"Look at this thing! Does he really think I'd take something like this out and use it against someone? Hell no. I think I'll have you give it to the king for safekeeping, okay?"

Sarah nodded. "You can if you'd like to, but I think you'd be dishonoring its creator if you choose not to take it with you tomorrow."

Still gazing fondly at his prized sword, Steve could only nod.

Chapter 14 – Exterminators

After spending a total of seven days charging the power crystals, including taking time to replenish their own personal jhorun, the emissaries from R'Tal were finally ready to fulfill the arrangement made with the dwarves. Outfitted in their brand new leather armor (except for Sarah, who was wearing a scaled-down lighter version), the troupe of humans, with Breslin as their guide, left Borahgg behind to venture into the recently dug eastern exploratory tunnels, last known location of the dreaded guur.

"I'm not kidding," Steve was saying again, his right hand resting on the hilt of his sparkling new sword. "If there's the slightest sign of trouble, I want you to get back to the city on the double. Okay?"

"No worries, honey. I hate bugs. I see a bug that big coming at me and I will give you my personal guarantee, on my honor, that the last person you'll have to worry about will be me."

"Have you practiced teleporting at all?"

"I have! You're going to be impressed! Watch this!" Sarah stopped walking, closed her eyes, and vanished.

The rest of the group disappeared into the tunnel when Rhenyon, about to step foot into the dark opening, noted Sarah's absence. Pausing in mid-step, he turned, raising an eyebrow at Steve. The male Nohrin held up a hand with one finger raised, signaling him to wait. Sure enough, moments later Sarah popped back into existence right next to her husband.

"See? No queasiness, no stumbling, no problem!"

Steve breathed a sigh of relief. One less problem for him to worry about. If things were going to get sticky, as he was certain they would become, it was a welcoming relief knowing that his wife could get herself to safety.

"So what changed?" Steve wanted to know. "Or did the queasiness just go away by itself?"

"Maelnar explained it to me," Sarah answered. "The reason I got so nauseous before, back in that tunnel, was of something they call 'the Barrier'. Basically it's a series of enchantments they have in place to prevent people like me from getting in the easy way. The Barrier was supposed to repel teleportation. Somehow, and I'm not sure how, I managed to sneak through."

"So your jhorun essentially defeated the security the dwarves put in place to keep strangers out, is that right?" Steve observed.

"That's exactly right."

"Cool!"

Following Steve closely, Sarah ducked behind her husband as he disappeared into the dark tunnel. Within moments they had met up with Rhenyon and the others, each holding a lit torch. The soldiers appeared to be in the midst of detailing their plans for the assault on the guur.

"We must assume that these creatures are wickedly fast," the captain was saying. "According to the dwarves, the guur's only weapon is its bite, so everyone keeps their armor on at all times. I do not care how cumbersome it feels to have all this on in here. Is that understood?"

Echoes of "aye, sir" resonated off the tunnel walls as each soldier checked their weaponry. Swords were unsheathed, inspected, and sheathed again. Three of the soldiers were wearing full quivers of arrows, each with a long bow already strung. Breslin pulled his axe off his back and checked the sharpness of the twin blades. Rhenyon pulled Steve and Sarah aside.

"Are ye prepared for battle, sir Steve? Lady Sarah?" Both Nohrin meekly nodded. "Keep your crystals ready. In fact, give several to Lady Sarah to hold for ye in case ye are too busy to get them out."

"Good idea." Steve pulled three mimets out and offered them to Sarah, who tucked them safely inside her pocket.

Silently, the group descended further into the depths of the earth. Pheron, being the logical choice to lead the group onwards, cautiously inspected tunnel after tunnel, only to find them consistently empty. Following the lieutenant was Breslin, quietly pointing out the minimal traces of spoor he could locate.

"Guur spoor," Steve snorted, chuckling to himself.

Sarah elbowed him in the stomach.

"Quiet."

Rhein, Kern, and Darius were all casting their torches about, looking for any traces of the huge insects. Following Darius were the Nohrin, nervously looking here and there for some signs of their adversaries. Bringing up the rear, Rhenyon kept an eye out behind them. It will be a cold night in a dragon's nest before he'd let anything come up behind them and catch them unaware.

It wasn't until they had finished their midday meal in a small cavern they had discovered when Pheron stiffened, motioning for the others to be silent.

Rhein and Kern were instantly by his side.

"What is it?" Rhein whispered. "What do ye see?"

"Perhaps two hundred paces away, along the back wall, two creatures have descended from a hole in the ceiling. They are presently about five feet from the ground."

Both men were shaking their head. They were unable to see that far away in the darkness.

"Are they the guur?" Kern asked softly.

"Insectoid, at least eight legs. No, make that ten," Pheron corrected, squinting at the far wall. "If that is something besides a guur, then we have more problems than we were led to believe."

From a safe distance, Pheron observed the two guur excavating a section of a stone wall. The insects' jaws were literally scooping mouthfuls of rock right from the surface of the wall, as though they were pulling the soft part of a piece of bread away from the crust.

"They are digging into the stone," he whispered, watching in awe as an opening to a new tunnel started to form. "Our armor is ineffective. They are digging into solid rock as though they were digging through sand."

"Good. Then this blasted armor is history." Darius pulled the buckles loose on his bulky armor, restoring his arms to full motion.

"No, wait!" Rhenyon's call came too late. The armor fell to the ground with a noisy thud.

In horror, Darius looked at Pheron. The lieutenant cursed as he stared at the far wall.

"Look out! Here they come!"

The two guur covered the distance across the small cavern in a matter of moments. Their ten segmented legs smoothly carried their heavily armored bodies towards the fresh meat they had just learned existed.

Watching the guur rapidly approach, Pheron whipped out his bow, fit an arrow, and fired it at one of the large insects in a single fluid motion. Disheartened, he watched as his arrow bounced harmlessly off the insect's thick carapace.

"Arrows are useless! No arrows! Use swords!" he called, pulling out his own sword. More shouts sounded behind him as the rest of his companions followed suit.

Rhenyon hastily pulled his own sword out and watched as his men attacked the two advancing guur. The bugs were incredibly fast, darting easily around the swords that were thrust at them. One of the soldiers howled in pain and went down as a guur managed to slip by the jabbing swords. Rhein feinted right, and as the huge bug went to lunge to the left, the short sword he was hiding behind his back whistled through the air, slicing the unfortunate bug in two. The remaining guur lunged for the fallen man, hoping to get in a couple of solid bites before the other bipeds could drive it off.

Breslin's axe suddenly whizzed by Kern's head, actually shaving off a few facial whiskers in the process. The attacking bug was neatly sliced in half, right down the middle. Such was the force of the throw that the axe actually embedded itself into a stalagmite several feet away.

Ignoring the grisly sight of squishy bug innards, Sarah pushed by the soldiers to kneel beside the fallen soldier. Darius was clutching his right leg, which had blood steadily pumping from an ugly gash on his upper thigh. Retrieving her precious vial from her medallion, she administered a single drop to the wounded soldier's leg. The bleeding lessened, but unfortunately did not stop. What was happening? Sarah stared at her vial. This was supposed to cure everything, wasn't it?

Breslin knelt down, inspecting the wound.

"His leg has been infected with guur venom. Elixirs will not help him now. He will need the help of a wizard."

Helplessly, she looked at her husband. "What do we do? How do we get Shardwyn here?"

Rhenyon leaned over to grasp Darius' arm. "Ye have fought well." He glanced at Sarah. "We cannot get Shardwyn here, but maybe we can get Darius to him. Think ye can take him all the way to the castle?"

Sarah sat back on her heels and thought for a moment. "Castle R'Tal is much farther away, but I think I can do it. If I get too drained, I'll just use one of the mimets I have. I'll be right back. Don't go anywhere." Leaning forward, she took the wounded soldier's hand. "Hang on, help is on the way."

Darius' glazed eyes focused on Sarah's. "Many thanks, milady. Sorry to be a burden. Sorry to be –"

"Don't start." Sarah closed her eyes, bringing up the familiar image of the throne room. "This is likely to cause a strong jolt to the system. Deep breath. Ready?"

Darius nodded.

In the blink of an eye, both people vanished. In the second blink, however, a raucous chittering had started and steadily grew louder.

"Uh, oh." Steve looked at the others. "That doesn't sound good."

A single guur appeared at the same entrance its brethren had previously emerged from. It stared for a moment or two at the intruders before making the loud clicking noise again. Instantly more guur came streaming out of the same tunnel. Clicking angrily, a group of at least twenty insects advanced on the small group of humans.

"Not good. This is not good at all." The dwarf was slowly retreating. "We cannot successfully face that many. We must fall back!"

"Not an option," Rhenyon snapped. "Lady Sarah will return here in a few moments. I will not let her arrive here to face these abominations alone!"

"And she won't," Steve declared, stepping forward. "This is my show. Time to put on a performance these little buggars aren't soon gonna forget." He looked back at the small group of soldiers, catching and holding Rhenyon's eyes. "Watch for Sarah to return. Keep her safe, okay?"

Silently, Rhenyon nodded, turning to watch the group of large insects advance. At that moment, Steve ignited both hands and faced the approaching Bugs from Hell.

The encroaching horde hesitated. Where had the fire come from? Could they still get to the meat they craved while finding some way to avoid their one, true fear? Greed and hunger prompted half the group to try, surging forward suddenly, pincers clicking furiously. Twin jets of fire appeared out of nowhere, incinerating those that had chosen to attack. Confused, the surviving guur turned to face the lone biped. Two of the biped's appendages were lit like torches. How could they make it to the meat they craved while avoiding the flames?

Dispatch the biped: the fire will be dispatched with it.

This single collective thought circulated throughout the remaining insects. In just a matter of a few seconds, all guur were focused on the same goal.

Steve watched as a wave of restlessness started with one insect and spread quickly throughout the rest of the group. It was then that he realized the clicking noise they were making had been steadily increasing in volume.

They're talking to each other, Steve thought with amazement. What could a bunch of bugs possibly be talking about? When to attack? How they were going to take me out?

"I never did like ants," Steve muttered, eyeing the large bugs distastefully.

All the remaining guur suddenly leapt forward in perfect synchronicity, something Breslin hadn't even known that they were capable of doing. If they could rush this One Who Wielded Fire, then perhaps with the instant onslaught of activity the biped would become confused and be unable to defend itself.

Unfortunately for the guur, Steve was fast becoming a pro at defending himself against a large group of creatures who all tried to rush him at the same time. As the bugs all leapt towards him, he ignited a jet of fire and kept it ignited, essentially turning his left hand into a flame thrower. Sweeping his arm in an arc, he ignited all of the leaping guur at the same time, one right after the other, which resulted in all ten guur falling back to the ground as flaming, charred husks.

At that moment, Sarah materialized back in their midst. Noting the burning piles, the horrible stench, and the tenseness of the soldiers, she went wide-eyed.

"What happened? Were you attacked again?"

"The moment ye left, actually," Pheron confirmed. "How is Darius? Will he survive?"

Smiling, Sarah shook her head. "Shardwyn is looking after him as we speak. Said he hadn't seen a bite that bad in some time. Don't worry, he said that he'll be fine."

"Excellent." Rheyon let loose a deep sigh of relief. "Do ye need one of yer power crystals, sir Steve?"

"Ummm, I don't think so." Steve ignited both hands, trying to determine if his jhorun was fatigued or not. Not sensing any type of weariness, he shook his head. "So far, I think I'm good."

"Keep one ready, nonetheless." Rhenyon gestured to the far cavern wall. "They came from that direction. Shall we?"

"So these things can inflict pain, whether we have armor or not?"

"So it would seem," Rhenyon answered, turning to address the soldier who had asked the question. "Why do ye ask, Kern?"

"If it matters not whether we are wearing this armor, then I would rather remove it."

About to protest, Rhenyon closed his mouth with a snap. Armor or no armor? If they could be hurt either way, what was the point?

Taking the captain's silence as permission, Kern started to unbuckle the protective leather padding he was wearing.

"Just a moment. We do not know if the armor saved Darius from losing a leg or not. I believe I will retain my armor. Whether ye choose to remove yer armor is yer choice to make."

Not wanting to risk losing any appendage, Kern hastily retrieved his pieces of armor that had fallen to the ground.

Up near the mouth of the guur tunnel, Pheron and Breslin were both peering into the dark opening, whispering together. As one, they slipped inside, vanishing from sight.

"Shouldn't they wait for us?" Steve wanted to know.

Rhenyon's head jerked up.

"Pheron! Breslin!" the captain snapped. "Get back here, on the double! Acknowledge!"

Silence.

"Lieutenant!!"

Suddenly they could hear distant shouting. With a curse, Kern and Rhein darted into the tunnel, followed closely by Steve and Sarah. Rhenyon brought up the rear, hurrying them along so that they could render assistance as quickly as possible.

"Sir Steve! Light!"

Steve ignited both hands as he ran, racing to catch up to the two sprinting soldiers, all the while straining to hear if Sarah was still next to him. No matter how fast the soldiers ran, he wouldn't dare try to outpace her. There was no way he'd leave her behind. Not in here. As they rounded yet another bend in the tunnel, he spared a few moments to glance behind him. There was his wife, just ahead of Rhenyon.

The shouting increased in volume as they progressed deeper into bowels of the earth. Without warning, the dwarf shot by them, heading in the opposite direction as fast as his short legs could carry him. A second later Pheron appeared, also running as fast as he could, shouting erratically. Breslin managed to avoid running into the humans, but Pheron wasn't so lucky. Coming around the bend he ran full-tilt into Rhein as Kern dove out of the way in the nick of time. Both soldiers went down in a tumble of arms and legs. Hot on their trail, however, were a group of guur. As the insects observed the two bipeds fall to the ground, they clicked their pincers hungrily. They were about to feed. Life was good.

Running up to the fallen men, the lead guur prepared to gorge on the highly coveted piece of meat it had finally caught up with. The larger version of these strange bipedal creatures were much quicker than the smaller ones!

Pheron and Rhein started to disentangle themselves from each other when a searing blast of heat was felt directly above them. Lying as still as possible, with one soldier still draped over the other, they waited, motionless, as the entire tunnel was illuminated. Loud screeching noises sounded all about them, and yet they still did not move for fear of being caught in the deadly stream of fire whizzing by less than a foot above them.

A few of the hardier guur managed to survive Steve's furious attack, only to stumble out of the roaring flames and quickly be dispatched by Rhenyon. These nasty insects weren't nearly as fast when they were being roasted alive! The captain glanced down at his two lieutenants, still lying sprawled on the floor of the tunnel as Steve fired off jet after jet at the swarming bugs.

"Rhein! Pheron! Stay as ye are!" Rhenyon ordered. "Do not attempt to move!"

"Fear not, captain," Rhein called, from underneath the bulk of Jheron's body. "We are quite content to remain here for the time being."

"Ye would not say that if ye saw what was trying to take a bite out of ye!"

Rhein twisted around on the ground to see for himself. Flat on his back, head tilted as far back as he was able to, all he could see between the jets of fire streaking over him were legs. Hundreds of insect legs.

"Wizards be damned!" Rhein started wiggling out from under Pheron, back towards the safety of the others.

All of a sudden Pheron let out a shout of alarm. From his ground-level vantage point, he had just caught sight of several of the large insects stealthily appearing out of the shadows behind them. Had he not been flat on his back, staring back at his companions, he would never have seen them.

"They approach from behind!"

Steve threw a quick look behind him. Sure enough, a group of about five guur were preparing to attack his companions where they were the weakest.

"Aw, crap. This is not good." He turned to his wife, who was trying to make herself as flat as possible against the tunnel wall. "This is about to get seriously ugly. You need to get out of here. Get out of here now!!"

"What about the others? If they are hurt, I can't help them!"

"We're gonna have to chance it. I'm not risking you. Not now, not ever!"

Steve shared a quick look with Rhenyon, who gestured in the direction of his men. Steve nodded, whispering instructions to his wife.

"Ready?"

Sarah nodded, hugging the tunnel wall as Steve simultaneously let loose jets of fire both in front of and behind them.

Rhenyon yanked Kern away from an advancing bug, while simultaneously plunging his sword through the insect's cranium. He pushed him towards Sarah.

"Ye will be the first. Go now! Wc are outnumbered here!"

Even in the midst of circumstances as dire as this, Kern bristled.

"With all due respects, captain, ye can take that suggestion and –"

Sarah lunged forward and grabbed Kern by the wrist. Both vanished right before their eyes, with echoes of Kern's curses fading away moments later.

Steve addressed the two fallen soldiers who still hadn't regained their feet.

"I'm going to fire off one helluva blast. Should be enough to back them off a bit. When I do, you two need to move, got it?"

Both fallen soldiers nodded.

Firing off a blast behind him to keep the bugs back there in check, he swung his right arm around to join his left. Before the guur could take advantage of the momentary lapse in their defenses, Steve fired off a massive wall of flames towards the carnivorous insects.

"Go!"

The two soldiers scrambled to their feet, joining their captain as they fought off more guur from the rear.

Sarah materialized right then, snagged Rhein by his ear, and vanished before his cursing could begin.

Pheron turned, noting Rhein's absence. He then swung his gaze around the area, taking a head count.

"Captain! We lost Kern and Rhein! Were they taken by the guur? We have to get them back!"

Sarah appeared again, right before him. Pheron suddenly understood what had happened to his companions.

"Lady Sarah, do not even think about –"

Sarah grabbed the shaking finger and the two of them both vanished.

"It is just the two of us now, sir Steve," Rhenyon called, hacking through the advancing horde of guur.

One guur hesitated, trying to decide which biped to sink it's fangs into. Its hesitation cost it dearly; the head and fangs went flying left while the rest of the body flew right.

"Make that three." Breslin retrieved the axe he had thrown, eyeing the surviving guur with undisguised hatred.

"I think I need a mimet!" Steve called out.

In a move so blazingly fast that he could barely follow him with his eyes, Rhenyon slashed viciously through an attacking bug, whirled his sword to decapitate a second guur, spun around Steve between bursts of fire, and then returned to his position facing the rear. Steve's mouth fell open, for in his mouth was the mimet that the captain had so deftly extracted from one of his pouches.

"Wow!" Spitting the disc into his hand, he replenished his jhorun before firing off a tremendous blast at yet another wave of insects tried to overwhelm them with sheer numbers alone. Fanning the air in front of him, Steve glared at the remaining guur, all of which were now slowly retreating. He cast a look behind. Three guur remained.

"Would you step aside a minute?"

Rhenyon nodded, flattening himself along the tunnel wall while Steve incinerated everything behind them. With retreat now a possible option again, the three of them turned to face the last of the attacking horde.

"Let's end this. I'm tired of smelling burnt bugs."

Steve's head swiveled as he counted the remaining insects. Seven left. Three leapt towards him. Make that four left, he corrected, nostrils flaring at the unpleasant odor of deep-fried guur.

The last four bugs paused to determine their next move. Attack or retreat?

Rhenyon lunged then, impaling one guur while decapitating a second. Their numbers halved yet again, the remaining two guur attempted a last ditch effort to eliminate this new foe. Deciding to attack the torso and the legs of the closest human simultaneously, both guur leapt in tandem. Both ignited in mid-jump; their charred carapaces landing with unceremonious thuds next to the captain.

"I really," Steve kicked the smoking remains of a guur out of his way, "really hate bugs," he finished.

In one fluid motion, Rhenyon cleaned his sword on the back of his tunic and slipped it neatly back into its scabbard.

"Nasty creatures, these guur," he observed.

"Let us find the female and be done with this," Breslin said. "Lead the way, master dwarf."

"How dare ye remove us from battle!" Pheron was bristling with anger. "I do not recall hearing an order for us to retreat. We left them to deal with those creatures without our help! Return us now!"

Sarah held up her hands to the angry lieutenant. "I know you're mad, Pheron, but it's what Rhenyon wanted. With us out of the way, they can go after that ant queen by themselves."

"How do ye know it's what the captain wanted?" Rhein wanted to know.

Standing in the plaza where not twenty-four hours ago they had a pleasant lunch together, Sarah explained her actions to the angry soldiers.

"Steve and Rhenyon were whispering together, and then he told me to get all of you to safety, myself included. Don't you understand? My husband was worried about me. He wanted me safe. So he looked to Rhenyon to see if that's how he felt about you three. And your captain agreed."

"The captain wanted us gone?" Kern was incredulous. "I do not believe that at all."

"I have a feeling that my husband is about to go nuclear," Sarah carefully explained. "Remember the attack in the orchard? The explosions? Something along those lines. If any of us happen to be too close when he does that, then it's all over for us." Taking a deep breath, she continued. "Now, Steve will only fight like that if he feels that he won't hurt anyone. Rhenyon and Breslin can take refuge behind him when that happens. Two people can do that," Sarah said quickly, observing Pheron ready to interject a complaint, "but not five, and certainly not six."

Rhein put an arm on Pheron's shoulder. "She's right. I certainly don't condone their decision, but I do see the logic of it."

"Do ye feel that?" Kern had squatted down to lay a hand on the ground. "The ground is shaking."

Pheron dropped to one knee, placing a hand on the rocky surface as well. "Aye, the ground is trembling. Is that from them?"

The rock floor continued to shake for a few moments more before slowly dissipating. The soldiers looked to Sarah for an explanation.

"I don't know, I guess it could be them." Sarah held up her hands. "Who's to say that the ground doesn't shake around here?"

Pheron straightened. "I can feel it trembling without even squatting down. It was not like that a few moments ago."

"I feel it, too. And I could not earlier, either," Kern helpfully supplied.

Rhein, still squatting, kept his hand firmly planted on the ground. "The shaking has increased in strength. They must really be going at it in there."

"Well done, Sir Steve!" Rhenyon fanned the air in front of him, trying to ward off the nauseating aroma of burnt bug. "Ye got near twenty that time!"

Replenishing his jhorun for the fifth time, Steve wiped his sweaty palms on his trousers.

"Stragglers?"

Breslin peered through the dense smoke at the retreating guur. "Five," he reported.

"Can you see which way they went? Sooner or later one of these suckers are gonna lead us to the female's lair."

"They took the right tunnel up ahead. We have them on the run! Come, lads! We must not lose them!"

The dwarf and two humans raced to keep up with the fleeing survivors. Sprinting through various tunnels, Steve quickly lost track of how many lefts and rights they had taken. Was anyone as concerned as he was?

"Breslin!"

"Aye, lad!"

"Dude, tell me you're not as lost as I am. Do you know where we're at? I don't want to have to worry about wandering around in these damn tunnels trying to find my way out!"

"I was born in here, lad," Breslin wheezed out, running slightly behind him. "I cannot get lost in my own home."

The tunnel they were following deposited them in a large cavern with several smaller openings dotted along the wall and ceiling. Guur holes? The retreating insects all disappeared into the same hole about four feet off the ground on the far wall. Running over to the tunnel to peer inside, Steve swore loudly.

"Cowardly sons of bitches! Think you're safe in there?? Have a taste of this!"

Placing both arms directly in front of the tunnel opening, Steve sent a brutal blast of fire and energy into it, watching with satisfaction as the tunnel's perimeter started to glow red. One order of guur flambé coming right up!

"Look out!!"

Rhenyon's warning caused Steve to snap his head up. A reddish-orange light had appeared directly above him and grew brighter by the second.

"They have set a trap for ye, sir Steve! Get out of there!!"

With a bemused expression on his face, Steve watched as the exorbitant amount of jhorun he had just expelled rain down from the ceiling above, completely enveloping him in a shower of pure fire.

"Sir Steve! Can ye hear me? Get out of there!!"

"Lad! Drop and roll!"

The fire storm finally tapered off, leaving Steve bare to his waist with only his nohrstaf harness criss-crossing across his chest. His magically enhanced dwarven gauntlets remained unaffected as well.

"Why is it always my damn shirt? What's the deal with that, anyway?"

Rhenyon ran up to him. Concern for his friend had him dropping formalities. "Steve, are ye alright? Are ye injured?"

"I'm fine. Lost my damn shirt, though." He peered into the still smoking hole. "Think I got 'em?"

Breslin nudged some debris that had fallen from the ceiling.

"I believe so, lad."

"Where now?"

Rhenyon turned to Breslin. "Master dwarf? Ideas?"

"Aye, we must go deeper. The female guur will prefer to have her nest situated on at least three sides by solid rock. The better to defend it from intruders. A guur nest will have to be close to a source of water. In fact," the dwarf paused, tapping his fingers on his axe, "I believe I have an idea where we might find her."

"Where?"

"We are near the source of Duvvin river."

"What river? I haven't seen any river." He glanced at the captain. "You?"

Rhenyon shook his head.

"It feeds the lake, lads. At the point where the river emerges above ground, there is a large cavern with several smaller caves scattered about. It would be a perfect place for a guur female to nest and hide. I have not actually laid eyes on that cavern in quite some time."

"Lead the way, master dwarf. Sir Steve, if ye please, flanking position."

"The rumblings have stopped," Kern reported. "Either they successfully destroyed the female guur, or else –"

Pheron smacked the soldier on the back of the head. Hard.

"Think before ye speak, soldier!" he hissed furiously at him. He indicated where the female Nohrin sat, a scant ten feet away. "Lady Sarah is right over there. Speak nothing of this to her, understood?"

"Aye," Kern lamely responded, rubbing the back of his sore head.

Sarah, in the meantime, had already detected the lack of vibrations in the rock floor. Since it was the one sure way she could tell that her husband was still alive, she had started praying for the trembling to begin anew.

Kern sat up and walked over to Lady Sarah to sit down next to her. Still electing not to say anything, they just sat there in total silence.

The dwarves had approached several times, offering food and drink, but all had refused. If their friends couldn't get anything to eat or drink, they reasoned, while they were battling those bugs, then neither would they.

A tremor hit just then, which had Sarah scrambling to her feet. She was closely followed by Kern, Rhein, and Pheron.

"Did you feel that? Did you? That's great!!"

Pheron smiled. The battle continues!

"Dammit! That was a crappy shot. My fault on that one!"

"No worries, sir Steve! Behold! They are all retreating to the tunnel Breslin wants us to take. He must be right. Come! Do not lose sight o' them!"

Dwarf and human surged ahead, with the weary fire thrower bringing up the rear. Every so often a guur would poke its head out of an overhead tunnel, and a searing blast of fire had it retreating back into the rock.

The guur they had been chasing paused suddenly, checking behind it to see if it had eluded the flames yet. It hadn't! The fire pursues! The urge to flee spurred the guur on once more. Up ahead was a known junction of at least ten subterranean tunnels. Chances of one or more of its hive mates being in the area was strong. With their help, it could rid itself of these aggressors once and for all.

Emerging into a small cavern, the guur bristled with excitement. One of its brethren was lying in ambush just inside the closest tunnel, waiting for the opportune time to attack. The smallest biped passed by first, followed by the much larger one. There, the final biped approached. Now was its chance! The guur clicked its pincers, signaling for the trap to be sprung.

Without warning, a guur's head appeared at eye level directly in front of Steve. Its jaws opened, pincers preparing to strike. He didn't even blink. Three years of taekwando kicked in even before he could even think about igniting his hands. His right fist lashed out as he twisted his body to the left, channeling all his strength into the blow. His fist, protected by the enchanted gauntlet, knocked the guur's head clean off. It rolled sickeningly down the tunnel before bumping into the captain's right boot. Rhenyon glanced down to see lifeless insectoid eyes staring up at him. Nodding with approval, he kicked the head away and watched as the rest of the guur twitched a few more times before dropping lifelessly to the ground.

"Ewww. Damn bugs."

"Excellent strike, sir Steve."

"Thanks."

Its chances of salvation dashed, the lone guur darted away as fast as it could.

The trio pursued the large insect through countless tunnels, passing by amazing rock formations, and numerous small caverns. What was that noise? Were they approaching the river? Something could now be heard besides the sounds of their own footfalls and the constant chittering of the guur. Yes, Steve decided, once he was able to hear it clearly past the sounds of his own labored breathing, they had to be getting close. Fumbling on his harness for yet another charged mimet, Steve restored his jhorun back to full strength and then slipped another crystal into his trouser pocket.

WHAM!

He had run full-tilt into the back of Rhenyon. Blinking his eyes profusely to clear the swirling stars from his vision, Steve gazed up at the captain. When had he stopped, anyway?

Rhenyon leaned over and offered an arm to help him up. The battle-hardened soldier hadn't even been thrown off balance by the impact. Impressive!

"Are ye uninjured, sir Steve?"

"Yeah, I'm okay. What's up? Why'd we stop?"

"Behold, lads," Breslin whispered, gesturing in front of them. "The source of the Duvvin. We must be careful. The female guur is here."

"How can you tell?"

Breslin gestured at the floor, where his axe was embedded. Steve squinted. He ignited his hands so that he could see better. There, on the floor, was a small guur. Half was on one side of the axe, and the rest hidden from view, presumably on the other side. Once again, the axe had buried itself deep in the rock. How strong was this dwarf, anyway?

"You got one, is that it? So there's more around?"

Breslin nudged one half of the guur. "This is a young guur. Note the size. The female is close, I tell ye. Be careful."

"Do ye think she's in one of those caves?" Rhenyon pointed at one of the shadowy openings down below.

"Aye, I do, lad."

"How do we find out which one she is in?"

"Let's introduce ourselves, shall we?" Steve ignited a chaser and threw it at the closest cave. It spiraled in and slammed against the cave wall. Three other chasers went rocketing into the other three caves, each exploding magnificently as they smashed into solid stone. Nothing.

"Two left," Rhenyon observed. "Which one do ye think it is?"

"Shhhh!" Breslin shushed them both, silently pointing at the third alcove to get hit with a chaser. "Observe!"

Something was moving about inside. A long, segmented leg extricated itself from the smoky ruins of the cave and dug into the rock, anchoring itself in place. Three more legs materialized out of the smoke to take their place on either side of the opening as the female guur emerged reluctantly from what was left of her lair.

The creature that appeared was unlike anything Steve had ever clapped eyes on. Whereas he could see the similarities to the 'drone' guur, the female was much larger, with what appeared to be two extra abdomens, and four extra legs to support the extended body. Numerous spiky protuberances were situated all along the carapace, with her head having an extra two sets of antennae that were constantly twitching about, testing the air. The female stopped to face the outcropping of rock that the three attackers were hiding behind. A loud, chittering careened off the walls as the female shrieked with anger.

"What's she doing?" Steve whispered. "Think she knows we're here?"

"Ye did just destroy her lair, lad," Breslin whispered back. "She knows we are here, that's for certain."

A swarm of about fifty guur materialized next to their queen, instinctively surrounding her to protect her from the unseen threat they knew was nearby. Several guur began herding the queen into one of the two remaining caves, intent on shielding her from harm as quickly as possible.

"Now is the time to act!" Rhenyon whispered, watching as the female was guided into one of the last two caves. "We must get to her before she retreats into another cave!"

The captain started to rise when both Steve and Breslin laid a hand on his arm.

"Wait. Let her go into the cave. Easier to hit her from here."

"Willing to wager that she is angling for a cave and not an escape tunnel?"

That silenced both Steve and the dwarf, who stared at the dark opening.

"All right, we attack on three. Ready? One… Two… Three!!"

"They must have found the female," Rhein reported, lying face down with his ear to the rocky floor. "That sounds like one hell of a battle."

"What do ye hear?" Pheron squatted next to his friend. Kern joined him moments later.

"Several explosions." Rhein was silent a moment as he sensed the faint vibrations in the rock. "The intensity is growing steadily stronger. Do ye think that the battle is in their favor?"

"There is no way to know." Pheron thought a moment. "Let me know the instant anything changes."

"Come on, you lily-livered, monkey-lovin', pea-brained pieces of shit! Come get me! Fresh meat!!"

The advancing guur clicked angrily as their hive-mates continued to drop around them, turning into flaming piles of goo. No matter how they attacked this wielder of fire, they kept sustaining incredible losses. The queen had retreated into the last grotto after narrowly avoiding being destroyed in the previous assault. A group of twenty guur had then been selected to sneak through the overhead tunnels to attempt an overhead attack. The rest were tasked with keeping the bipeds preoccupied while more reinforcements could be summoned.

Three of the most aggressive guur chose to attack the largest of the bipeds. As they rushed to overtake the human, a fireball slammed into two of the large insects, reducing them to deep-fried status. The third actually made it to the ungainly biped. Chittering victoriously, it leapt at its prey. It was then that it realized part of its abdomen had stayed behind, while the half with its head still attached learned what it was like to become a shish-kabob.

Breslin whistled in admiration. That human was insanely fast with his blades.

Pushing the remains of the insect off his sword, Rhenyon glanced around the cavern. Breslin was now advancing on the guur that he had been facing, hacking the bug into little pieces much like a chef would dice an onion, all the while deeply scarring the rocky floor in the process. Apparently the dwarf liked these things as much as he did. Speaking of which, what happened to the rest of the horde he had just seen? What were they up to?

"They just left their queen unprotected," Steve observed, also noting the strange absence of the guur horde.

"I trust this not, sir Steve," Rhenyon murmured. "Do not let yer guard down."

"I hear that." Steve looked at the last remaining alcove. "Time to finish this once and for all."

At that moment, however, it started raining bugs. Big ones. The rest of the guur horde had reappeared, streaming out of numerous holes scattered all across the ceiling. Some chose to scuttle down the cavern walls while others elected to simply drop down, hoping they could score a hit on the deadliest adversary they had yet to encounter.

"Get back! Get back now!" Steve turned, grabbed Rhenyon by his right wrist, and executing a move that would make his old taekwondo master proud, hurled the startled soldier back amongst a group of fallen boulders, knocking Breslin down with him as well. At that moment, Steve's jhorun, correctly guessing that some dire action was needed, once again took the guesswork out of his hands.

The very air in front of him detonated, generating a large, intense sphere of fire and heat that expanded rapidly outward in all directions. It caught the guur completely unaware, vaporizing soft tissue instantly, leaving nothing but empty carapaces everywhere along the ground. Dead, smoldering guur began falling from the ceiling overhead.

Echoes of the explosion continued to reverberate throughout the surrounding rock until eventually fading away, leaving a silence that was inexplicably deafening. The singed head of the captain appeared over a large boulder.

"Wizards be *damned*, Sir Steve!"

"What the hell was that?"

All three soldiers had leapt to their feet. Sarah joined them moments later.

"Did everyone feel that?"

All those present nodded.

"That was no simple tremor. The very ground shook! Was that Sir Steve?"

Sarah nodded again, staring numbly ahead. "In dire circumstances, he has been able to generate a blast that can incinerate everything around him."

Curiosity had numerous dwarves poking their heads out of their houses. Windows and doors opened. Younglings appeared, chatting excitedly amongst themselves. Maelnar, along with several members of the Council, approached.

"What was that, lass? Was that yer husband?"

Sarah could only nod. Until she knew that her husband was okay, she didn't trust her voice.

Noting her discomfort, along with the unease exuding from the human soldiers, Maelnar sat down next to Sarah to wait with her.

"Did I get them all?" Steve fanned the air in front of his face. That was the fourth blast he had generated and each had been more powerful than the previous one. Cool! "Anything moving besides us?"

"Nay, lad."

Breslin was poking several of the smoking carcasses. No signs of life anywhere. Suddenly remembering that their primary objective should be in the vicinity, the dwarf's head jerked over to the last remaining cave. It had suffered a cave-in! Tons of rock had fallen from the ceiling, smashing everything flat!

"Lads! Behold! The last cave has been demolished!"

They approached the destroyed cave cautiously, waiting for the last bits of debris to clear the air. Steve sneezed. The dust kept tickling his nose.

"Think she made it out?"

Breslin approached the ruins of the guur queen's lair. Nudging aside some of the smaller rocks, he let out an exclamation of surprise. He pointed at an object in the pile of rocks.

"Look there, lads. There can be no doubt. The female is no more!"

The two humans joined the dwarf by the pile of debris. There, protruding from beneath an enormous boulder, were two large smoldering insectoid legs.

The captain clapped Steve on the back.

"Ye did it, sir Steve! The female guur has been destroyed!"

"Let's get the hell out of here. We need to let everyone know that we are alive and okay."

"Agreed. Master dwarf, lead the way."

Guur drone

Chapter 15 – Key

Tumultuous applause erupted as the three weary fighters emerged from within the depths of the earth. All three soldiers embraced their captain, giving him a royal welcome. Only after they had verified he was uninjured did they all let their accusations fly. Sarah pushed by the cheering dwarves and the angry soldiers to pull her husband into a tight embrace.

"Are you alright? What happened in there? And what happened to your shirt?"

"I'm alright. A little tired. About my shirt, though," Steve looked down at his bare chest. Was it his imagination or did it look like he was losing some air in his spare tire? Will have to ask Sarah for an honest opinion later. "It's a long story. Tell you all about it tonight."

Thinking back to their quarters in the dwarven city, Sarah teleported a fresh tunic for her husband, who hastily pulled it on. He never really was comfortable without his shirt, Sarah mused. She wasn't sure why. Watching Steve stretch his arms up to slide the tunic over his head, she couldn't help but notice that he really should go without a shirt more often.

Properly attired once more, Steve turned to Maelnar, who was approaching with several other members of the Council. Pheron, temporarily finished with chewing out his superior, followed the captain to the impromptu meeting with the dwarven council.

"We are relieved to see ye safe and well. I take it ye were victorious, were ye not?"

"The female guur has been destroyed," Steve confirmed. "Along with I don't know how many of the drones."

The elderly dwarf turned to Breslin. "I am relieved that ye are safe, my son. Have ye any idea how many of the drones were destroyed in the process?"

"We did not keep an accurate count, father," Breslin began, "but if I were to venture a guess, I would say we destroyed maybe three or four hundred. They kept trying to overwhelm us with sheer numbers, and fortunately sir Steve was able to incinerate anything that attacked us."

Maelnar clapped his hands together. "Excellent! Ye have exceeded my highest expectations, all of ye." The dwarf gestured to the large council chambers. "Do ye mind? We would all like to hear about yer splendid victory over the guur."

Breslin looked at his companions. Rhenyon was yawning profusely while Steve appeared to be asleep on his feet.

"Perhaps we could all convene tomorrow, father," Breslin answered. "Speaking for myself and my companions here, I think we would all appreciate a night of rest and relaxation. What say ye, lads?"

"He has my vote," Rhenyon muttered.

"That sounds like an awesome idea," Steve yawned through his response. "Sorry."

Maelnar was nodding. "No apology necessary, lad. Rest and recovery is more important. We shall convene on the morrow, then."

Steering her husband gently away from the throngs of well-wishers, Sarah guided him towards their assigned quarters.

"You look dead tired, honey. Are you sure you're okay?"

"All things considered, I'm not doing too bad. Just really tired. Wouldn't mind grabbing a bite to eat, though. Must have something to do with expelling all that jhorun."

"How many of those mimets did you end up using?"

Steve patted the pouches along his chest, pulling out various crystals to see if they were hot or cold.

"I have seven left, plus I'm missing a couple."

"I still have the three that Rhenyon gave me. Two hot, one cold. I used one to replenish mine after the trip to the castle. One round trip and I was wiped out." She gave the crystals back to her husband, who had to pat himself down again to find the empty pouches they belonged in.

"Okay, make that nine, then."

"So you used close to half. That must have been one huge battle."

"More like three or four huge battles, one right after the other. I'm surprised I didn't deep fry Rhenyon or Breslin." Steve laughed. "You should have seen me, babe. I was firing off blast after blast at anything that moved. It was like that whack-a-mole game. There were so many holes everywhere and these things kept popping out of them all at the same time."

As Steve continued to relay the events that had transpired after she and the soldiers had left, several dwarven guards appeared out of nowhere and discreetly started clearing the road back to the guest quarters. With Rhenyon and Breslin both following silently behind, they navigated their way through numerous streets and alleyways, all the while being congratulated by every dwarf they encountered. Numerous well-wishers had lined the streets, all cheering loudly and clapping everyone on the back, including Sarah.

Bidding their friends good night, the two Nohrin retired to their chambers. Pushing the door gently shut, she turned to her exhausted husband and suppressed a smile. Steve was attempting to pull off his boots, which were refusing to cooperate due to the laces still being tied. Coming to his aid, Sarah untied his laces and then helped unbuckle the dragon sword. Sighing heavily, Steve stretched out on the bed.

"Haven't been this tired since I did that cabling job in Los Angeles," Steve remarked. "Only had about two hours of sleep a night for about a week straight."

"You were tired, that's for sure," Sarah agreed, helping him undress. "Just try to get some –"

Steve's snoring had already begun. Fortunately, the snoring was soft, and non-disturbing. Moments later, Sarah joined her husband. Her soft breathing mingled with her husband's and together they slept like the dead.

"So how did ye manage to find the female?" Maelnar asked, once everyone had breakfasted on the celebratory feast assembled in their honor.

Mouth still full of food, Steve hooked a thumb at Breslin. "It was his idea. Said he had a notion where the female was hiding, by the source of some river. I forget which one." Noting Sarah's disapproving frown, he followed her eyes down to his plate and the area around him, which was now speckled with flecks of food. Nonchalantly scraping the remnants of his meal onto the floor he gave a sheepish smile to his wife. Kern, Rhein, and Pheron all quickly wiped their areas clean before Sarah could notice.

"Ah, Duvvin river. I forgot about that. So she was hiding in Dyr'gyst Cavern, was she not?"

Breslin nodded. "Aye."

"Are ye certain that she was destroyed?"

"We saw the remains," Rhenyon confirmed. "She was crushed in a cave-in. She had just set a trap for us when it backfired on her."

"How so?"

Breslin spoke up. "When we arrived in the cavern, we noticed the caves along the river. Six I think, was it not, lads?"

Steve and Rhenyon both nodded.

"We wondered how to lure her out when sir Steve figured out a better way to get her attention. He sent four fireballs into the first four caves, and was preparing to send two more to the last two when the female emerged from one of the previously hit caves."

"Nasty, ugly sucker," Steve agreed, picking up the thread of the story. "As soon as she came out there were like fifty bugs around her, protecting her. Had no clue where they came from. One minute it was just her, the next, a whole swarm of 'em."

"Aye, they were trying to make her go into one of the last two caves. Damn near got her in one but a whole wave of them rushed us, causing sir Steve to miss. The cave was destroyed, but she managed to retreat into the last one."

"What happened then?" Maelnar and the rest of the Council were spellbound, leaning forward in their seats and hanging on every word that was spoken.

"If I did not see it with my own eyes, I would not have believed it," Breslin declared. "She ordered a group of them to attack from above."

Maelnar's eyebrows shot up. "Ye say ye heard the female guur order the drones to attack from above?"

"She shrieked, and half of them disappeared. We had no idea where they went," Steve explained.

"Where did they go, then?" one Council member asked, nervously twisting his beard around a finger.

Getting into the moment, Steve paused for dramatic effect. Grinning, he eyed his captive audience. "Well, that's just it. We didn't know. Rhenyon was warning me that they were more than likely planning something, but the only thing I could see is that they pretty much left their queen unprotected. I was ready to throw a chaser at her when –"

"Excuse me, please," one Council member interrupted. "What is a 'chaser'?"

"Oh, sorry, it's a ball of fire that will pursue the intended target, no matter if the target is fleeing, moving in different directions, etc. Hence, it is 'chasing' the target."

"Ye can produce these 'chasers' at will?"

"Yeah. I've used a couple before when I was attacked back at castle R'Tal."

The dwarf stroked his beard. "Interesting."

Deciding that Steve shouldn't have all the fun relaying their exploits, Rhenyon picked up the thread.

"As sir Steve was preparing to throw his chaser," the captain began, "the group of guur that had disappeared suddenly reappeared, falling down on us from above."

Several dwarves let out curses as they imagined the feared guur falling on them from the ceiling.

"I believe someone yelled a warning. Might have been me," the captain grinned, "but the next thing I know I was flying through the air and colliding with Breslin here. Together we were thrown to the floor, which was damn good timing, because at that moment there was an explosion in the cavern the likes of which I have never seen before."

Breslin had been nodding through Rhenyon's narration. "I was trying to find a better angle in which I could throw my axe when a large, heavy human lands on me, knocking me flat." Several dwarves laughed. "The explosion sounded and everything went quiet. Methinks I lost my hearing, it was so quiet in there, until this oaf," he elbowed Rhenyon in his gut, with several more dwarves snickering; the captain grinned, "let out an exclamation of surprise."

"What did ye do, sir Steve?"

"I wish I could tell you," Steve answered, shrugging his shoulders. "It's happened a couple of times to me. The situation has become so dire that I honestly don't know what to do, and that's when the explosions usually happen. Fried an arrow in mid-flight once, to save Sarah. And then it happened twice more, when we were attacked outside the castle."

Resuming the role of storyteller, Steve straightened, pretending to look surprised at the carnage his blast had created. "I looked around, startled to notice that I wasn't blown on my ass like I usually am when that happens."

This time, the four human soldiers all snorted with amusement.

"Bugs were still falling from the ceiling," Steve continued, "but they were just charred remains. Apparently the blast had travelled well up into the tunnels in the ceiling, frying everything in its way. And, consequently, the blast broke apart the ceiling in the last cave."

"Ah! So that is what caused the cave-in!"

"That's right. Breslin saw it first, and was able to find the burnt, squished remains of the *last female guur*." As he spoke the last three words, he met a different Council members eyes each time.

At this, the cheering began again as dwarves he was familiar with, as well as those he wasn't, congratulated them yet again on their spectacular victory.

Sarah smiled. Her husband had always told her that he didn't like to be the center of attention at any type of party. But watching the way he was smiling and joking with everyone present, she would have to argue the point. He was completely comfortable being in the spotlight, that's for sure!

Smiling, Steve turned to Sarah and held out his hand. She rose to take it, all the while beaming at her husband. Together, they turned to the dwarf keymaker.

"Now. I would say we've upheld our end of the arrangement, don't you think?"

Smiling, Maelnar nodded.

"How's it going with our new key?"

"I was wondering when ye were going to ask about that, lad." Maelnar grinned up at the two tall humans. "It will be finished in about two days. The crystals need to be tuned. And I was going to ask the two of ye about that. I will need yer help."

"Sure. What do you need from us?"

"I will need the two of ye to concentrate on something from yer homeworld so that I can tune the key in to it. It has to be a strong, vivid memory so that the crystals can detect it."

"Like the gate itself?" Sarah asked.

"Aye, that would be perfect. When ye have a moment, come find me at my workshop so we can finish yer key."

Steve and Sarah shared a glance. "How about now?"

"So what do we have to do?"

"The two of ye sit there," Maelnar instructed, indicating two wooden stools with worn, leather cushions. Taking their places, both humans waited as the dwarf withdrew a felt, drawstring pouch. Reaching in, he pulled out a sparkling crystal key, but this time it was purple! A deep, rich amethyst embossed with several ancient symbols that weaved themselves together, resembling several Celtic patterns Sarah had seen before.

"It's purple!" Sarah was delighted. This was much better than the green key from before!

"Why's it purple?" Steve wanted to know. "Will it change color once it's tuned to our world?"

"The green crystal from the previous key was not ready for harvesting. The purple was in abundance, so I used that. I do hope that ye do not have a problem with the color, 'cause that is what ye get, human."

Elbowing her husband aside, Sarah let out a shout. "Don't you dare change the color! I love purple!"

Grinning from ear to ear, Maelnar chuckled to himself. He had grown quite fond of these two.

"Now," the dwarf began, "I will need ye to focus on the gate on yer world. Picture it as vividly as ye can. Hmmm, Sarah, maybe ye should be the one to do this."

"Hardy har har," Steve grumbled, but obligingly pulled his stool farther away so as not to disturb his them.

"What would you like me to do?" she asked the dwarf craftsman.

"Come sit next to me, lass."

Sarah pulled her stool over to Maelnar's work table. Pulling out the purple crystal key, he laid it down on the surface and pulled out a complex set of tiny tools. Laying the instruments all about the table, he started making adjustments on several of them.

"Now, I need ye to vividly picture something from yer world in yer head. Ye mentioned before ye might be able to visualize the portal gate itself. Think ye can do that, lass?"

Sarah nodded, bringing up a mental image of the carving spanning the two massive doors back home in Idaho. The Kingdom of Idaho, she thought wryly. Sure enough, the image formed.

"I have the gate pictured," Sarah reported, eyes closed. "Quite clearly, actually. The portal is off. I mean, the doors to the room are closed, no portal." In her mind's eye she could see the intricate details on the gigantic double doors. There, as before, was the beautifully carved castle. Was her mind playing tricks on her? She could actually picture the green crystal key sticking out of the window/keyhole.

Seeing her expression change, Steve stood. "What is it? You're frowning. What's wrong?"

Keeping her eyes closed, she shook her head. "It's nothing. I was just mentally picturing the door, and I can imagine that green key is still sticking out of the keyhole in the window. Remember that?"

Forgetting that his wife's eyes were closed, Steve nodded. "Rather hard to forget."

"Anyway, I can actually see it in the keyhole. Makes me think that I could teleport the crazy thing here."

Inexplicably, the infamous green key appeared in her hand. Sarah shrieked, dropping the key on the ground. It clinked several times before it came to a noisy stop, resting up against her foot.

Steve had leapt to his feet yet again. "What is it? What's the matter?" His gaze dropped to the floor where it landed on the key. "Is that what I think it is?"

Tentatively, Sarah stooped down to pick it up. Holding the familiar key in her hand, she turned to stare at her husband, whose shocked expression mirrored her own.

"It's the key! What the hell! How did you get that thing here? What did you do??"

Maelnar walked over to speechless human female and took the key from her. He hefted it in his hand, and then held it close to his face, studying it meticulously. His sharp gaze found Sarah's. "This is the key I crafted for the Scribes! If ye could have teleported it here at any time, why the ruddy hell did ye have me craft another one?"

"Like I knew I could do that!"

Steve took the key from the dwarf. Holding the blasted thing in his hand, he turned to his amazed wife. "So we just risked our lives for nothing? We could have gotten this damn thing at any time?"

Sarah shook her head, taking his hand. "No, I'm pretty sure we could not have. Until we learned how to use our jhoruns, I would never have been able to teleport this thing here. I had to be able to clearly see that key in my mind. Until I could picture what I wanted, I wouldn't have been able to retrieve it. I had to *learn* how to do that."

"You know what this means? We can go home!"

"Not for another two days yer not," Maelnar gruffly corrected. "Ye asked for this cursed key, and ye will get yer damn key. Then ye can go."

Rhenyon studied the green portal key, turning it over and over in his hand while Pheron and the others admired the new amethyst-colored one, admiring how the many faceted key created little spots of light everywhere.

"If ye could get this key," Pheron began, "then why did ye need –"

Sarah held up a hand, cutting him off.

"Don't. Don't ask. I didn't know I could get it. Never dawned on me to even try."

Rhenyon looked up, eyeing Steve first, then Sarah.

"This completes our mission. This is what we came to get, is it not?"

Steve nodded, pointing to the purple key. "We came for that one, but without realizing it, we acquired our old key, which is this one."

"And both will take ye home?"

Both nodded their heads.

"Their majesties will be most pleased. We can begin our trek home tomorrow. We should be back in the castle in about three days."

"The trek to the castle?" Sarah sputtered. "Three days? I think you're forgetting who you're talking to, mister."

The captain bowed, giving Sarah his trademark sheepish smile. "I stand corrected, milady. With yer help, we will be back in the castle by tomorrow."

Maelnar emerged from within the council chambers, with the entire Council following closely behind.

"Lads, lass, ye have done the Kla Guur clan a tremendous service. We cannot let ye leave without a proper celebration, as ye have given us much to commemorate. Tonight, we feast in yer honor!"

Without waiting for a response, Maelnar turned and strode off, with the rest of the Council following behind like obedient puppies.

"They sure enjoy their celebrations, do they not?" Rhenyon chuckled. "What is one more? We have feasted to the death of the female guur, to the safety of the tunnels, and to the ancient pact of dwarves and humans. Have I missed any?"

"I believe ye have missed the feast in honor of our bravery," Pheron answered, chuckling. "That was feast number three, methinks."

"Aye, right. Forgot that one. My memory escapes me at times."

"From age or from ale?" Rhein asked, causing the captain to cough up half the ale he had just swallowed.

"Ye have gone soft, sir," Pheron said, slapping him on the back to help clear his lungs. "Imagine having to have help in defeating those guur. What kind of captain are ye, anyhow?"

"Keep it up, lieutenant, and ye will find yerself mucking out Bredo's moat before ye can even blink an eye."

Knowing full well that his captain would never bestow such a chore on him, Pheron grinned.

The dwarves of the Kla Guur clan pulled out all the stops for their celebratory feast that night. The plaza in front of the council chambers had as many tables crammed together as would fit. Temporary hearths had been set up all throughout the city, providing additional light and warmth for those that needed it. Musicians filled the night air with gaily played ditties, encouraging those within hearing range to come dance a jig. The dwarves of the Council were decked out in their finest, displaying various ornamental robes, belts, gilded instruments, and the like.

Steve and Sarah laughed, ate, and danced well into the night. Steve quickly lost count how many times he had recounted their adventures in the depths of the earth. After succumbing to an underling's request to hear yet again how the female guur had been defeated, Steve departed, leaving Sarah sitting alongside Pheron. With a grin, the lieutenant leaned forward and asked Sarah a question. Smiling, she accepted Pheron's invitation for a dance, followed closely by invitations from Rhein and Kern. Keeping an eye on her husband, Sarah even managed to pull the reluctant captain out into the center of the square.

"Not a good idea," Rhenyon protested, staring down at his two left feet. "Ye are apt to get stepped on if ye persist. I am not much of a dancer, and I do not know this tune."

"Good. I don't know it, either."

Rhenyon stared at her for a few moments.

"But ye have been dancing now for nigh half an hour! How can ye do that if ye do not know the music?"

Smiling, she took the captain's hands. "Here we go. Eyes straight at me. Listen to the beat," Sarah instructed, leading the hesitant soldier through some basic steps. "No, don't look at your feet. Keep your eyes on me."

Finished with his latest bout of storytelling, Steve turned, looking for his wife. He finally spotted her dancing with someone who was clearly way out of his comfort zone. Rhenyon was shuffling along, doing his best to keep up with the fast tempo the song demanded. Suffering sympathetic pains, Steve winced as the captain went to move right, catching his partner unaware, and stepping solidly on her foot.

"Ouch!"

"Many apologies, milady."

"It's okay, you're learning."

"How did ye learn the steps so fast?"

"It's something I could always do. I watch and listen, and though my steps might not be exactly right, it's close enough."

"Ye are an exquisite dancer, milady."

Unwilling to wait for the end of the song, Steve deftly cut in, sending a smiling Rhenyon back over to his comrades. Waiting in the wings for the prime opportunity, two of Maelnar's five daughters approached the now famous soldier, asking politely if he'd honor them with a dance. Throwing his face into neutral, Rhenyon swallowed his surprise and graciously took the hand of the closest female dwarf. If not for the long, braided beard that was tucked into her belt, she might actually be fairly attractive, the captain mused.

The festivities lasted well into the night, with people dropping off to sleep wherever they were, regardless if they were sitting or standing. Apparently dwarves could nod off even if they were standing upright. Maybe this explained her husband, Sarah thought with a giggle. Seeing her husband fall asleep propped up on his elbows, or reading a book, maybe it was because he had some dwarven blood in him. Casting a sidelong glance at Steve, who appeared to be asleep on his feet with eyes partially closed and a lopsided grin on his face, she smiled. She was honestly surprised that he had enough mental prowess left to keep those legs moving.

For the second time in a row, Sarah had to tuck her husband into bed, and also for the second time, he was snoring before she could even remove her shoes.

"On behalf of the Kla Guur clan," Maelnar was saying, "we cannot thank the likes of ye enough. The tunnels are safe once more."

"I'm glad we could help," Steve said, shaking the proffered forearm. "This has truly been an experience that I won't ever forget." Remembering Sarah's last comments to their dragon friend, Steve smiled. "We count ourselves lucky to call the Kla Guur clan friends."

"Friends, hell," Maelnar muttered, pulling Steve into a hug. "Ye are family now. Do not ever forget that, lad."

The four soldiers approached, greeting each member of the Council in turn.

"We thank our human brothers for their assistance," Maelnar began, much more formally. "Ye have affirmed the wisdom of our ancestors in creating the pact with the humans. We are proud to honor that allegiance whenever the need arises." The dwarf glanced across the room, where a contingent of dwarves, led by Kharus, had just entered. Smiling, he turned back to the humans. "As a token of our appreciation, our esteemed master Kharus has commissioned special armor for everyone, including yer fallen comrade. Master Kharus?"

Steve's former boss turned to his group of assistants and began unwrapping packages. Assembling the first suit of armor, he called the captain over. With skilled movements, they had Rhenyon outfitted in the finest set of armor that he had ever seen. Repeating the process with the other three soldiers, Kharus then called Steve over, outfitting him with the same suit as the one the soldiers were wearing. While Steve admired the latest addition to his wardrobe, Kharus turned to Sarah, smiling warmly.

"Ye are next, lass."

Not sure what to expect, and not really wanting (or needing) protective clothing, Sarah approached. However, the garments Kharus held out to her had her staring open-mouthed. The fabric the dwarf craftsman presented to her didn't even come close to resembling the suits of armor the others were wearing. What she was looking at was a much thinner, much stronger variant of the dwarves' special metal, bryl, which had been deftly woven into the fabric of the light purple gown being presented to her.

This was armor? Sarah ran her fingers through the material, rubbing them together. The fabric felt like silk! This was even finer than the armor given to her by Quisen however long ago that was. This gown could effortlessly be worn to the most formal of occasions, while easily being worn out to dinner at their favorite restaurant. This had to be the finest dress that she had ever been given. Then she thought back to the closet full of gowns back at the castle. Her wardrobe here certainly outshone the one from back home, that's for sure.

One of Maelnar's daughters approached, gently tugging her arm, indicating she was to follow.

"Guess I'm changing," Sarah told her husband, as she was herded out of the room. "Be right back!"

While the soldiers all admired their new armor, master Kharus smiled mischievously. He had yet to present his finest gifts to their intended recipients. Pulling out his final wrapped bundle, he took his time removing the fabric coverings, making a show of exposing as little of the concealed item as possible until he was ready. The chamber suddenly hushed as all eyes turned to look at the newcomer. Steve sucked in his breath.

Sarah had reentered the room, wearing her new "armor", although it appeared to everyone else that she was now decked out in her finest apparel, meshing nicely with the finely attired dwarves. The gown was a perfect fit, extending all the way down so that it gently brushed the floor. There was the slightest rustling of fabric as Sarah joined her husband at the front of the procession, delighting the dwarves with an elegant curtsy. In unison, the Council of dwarves bowed in return.

"You look beautiful! Just like a princess!"

Sarah beamed at her husband. "Thank you. I'm not comfortable being the center of attention like this."

"Better get used to it when you look like that."

Doing her best not to blush, Sarah smiled.

Still smiling at Sarah, Maelnar turned to Kharus. "Are ye ready?"

"Aye."

Quizzically, Steve and Sarah returned their attention to the blacksmith, who was busy unwrapping the last package. Finally removing enough coverings to pull a smaller bundle free, every human present gasped as the final piece of fabric was removed, revealing a magnificent two-handed broadsword. But what caught everyone's attention was the blade itself. It was blue! Sidling a bit closer, Steve gazed admiringly at the magnificent masterpiece. The sword measured close to four feet in length, from pommel to sword tip, with ancient dwarven runes etched into the colored blade on both sides. The grip was wrapped tightly in black leather, with a griffin on each end of the golden guard. Brilliant sapphires were set into the hilt in various places. Steve whistled in admiration.

Holding the sword up high so that everyone could admire the unique weapon, Kharus presented it to the human captain.

"In honor of yer bravery and courage, brother, we are honored to present ye with this token of our appreciation." The dwarf held the hilt out to the captain, who stood there in shock. Seeing no move to take his gift, Kharus placed the sword into his hands. While Kharus turned back to retrieve the second bundle, Rhenyon continued to stare in awe at the exquisite work of art now in his possession.

"Breslin, step forth."

Surprised, the dwarf moved next to Rhenyon. Casting a quick, admiring glance down at the sword his friend was holding, the dwarf turned to see what the skilled blacksmith was unwrapping next. His eyes widened as the cloth on the double-bladed ax fell away. As with the sword, the first thing Breslin noted was the color. The blades were a striking red, also with the ancient runes etched into both sides. The same griffin was carved into both sides of the ax head, with a large ruby set into each side of the ax. Mouth open in shock, Breslin took the weapon Kharus presented him.

Sliding the coverings off the final weapon, Kharus presented Steve a twin to Rhenyon's sword, only this time the blade was forest green, with emeralds adorning the hilt instead of sapphires. Steve stared at his sword, admiring the detail of the carved griffins and the ancient symbols on the blade.

"Behold the Mythra triad, crafted solely for the three of ye. Sir Rhenyon, ye be holding Mythron, of the blue blade. Breslin, ye have Mythryd, with its double red blades. Finally, sir Steve, ye be holding Mythrin, of the green blade." Smiling profusely, Kharus surveyed the recipients of his gifts. "Each blade will forever hold its edge," the dwarf explained, "while simultaneously being able to slice through practically any material. Use these weapons well."

The two humans were unable to speak, still staring incredulously at their gifts from the dwarves. Breslin, testing the sharpness of his ax blades for the fourth time, bowed in appreciation to master Kharus, who bowed in return.

"I will treasure this always. I thank ye."

"That goes for me, too," Rhenyon finally managed to say.

"Same goes," Steve murmured.

Returning to their quarters to collect their belongings, the departing guests decided to honor their hosts by remaining attired in their new armor, with Steve and Rhenyon both displaying their new swords. For Steve, however, it was a little more difficult. Wanting to display both of his new weapons, the avid sword collector decided to wear both on his back, each handle over a shoulder. As they left the chamber that they had thought of as home for the last two weeks, Sarah snorted, stifling a chuckle.

"What is it?"

Sarah glanced at her husband, eyeing the two swords strapped across his back.

"I feel like I'm following a walking map."

"What?"

"You have a big 'X' on your back. 'X' marks the spot!"

"Zip it."

"What are you going to do with two swords?"

"Well," Steve admitted, the corners of his mouth turning upwards in a smile, "actually its three swords and an axe. Rhenyon gave me his old sword and Breslin gave me his axe."

"What in the world for?"

"Are you kidding me? Authentic Lentarian weapons. I'll put 'em on the wall in my office back home! How cool will that be?"

Sarah shook her head. "Men."

Arriving at the plaza where they had previously partied all night, Steve and Sarah bowed to the dwarves, who reciprocated the gesture. Rhenyon and his men arrived moments later, each carrying their belongings in a type of duffel bag slung across one shoulder. Saying their final goodbyes to their new friends, the small group assembled in front of the teleporter.

Sarah chuckled, shaking her head.

"Guys, guys, this will never work. We can't have you gentlemen arriving back at the castle decked out in that fine armor, with your dirty clothes slung across your back."

The soldiers all grinned at her, inspecting their own appearance and that of their companions.

"Drop your bags in front of you," Sarah ordered.

Without waiting for their captain's approval, three bags plopped unceremoniously onto the ground. A moment later, they all vanished, having been transported back to the castle. Smiling, Sarah looked at Rhenyon, who sheepishly held out his own pack. It vanished moments later, joining the others back in the throne room of castle R'Tal.

"I've charged several more crystals," Steve informed her, automatically patting several of the pouches along one strap of the nohrstaf harness. "I have plenty in case you need to use them for this jump."

"Thanks, I'm pretty certain that I will." Sarah turned to the men, who were now trying to suck in their stomachs. "Okay, who's first?"

"I will be the first," Rhenyon declared, stepping forward.

Taking Rhenyon's arm, they vanished. One by one they were teleported back to the castle, taking only enough time for Sarah to recharge her jhorun between each teleportation.

With Sarah gripping his arm tightly, Steve materialized in the Great Hall, being the last to make the journey. Both thrones were currently occupied, and the entire hall was filled with the castle's nobility, all wearing their finest. Either they had just interrupted some important function, or –

The room erupted into cheers as everyone started clapping and whistling, hailing the famous Nohrin and their brave companions. When the exuberant applause finally died down, Kri'Entu stood.

"Made some new friends, did ye?"

Grinning sheepishly, Steve nodded, while Sarah smiled at the queen.

Directing his gaze over to his captain of the guard, the king grinned.

"Looking good, captain."

"Thank you, sire."

"May I see… what was it called again? Mythron? May I see Mythron?"

Shocked, Rhenyon unsheathed his prized sword and presented it to the king. "How did ye learn of this? We only received them no less than an hour ago."

"I make it a point to stay informed, especially when denizens of this castle are guests in another city."

"Someone told you what was going on?" Steve asked, shocked. "Who? I thought it was supposed to be an unknown city!"

Enigmatically, the king smiled at Steve. Returning his gaze to the magnificent blue sword, he sighed. This was truly a masterpiece, the king thought. They could not have selected a more deserving person to give this to.

"Would his majesty care to see Mythrin?" Steve reached over his right shoulder and started pulling the sword free of its scabbard.

Sarah giggled. "Wrong shoulder, honey."

His hand freezing in mid pull, Steve sighed. Naturally. He had had a fifty-fifty shot of executing a move he'd only seen in movies, where the hero gracefully reaches over his shoulder and pulls out his sword. Returning the sword he'd had helped create back into its scabbard, he reached behind his other shoulder to unsheathe his gift from the Kla Guur clan. Presenting it hilt-first to the king, Steve gave a small bow.

Returning Mythron to its owner, the king admired its green twin.

"These are truly magnificent. Yer other sword, is that the sword that ye had a hand in fashioning?"

Steve pulled the dragon sword free, electing to hold it himself rather than tie up both of the king's hands. "This sword was the result of sheer curiosity."

"Oh? Please explain."

"We were exploring the city and decided to check out one of the numerous workshops. It turns out that the place we stopped was the workshop of master Kharus, who apprenticed under Maelnar himself. I wanted to see what it was like to be a blacksmith, so he had me strike a few blows on a shield he was just starting to create. Liked what he saw, so I was *drafted* into service."

Ny'Callé stifled a chuckle. "Ye would make a good bard, sir Steve." Smiling at Sarah, the queen leaned forward. "I do like yer gown, Sarah. A gift from the dwarves?"

"Yes, it is. I love it. Believe it or not, it provides the same amount of protection that a suit of armor does. You should feel this material!"

Forgetting that she was formally addressing a queen, Sarah hurried over to Callé's throne. More interested in the dress than the story Steve was relaying, the queen rubbed a piece of the fabric between two fingers.

"It feels like silk. This has the strength of armor??"

Sarah laughed. "That's exactly what I said after Kharus told me the same thing."

"Impressive. I am glad ye have returned safely, Sarah."

A sudden disturbance attracted everyone's attention. Several of the soldiers let out shouts of surprise. Darius had emerged, slowly limping towards his companions.

"Darius! Are ye well?"

"How the ruddy hell are ye, Darius?"

"Ye have a gift from the dwarves," Rhenyon stated, turning to go through the pile of belongings Sarah had teleported back. "Hold still for a moment."

With Darius outfitted in his new armor, the injured soldier moved to stand next to his captain. "Why did they gift me with armor?" Darius asked miserably. "I lasted all of, what, ten minutes into the first battle? What kind of soldier is that, anyway?"

"Join the club, mate," Pheron whispered back. "We were sent away during the heat of the battle."

"What? Who eradicated the guur then?"

"Sir Steve, the captain, and Breslin. It was sir Steve who destroyed the female guur."

While Pheron attempted to restore Darius' self-esteem, the queen sat, mesmerized, while Sarah recounted some of their more harrowing exploits.

When their story had been told for what felt like the hundredth time, the king and queen both took their respective places on the thrones. Kri'Entu leaned forward, addressing Steve.

"Ye may be interested in meeting the newest liaison to this castle."

"Umm, okay."

"May I present Pheris, newly-appointed liaison to the griffins."

"Pheris? The same Pheris who –"

"The very same. A contingent of griffin visited the castle not long after yer skirmish to express their gratitude for yer gift of the elixir and the meal. We started a dialogue, and am now pleased to say a new human-griffin alliance has been forged. Ye have my thanks, and the thanks of the kingdom of Lentari."

A familiar griffin appeared, quietly taking up residence close to the queen. Pheris bowed in Steve's direction. Bemused, he returned the bow.

"May we see the portal key, please."

Always the smart-mouth, Steve blurted out his response before his mouth could censor itself.

"Which one? The new one or the old?"

"Sorry? Have ye more than one?"

Nodding, Steve pulled out the green portal key, presenting it to the king. Still standing beside the queen's throne, Sarah retrieved the sparkling purple key and handed it to Ny'Callé. Confused, the queen met Sarah's eyes.

"Ye need two keys to activate the portal? I thought ye needed just the one."

"They do," the king confirmed. "This," he held up the key he was holding, "is the key that my father presented to the Scribes nigh thirty years ago. I do not recognize the purple key."

"That is the new one," Steve explained. "It wasn't until the purple one there was practically finished when Sarah somehow managed to teleport the gate key from our world to here."

The king's eyebrows shot up. He turned to Sarah. "Ye teleported that from yer world? How?"

Sarah shrugged, spreading her hands. "I wish I knew. I've tried countless other times to see about teleporting something else, but nothing has worked. I just don't know what I did to do it the first time. It's very frustrating."

"I will consult Shardwyn. The level of jhorun necessary to move an object between worlds, no matter how small it may be, is unheard of. There must be some type of explanation."

"Well, when you figure it out, please let me know, too."

"I will, Lady Sarah."

Steve stepped forward and bowed to the king and queen. "Umm, I don't know if this is a good time to ask this, but is your son packed and ready to go?"

"Mikal is indeed ready to depart, and depart he will," Kri'Entu said, "but that will be tomorrow. Tonight, we feast in yer honor."

A small groan sounded from somewhere behind Steve while several soldiers snickered. Careful to hide his rolling eyes from those of royal persuasion, Rhenyon sighed.

The celebratory feast held in the Great Hall was no less spectacular than those held by the dwarves. Musicians lined the hall, encouraging passersby to dance a jig or two. Heavily laden tables of food were everywhere, tempting even those with full bellies to have another morsel or two more. Everywhere they walked people stopped what they were doing and bowed, murmuring their names as they passed.

Rhenyon surprised Sarah by asking her to consent to one last dance. Giving the grinning captain one of her famous million-dollar smiles, and a small curtsy, Sarah allowed herself to be led out into the throngs of people, all dancing a slow waltz.

Feeling a small tap on his shoulder, Steve turned, surprised to see the queen before him. She gave him a small curtsy as well, holding out her hand for him to escort her to the dance floor. Swallowing loudly, Steve bowed in return, and took the queen's soft hand in his. Thanking his lucky stars that his wife had talked him into taking a ballroom dancing class several years ago, Steve managed a passable waltz, guiding the smiling monarch around the dance floor without once stepping on her feet. He even spun her through one turn, much to the queen's delight, her eyes opening wide with amazement.

Feeling another small tap on his shoulder, Steve turned again, discovering himself face-to-face with the king.

"May I cut in?" Kri'Entu politely inquired.

"By all means, your majesty."

Finally able to breathe again, Steve ran a shaking hand through his hair. Where was his wife? A quick scan of the dance floor provided the answer: dancing with the young prince. Mikal, it would seem, had been well trained in the finer art of dancing, leading a laughing Sarah through several styles of dance, even spinning her much more elegantly than he had ever been able to.

"Show off," Steve muttered, chuckling.

The following morning found everyone assembled in a smaller chamber off the Great Hall. Looking around the richly decorated room, Steve realized he hadn't ever been in this part of the castle before. Tapestries lined the walls, and numerous tables were scattered about. Maybe this was a conference room of some sort? Steve shrugged inwardly. Giving his immediate surrounding a quick, cursory glance, he was startled to discover that the room didn't contain a portal or at least something he could recognize as one.

Walking over to the far wall, Kri'Entu gave several tugs to the huge floor-length twenty foot tapestry that was hanging unobtrusively from several pegs. Dislodged from its holders, the tapestry plopped to the ground, revealing a ten foot tall door frame, complete with ancient runes carved onto every square inch. This time, the carved relief depicted castle R'Tal, in its entirety. There, smack in the middle of the closed drawbridge was a hole. A keyhole.

The king turned to the Nohrin. "Sir Steve, if ye please."

Figuring this would be a great time to test their new portal key, Steve stepped forward and inserted Maelnar's latest creation, automatically twisting it clockwise. Returning to his wife's side, together they watched as the newly activated portal rapidly came to life. Grinning like a couple of enthusiastic school kids, Steve and Sarah each held their breath as the familiar chiming was heard. The surface of the wall fuzzed out, replaced by a very welcoming scene: a comfortable sitting area, with a window overlooking an immense Victorian garden.

"Okay, kiddo," Steve said, grinning down at an amazed Mikal, "ready to check out another world?"

Nodding his head in wonder, Mikal looked back at his parents. The king was smiling, nodding his head in encouragement while the queen was doing a remarkable job of not bursting into tears.

Taking Mikal's hand in her left, while simultaneously taking her husband's in her right, Sarah led them into the portal, leaving the Kingdom of Lentari behind.

Chapter 16 - Surprise

"Are we back? Is this really home?" Sarah ran to the window to look outside. Sure enough, she could see the beginnings of the Victorian garden on the southern side of their newly inherited mansion. There, parked out front, was their SUV. Turning, she saw the young prince waving enthusiastically at his parents, still visible in the open portal. The Kri'yans, however, were snapping out last minute instructions to their son.

"Ye are to be on yer best behavior at all times, young man. Do ye understand?"

Mikal sighed. "Yes, father."

"Do as ye are told. I do not want to hear of any disobedience, is that understood?"

Another sigh. "Yes, father."

The king's tired eyes swiveled to Steve's. "Keep him safe."

"Count on it, your majesty."

With that, the portal faded back into the carved likeness of Lentari. The sudden quietness of the house spooked Sarah. Nervously, she looked around.

"This feels so weird! After all we've been through, I can't believe we made it back. I mean, we must have been gone at least two or three weeks, right?"

Steve was nodding. "I'm figuring at least a month." He absent-mindedly patted his pockets. "Without a watch, I really have no idea how long we were gone. I usually just check my cell for the date and time, and I don't have my cell anymore. We need to find a phone. We have some serious damage control to do, my dear."

"Could your cell be in the pack?"

He thought a moment. No, he was pretty sure his cell was still a resident of that shabby cottage where they were temporarily held prisoner.

"No, it's gone. Gonna have to get a new one. What about yours?"

"It's not in my purse, or else I would have seen it. Wait! We had it charging in the car just before we got here, remember?" Sarah took Mikal's hand as she moved to follow her husband down the two flights of stairs. Blinking profusely, they emerged into the bright sunshine. Without stopping to admire the scenery, Steve went straight to their SUV, checking the interior. With a shout of triumph, he emerged with her cell. However, as was the case with most car cell phone chargers, when the car's engine was turned off, the ability to charge the phone was turned off, too. The cell phone was dead.

"Not a problem. We can charge it for a bit." Certain he wouldn't be able to find his keys, Steve climbed behind the wheel and reached beneath the seat to retrieve the spare. The black SUV purred to life as soon as he twisted the key. Plugging the phone back into the charger cable, he was rewarded with a soft musical chime as the cell recognized a valid power source. Mikal was staring open-mouthed at Steve. He climbed out.

"What?"

"What is *that*?"

"What is what? The car?"

"You're talking to someone who has never seen a car before, honey."

"Oh. Right. Sorry about that. This will take some getting used to. You see, a car is –"

At that moment shouts could be heard coming from within the house. Alarmed, Steve bolted back inside, igniting both hands as he did. Impossible! There's no way someone could have followed them through that portal!

Sarah, however, had skidded to an abrupt stop. She was staring at her husband.

"Good, stay there," he called as he disappeared inside the house, bolting up the stairs two at a time.

Several moments of silence ensued, followed shortly thereafter by Steve's laughter. Sarah blinked. He was laughing? What now?

"What is it? What's going on?"

"Stay there," Steve called down, still chuckling. "We'll come down to you."

"We? Who's there with you?"

Emerging back out of the house, Steve was shaking his head. Someone was moving behind him. It was –

"Tristan? What are you doing here?"

"As I understand it," the soft-spoken soldier said, "the reason the two of ye went through so much turmoil in Lentari was that ye activated yer portal and then went through without the key to return, is that right?"

Sarah stared at her husband. "You forgot to take the key, didn't you?"

Sheepishly, he handed her the sparkling purple key. "Okay, we can call this even." He smiled at Tristan. "We still have another one. We could have just gotten the new one when we report back in, what was it? Six months? Nine? A year? Man, I can't believe I don't remember."

"You can't believe you forgot already?" Sarah giggled. "I can. I married an old –"

"Hey! Play nice!"

"The whole purpose of having young Mikal on this world," Tristan interrupted with a smile, "was so that no one from ours could make it here. If we have a key to yer world on ours, then he would not be safe. Besides," he continued, "it has been decided that it is very important for the prince to maintain his studies, and since he is destined to be ruler one day, he will need to have an adequate understanding of our kingdom and its laws."

"So you're going to be his tutor, is that it? Sure, why not? Join the gang!"

"My thanks, sir Steve."

"While you're here, you had better just call us Steve and Sarah so that you don't stand out," Steve explained. *More than you already do*, he silently added.

"Aye, I will try to remember."

Sarah grabbed her husband's arm, spinning him around.

"You just ignited your hands!"

"So? I've been doing that for a while now."

"Not *here* you haven't."

Realization sunk in. His jhorun was working here? How could that be? Bewildered, he looked at his hands and ignited them again. Sure enough, both hands became engulfed in flames. Snuffing them out, he looked at his wife.

"You try something."

Sarah paused, thinking of a location back inside the house. Moments later, she vanished. The upstairs window opened. She poked her head out.

"Am I supposed to be able to do this?"

"Come on back down here."

Pulling her head back inside, Sarah closed the window and then materialized next to her husband. Steve turned to Tristan.

"No one ever told us that our jhoruns would work here."

"Because they do not, sir Steve."

"You just saw it work. Both of us can still use our jhoruns. Can you?"

Tristan was silent a moment as he asked his jhorun to summon a small dagger. Nothing. He again ordered his jhorun to summon a dagger, dirk, anything. Nothing appeared.

"See? I told ye that jhorun is ineffective here. The Scribes have long told us that their own jhoruns did not work here, either."

Steve ignited his right hand, holding it before Tristan's face. "And what do you call this, then? Think I can spontaneously combust that often?"

Tristan looked at the flaming hand in front of him. "I cannot answer ye, sir Steve. That goes against everything I was ever told about yer world."

A car's engine revved in the distance. Then they all heard the faint, but distinctive clang as a set of iron gates were pushed open.

"There aren't any other driveways with gates," Sarah recalled, eyeing her husband. "Someone's coming."

"Someone has keys to this place? Mikal, back inside the house. You, too, Tristan."

Boy and tutor scrambled inside the mansion, closing the front door behind them.

The sound of crunching gravel steadily increased as the car moved closer, finally rounding the bend and coming into view. Of all the vehicles he imagined he could be looking at, this one wasn't anywhere on the list.

The old, beat-up blue and white truck came to a stop just before the house. Stan Miller emerged, staring hard at his son and daughter-in-law.

"Steve? Sarah? What – where have you been? Where'd - you were not here last night. I searched that house from top to bottom!"

"Well, we just got back. Literally. What are you doing here, dad?"

"What do you think I'm doing here? You vanish for over a month and you think your mother and I aren't going to worry?" He stared at his son, as if seeing him for the first time. He looked at Sarah. Had they been to a costume party? "What are you wearing? Where were you?" he repeated.

"You wouldn't believe me. Not by a long shot."

"Hold on, we need to call your mother. And, you get to do all the talking." Stan pulled out his cell and got his wife on the phone. "Hon, there's someone here that you are going to want to talk to."

Steve took the phone. Wincing, he held it up to his ear. "Hi, mom."

Even though Sarah was standing a full five feet away, she could still hear the distinctive squawk his mother had let out.

"No, I'm fine, really. Sarah, too. What? Ummm, I don't think you'll believe me. You see, we… what? WHAT?! What the f-… How could you possibly know that??"

Perplexed, Sarah studied her husband's face. Did his mother actually suspect where they've been? How could that be??

"What is Steve doing, holding that thing to his ear?"

With the unexpected appearance of Steve's father, Sarah had momentarily forgotten about Mikal and Tristan, who had just now emerged from the house. Sarah looked down at Mikal, then over at Stan. Her father-in-law stared at the boy then at the strange man.

While Steve held a fast and furious conversation with his mom, Stan sidled closer to Sarah. "Who are these two? Are they friends of yours?"

"I'll answer that if you answer me this: what are Steve and his mom arguing about? Do you know?"

Stan scoffed. "Bonnie had some outrageous notion that since this was my parent's house that you two might have been unarguably out of the country. Horse crap, if you ask me. What is that supposed to mean, anyway? How could you two have been out of the country?"

"Stan, what if I told you that not only were we out of this country, but out of this world, too?"

"Not you, too," He groaned, running his hands through his hair. "Why would you go along with this charade? What you suggest is impossible."

Sarah was nodding. "And if I can prove it to you?"

"How? How can you possibly prove it?"

Sarah turned, pointing to the third floor window overlooking the garden that she had previously stuck her head out of. "See that window up there? Top floor with the white trim?"

Stan gazed up at the closed window. "Yes, I see it."

"Keep watching it."

"And what am I looking for?"

Suddenly the window opened. Sarah leaned out and waved to her father-in-law.

Stan's neck actually cracked as he snapped his head around to the spot Sarah had just vacated. "What the hell?" Stan rubbed the painful kinks that were beginning to form in his neck. "How did you get up there so fast?"

"Teleportation," Sarah called down. "A gift I was given upon setting foot in Lentari. One I didn't think I'd still have once we returned. But, there you go."

"You expect me to believe that you magically appeared up there?"

"Look around you. Clearly I'm not down there, right?"

"Not unless there are two of you," he admitted. Returning his gaze to the window, he was startled to discover Sarah was gone. A soft tap on his shoulder had him spinning around yet again. There she was!

"But…you… Do that again."

"Let's try this. I'll stay in your line of sight. See that stone bench in the middle of the garden over there?"

Stan looked beyond his daughter-in-law and saw the bench about fifty yards away. "I see it." He blinked. A figure had just materialized out of thin air and was waving at him.

"Stay there," she shouted to him. "I'll come back."

Deciding to watch the spot that she kept disappearing from, Stan reeled in shock as Sarah materialized beside him. His look of disbelief was very rewarding.

"You teleported yourself! You actually teleported from here to there!"

Sarah smiled, nodding her head. "Trust me, no one was more surprised than I was once I learned I could do it." She took Stan's hand in her own. "Please believe me when I say that Steve and I were stuck on another world for the past month or so. Once we learned we had inherited this house, we came up to take a look. We discovered the portal, and without realizing what we were doing, activated it and stepped through, without having any way to return home."

"What was it like?" His voice had changed. There was no malice, no venom, just sheer unbridled curiosity.

"We'll have to take you there. It's very picturesque. It can be dangerous though, if you don't know what you're doing, but as long as you have Steve around, you'll be fine."

Stan looked over at his son, still deep in conversation on his cell. "Why do you say that? Does Steve have some magical ability, too?"

"Steve has the ability to summon and control fire. Very handy to have when being attacked by griffins, or trying to impress dragons, or battling huge bugs."

"Griffins? Dragons? Are you serious??"

"Yeah, I am. Apparently us showing up there was foretold in some ancient prophecy of theirs. We have the ability to protect their future king, which reminds me. May I present Kre'Mikal, prince of Lentari. Mikal, this is Steve's father, Stan."

Stan looked down at the small boy, who returned his gaze with equal fascination. Pausing only a few moments, Stan extended his hand. His manners kicking in automatically, Mikal grasped the forearm of the father of one of his two protectors. "Pleased to meet ye."

"Nice to meet you as well, Mikal," Stan answered, noting the strange manner in which the boy spoke.

Tristan stepped forward, giving a slight cough.

"Stan, I'd also like you to meet Tristan, who will be Mikal's tutor while he's here."

"And are you going to be taking care of him?" Stan asked, after shaking hands with the silent, bald man.

"We are his official bodyguards," Sarah confirmed. "Until things are safe again in his kingdom, we will be looking after him."

Amazed, Stan looked at the boy again. At that time, Sarah heard her husband finally say goodbye and then heard the distinctive snap of a cell phone being closed. Steve joined them moments later.

"You'll never believe this," he told his wife, momentarily forgetting that his father was standing quietly nearby. "Mom knows about Lentari. Apparently the Scribes, I mean grandpa Simon, actually told her a little about -"

"Did you just call your grandparents 'the Scribes'?" Stan interjected.

Realizing his father was still present, Steve grinned. "Yeah, that's what they were called in Lentari. They were the court scribes, restoring ancient Lentarian manuscripts and cataloging the royal library. They've been performing tasks for the king and queen there for years now. That's where we've been. We were stuck there until we could get the key to come back. Long story."

Stan's head was spinning. All those stories his parents had told him were true? He had just figured they were pathetic attempts to excuse their behavior for the past thirty or so years.

"Sarah says you can control fire?"

Amazed, Steve stared at his father, and then at his wife, who nodded her encouragement for a demonstration. "Yeah, I do. How did you - never mind. Wanna see?"

Without waiting for a response, he ignited both hands, holding them up for his father's inspection.

Stan blinked. Both of his son's hands were now completely engulfed in flames, yet he didn't appear to be in any pain! Incredible! Realization finally started to settle in, and a profound sense of guilt slowly reared its ugly head.

Steve shared a glance with his wife. He suddenly knew what the rift had been between his father and his grandparents. The guilt his dad must now be suffering had to overwhelming.

"There's no way you could have known that they were on another world, dad," Steve said softly. "I wouldn't have believed it, either."

Nodding appreciatively, Stan met his son's eyes. "I just felt that they had to be telling lies. All those attempts at telling me stories about griffins, and magic." Sighing heavily, he leaned up against his son's Santa Fe. "You actually met a live griffin?"

"About thirty of them," Steve confirmed, smiling at his dad. "Would you believe some can actually speak? I even made friends with several of them."

"I wish your mother was here."

Looking closely at his father, Steve gave his wife a sidelong glance, raising an eyebrow. Taking the mimet from Steve's outstretched palm, Sarah closed her eyes.

Let's see, Sarah thought. *If my jhorun truly works here then I should be able to picture something to reference.* An image formed: a quaint living room in Bonnie and Stan's house. She'd been there a few times, enough to be able to visualize where everything was. Taking a deep breath, she teleported.

Sarah vanished, right before Stan's eyes.

"Where'd she go?"

"To see if she can bring mom here."

"What?! Can she do that?"

"She was teleporting people across the kingdom of Lentari not three days ago."

"How? How can she move people around like that?"

"Essentially, it's magic. Whether you believe it or not, it exists. You watched me light my hands on fire. Sarah just teleported right in front of you. Take it from someone who had a very difficult time believing in all of this. Magic is real, and exists on Lentari."

"And here, too, apparently," Stan observed.

"Yeah, I can't figure that one out," Steve said, shaking his head. "Why are we still able to –"

Sarah materialized then, with a short, middle-aged woman clutching her arm, eyes squeezed tightly shut.

"Hi mom."

Bonnie Miller cracked an eye open. Good lord! There was her son! It worked! Sarah had just teleported them over thirteen hundred miles north! Rushing to hug her son, Bonnie caught sight of a small boy with a strange bald man standing silently nearby.

Introductions were made while Sarah snuck off to call her sister. Much to Sarah's surprise, before she could get a word out edgewise, Annie hit her with, "Must be nice to be able to take such a long vacation! Coeur d'Alene must be very pretty."

"You weren't worried?"

"Should I have been? Mom got a call from Steve's mom, saying that you were probably going to be gone longer than planned and that they don't have cell service there."

"She did, did she?" Clever woman! She had surmised, correctly, that when they were gone longer than anticipated, that they were more than likely out of the area. Way out, Sarah thought with a chuckle. A quick phone call to her mother confirmed Annie's story. Her mother was pleased she that she had a good time and to call later that night to hear how things went. Her mother-in-law had just saved her from a major headache!

Rejoining the rest of the group, she was shocked to see Steve's parents embracing, with his father doing his best not to get teary-eyed.

"How'd it go?" Steve inquired. "Were they all freaked out?"

"Nope, not at all. And I have your mother to thank for that."

"Excuse me? What did my mom do?"

Detaching herself from her quietly grieving husband, Bonnie approached her daughter-in-law. "I do hope you don't mind, dear, but I had told myself that if we ever lost contact with the two of you, especially going up there, that there was a chance that you could have found the portal. You two are the most intelligent people I have ever met, so if anyone would have been able to figure out how to activate it, it would be you two." Smiling warmly at her son, standing next to his beautiful wife, Bonnie continued. "After two weeks with no contact I just knew the stories were true. Lentari did exist, and you two managed to find your way there. So I called Sarah's family, assuring them that that you were okay, and chose to extend your stay."

"And that we were out of cell phone range," Steve said, nodding his head.

"Like that trip you two took to that small town in Oregon," his mother confirmed. "They didn't have cell phone service there, either. Sarah, your mother was very understanding. If she would have called to inform me that you two were out of cell phone range, and taking even more time, I would have panicked."

"That's my mom," Sarah laughed. "She's very laid-back."

Assuring her in-laws that they were fine, Sarah set about preparing to transport the both of them back to Phoenix, with Steve's father agreeing to leave his truck behind.

"I can drive it back down at Christmas, if that's okay," Steve had told his father.

"Son, that's fine with me. You just saved me a twenty hour trip. Your mother and I can use the car for a while."

Tucking several mimets into her pocket, Sarah returned the Millers to their home. Moments later, she reappeared, smiling at both Tristan and Mikal.

"You are gonna come in really handy," Steve observed, giving his wife a hug.

"I can't wait to tell Annie all about what's happened to us!"

"How much are you going to tell her?"

"Everything. I don't keep secrets from her."

"Sorry, I knew that. What I meant was, how much are you going to hit her with at one time?"

"Oh. Probably all of it. She's a smart girl. She can handle it."

"We'll have to set up some type of get-together, really freak her out. Just show up suddenly on her doorstep. What do you think she'd do?"

"We're not going to do that," Sarah shook her head. "You want to surprise your family all the time, that's fine, but we're not doing that with mine."

"Spoilsport."

The two of them took the remaining part of the day to set their affairs straight. Steve had indeed been let go from his job for his extended absence, a fact which didn't trouble him in the slightest. He had been itching for an excuse to leave and start his own computer consulting business for quite some time. Sarah's employer, a medical billing company, had a much more mom-and-pop feel to it. Her company had no choice but to fill her position with someone else. However, not only were they thrilled to learn Sarah was safe, they even offered to let her work remotely when they were finally settled in Coeur d'Alene. All she needed was a computer, a high-speed Internet connection, and a phone. She thanked her bosses profusely, but declined, explaining that she and Steve needed to focus on their family.

A phone call to their apartment manager confirmed their apartment was still in order, with action just now ready to be taken to locate the missing tenants. They gave their notice and promised to move out in thirty days.

Draining the cell phone battery for the second time that evening, Steve finally took a seat in the huge, luxurious sitting room on the ground floor. Mikal followed suit moments later. Sarah and Tristan rummaged through the kitchen, finding not one crumb of food in the entire house. Squeezing enough power out of Sarah's cell to make one more phone call, Steve delighted the young prince with his first pizza. Tristan was less than enthused, but politely ate a few slices.

"We'll get some proper food soon," Sarah promised. "As soon as we find a grocery store." Tristan nodded his appreciation.

Mouth full of pepperoni, Mikal grinned. "I like pizza! Can we have this again?"

"Pizza is only the start of it," Steve promised. "There are hamburgers, fried chicken, and burritos, just to name a few. Then there are video games, which, just to give you fair warning, I am the king. And movies! Don't get me started!! Trust me, sport, you're gonna love it here!"

THE END

The story continues in Bakkian Chronicles, Book II – Insurrection!

2696539R00181

Printed in Great Britain
by Amazon.co.uk, Ltd.,
Marston Gate.